Annie of
the Point

by
Mark Weir

GWL
PUBLISHING

First Published in 2018
by GWL Publishing
an imprint of Great War Literature Publishing LLP

Produced in United Kingdom

ISBN 978-1-910603-52-9 Paperback Edition

GWL Publishing
Forum House
Sterling Road
Chichester PO19 7DN

www.gwlpublishing.co.uk

Mark was born in Portsmouth and has lived on the south coast almost all his life. He attended Fareham College where he studied art with art history, and the social and economic history of Great Britain since 1834. Through these studies, he developed a love of history, which was enhanced by his reading of horror stories. He particularly enjoys books by Stephen King, as well as ghost stories, such as *The Signalman* by Dickens.

He lives in Gosport and is married with two grown-up children.

Also by Mark Weir

Randall Crane and The Whitechapel Horror
Special Medicine

Dedication

This book is dedicated to my wife and family. How Julie suffered with all those long, sunny days in the beer garden of the *Still and West* pub, sipping beer and watching the world go by; all in the name of research.
Look how it paid off!

Here's to the follow up, and more hard research… oh, and another beer of course!

Acknowledgements

I would like to thank all those who keep the past alive, especially local history. Without your knowledge, this book wouldn't have been written. Also, thank you to the fantastic team at the Portsmouth Central Library History and Archive Centre, who showed me gems from the past which helped enrich the book with detail that, without their help, would have been missing.

Thank you.

Prologue

For King and Country

Annie Crowther's dress flapped in the unforgiving wind like a flag of surrender.

She cut a lonely figure on the Camber, staring out beyond the harbour mouth. Out there in the dark depths of the Solent, behind the veil of rain that swept in, the silhouetted shape of the Isle of Wight blackened the horizon like a thick charcoal line. The twinkling lights danced on the many ships that anchored in the waters off Spithead, and Annie thought them surreal, almost ghost like, floating in the murk. Choppy waves squeezed into the narrow mouth of the harbour, carrying flotsam and jetsam in their swell, and she wished that those same waves would carry her man back to her. The sound of voices whispered on the wind, blowing in from the icy sea. Faint and wraithlike, they were barely audible, but Annie was sure that she could hear him in the gusts. Tonight, fortune rewarded her patience. He was calling to her, calling her name, and it lifted her heart. Then the voice was gone, carried into the distance as the wind changed direction on the squall, twisting and turning, and all that was left in the silence was doubt. Doubt that the voice was his, a trick of a tragic mind, a hoax played upon her by lovesick ears, desperate to cling to anything that reminded her of her man. Annie looked up at the sky, its celestial beauty always so evident on the most violent of nights. Through a gap in the thickening clouds, millions of stars shone above her like tiny lights in tiny windows, looking into heaven. She imagined angels staring out of those windows and hoped that they felt her plight, that they conveyed her pain to the feet of the Almighty. Annie wasn't given to praying but she would if it helped bring him back.

She came to this spot most nights, to say goodbye to him, to reconcile herself with the loneliness that he left inside her and – despite her desolation – to cling to hope. Flimsy, fleeting hope was the one thing that she had left, but as the days became weeks, months and years, it was waning. Perhaps he would return, she reasoned, and then they would be a family again. Perhaps she would feel the warmth of his skin once more, or his breath on her cheek. She touched her hand to her face and held it there for a moment, imagining his presence. The spray from the sea and rain wetted her rosy cheeks, soaking her to the core. And yet here she stayed, oblivious to the conditions. Perhaps God wanted nothing to do with her and had summoned the stormy night to dampen her faith even more. Not even the lure of her child's love could break her melancholy, or show her a path back to happiness. She closed her eyes and lifted her face into the falling rain as the ghostly image of her love appeared in her mind. With each passing day it grew more imperceptible and she tried with all her might to cling to the last scraps of the man who had been wrenched from her so cruelly on that fateful day. There was comfort in the pain – and there was a connection to this spot on the harbour side. The 10th of March 1803 was when her world had changed forever. That was the day that her world had fallen apart.

Dark clouds were gathering in the skies above, as dark as the clouds that were gathering in her life.

****

In the beginning…

"Quiet tonight," said William Juxon, the landlord of *The Camber Inn*. Sam Crowther slouched in the wooden chair next to the fireside, nodded without uttering a word and took a large gulp from his tankard of ale. The fire crackled and spat in the hearth, shooting hot embers on the flagstone floor of the pub, one of many drinking establishments that vied for custom on the few acres that made up the Point in Portsmouth.

The Camber Inn wasn't a welcoming place but it was familiar and it was Sam's sanctuary for the evening. The landlord rested his elbows on the counter and surveyed the empty chairs in the room, with a grumpy expression fixed to his face. He sighed loudly and grabbed a cup, filling it with ale. Sam looked over at him and pondered how little William had changed. Sam had lived on the Point all his life, never wanting to know what it was like to live on the other side of King James Gate. He worked at the Dockyard on the Hard, and every day on his short journey to work he passed by the streets of the old town. To Sam it was another world. In his world there were constants; unshakeable things that added weight to his feelings of awareness and reluctant fondness for the Point. He belonged, and part of that familiarity was the miserable, ugly and some might say, downright scary face of William Juxon, pub landlord, dyed in the wool *Pointer* and all round cheerless man.

Sam had been drinking in this establishment for as long as he could remember, certainly for as long as he could reach the counter on tip-toes, and in all that time he struggled to recall ever seeing William Juxon with a smile on his face. As he swallowed the last dregs of the muddy brown fluid that passed for ale, his thoughts returned to the argument that had led to him storming out his home. His wife, Annie wasn't happy, and he knew that he had to do better by her and learn to curb his jealousy. He felt blessed that she was his wife, especially as he wasn't rich or gifted at anything that would change their fortunes, but he knew that one man in particular wanted her more than all the others: a rich and violent man who was used to getting his own way. The demands of George Brownrigg were not to be ignored, not unless life had lost its lustre and was the preserve of others. The Point was beyond the control of the city and its lawmakers. The gate saw to that and all the while George grew fat on the takings from his ill-gotten businesses of prostitution, protection and peddling stolen goods. Nothing moved on the tiny outcrop of land without Brownrigg's knowledge or say-so. He was the law and the self-styled King of the Point. Sam's mind replayed the events from earlier in the evening…

"I seen the way George Brownrigg looks at you. I see that look in 'is eye." Sam had grabbed Annie by the wrist and spun her around to face him. She'd resisted, trying to turn away, snapping free from his grip, and he'd raised his arm.

"Don't you dare, Sam Crowther," she said. "Don't you dare at all. I ain't got no interest in the likes of Brownrigg."

"Maybe not, but 'e's got an interest in you."

"I'm taken," said Annie trying to lighten the moment with a weak smile. "Besides 'e's a big, odorous man."

"'E's a rich man is what he is," countered Sam, lowering his arm with a sense of shame. He knew that he couldn't hit his wife, nor did he want to. He wasn't that sort of man. It was the other lads at the dockyard who told him that he needed to stamp his authority. What was he thinking? Sam was different. He didn't want his family to live in fear of his temper, like the other wives and children on the Point. He'd seen how they cowered when their men folk returned from a night's drinking and he'd seen their bruises the following day.

Annie supplemented their income by taking in washing from those who could afford it, and Brownrigg was one such man. Sam had left work a little earlier in the day and, as he'd passed through King James Gate he was looking forward to spending a little extra time with his wife. He'd stepped onto Broad Street, heading for home and turned the corner from Broad Street into Bath Square, and that's when he'd seen George Brownrigg pressing himself against Annie by their front door. She struggled with the man, pushing him away, but all Brownrigg did was laugh at his wife's futile struggle and the veins in Sam's forehead had started to pulse. He wasn't a man of violence and George was. George saw Sam approach and released Annie from his grip. He stood with his hands thrust into the pockets of his great coat and smirked at Sam as he drew nearer. Sam went to say something but Annie stepped between the two men before he could do anything that would lead to a fight, steering her husband into their small lodgings. George watched with amusement and all Sam could remember was that he'd wanted nothing more than to wipe that stupid grin from his face. If Annie hadn't slammed the door shut, Sam was sure that the events of earlier would have ended very differently and he knew that George Brownrigg wasn't a man to be messed with.

"'E was hard for you, Annie. Make no mistake."

"Don't be so vulgar. It's 'is way of bein' friendly, that's all. You know, just larks." Annie did her best to laugh it off, but she wasn't fooling Sam. He'd known that his wife was trying to protect him. He didn't know that Annie had the measure of men like George Brownrigg and that it wasn't the first time he'd pressed his considerable frame against her.

"I don't want you taking that man's washin' no more," demanded her husband. "George Brownrigg is bad news. You know how 'e makes 'is money, don't you?"

"'E's a thief, 'e's violent. I know that. But 'is money is as good as the rest, and we need 'is money."

"We don't need it. I take care of this family. You and Bessie are mine and mine to care for."

Annie snorted in derision. "If that's the case, why've I gotta stick me 'ands in shitty piles of washing. Why do I spend hours washing stains from the likes of Brownrigg's smalls?" Her caustic words had the desired affect and Sam's shoulders slumped a little, and he glanced at the floor.

"That 'urts," said Sam as he glared at the ground. "Tellin' a man that he don't take care of 'is family is as good as tellin' 'im that 'e ain't a real man."

Annie said, "I'm sorry, Sam. I didn't mean it." She took a step towards him, holding out her hands and he took a step backwards towards the door. His face turned scarlet with rage and he shook with anger.

"Sam, please… I didn't mean…" Before Annie could finish her sentence, Sam had turned and thrown open the front door, rushing into the night. Annie went after him and called across Bath Square, "Come back. I'm sorry for what I said."

Sam Crowther had kept on walking, picking up his pace, without looking back. His wife's words barely registered and his burst of anger had suddenly given him an almighty thirst.

So, he sat by the fireside and played with the dregs in the bottom of his cup. Juxon was right, it truly was a quiet night in the pub. It had been quiet all week, ever since the rumours that the Impress Gangs were back on the prowl, eager to dish out the King's shilling. Four men had gone missing in that week alone and the menfolk were conspicuous by their absence.

The door opened and a small girl, probably no older than ten, stepped into the dirty room. She had bare feet and rags for a dress. It was ten o'clock, way past the hour that a little girl should be up. William Juxon looked up from his own drink and stared at her with his lopsided face. William was a scary man to look at, having suffered a heart stroke that severely affected the left side of his face. He was once given the nickname, 'Candle Wax William' by a foolhardy man back in the day, on account of the fact that his skin looked like it was melting clean off his skull, but it was short lived. William Juxon was not a man to cross and made sure that the nickname, along with the man, were quickly forgotten.

The girl shrieked and took a step away.

William approached all the same, oblivious to the effect that he had on her.

"What's a mite like you doin' out at this hour?" he said.

She thrust a coin on the bar with her tiny shaking hand, alongside an empty wooden jug with a stopper in it.

"Cat got yer tongue, eh?" said William, snatching up the jug. "Old man havin' withdrawals, is 'e? Why don't 'e come 'imself?"

The girl shrugged and said nothing. She turned and stared straight at Sam, who smiled at her, but the girl didn't smile back. Sam recognised her as Kitty Hawkchurch and knew that the poor girl would have been sent out on pain of a beating if she didn't come back with the ale, such was her father's nature.

"Shy little thing, ain't yer?" said William, filling the jug from a large barrel that stood on a rickety shelf behind the bar. He put the stopper in and handed it to the girl, snatching up the coin from the counter. "You tell 'im that if 'e wants any more, 'e'll 'ave to come 'imself next time."

The girl nodded and scampered out of the door. As it swung shut, a cold breeze blew in and the fading flames in the hearth leapt into life, dancing vigorously. Sam stood, stretched and sauntered to the bar.

"Her father is a bad-un," he said. "Ivan Hawkchurch is a miserable drunkard, and no stranger to violence."

Juxon nodded but didn't respond. Sam placed his empty cup on the counter.

"I thought you was gonna make that drink last all night," said William.

"Not me," said Sam. "I'm done. I gotta get back to the missus."

"Got you on a short chain, eh?" laughed Juxon. "Worried that the Impress'll get you?"

"No," said Sam indignantly. "I'm tired is all."

Something in William's expression sat uncomfortably with Sam. He'd caught a brief glimpse in the landlord's eyes and it made him uneasy. *Was it panic?* Sam couldn't be sure.

"What's that look?" said Sam.

"What look?" Juxon shrugged his shoulders.

"You looked sorta jumpy."

"Just a bit slow in here, that's all," Juxon said. "Has been all week, what with them bastards stealin' folk away for the ships. Takin's are down and 'ere you are leavin' me to an empty pub."

"'Tis bad news indeed. Charlie Babcock's been taken. So 'as Loughton. I expect that'll be that last that we'll see of 'em," said Sam.

"What say I offer you one on the 'ouse?" said William, trying to change the subject. He backed up his offer with a weak, lop sided smile.

"I been drinkin' in this shit 'ole all me life and I ain't never seen you crack a smile, nor offer me a free drink, and now you offers me both. What's up? You found Jesus or somethin'?"

"You ungrateful…" William rolled his eyes. "Sam Crowther, I offer you a free drink this once only. Do you accept?"

Sam nodded and smiled. "Bein' as you put it so nicely, I do. The missus can wait."

"That's the spirit, my boy. You let her know who the boss is."

William refilled his tankard and Sam went to resume his place by the fire. Speckles of water mottled the dark panes of glass and Sam was glad he was in the warm, candle-lit pub. He was also glad he'd accepted the free drink, deciding to wait until the rain stopped before heading home.

The door opened again and two men entered. They were soaked through from the downpour and stood at the bar, shaking off their long coats. The taller of the two scanned the room and his gaze fell upon the solitary shape of Sam sat by the fire. His tall hat sat on his head at a jaunty angle. The other one went to speak to William Juxon at the other end of the bar and Sam saw that same flash of panic in William's eyes as he looked over at him. He heard the smaller man say something in low tones to William but couldn't quite hear what it was and the landlord nodded, occasionally darting his eyes over in his direction. It was as if the pair were sharing something clandestine, and then he poured the strangers a drink. Sam thought it was odd that neither man offered any reimbursement for their ales and Juxon seemed disinterested in asking for their money. Sam hadn't seen the pair on the Point before and it wasn't a place that people stumbled across by accident. For one thing, King James Gate was more often locked by seven at night to keep the respectable folk separated from the iniquitous peninsular. The taller man still hadn't averted his stare.

"Got a problem?" said Sam gruffly, taking his cup, glugging back his ale and wiping his chin. Something was telling him that it was time to leave.

The stranger smiled at Sam then turned to face the bar and converse with his companion. Sam downed the remaining contents of his drink and slammed the tankard on the dusty table. The clattering sound made the two strangers at the bar jump and, once again, the taller of the two stared at him as he stood.

Where's William? Sam thought to himself, scanning the bar and noticing that he was nowhere to be seen. *That's odd. He never leaves the place unattended.*

He passed the two men and squeezed out of the door. As he did, he noticed out of the corner of his eye the smaller one nudge the taller man and nod. He turned just as the door closed and saw the taller one staring at him again. This time he was grinning from ear to ear with his hands on his hips.

The penny dropped. *Shit, it's the Impress, come for me.* Sam turned on his heels and bolted for home. As he did, he didn't notice the small group of dark shadows huddled at the corner of the pub just out of view. Something tangled with his feet and Sam could feel himself start to topple. With a heavy thud, he slammed into the cobblestone ground and his head clattered heavily against the path. He gave out a loud groan and tried to sit. He saw the door to the pub open and the blurred shape of the two men appeared in the light of the doorway.

"How old would you say he is?" said a voice from behind him.

The taller man leaned in closer to Sam and he could smell the foul stench of his breath, like that of a stray dog. "Easily thirty or so. This one's lean too, perfect for old Horatio." There was a sudden burst of laughter from the assembled group behind him and Sam struggled to stand.

"Please," he slurred. "You 'ave to let me go. I 'ave a wife an' child." He was nearly on his feet when a heavy boot connected with his stomach and he doubled up in pain.

Another voice said, "C'mon. Let's stop wastin' bleedin' time and give this man 'is shilling."

The tall man slipped a coin into Sam's hand and said, "Good boy," then patted the side of his face. "You are now in the employ of His Majesty's Navy."

"Cunliffe," said the shorter man, "stop wasting time and get this man to the boat."

"Boat?" cried Sam. "I don't wanna get on no boat."

A heavy fist struck him on the side of the face and he blacked out.

The last person to see Samuel Crowther on the Point was William Juxon, peering from the doorway of *The Camber Inn*, as he watched the Impress Gang carry him across the dockside to a waiting boat at the Camber.

Chapter One

Still Missing…

Annie Crowther pulled the wiry blanket from her body and sat to rub away the frost from the small window that faced into Bath Square. She glanced up at the sky and saw that it was slate grey; one solid block of matt shade that stretched across the horizon from the Point to Spithead and Gosport beyond. Annie searched for the sun, just making out a milky, peach coloured orb low in the distance. It reminded her of a candle burning behind a curtained window. The daylight was there, but night was clinging on for all it was worth. The sun's radiance was trapped behind a veil of cloud which prevented any heat reaching the chilled ground on this damp December dawn. Annie sighed at the thought of another day's toil beneath a leaden firmament, and another day without her beloved Sam.

Mornings were the worst part of the day for Annie. She missed the reassuring warmth of his body and the gentle kiss on her shoulder or neck to excite her and light the fire within. She cast her mind back and he was there, right beside her, reaching into her clothes with his cold hands, snaking his way up her back. His warm breath tickled the nape of her neck.

"Control yourself, Sam Crowther," she whispered, closing her eyes and allowing his touch to entice her. "You'd best be up or they'll lose patience with you at the dockyard."

"Just one kiss is all," said Sam, persevering with his wandering hands.

Annie felt them slide around her waist and climb up her stomach. She slapped them away and said, "Not while Bessie sleeps. Control yourself." She leaned back against his strong frame and sighed. And then he was gone. The room was as cold and silent as before and the scent of her husband was just a figment of her dream.

"You may 'ave that kiss now," she said to the darkness. "Just come back to me and I will grant you your 'eart's desires."

Just having him here again would help her face the day, whatever the weather. It had been so long since she had felt his touch, she resigned herself to another empty day. Mornings without her Sam were much like this sky; grey, featureless and bland, and to Annie, he was like this ghostly sun, distant and impalpable, yet definitely there in her memory.

The small shape in the bed beside her stirred and Annie held her breath, biting down on her lip. Bessie, her nine year old daughter, was sleeping and Annie prayed that she didn't wake. Whilst Bessie's sleep had been fitful of late, she knew that the last few hours of slumber just before the dawn were the most peaceful for her little girl. Many a night she had woken in the small hours, disturbed by her daughter's mumblings. Many a night she would sit and wait for the hue of first light, watching Bessie's face as her eyes flickered beneath her eyelids and Annie knew that she was dreaming about her father again. The last embers of dark morning saw Bessie settle and in that moment, Annie knew she was calm. She had suffered immeasurably after Sam disappeared and Annie didn't want the reality of another fatherless day to come too soon. In those few moments before she opened her eyes, she was sure that Bessie was mercifully rid of the memories and images of her father's face. Bessie's breathing regulated and Annie allowed herself a small breath, which fogged in the air before her.

She took in her surroundings and in her mind, counted the few things that she had in her life. She supposed that if there was one word to sum up her life, to best describe her surroundings and chattels, then that word would be *meagre*. There was her little girl, independent spirit, beautiful features and raven black hair that matched her mother's. She was the most precious thing in all the world. She was her reason for waking, for pushing on and not giving in. She was the link to her missing man; his flesh, his blood.

Their two room house had a tiny store and food preparation area at the rear on the ground floor. There was a chimney breast with a small fireplace and, next to the chimney, stood a bench and table of rough, hand-carved wood. Sam had made that table and they had both laughed at the poor carpentry skills that he displayed. Thinking of that day when he'd presented it to her, so proud of what he'd achieved, brought a rare burst of happiness within her and she smiled for what seemed like the first time in ages. She remembered how she'd tried not to laugh at him on that day, biting back the urge until she thought it would hurt. Luckily Sam saw the funny side and they both fell about cackling like drunken fools. That table didn't seem so foolish now, with its gnarled top and mismatched legs. There were scant other belongings and that room's only source of natural light on the ground floor came from a small window next to the doorway that faced onto Bath Square. With only an upstairs window for additional light, the house rarely looked bright, even on the sunniest days. The fire hadn't been lit for a week as wood and firelighters were costly. The upstairs room was mostly taken up with a large bed that Annie shared with Bessie to keep warm. It wasn't luxurious, consisting of a straw mattress that prickled and scratched, and a rag filled pillow. The bed had wooden slats that the mattress sat upon, but some were missing and it sagged like a hammock in places.

Annie shivered and wrapped her arms around her knees, hugging them tight for warmth and Bessie stirred once more, fidgeting and rolling on her back before opening her eyes. It took a while for Bessie to adjust her vision, giving the impression that, whilst her eyes were open, her sight was some way behind, attached to a piece of rope and trying to catch up.

Annie knew what was coming next.

"Are you there, father?" muttered Bessie in a state of lethargic half-sleep. Those were the same four words that she had muttered yesterday and the day before, stretching back almost every day since Sam went.

"Shush child," whispered Annie tugging the blanket and tucking it under her daughter's chin.

Bessie yawned and muttered something else, which Annie thought sounded like 'please come back,' then closed her eyes. She ground her teeth and her breathing grew heavier and Annie could tell that she was falling back into a deep sleep. It had been over two years since Sam had disappeared and Annie remembered that night as if it was yesterday. It was burned in her memory with a mental branding iron. That was the night that her life had changed completely. A single tear splashed onto her cheek and made a clean track down her face, washing the grime from her soft milky skin as it went. She wiped it away, sniffed back the deluge that threatened to follow and took a deep breath.

"Not today," she told herself quietly. "Not tomorrow neither."

Self-pity wasn't going to serve anyone well, least of all her sweet daughter. With one parent gone, Annie knew that she must carry the responsibility of being Bessie's mother and father, at least until his return, and she was sure that one day he would. It was that hope that she clung to above all others, and for that reason Bessie deserved a strong mother at the very least.

Down in the square she could see her friend Mary Abbott. Annie watched as Mary stuffed her lit pipe into her mouth, wrapped her dirty shawl around her shoulders and stamped her feet to ward away the cold. Her boots, laced with string, landed near three piglets that were searching for scraps and they jumped and scampered away. Annie watched as Mary chuckled to herself and yawned, a cloud of tobacco smoke billowing around her head.

She slid from the bed, still clothed in her only dress and clambered down the ladder stairs in her bare feet. It was freezing in the ground floor room and she struggled to stop her teeth from chattering. It left her feeling very grateful for the body heat that the pair had generated upstairs. She glanced at the dark, empty fireplace and scowled. It seemed to her that its soot encrusted aperture was somehow mocking her with its toothless grin. There would be no pot of warm water for Bessie and she would have to go without her wash again. She put on her boots, opened the front door and a blast of cold air slapped her across the face, making her catch her breath. Across the small square, Annie caught her friend's attention and the pair exchanged a wave. She stepped through the door and held her breath at the chill wind that whipped in from the harbour. There was a dampness in the air; the sort that penetrates to the core and wets bones from the inside out.

"Mornin', Annie," said Mary, sweeping a pile of straw and pig droppings away from her front door with the toecap of her boot. "Cold one, eh?"

"Seems to me that we've been trapped in winter forever," said Annie, hugging her slim frame. "I hate it," she concluded with a scowl, more to herself than for the benefit of the conversation.

"Had a drink yet?" said Mary trying to sweep the conversation away from her friend's melancholy.

Annie shrugged. "No. I'm out of ale and I got no money."

"Come in, sweet. Charlie's got some inside," said Mary opening the front door.

"Won't 'e be cross when 'e sees it's gone?"

"That man is drunk more than 'e's sober. I s'pect he will notice soon enough, but by then 'e'll be too pissed to care." Mary winked at Annie and pulled her into the house. Her place was almost identical to Annie's, but because there were two incomes, the furnishings were softer and more comfortable. In the hearth was a wood burning stove with a raging fire inside. Warmth flooded the room and instantly Annie felt cosy. She could feel the heat prickle on her frosty cheeks and her whole body itched as it warmed up.

"Sit down, girl. I'll fetch the ale." Mary rooted noisily inside a cupboard as Annie plonked her slight frame in a chair. She slid off her boots and allowed her frozen toes to defrost in front of the stove.

"You're one lucky bitch, Mary Abbott," joked Annie. "That fire would suit me. If I 'ad a fire like that, I'd think I'd died an' gone to 'eaven."

From the depths of the cupboard, Mary's muffled voice answered, "Charlie put that stove in for us. I'm only lucky cos I got a man about the 'ouse. Now, where is that bastard jug of ale? If 'e's drunk it, I'll swing for 'im." Mary pulled her head out of the cupboard and thrust the jug of ale triumphantly into the air like a trophy. She looked at Annie, who had fallen silent in the chair.

"Oh Annie, sweet. I didn't mean what I said. I didn't think, is all." Mary crossed the room and squashed her young friend's face into her bosom, patting her on the back. "There, there," she said, letting her go.

Annie's bottom lip trembled as she spoke. "If only I knew where 'e was. Or if 'e is alive at all. It's the not knowin'."

"That press gang's 'ad 'im for sure. You'll see," said Mary. "Mind you," she said, with a mischievous look upon her face, "why not let 'im 'elp you with the bills, food and what not. If nothin' else, 'e 'as money."

"'Im? 'Im, who?" said Annie.

"George Brownrigg is who. That man 'as the means an' the desire... an' 'e's not unappealin' to the eye either."

George Brownrigg ran the Point, leading a gang of villains called the *Riggers*. He took a percentage of the gains made from whoring on the Point and in return he offered his protection to the women who worked the streets. He also offered protection to the ale houses and pubs on the Point. In return for his unique brand of law, George charged the landlords a sum of money – and it was very lucrative work. George Brownrigg was a feared man.

"George is an attractive man, I admit that," said Annie. "But are you suggestin' that I forget my marriage?"

"So, for the first time you admit that he is attractive?" said Mary pointing at her friend and wagging her finger. "You could do a lot worse. 'Sides, Sam's been gone for such a long time now."

"And I s'pose your goin' to tell me that 'e ain't comin' back, is that it?" Annie folded her arms and stared at the floor.

"What's the point in hangin' on to the past? What if Sam don't come back? What then?"

"I am waitin'. Do you 'ear me, Mary Abbott? I will wait until hell freezes over."

"An' I admire that in you. We all do. I dare say that George is thinkin' that you're a loyal lass an' recognises it in you."

Annie stood and thrust her face at Mary who took a step backwards. "I wait cos I love 'im. Is that so 'ard for you to understand?"

"Not in the slightest," said Mary. "You seem to be labourin' under some idea that I don't understand the depth of feelin' you have for the man. I knows you better than anyone, and I understand, but that may be your past an' I was just thinkin' of the yet to come. Won't you at least think about it?"

Annie shook her head. "George Brownrigg is a bad man. He does bad things."

"'E's a rich man is what 'e is, an' 'e's fair smitten with you."

"I know that. Before Sam was gone, George would try 'is luck and it seemed the more I resisted, the more 'e wanted to try. I don't think 'e ever thought I'd give in, so it seemed more of a game to 'im. It didn't matter that Sam was there, George saw me as some prize to be won," said Annie. "And Lord knows 'e's tried. I've lost count of the advances and comments. 'Ow I kept 'im at bay all this time I'll never know."

"When it comes to you, George is different. I reckon he's prepared to wait."

"In what way?" said Annie.

"Look at you, girl. You are the prettiest woman in all of the old town. Everyone knows it, an' so did Sam. George is in love with you. Always 'as been, an' everyone except you can see it from as far away as Bembridge on the Island." Mary patted Annie's shoulder. "That's what kept you safe all this time. George wouldn't lay a finger on you in anger because 'e respects you."

"Respects me? That man respects no-one but 'imself."

"It's true," said Mary. "Just look at the way 'e treats the other women. Look at the way 'e treats me. With you it's different, like 'e sees you as a precious object. Some jewel in his crown. That's why 'e's waited all this time. It's like 'e wants you to want 'im. Playin' it nice an' slow." Mary winked at Annie. "So what 'ave you got to lose?" she said.

"My 'usband for a start," said Annie. "When he returns."

"*If* 'e returns."

Annie stormed towards the door. She threw it open and turned to Mary. "Stop sayin' that Sam is gone for good. I can't talk of this anymore."

Mary threw up her hands and said, "I'm sorry. I didn't mean to upset you so. If it makes you feel better, I 'opes he does come back an' all this can go away." Eager to dissipate the ill feeling, she continued, "The press gangs 'ad 'im fer sure. You'll be sittin' at home and 'e'll walk through the door like nothin's changed. You mark my words, sweet." Annie shut the door and turned to her friend. Mary handed her a wooden cup filled to the brim with ale. "'Ere you go," she said. "Now calm yourself down and sit."

"It's been such a long time now. So long that I lose sense of it, and still not a word." Annie accepted the wooden cup, set it down on the table and sat back down, tracing the ridge of the cup with her finger. "What if he's…?" Her words trailed into silence and she seemed lost in her thoughts.

"Don't think like that," said Mary. "Those press gangs have a lot to answer for, breaking up families indeed. What fuckin' right have they got?" Mary downed her cup of ale in one and wiped the dribbles that ran down the front of her dress. "You keep 'im alive, in 'ere." She pointed to her head. "And in 'ere." Now pointing towards her heart. "For King and Country indeed. What about for wife and family. Who speaks up for them? Who defends them?"

Annie loved Mary like a sister. She admired the woman for so many reasons. She was smart. Not smart in an educated way, like those who lived on the other side of the gate in town houses and had servants; but smart in other ways. She knew the Point and its ways. And fools got short shrift. Mary was a woman known for speaking her mind… and she was tough, fierce and loyal. She was Annie's protector, an aunt to Bessie and the one person who kept Annie going. She was under no illusions that, without Mary, she and Bessie would have starved. It was Mary who'd told her that she had two choices after her husband had gone, she could either apply to the Poorhouse at Portsea, or she could seek employment of sorts. Annie knew that 'employment of sorts' meant selling her body and on this subject Annie was resolute. She cast her mind back to the conversation…

"There are some things I ain't prepared to do," Annie had protested, "and betrayin' 'is memory's one of 'em."

Besides, wasn't she already a washer woman, to which Mary had laughed and said, "You think that the money what you earn from washin' is gonna save you from the poorhouse?"

"But the poorhouse, Mary. I 'ear things what go on there. Bad things." The stories that were told were awful and it seemed, to many, that starvation and destitution on the cold streets of the Point were better bedfellows than the kind of benevolence that was handed out in that place. "They claim to be Godly folk," said Annie, "but I knows the truth. They claim to be kind hearted and pure, but the reality is far worse than their noble intentions. Behind their starched clothes and leather-bound bibles, they are as immoral as the rest. Everyone knows they blame the poor as the creators of their own misfortune. Too stupid or lazy to improve their situations." Annie had felt herself growing angry. "At least the streets don't judge. The cold and damp don't care who's at fault." Annie knew that well-meaning folk were in short supply and in the *Portsea Poor House*, they were very thin on the ground indeed. Stories circulated about children being taken from their mother's breasts and sold to the highest bidder. Molestation, starvation and disease were as rife inside the walls as they were on the outside. Annie didn't want to subject Bessie to that. Anything was better than that life…

Annie's thoughts were interrupted by Mary's voice pulling her back to the present. Annie said, "Do you remember the time you told me to make money by sellin' my body?"

Mary looked sheepish. "I was just lookin' out for you is all. You was facin' the poorhouse."

"I still am."

"I wouldn't see you in a place like that anyway," said Mary. "If you remember, I was just sayin' that you gotta think of earnin' some money in other ways." Mary smiled at Annie and said, "All the while there's food on my table, there's food on yours."

"I do love you," said Annie. "You've been dear to me and Bessie."

"You're such a mawkish cow," laughed Mary, refilling Annie's cup. "You'd do the same for me if the boot was on the other foot."

"That I would," said Annie, "that I would."

The two women chatted until the light came up fully and the sun finally put in a pathetic appearance. It trickled through the slate grey sky and dribbled the ground with tentacles of pale golden light. Outside the house, people were starting the day's chores.

"Look lively, my girl," said Mary observing the changing light, "busy day's work ahead."

"What ship is it today?" said Annie.

"The *Foudroyant*. Due in after noon. William Juxon says that she's to be anchored off Spithead until she's ready for her repairs."

"It's not just the ship needin' a service," said Annie. "You're gonna be a busy woman, Mary Abbott."

"It puts food on the table and beer in me belly," said Mary. "It could do the same for you, if you just swallowed that stupid pride of yours."

"I couldn't. I wouldn't," said Annie. "I'd 'ave to be desperate to resort to that."

"An' you ain't desperate now?" said Mary. "Doin' the laundry ain't makin' you enough. I worry for Bessie's 'ealth."

"Bessie is fine. She's just a little pale, that's all," said Annie indignantly.

"And thin," countered Mary. "When was the last time that girl 'ad an 'ot meal? And you, come to think of it?"

"I don't matter," said Annie. "Only Bessie matters."

"Oh, is that so? And I suppose Bessie will fend for 'erself when you die of starvation."

Annie fell silent and stared at her toes. After a while she said, "I still couldn't. There 'as to be another way. Resortin' to fornicatin' with strangers would be like acceptin' that Sam was dead, an' that would be the death of me." She shuddered at the thought and said, "I couldn't think of anythin' worse than workin' for George Brownrigg."

Mary left the room and returned with a rag soaked in cold water. She hitched up her dress and wiped herself with the rag, sucking air through her teeth and said, "That's fuckin' cold and no mistake."

"I'd best be getting' back. Bess will be wantin' her food." Annie slid the dregs of the beer down her throat and handed the cup back to her friend.

"What food have you got in the 'ouse?" said Mary with a kindly look.

Annie shrugged and stared at the floor, avoiding her friend's gaze.

"I can read you like a book, Annie Crowther," said Mary with a chuckle.

"Who you tryin' to kid. You can't bleedin' read," said Annie.

Mary slapped her on the arm playfully and went to the cupboard, pulling out a cloth bag. Inside there was some bread and cooked meat. She broke a chunk of bread from the loaf and ripped at the meat. "Here." she said, handing the food to Annie.

"Thank you," she said, taking them. "You are such a good woman, Mary."

"Like I said, you'd do the same for me."

Annie hugged her and left the house. By the time she crossed the square, the sun was fully up and a grey mist clung to the ocean like smoke from the dying embers of a fire. It drew her to the edge of the harbour, by the sea wall where she'd stood so vigilantly, so many nights past. That familiar sight transported her back to her younger days, to when her father used to tease her that the sea-mist was the fogged breath of a giant serpent lurking just below the surface. Sometimes he called it sea smoke. In the distance, she could just make out the guard ship *HMS Fortitude*, and she wondered about the poor wretched souls incarcerated in its wooden belly. Its massive hull sat on the water like a sea monster rising above the waves. Ships dotted the horizon as far as the eye could see, stretching around Spithead, heading towards Gosport and beyond. Annie wondered if her husband would ever come back and, if he did, what would he make of her now, and the life that she led? Would he be ashamed of her if she sold her body to put food on the table? Would he still love her? Annie doubted that he would, but then again, she wasn't the same woman that he'd left all those years ago. She was tougher now with more sharp edges, jaded by her experiences. She knew that she only resisted Mary's pleading that she follow her into prostitution because she wanted to keep herself clean for when he came back. She couldn't have another man be intimate with her, not while she still burned a candle for her departed love. *He **was** missing*, she told herself many times, *he was **not** dead*. She had to become this person for the sake of Bessie. In her mind it wasn't a choice like Mary had said, either the poorhouse or prostitution. It was always a choice between harden up or give up, and Annie was no quitter.

The noise of shouting across the square diverted her attention from looking out to sea. She turned and saw the hulking frame of George Brownrigg, standing at well over six feet, towering above a man who cowered on the ground in the centre of a swell of people. She could tell it was a man from his wailing. George gripped his club headed walking stick in his right hand and brandished it above the stricken man's head. Behind George, Liz Beddows, another one of his women, clawed at him screaming like a banshee. Annie could see that she had a black eye. George shoved her to the ground and she landed in a stagnant puddle. The man wailed for mercy but George wasn't listening. Annie edged closer to hear what was being said as the crowd that surrounded them squeezed the circle tighter. Calls came from the back of the throng, a woman shouting to see blood. Another echoed her, "Kill the bastard."

"Please don't hurt me," screamed the trembling man who must have been half the size of Brownrigg. "She's my wife for pity's sake, George."

"She may be your wife but if you beat 'er, she ain't worth shit. No one will pay for 'er in that state."

Annie held back from the crowd but lined her sight directly with George's. She stared at him, willing that he would look up in her direction. She would not allow this man, this bully, to do this to that poor man. She watched as George gripped the man by the scruff of his coat and lifted him off the ground with one powerful arm, squeezing his face closer to his intended victim. Annie saw him mouth something to him.

"George Brownrigg!" she screamed. "You let that man be." The crowd turned and faced her. George dropped his intended victim to the ground and stared at Annie through the sea of people. His expression softened, as though coming out of a trance. The man scurried away, pushing through the booing crowd, who took advantage of the situation and kicked and punched him as he escaped.

"There'll be no killin' 'ere today," said George Brownrigg, still fixated on Annie. "Now clear off, the lot of ya." He swatted at the crowd, shooing them away and started to cross the Camber towards

Annie. She shifted awkwardly on the balls of her feet as he drew nearer. It hadn't occurred to her what she might say to this man mountain, or for that matter, what he might be about to say to her. Hadn't she just rebuked the self-styled 'King of the Point' in front of his people?

When he was close enough, she steeled herself and said, "I see you were about to mete out your usual brand of justice, George Brownrigg."

He smiled at her and said, "I see your low opinion of me is matched only by the high esteem with which you hold yourself, Annie Crowther." He bowed to her mockingly and tipped his hat. As he did so, she noticed him wink at her. "Had it been anyone else, I am certain that my mood would not be so forgiving, but as it's you…"

"And I see that you are so resolutely jovial in the face of such violence."

"I prefer to call it discipline," he said wistfully. "Discipline an' good humour are the backbone of a successful day, Annie Crowther. You will notice that the man lives, does he not?"

"I concede that 'e does but 'e might not, 'ad I not caught your attention."

"I cannot deny that you might 'ave 'ad something to do with the outcome."

"An' is your day successful?" said Annie.

"I believe it is becoming more successful by the minute," said George. Annie blushed and George said, "So I see a crack in the stony façade."

"You see nothing," said Annie, turning away briefly. George reached for her cheek, gently turning her face toward his.

"You have a tender touch for one so violent," she said.

"An' you 'ave a conviction rarely found in one so gentle."

"Who said I was gentle?" said Annie. "Raising a daughter, feeding an' clothing 'er whilst yearning for an absent 'usband can steel a girl, give 'er fight to see the day through to the next, even when there's little that brightens life. These traits are steadfastly the opposite of gentle."

George burst into laughter and immediately said, "Forgive my laughter. I see you, I know you. 'Ave we not spoken many times before today on matters of the 'eart? It is precisely that strength you show that attracts me to you. You have a strong will an' I like that, even if it sits awkwardly with me. I cannot think of another I would rather be with than you."

"But you must," said Annie.

"Why must I?" said George. "Think what great things we could achieve if we joined together. With your determination an' my head for business we could rule this place for years."

"I am taken," said Annie.

"Taken in spirit and in the eyes of the church, yes. But in practice, alas no."

Annie jabbed her finger to her breast and said, "I am still taken in my 'eart. 'E lives in here."

"Face the facts. Sam has been absent now for well over a year," said George. "You don't even know if you'll see 'im again."

"Well over *two* years now. I should know," she said jabbing her finger to her chest, "it's engraved in my 'eart. So will everyone stop tellin' me that Sam's not returnin'? First Mary, an' now you."

"So I'm not alone in my thinking?" said George.

"But it appears I am alone in mine," said Annie.

Suddenly George clasped his hands to his heart and said, "Please will you let me help you? I 'ave much I can give – not least money, food an' security. Can we at least not be friends?"

"And what price friendship?" said Annie. "What toll must be paid?"

"I seek nothing from you, other than the melting of this constant winter that seems to exist between us."

"I will consider your proposal," said Annie, turning and heading away.

As she walked George shouted, "You make me want to be a kinder man, Annie Crowther."

Annie could feel his dark eyes boring into her back all the way to the corner and, once out of sight, she raced back to the house at number three. Bessie sat at the table with her forehead resting on the cold wooden surface.

"Are you hungry?" said Annie.

Bessie barely looked up, but when she did, she looked at her mother with pale, dark ringed eyes and said, "No." She coughed violently and it sounded like the bark of a dog. Her skin had a ghostly pallor and Annie knew immediately that something was wrong. She sat next to her daughter and placed the back of her hand on Bessie's forehead.

"Child, you are burnin' up," she said. "'Ow long 'ave you been feelin' unwell?"

Bessie pressed her head onto her mother's hand, grateful for the reassurance that she got from its touch. She didn't answer Annie.

"Bessie, answer me. How long have you been feelin' unwell?"

"Just this mornin'," said Bessie. "I woke with a fever and my throat is sore."

"Let me see?" said Annie angling her daughter's head so that she could look at her throat. "Open up, there's a good girl." She lit the candle on the table and held it in front of Bessie's face. The flame danced, casting soft light over Bessie's pasty features. It seemed to Annie that her daughter's skin was almost opaque, with a greenish hue.

Bessie did as she was told and Annie peered down her throat. At the back, in the darkest recess near the tonsils, she noticed a greyish patch. She strained in the candle light to see what it was. The light from the flame wasn't bright enough and Annie closed her daughter's mouth gently, pressing her left hand on her neck, just below her chin. "Does this 'urt?" she said.

Bessie nodded, pulling herself away.

"Do you want to go back to bed?" she said, placing the candle back on the table and pulling her daughter close to her bosom, squeezing her thin frame. If only she knew what to do. Was this her fault for not feeding her child properly?

Bessie nodded and tried to stand, but in her state of weakness, she stumbled backwards, almost falling to the floor. The sudden movement brought a gasp of pain from the little girl.

"Are you alright?" said Annie shooting out her arm to steady her from the fall. Bessie closed her fingers around her mother's grip and smiled weakly.

"I want to go to bed," she said.

Annie lifted her child into her arms and climbed the ladder to the first floor room. It surprised her just how light Bessie was. Fear crept into her doubtful mind. Fear that she had caused this because of her stupid pride. If only she knew what to do.

Annie tucked her child into the bed and pulled the scratchy blanket around her. Bessie's teeth chattered, even though she was running a high temperature. She knew that medicine was expensive and Annie didn't have enough money for food, let alone remedies, or the cost of a physician. Mr Smallcoates was the only doctor she knew of. He had a small practice on the other side of the gate, in the High Street, but there was no way she could afford his fees. Annie tucked the blanket around her body and pulled Bessie onto her, rocking her slight frame back and forth, soothing her to sleep. Her feelings of uselessness hung over her like a dark cloud, ready to soak her in misery. Why hadn't she just listened to Mary and taken the work that was offered by Brownrigg? She might have dented what was left of her dignity but losing dignity didn't compare to losing a daughter. Bessie's breathing was irregular and, every now and again, she would flutter open her eyes and stare at her mother. There was a distance in her gaze. She seemed to stare through Annie as though there was little recognition of her mother's presence.

Through the window that looked down on the square, Annie saw George strolling by with his hefty stick at his side. He stopped to chat to Pete Bookbinder, one of his men and then as the two parted he stared at Annie's tiny little house. Annie slid away from the window, hoping that George would soon be gone. She couldn't face him again today, not with Bessie being so poorly.

Chapter Two

The mighty *Foudroyant*, an eighty gun third-rate ship of the line, sat proudly in the bay, anchored off Spithead with its hulking frame dwarfing the surrounding boats that bobbed on the winter waves. The first Pinnace arrived shortly after three o'clock, greeted by a gaggle of local dollymops, lining the harbour walls, eager to get a glimpse of the sex starved crew, and pretty soon the Point was teeming with sailors, all looking for food, fun and ale. The pubs and grog shops were full to bursting and the chaotic sound of money-making filled the narrow streets.

Annie was woken from her slumber by the bustle outside her house. She had drifted off to sleep while she sat with her daughter. She looked down at Bessie's ashen face, more akin to an apparition than that of a little girl, and bit back tears. She was sleeping soundly in her mother's arms but her breathing was erratic and the fever had really gripped her small frame, with Annie convincing herself that it had grown worse since the morning.

"Bessie," she whispered in her daughter's ear, "wake up."

Bessie stirred, her long lashes flicked open briefly and she stared at her mother vacantly. No sooner had her eyes opened, they closed again and she slipped back to sleep.

"It's me, Bessie. Don't worry, I'm 'ere." Annie did her best to not sound panicked and brushed stray hairs from her daughter's face.

Suddenly, Mary's voice called from the open doorway of Annie's house.

"Are you there, sweet?" she said. "I'm off to work. Do you need anythin' while I'm out?"

"Mary?" Annie called back. "Can you come up 'ere?"

Mary tutted and said, "Okay but I'll 'ave to be quick. I'm late as it is."

"Please, Mary," said Annie.

After a second, Mary's face appeared at the top of the ladder and she smiled at her friend. She climbed onto the bed and said, "In bed at this hour? Whatever is the matter?"

"It's Bessie," said Annie, finally allowing the fears that she had held inside to overwhelm her. She lowered the blanket to reveal her daughter's face and Mary's countenance was one of shock. "She 'as a fever and an awful cough," said Annie, biting back the tears.

Mary clasped her hand to her mouth and gasped in fright. "What is it that ails her?"

Annie shrugged at her friend. "Dunno. She was sick when I got back from yours earlier. I'm scared, Mary."

****

William Juxon stood in the doorway of *The Camber Inn,* waiting for Mary, knowing Brownrigg would be very unhappy is she was late again. He thrust his hands into his pockets and tried not to think about the cold that penetrated every muscle and sinew of his body. A shape floated into view, coming from the direction of Broad Street and William instantly recognised its familiar contours. Brownrigg's ever present Derby hat sat on his head in a jaunty manner, giving the impression that there was something of the comical about the man. But Juxon knew better. Everyone knew better. There was nothing comical about George Brownrigg. Nothing in the slightest. As George got nearer to the pub, he raised his hand in greeting.

"Bleedin' cold one today," he called to Juxon, puffing steam through his nostrils and rubbing his hands together.

William Juxon nodded. "Let's get inside. There's a fire lit."

"Was Mary on time?" said George drawing to a halt.

Juxon paused, shrugged and said, "You knows what she's like, George. That woman is never on time."

"I thought you were goin' to 'ave words?" said George. "Make it clear an' all that."

"An' I did, George. Couldn't 'ave made it any clearer."

"I am goin' to teach 'er a lesson when she gets 'ere." George screwed his fists into a ball and spat on the ground. "Go an' fetch 'er," he commanded.

"Can't we give her a bit longer?" said Juxon. "She will be 'ere."

"That's your fuckin' problem – too soft by arf. Go an' get her," said George through gritted teeth. "I won't ask again."

William Juxon brushed past Brownrigg and scampered in the direction of Mary's house. He passed the open doorway of Annie's house, and crossed the street, stopped at Mary's door and knocked. When he got no response, he knocked again and muttered under his breath, "Look lively, girl, or this day will be a bad one."

Across the square, Annie was pleading with Mary.

"Please, I don't want anyone to know about this."

"But why?" said Mary. "If you can't afford the doctor, someone might 'elp."

"Like who?" said Annie. "This place 'ain't famed for its kindly spirit. People will point an' say cruel things. They'll chase us away from our 'ome."

"No they won't. They'll understand."

"Really? Is that what you think?" said Annie. "You seem to forget what 'appened to Susan Rawridge. She was run out of town when 'er Bert got the small pox. They said he 'ad the plague an' damn near burnt their place down."

"That was different," said Mary. "Susan wasn't well thought of to begin with. Folk round 'ere used the plague as an excuse."

"Even so, I 'ain't willin' to put Bessie through that."

"But…" said Mary.

"No buts. Folk can be cruel. I ain't 'avin' this poor girl goin' through that."

Mary grasped Annie by the hand and squeezed it. She said, "For Bessie's sake, please let me get 'elp. That poor girl doesn't 'ave the strength to make it on 'er own."

"You think that thought ain't crossed my mind already? I fear the worst," said Annie.

"Then for the last time, let me 'elp. I know someone who has the means."

"'As the means? You mean Brownrigg? I don't want him knowin' about this, if that's what you're thinkin'," said Annie. "I don't wanna be in debt to 'im. I'll just 'ave to find another way."

"But 'e's got money. More than enough to get this girl the medicine that she needs."

Suddenly William Juxon's voice echoed in the small room downstairs, "Annie, are you there?"

Both women froze, holding their breath. Annie looked at Mary and shook her head as if to say, *keep quiet.* Juxon called again,

"Hello. Are you there?"

Mary stood slowly, shifting her weight and stepped on a squeaky floorboard.

"I can 'ear you up there," said Juxon grabbing the ladder and climbing. He poked his head through the gap in the floor, just as Annie threw the blanket over her daughter's pale face and said, "What's goin' on 'ere?"

"I was just comin'," said Mary with a hint of panic in her voice. "Annie needed me."

"Annie needed you? What about Brownrigg? 'E's got a room full of sailors waitin' for their greens. Lizzie's already there earnin' 'er keep, an' so should you be."

"I know an' I'm sorry. I'm comin' now." Mary shot Annie a telling look that said she had no choice but to leave. As she started down the ladder she said, "I'll look in on you later."

Once at *The Camber Inn,* Mary encountered George's humourless disposition. He scowled at her as she entered the bar.

"What time d'ya call this?" he said, glugging back a generous slug from his cup. "Look around, girl. I got men with money an' no-one 'ere to take it from them." He stood and grabbed Mary by the arm and pulled her into the centre of the room.

"You're 'urtin' me, Mr Brownrigg," protested Mary as she wriggled in his grip.

"Good," said George pressing his mouth to her ear. "You count yourself lucky that I don't cut you for this. Now get to work and maybe I'll look upon you more kindly by the end of the night." He released his meaty fingers from her arm and Mary breathed a sigh of relief. She glanced at the gaggle of men seated in the pub and knew that she was going to be very busy. Lizzie Beddows smiled at her as she guided a portly customer through a door at the rear of the room that led out into the alley at the back. From there she would take him to the stables in the small yard. It was private and reasonably warm.

Mary brushed her hair from her forehead, planted the most insincere smile on her face and said, "Who's first?"

By the end of the night, Mary was exhausted. She had made enough money to keep her and her husband Charlie in food and ale for the week, and for that she was grateful. Juxon moved about the room, scooping up cups and tankards and depositing them on the bar. The room was empty, save for a drunken man in the corner who had slipped into infused slumber, resting his head on the table and snoring loudly. Juxon gave him a sharp boot in the side, toppling the chair that he sat upon, and the man fell to the floor with a groan.

"C'mon. Fuck off 'ome," he shouted and the man scampered towards the door in a dazed state. Juxon cleared the rest of the tables in silence. Mary watched him from her chair in the corner and puffed smoke from her pipe.

The door opened and Brownrigg entered. He glared at Mary and said, "Right, girl, let's see whether you've managed to redeem yourself. How much 'ave you got." He held out his shovel sized hand and Mary pulled a cloth bag from deep within her cleavage and handed it to George, who lifted it up and smiled.

"Good weight of coins. Looks like you might 'ave succeeded in liftin' me mood." He opened the bag and poured its contents on the bar. George divided the pile of coins into three; the largest pile was his and he slid it into the pocket of his great coat, the next stack was for Juxon, who accepted his payment without the slightest hint of gratitude. He simply grumbled, wiped his nose with the sleeve of his shirt, turned and went back to his chores. Mary's was the smallest pile.

She was grateful for her share and said, "Thank you, Mr Brownrigg," sliding the money into her small purse that she kept in a hidden pocket in the underside of her dress.

"Get off 'ome an' rest, cos there'll be another lot to see to tomorrow."

Mary nodded and went through a doorway to the right side of the bar to fetch her shawl. The door shut behind her and all she had to light her way was a single candle that burned in its holder on the table. Next to the candle were some supplies. There were firelighters, spare candles and a white cloth that covered something. Curiosity got the better of her and she lifted the cloth and peeked under. On a wooden plate sat some bread, some pottage, an apple, a pear and three pies. Immediately, her thoughts shifted to Annie and her sick and starving daughter. Mary's heart raced as she contemplated what she was about to do. She lifted one of the pies from the table and slid it into the secret pocket in her dress. Next she slid the apple into her hand and turned to leave. Suddenly the door opened and Juxon entered the room, spying the apple in Mary's hand. His eyes widened.

"What you doin', Mary?" he said shifting his gaze from her face to her hand and then back again. "That's mine," he said.

"I was just lookin' at it, is all," said Mary feigning innocence.

"No you wasn't. You was stealin' it." Juxon grabbed her by the arm and lifted it in the air. He prized the apple from her small fingers and checked it for damage. "I didn't 'ave you for a thief, Mary Abbott. What else you got 'idden?" Juxon pulled Mary towards him and Mary screamed. From the bar, George called out,

"What the fuck is goin' on in there?"

Mary screamed again as Juxon pressed his large frame against her, pinning her to the wall. His breath stank of tobacco and stale beer. "Where's that pocket of yours?" he said, lifting her skirt and rummaging underneath. "I know you got a pie cos there were three on that table."

Brownrigg stood in the doorway, blocking the light from the other room. He saw Juxon with his back to him with his hand up Mary's skirt and thought the worst, grabbing the landlord by the collar and yanking him away. Mary stepped towards the door, trying to squeeze past George but he blocked her path with his elbow.

"What the 'ell is goin' on? William, what were you thinkin'?"

"I caught this bitch stealin' from me. Red 'anded and as brazen as you like."

George turned to Mary, who didn't look him in the eye, opting to stare at the floor instead. "Is there truth in this?" he said.

Mary didn't answer and continued her prolonged gaze at the floor. Suddenly, Brownrigg's hand gripped her by the chin and lifted her face upwards. She blinked at him and said, "It wasn't for me, Mr Brownrigg. I wasn't takin' it for me."

"Then who was it for?"

"I cannot say. I am forbidden."

"Then you leave me no choice. I'll deal with you like I deals with all the traitors among us." He clenched his fist and William Juxon turned his face away.

Mary clasped her hands together and pleaded with George. "Please don't. I am no thief, an' you knows what I'm like." Mary gripped Brownrigg's arm. "I'm as trustworthy as the day is long." She turned towards William Juxon gripping his arm instead. "I ain't never taken from you before, 'ave I? You gotta believe me when I say it wasn't for me that I took it."

William sighed and said, "I know you, Mary, an' I know that you don't normally steal, but this behaviour is unacceptable." He threw his hands in the air in exasperation. "The only way you is goin' to avoid a beatin' is if you tell us who you were stealin' the food for."

Both men fell silent and watched as Mary's bottom lip started to quiver. George crossed his arms and waited. Eventually, she said, "Promise me that if I tell, you won't breathe a word of it?"

"Speak, woman. My patience is as weak as the beer in this place and I pine for me bed," said George, adding, "Who is it for?"

"It was for Annie. Her daughter Bessie 'as the fever and I thought that a full belly might make 'er feel well again."

"'Ow long as she been like it?" said Juxon.

"Just today, but she's proper pale an' 'as a cough that would shame a barkin' dog." Mary wiped her eyes with the heel of her palm. "That poor child needs medicine but Annie don't 'ave the money. As I live an' breathe, I swear to you that I was stealin' for that little girl."

A smile curled on the unkindly face of George and his eyes sparkled with mischief as he placed his hand on her shoulder. "Annie Crowther, eh?" He pondered for a moment, as if in private conversation with himself, then he turned to Juxon.

"Give her the apple and some beer. What else is under that rag?" he said.

Juxon muttered something barely audible and lifted the cloth. He picked up one of the pies and tossed it towards Mary who caught it deftly in her left hand. "Take the lot if you must," he said.

"I don't want to take your food, Mr Juxon. Just the pie and apple will do."

William Juxon glared at George. "S'pose I got no say in all this."

Brownrigg stepped forward and slapped Juxon across the cheek. "Keep your tongue an' find your manners," he said. "Remember to whom you speak." He emphasised his point with a jab of his forefinger in Juxon's face. "There is a child in need 'ere," he said pacing the room, rubbing his meaty hand over his chin. "There is a woman, an' a fine one at that, in need too. It is not beyond our powers to grant a brief cessation in their sufferin'." Brownrigg stopped pacing and turned to stare at them both. With a click of his fingers he said, "An' that is what we shall do."

"What shall we do?" said Mary. "What *can* we do?"

"I'll fetch Smallcoates the physician in the mornin'," said George. "You tell Annie that we will do all we can to aid 'er child's recovery. You tell 'er that kindly ol' George is gonna look after 'er from now on." He leaned over and squeezed Mary's arm. "You tell Annie Crowther exactly that." George was now so close that Mary could smell his breath. He patted her cheek and said, "Now run along, there's a good girl, an' deliver my words. Be sure to get 'em right."

Mary left the pub and rushed to Bath Square. The sky was clear and, for the first time in what seemed like an age, the stars put on a show of dazzling beauty. Mary played Brownrigg's words in her mind as she made her way across the Camber. Had she just given that brute of a man a reason to hope? Had she just opened a door – one that would not be shut so easily? She hoped that Brownrigg's money would save Bessie, and for that she would be glad for her actions, but something gnawed at her conscience like a rat chewing on the rotten toes of a dodger in a debtor's prison cell.

Mary crossed the Camber, turning past *The Coal Exchange* pub on her left and made her way to Annie's. She worried that her friend would not like what she was about to tell her, but a small piece of Mary felt that she had done the right thing. She knew that Bessie needed medical care and she hadn't been at all surprised by George Brownrigg's reaction. He was a man well versed in the art of sniffing out opportunities and Annie was the greatest prize of them all. For that reason, Mary resolved that she would mention her conversation with George and the kindness that he'd shown, but not mention the bit about Smallcoates. How else was she supposed to explain away the gift of the food? Annie had enough on her plate without adding to her worries.

Mary pushed open the door and entered the dark little house. In her hand she held the bright apple.

Chapter Three

Gilbert Smallcoates, Physician...

There was a timid, almost frightened little knock at the door. At first it was barely audible, but the knock came again, slightly more assured than before. Annie hadn't slept at all and stared out of the upstairs window. It was light outside and the Point was busy. The knock came again and she opened the window and called down impatiently,

"I'm comin'."

She pressed her hand to Bessie's body and the heat that the small girl generated made her skin feel clammy. Annie knew that her fever was raging and that her child was getting worse. She climbed down the ladder and opened the door. Standing before her was a pinched, waif of a man with a thin nose that seemed to have no other purpose than to hold his eye glasses, and a pursed lip that any fishwife would have been proud of. He offered her his card, which Annie took, saying, "I cannot read it, sir."

The man cleared his throat and announced himself.

"Good morning," he said. "I am Gilbert Smallcoates, Physician, and I am sent to treat your sick child." He spoke in a shrill little voice that reminded Annie of early morning birdsong.

"I ain't sent for no doctor," said Annie, sounding confused.

"You are Mrs Crowther?" said Smallcoates and Annie nodded.

"And this is number three Bath Square?" Again she nodded.

"Good, then all appears as it should be. Now, may I come in?"

Annie stepped aside, allowing Gilbert Smallcoates to brush past her and the way he moved reminded her of a bird with clipped wings. He walked in a strange fashion, much like a chicken clucking in the yard. The sweet aroma of his perfume filled the air. Annie shut the door and said, "I don't 'ave any money."

"Money isn't important, Mrs Crowther. I am sent to you and that is that." He gave her a small bow and offered a version of a smile. His tiny little eyes sparkled like black jewels set against a backdrop of paleness. Annie's mind was a whirl of emotion. She couldn't believe that her little girl was going to get proper treatment, but she suspected that this funny little man before her was part of a slippery slope of indebtedness to one man. She swept away her fears and reasoned that her daughter was her priority.

"Who sent you?" she said.

"I am not at liberty to divulge. Client confidentiality is paramount. Suffice to say that I am here to help. Now, where is the patient?"

Annie pointed to the ladder.

"Very good," said Doctor Smallcoates. He looked around the room, scowling slightly. Annie had the distinct feeling that he was offended. "Just as I thought," he said absently under his breath.

"Just as you thought?" said Annie. "What do you mean?"

"Forgive me, Mrs Crowther. I mean no offence when I say that this abode is... how should I put it?" Smallcoates fished for the least offensive words. He clicked his fingers and said with self-congratulatory delight, "A little limited."

"It ain't much," said Annie, "but it's my 'ome. We can't all live in grandeur."

The doctor ignored her and said, "Will you fetch me some fresh water?" There was no hint of kindness in his tone. He placed his hat and coat on the wooden bench and wiped his hands on his waistcoat.

Annie said, "Fresh water? You're 'avin a laugh. We don't 'ave fresh water 'ere."

Smallcoates replied, "No matter," and tapped his bag. "I have my own supply just in case. Now do you own a bowl?" Annie left the room and returned with a bowl, and a rag for a towel.

She placed the bowl on the table and watched while Smallcoates filled it with water from a bottle, asking him, "What are you goin' to do?"

"I understand that your child suffers with the fever." He didn't wait for Annie to reply and continued, "The cure will be based on the four humours that are the mainstay of modern medicine." He turned and climbed the ladder, offering no further explanation to his words. Annie shrugged and supposed that he knew what he was doing for such a learned fellow. Smallcoates disappeared through the hatch, carrying his bag with him and Annie followed him up the ladder, carefully balancing the bowl of cold water and the rag.

The doctor knelt down and stared at Bessie. "This child is painfully thin. Does she not get fed?" he said, lifting her arm.

Annie felt a wave of shame. She had done this to her child. Whilst she herself hadn't eaten properly in weeks, opting to give the scant supplies she had to Bessie, she still knew that it was because of her circumstances that her child was at death's door.

"I do my best," she said, "but there is little money comin' in."

"This child needs nourishment. Her bones are not growing and that may be why she has suffered with fever." Smallcoates opened Bessie's mouth and stared inside. "Mm," he said.

"What is it?" said Annie. "What do you see?"

"There is a something attached to her throat at the back," said the doctor. "That isn't good."

Annie knew that he must have meant the growth on her tonsils. "Do you know what it is?" she said.

Smallcoates closed Bessie's mouth and turned to Annie, sliding his spectacles down his nose, and balancing them on the tip. "I'm afraid I know what ails your daughter. Have you ever heard of Boulogne Sour Throat?"

Annie shook her head.

"I'm fearful it is what she suffers from," said the doctor. "Tell me, does she have trouble swallowing, breathing and so on?"

"She complained of a sore throat yesterday and she is without her appetite."

"Exactly as I thought," said Smallcoates, opening his bag and pulling out a small knife.

"What's that for?" said Annie in a state of panic.

"Bloodletting. We need to drain the disease from her body, Mrs Crowther," said the doctor. "Please be kind enough to hold your child's head still."

"What are you goin' to do to her?"

"One must think of the body as a machine, or a pump. The bloodletting acts like a valve and will allow the body to rid itself of the disease thus lowering the pressure within."

Annie did as she was told and gently, but firmly, gripped her daughter's head, soothing her pale skin and whispering calming words to her. She doubted that Bessie could hear her voice but it made her feel better for it.

"Mrs Crowther, I must stress that you need to be extremely still. I am about to make a cut in the vein just under her tongue."

"Will she feel any pain?"

"I suppose so," said Smallcoates,. "But I also suppose that the alternative if the procedure remains undone would be much worse."

"Be quick about it then," said Annie. She was mightily grateful for the services of such a knowledgeable man, but she was beginning to find him pompous in the extreme.

Smallcoates reached inside Bessie's open mouth with the knife and lifted her tongue. He slid the tip of the blade along the vein where her tongue was joined with the base of her jaw. Bessie twitched and opened her eyes, staring up at her mother.

Smallcoates snapped, "Please keep the patient still." He peered at her over the top of his spectacles and his features further reinforced Annie's image of him as a bird; a sparrow perhaps, in a man's clothing. After a moment or two he dabbed at Bessie's bleeding mouth with the rag and said, "There. We are done."

"What now?" said Annie. "Is that it?"

"On the contrary, Mrs Crowther. We have still to apply the balm." The doctor reached into his bag and produced a tiny bottle of powder with a blueish tint. He uncorked the top and said, "You can release her head. Some water, if you please?"

Annie handed him the bowl and watched as Gilbert Smallcoates poured a small amount of the powder into a tiny bowl, again produced from his bag. He dipped his finger in the bowl of water and added a drop or two and, using the same finger, smoothed the floury mix into a paste.

"Do you have any honey, Mrs Crowther?" he said.

Annie shook her head.

"Never mind. Here," The doctor once more reached into his bag and pulled out a clay jar with a cloth lid. He handed it to Annie.

"What's this for?" she said.

"It is to sooth the redness in the throat. I suggest that she swallow a mouthful every evening before bed to aid her rest. Other than that, you can apply as liberally as you wish."

"Thank you," said Annie. "What's in that powder?"

"This is Devil's Bitt," said the doctor, holding the bowl aloft, "an ingenious little flower that is commonly found in this country. Once picked and dried it is ground into a powder. It has been discovered that it has a particular use when dealing with Boulogne Sour Throat. I have used it before in similar circumstances and I have to say that the results have been favourable in thirty percent of the cases."

"It looks expensive," said Annie eying the paste in the bowl.

"Extremely," said Smallcoates without a thought for her embarrassment.

Annie swallowed and said, "An' you're sure that there is to be no recompense for your services?"

"I was summoned on the instruction that your daughter was to receive the finest care, whatever the cost." Smallcoates again stared down his nose at Annie. "I daresay that you have wealthy friends indeed, Mrs Crowther." He looked her up and down and surveyed his surroundings and said, "Although, lord knows why."

"I'm sorry that we don't live in splendour like you," said Annie.

Smallcoates, realising the error of his words, hastily said, "This treatment is expensive but free to you, my dear."

"An' if I begs, you still won't tell me who sent you?"

"I have no doubt that in due course he will become known to you, but for now he will remain masked."

"Ah," said Annie with a hint of triumph, "so you admit that it is a *he* at least." And Annie knew who it was.

The doctor squeezed his eyes shut and muttered something barely audible, but she supposed he was giving himself a stern dressing down for the slip up. Smallcoates opened his eyes and ignored her question. He said, "Kindly open the child's mouth so I can apply the balm." He reached in with a globule of the paste on the tip of his finger and spread it skilfully over the sore on Bessie's throat. "There," he said, "that is that." He dipped his finger in the bowl of water and wiped it on the rag. Smallcoates stood suddenly and quickly deposited his things back in the bag, then started down the ladder. Annie followed him with the distinct sense that, now he had carried out his duties, he had little desire to stay in such a lowly place and was at great pains to leave. Once on the ground floor, the doctor said, "She needs as much rest as possible. You must keep her cool, so I might suggest that mopping her skin in cold water will help reduce the fever. You already have the honey and will follow my instructions?"

Annie nodded.

"Good," said Smallcoates. "Now I must stress that your daughter has a long road to traverse and it will be fraught with danger. May I be candid, Mrs Crowther?" For the first time since his arrival, Annie detected a hint of kindness, of softness in the doctor's voice. He leaned closer to Annie and stared into her eyes. She nodded and bade the man to continue. "Then I feel that it would be remiss of me if I did not point out the possibilities should the treatment not work." He paused while she digested his words. When he was sure she had, he continued, "Mrs Crowther, there is the chance that your daughter might die."

"Die?" said Annie clamping her hand to her mouth. "Please say it ain't so? Please tell me that there is 'ope?" She gripped the featherlike hands of the doctor and squeezed them. He looked embarrassed and took a step backwards, as if scalded by her touch.

"Mrs Crowther, there is always hope. Without it I wouldn't be here." He pulled his coat on and placed his hat on his head. "I must emphasise that she needs to be kept cool. The fever will worsen over the next day or so, but with the will of God and my skilled treatment, hopefully we should see a break in her temperature within the week. I will return in two days to administer some more of the balm." He gave a small bow and said, "Until then."

Doctor Smallcoates opened the door and disappeared into the throng of life outside. Annie shut the door and rested her head against the cold wood listening to the sound of her heartbeat and for the breathing of her daughter upstairs. Her mind was a mess of thoughts, cramming for space in her brain. *He said she might die. She mustn't die.* Annie slid down the door and sat on the floor in a heap. It had all become too much for her to cope with and she let the river of sorrow flow. She sobbed and sobbed until the well of tears ran dry. Eventually she stood, wiped her eyes with her sleeve and crossed the room, sitting at the bench to gather her thoughts. Smallcoates had said that the mysterious friend was a *he* and Annie knew exactly who *he* was. Mary had told her the previous evening about the incident in *The Camber Inn* and it was George who had showed her kindness. It was George who heard of Bessie's plight and so it followed that it had to be him who paid for the doctor. Her heart swelled at the thought that such a bad man, a violent and feared man, could do something so good. She supposed that he had done it for selfish reasons, because Brownrigg liked her and that he hoped her gratitude would elevate into something greater. Annie was under no illusion that if Bessie recovered, she would indeed be indebted to him.

Bessie coughed upstairs and cried out to her mother.

"Coming," called Annie, crossing the room and climbing the stairs. As she rested her daughter's head on her lap, she resolved to visit George later that day and thank him.

****

George stood by the bar of *The Camber Inn* and sipped his beer. He read the note that Doctor Smallcoates had given him. It was a bill for his time and expenses for attending the Crowther child. He folded it into four and slipped it into his coat pocket. In the corner of the room a small group of sailors, fresh from *H.M.S Foudroyant*, were busy slapping each other's backs. They were a bawdy bunch of drunken men who had been in the pub for most of the day. They had sampled the local women and one in particular, a scrawny man, known simply as Guppy, was becoming more vocal about his dissatisfaction with the woman he had paid for.

"She was a sizeable thing," he said, glugging back his ale, taking in the merriment of his friends. "I tell you," he shouted, "she wasn't worth what I paid. I wouldn't be surprised if she gave me somethin' down below." He glanced down at his groin and scratched comically, which amused his shipmates immensely.

Someone in the group suggested that if he were so disappointed he should request a refund. A few of the others agreed.

"A refund, eh? Maybe you're right." Guppy stared around the room and said, "Which of these men is 'er keeper?"

"The big fellow at the bar," said one of his friends. "'E's the one you wanna see."

Guppy stood and approached the big man at the bar. George, who had been deep in thought about Annie and her sick child, turned to stare at the twig in breeches that stood before him.

Guppy said, "Is you the one what keeps the whores?"

"Who wants to know?" said George dismissively.

"Me an' my mates want a refund. We wasn't 'appy with the woman that you sold us." Guppy looked back at the noisy table of sailors in the corner and winked. They fell about in fits of laughter, raising their ales to Guppy. Buoyed by their encouragement, he pressed on, "I wanna know what you intend to do about it?"

George turned his back on the sailor without a word and stared straight ahead at the bar, never once averting his gaze. He sipped his beer calmly.

Guppy poked him in the arm and said, "Are you listening to me? We wanna refund."

Brownrigg slammed his cup down on the bar and stood slowly. As he rose from his chair he grabbed the thick club-stick that rested against the wooden side of the counter. He turned to the slither of a man before him and through gritted teeth said, "You 'ave about ten seconds to get the fuck outta this pub and off my patch."

Guppy took a step backwards and glanced at his foolish mates but they just egged him on. Not wanting to lose face, he swallowed and said, "Not until we gets what we want."

Suddenly, George grabbed Guppy by the collar and dragged him towards the door. He pushed him out into the cold evening, using his face as a battering ram against the heavy door. Outside, Davey Turner and Pete Bookbinder were deep in conversation when they saw their boss dragging Guppy to the floor. They raced over just as Juxon emerged from the pub with another two of the drunken sailors in his grasp.

"These two can join 'im," said Juxon, shoving them into the square. He turned to Pete and Davey. "You two follow me. There's a couple more inside that need shiftin'."

Guppy climbed to his knees just as Juxon and the other two disappeared back into the pub. His two shipmates hauled him up and the three sailors squared up to Brownrigg.

"Lookin' for a fight, eh?" said George swinging his club-stick in his right hand. "There's three of us and one of you. I likes them odds," said Guppy.

The seamen rushed at George and he side-stepped their advance. In their drunken state they didn't keep their balance and toppled in a heap on the wet ground. George wasted no time in grabbing Guppy and swinging his club. Guppy screamed as it connected with his head and his two mates suddenly lost their appetite for violence. They ran towards the Camber and the empty Pinnace tied up in the harbour. Guppy pleaded with George.

"Please," he said dripping in blood, "we didn't mean anythin' by it. We was just havin' a laugh, is all."

The remaining two drunkards suddenly flew out of the door of the pub and landed in a puddle. They saw the blood on Guppy's face and ran for the Camber to join the others.

"Looks like you're all alone now," said George. "It's a shame, cos I was itchin' for some fair odds." He raised the club over his head and brought it down with all his might. Guppy's scream could be heard in the harbour as the four cowardly sailors rowed for all they were worth back towards the ship.

Chapter Four

Burrow Island…

Guppy's body was gone by the time Annie crossed the square in the direction of *The Camber Inn*. So were the tell-tale signs of a struggle. George couldn't afford to have a dead sailor on his patch; he knew that the ones who escaped back to the ship would alert the ship's officers and they would come knocking. She passed the spot where Guppy had lain, face down in a puddle, completely unaware of the murderous act of the man she was on her way to thank for his kindness. Annie had slipped out when Bessie seemed at her most restful, concluding that a few moments alone wouldn't harm her. Tears clouded her vision and the speckles of water in her eyes made the lamps that burned in the many windows on the Point appear disjointed and floating, like hundreds of fireflies. A light mist had descended and the air was cold and damp. Annie glanced back at her house as her footsteps muffled on the wet ground and the iridescent glow that illuminated the window, throwing pale light into the square, looked warm and inviting.

Annie turned away, playing out in her head what she was going to say to George. She wanted him to know that she was grateful for his intervention, but at the same time, she didn't want to give him the wrong impression, that his kind deed meant there was something more between them. Bessie had to get well, that was the priority, but Annie knew that she would have to tread very carefully indeed along the narrow path of gratitude and indebtedness, which stretched from her to Brownrigg's door. In some respects she had hoped that her kind benefactor could have been anyone other than the man she now made her way to see.

She stared out to sea at the beautiful moon hanging in the sky like a silver medallion, casting shadows on the calm waters below. Lights danced in the distance like tiny beacons floating on the breeze; dozens of torches burned aboard the ships anchored off the Point and around the harbour and Annie imagined that they were dark, blinking giants. They stretched from Priddy's Hard in Gosport all the way round the shoreline to Fort Blockhouse and into the open waters of the Solent, beyond the protective chain at the harbour mouth. Annie could just make out the hull of *The Foudroyant* with its tall masts stretching so high, silhouetted against the moon's glow, and she imagined a small cabin boy could run up their length and reach out to touch the surface of the moon above. The ships were a truly remarkable sight and Annie supposed that her beloved Sam was on a vessel much like those in the harbour. Every time a ship came in, desperation drove her to ask the sailors that came ashore if they knew of her husband's whereabouts, describing him in the greatest detail. Their answer came as it always did, with the shake of a head or a shrug of the shoulders. Someone somewhere must have met Sam, must have served with him? How could they not know his face? Annie resolved to keep asking until she got the answer she desired.

She tried to imagine the hardship that he must be enduring and the sense of lost time that he too must feel. She had Bessie, but Sam had no one. The gentle lapping of the waves against the Camber wall soothed her troubled mind and the hypnotic shimmering of the moon caressed her eyes. Annie stood, rooted to the spot, for what seemed like an age before a sound behind her snapped her back from her thoughts. She turned to see what the noise was and found that she was virtually alone on the harbour side. Whoever had made the sound had disappeared. The thin light that radiated from *The Camber Inn* pulled her towards it and soon she found herself at the door. She went inside.

The pub was empty, except for William Juxon who was busy wiping down the tables with a dirty rag. He was so engrossed in his work that he didn't see or hear Annie enter. She cleared her throat and the publican nearly jumped out of himself in fright.

He turned and said, "What the fuck?"

"Sorry, William. Did I startle you?"

"Startle me? You fair nearly killed me with fright, Annie Crowther. What the 'ell are you doin' 'ere at this time of night? You know it's not safe to walk alone."

"Like I don't know the place where I live? Am I not among friends here?" said Annie, laughing.

"I wouldn't mock, girl. It's not your friends that you should worry about. Skinny Jim's been spotted sniffin' round the gate. That man is bad news… almost as much as George is."

"Skinny wouldn't dare come onto George's patch, would 'e?"

"Anythin's possible where there's a profit to be made. Besides, I doubt the man 'imself would do the work. More likely he'd send a couple of 'is lads to see what's what. Just be careful when you leave, cos darkness is no friend, let me tell you."

Annie nodded and said, "I was 'opin' to catch up with Mr Brownrigg, if 'e's around?"

"Missed 'im, girl. Went 'ome about an hour ago. What do you need 'im for?"

"I wanted to thank 'im fer sendin' that doctor," said Annie. "The doctor didn't say who sent 'im but I knows it was Brownrigg all the same. Do you think I should go an' knock?"

Juxon threw the damp rag over his shoulder. "I wouldn't bother 'im tonight. He'd had a fair few by the time 'e left, so I suppose 'e's fast asleep by know. And the girl, is she on the mend?"

"Too early to say."

"Is there any message that I can give George, if I sees 'im?"

"Just tell 'im that Annie Crowther is grateful for what 'e's done this night, an' if he saves Bessie's life, I will be forever indebted to 'im."

"Be careful what you promise," said William with a wry smile.

"I ain't indebted in *that* way," said Annie. "I don't want to mislead 'im."

"George don't need much of an excuse to be misled where you're concerned. Reckon he misleads 'imself most of the time."

"Don't worry, William. I'll make it clear."

"What did the doctor say?" said Juxon pulling out a chair for Annie and then pulling out one for himself. As he sank down, he lit his pipe and a plume of grey smoke drifted upwards, hovering above his head. The last embers of the night's fire spat in the hearth behind Annie.

"Bessie is sick… really sick. Doctor says she's got somethin' called Boulogne Sour Throat, whatever that is."

"It's nasty is what it is, my girl. I've 'eard tales from the sailors returned from the continent, and they say it's rife over there. Whole crews have been lost to it." Annie's face dropped and Juxon quickly said, "I 'ave seen some survive if caught early. You take care of that child and see that she pulls through," said Juxon gripping Annie's hand tightly. She could see tears in his eyes and was shocked, as William Juxon was not a man taken to shedding tears.

"I will do my best, William, but Doctor Smallcoates said that she might die."

"That man's as pompous as they come. You tell that Smallcoates that he better save her, or else 'e'll 'ave William Juxon to deal with."

Annie smiled and patted the back of his hand. "I will," she said. "I will." She stood and turned to leave. "I must be gettin' back in case Bessie wakes. Tell George that I'll pop in to see 'im tomorrow."

"I will. You give her a kiss for me, an' tell 'er that we is all wishin' 'er well."

Annie paused and said, "Do you really think that Skinny and 'is boys are plannin' somethin'?"

"Well, put it this way, I 'ave friends on the other side of the gate an' one in particular, tells me that Jim an' 'is rabble 'ave been takin' a keen interest in this place."

"But George will stop 'em, right? 'E knows all about this?"

"George knows what I know," said Juxon. "And I don't think that Skinny Jim nor the devil 'imself are goin' to take this place, nor 'arm the people in it. 'Sides, the gate is shut after dark, an' old Stanley stands guard. Without 'is say so, 'ow they goin' to get across the drawbridge?"

Annie nodded and said, "Oh yes, I forgot about Stanley." She thanked William for his kind words and said she would indeed give Bessie a kiss for him. She opened the door to the pub and stepped outside, wrapping her shawl a little tighter than normal. The shadows seemed longer and deeper somehow, after William's words. Something moved to the left of her and she jumped, stifling a small scream. "Get a grip, girl," she scolded herself. Annie scuttled back to the house.

****

The small boat slid silently on the murky brine. Davey Turner and Pete Bookbinder sat in quiet contemplation. Davey rowed expertly and they made good progress. To their left the large dark mass that was the guard ship *HMS Fortitude* loomed large. Lights burned on board, lifting the darkness a little and guiding their way. Faint voices from the deck carried on the lazy breeze. Between them, in the centre of the boat, lay the body of Guppy with a sack cloth covering his face. Ahead of them lay Burrow Island, or Rat Island as the locals called it. Tall trees lined the shore and a narrow stretch of beach came into view. Behind the trees, entwined in the vegetation and undergrowth, the crumbling remains of Fort James could be seen jutting out of the ground. Once an important fortification, it now stood abandoned and forgotten. The modern Navy had no more use for it, or the island, and so used the small stretch of land as a dumping ground for dead prisoners of war and the entrails of animals that were discarded by the naval stores depot at Royal Clarence Yard. Pete tapped Davey on the shoulder and pointed to the beach in silence. They couldn't alert anyone to their presence, George's was insistent on it.

"Don't get spotted, or we'll be done for, gentlemen." The sound of his voice rang in their ears. Neither of them wanted to incur the wrath of George Brownrigg.

The boat bumped gently on the shore and Davey jumped out, closely followed by Pete. Both men hauled the small vessel onto dry land and out of view of the surrounding ships that filled the harbour.

"Why us, eh?" said Davey, grabbing Guppy's legs.

"Stop moaning. 'Tis the life we chose, is it not?" said Pete taking Guppy's arms. Both men lifted the dead man from the boat and swung him over the side, laying him on the ground.

"Grab that shovel," said Pete. Davey did as he was told and tucked it under his arm as they lifted the corpse and stumbled into the dense vegetation.

"Do you suppose that one day we'll end up buried on this island?" said Davey.

"Anythin's possible. Keep talkin' like you are, an' I'll put you in the ground this very night," said Pete. He paused, casting a wiser eye over his young friend and said, "Why do you ask?"

"Cos George is a bit, well… he's a bit brutal."

"Brutal? That ain't the half of it, my boy. That man is bad to the core, which is why you would do well to keep your mouth shut."

"'E scares me," said Davey.

"Me too," said Pete. "But that's just it. You're meant to be scared or 'e wouldn't be the King of the Point now, would 'e?"

"S'pose not," said Davey absently. "This place scares me," he said, looking around in the gloom. "I swear these trees are watchin' us, and the bushes are talkin' bout us. Listen?" Davey fell silent and listened in the darkness. A light breeze brushed the thick vegetation that lined the woods and the leaves rustled in response to Davey's superstitious fear.

"This island is deserted. There's nothin' 'ere to scare you," said Pete. He was feeling a little agitated himself, but he was careful not to let it show. He'd heard rumours that the dead walked the island and that every rat on this godless place was possessed with the soul of a deceased prisoner. Pete shivered and banished scary thoughts from his mind. The men pushed into the vegetation, heading for the centre of the island.

"Let's dig 'ere," said Pete, stopping in a clearing and feeling the ground with the heel of his boot. "Seems soft enough."

Guppy was dumped on the ground and the two men worked in silence until they had dug a man-sized hole, roughly three feet deep. Pete stood and wiped his brow with a muddy palm, smearing dark soil over his face, making it look like he was wearing war paint.

"Here, Davey, give us an 'and, will you?" Pete had hold of Guppy's legs. "Grab 'is arms."

Both men lifted the dead sailor and dumped him in the hole. After an hour, they had piled the soil back into the grave and all that could be seen was a small ridge in the ground.

"That'll do," said Davey. "Now let's get outta 'ere." He pushed through the trees, following the same route back to the boat, with Pete following. Suddenly something moved to his side and Davey froze, grabbing Pete's arm.

"What is it?" said Pete.

"Listen! Did you hear that?" The rustling noise came again. "It's the souls of the dead walkin' about the place." Davey started to shake.

"Get a grip, Davey. Dead souls don't rustle around in bushes. Most likely it's a rat."

"This place is cursed, I tell you," said Davey. "And dead souls can do whatever the 'ell they like."

"The stories about this place are just that – stories," said Pete.

"I don't care. Let's get outta 'ere." Davey ran across the shingle strip that led to the water. He threw his shovel into the boat, grabbed the bow and started pulling the vessel towards the sea. Pete caught up with him and pushed the boat from the rear. The waves splashed over their feet, both men climbed in and started rowing back to the Point.

****

Skinny Jim McDowell blew warm breaths into his hands, stamped his feet and winced at the pain the dampness in the air infused in his middle-aged bones. He hugged the ill-fitting coat around his emaciated frame and patted the chill away. Skinny was a man of means, but was thrifty. Some would say mean. He'd been waiting for the Knox brothers, John and Henry, for half an hour and was beginning to wonder where they had got to. He stood at the entrance to St Georges Square and stared at the water that filled the inlet which ran all the way towards the sea mill. Its large sails turned slowly in the breeze.

Skinny heard voices approaching through the gloom and pressed his rakish frame deeper into the shadows. He was a feared man in Devil's Acre and The Hard, but even he wasn't above the Impress gangs that roamed these parts looking for drunks, the homeless and the misplaced to fill the wooden guts of Nelson's galleons. Skinny listened from his obscured position and quickly recognised the voices as those of the Knox brothers. He stepped from the blackness and waved at the dark shapes that approached. They waved back and drew closer.

"Sorry we're late," said John. He looked a little the worse for wear.

"Been drinkin' 'ave you?" said Skinny sniffing the air in front of his face.

"I been in *The Camber Inn*, on the Point like you said," said John indignantly.

His brother, Henry, nodded in agreement and said, "Like you said," echoing his brother.

"Like I said, eh? Bleedin' clowns. I said to get news, to spy, not get pissed at my expense." Skinny lit his pipe and blew smoke at them.

"The landlord, 'e made us buy drinks, or 'e was gonna chuck us out," said John.

"Alright, lads. I ain't come out tonight to discuss your drinkin' 'abits. What you learned?"

"Brownrigg's got quite a little business empire on the Point. From what I can see, 'e is protected by the gate. No-one enters or leaves without the say so of the guard. George 'as a captive audience and they're all too pissed to care." Henry rubbed his hands together to ward away the cold. "He's got whores, stolen goods, smugglin'. You name it, 'e's got 'is fingers in it. Quite a business indeed."

John nodded and said, "You wanna see the money they is rakin' in. Place is full most nights with tars with weighty purses."

"Go on," said Skinny.

Henry continued, "They take a percentage of the profits. I 'eard one of 'em, a fella called Davey, boastin' to another man about 'ow much they were makin'. Seems the gang also take money from the inns and grog shops to ensure that the peace is kept."

Skinny looked across at the harbour and the lights that floated above the water, towards the Point. It was a twinkling peninsula of opportunity, money, and of sin and sex, and Skinny wanted it. He wanted to prise George Brownrigg's jewel from his dead fingers. A thin smile wriggled across his cruel face

"Lots of ships out there, boys. Lots of sailors," he said distantly.

"Sure is. The Point was teemin' with 'em. We could make a killin'," said Henry Knox.

"That's the plan," said Skinny.

"What you got in mind?" asked John. "Are you gonna take on Brownrigg and 'is boys?"

"Brownrigg is nothin'. The *Riggers* are nothin' compared to the *Squeeze Gut Boys*. I say we call in the rest of the lads and plan a visit to the Point. I say we go and see what's what."

Chapter Five

Surprise visits...

Annie was up early the following morning, the chores of the day a welcome relief from another night of troubled sleep. Bessie had woken several times complaining that she was too hot or too cold, that her throat was burning, and Annie did exactly what the doctor had said, bathing her pale skin in cold water and soothing her enflamed gullet with the honey that he had given her. At first light Bessie settled, more through fatigue than wholesome sleep, giving Annie the chance to slip out of the bed and creep downstairs. She spent the next few hours immersed in the numbing monotony of the housework, and was thankful for it.

Annie was busy sweeping up when a loud banging rattled her front door, making her jump and drop the twigs that she'd bound with twine to make a brush. She squinted through the window and saw that the sun had risen on the harbour. On the other side of her door stood the rugged shape of George Brownrigg. Annie straightened her dress and reached to open the door. Upstairs Bessie slept soundly, oblivious to the noise outside. Suddenly, the door was banged impatiently again, followed by the sound of his booming voice.

"Annie Crowther, are you in there?"

She opened the door and said, "Mr Brownrigg, what a pleasant surprise."

"I thought you was dead or somethin'. Didn't you 'ear me knockin', girl? You knows I'm an impatient man." George's face didn't lend itself well to smiling, but he tried it all the same, only managing to look like he was in pain. He gripped his tall Derby hat in his large hands. Annie didn't think that a couple of knocks constituted a long time, but decided to bite back any comments before they landed her in hot water.

"Would you like to come in?" Annie stepped aside to allow him to pass. George stooped to avoid banging his head and stepped into the small room.

"I 'spect you're surprised to see me?" he said more softly.

"Well, now that you mentions it, yes I am, Mr Brownrigg."

"Juxon called on me this mornin' and said you was lookin' for me last night?"

"I came to see you at the pub but you was gone, Mr Brownrigg."

"Please, call me George. Mr Brownrigg's so formal, don't you think?" Again he made an attempt to smile and this time he succeeded in softening his stern façade.

"Well, if you're sure, George." Annie sounded a little embarrassed. "I can't offer you nothin'. I got no beer or food." She felt a pang of guilt, knowing that the morsels Mary brought her were being saved for when Bessie regained her strength.

George fished in the pocket of his long coat and brought out a small package wrapped in cloth. He thrust it at her.

"What's that?" she said nervously.

"Open it," he said. Annie didn't need to be asked twice and snatched the cloth from his hand, placing it on the table and unwrapping it.

"Thank you, George. I'm grateful. But why you bringin' me food?" On the table was a small stack of dry crackers and a lump of cheddar. "I ain't goin' to pretend that it ain't a struggle each mornin'."

"Call it an act of kindness," he said with a jovial bow. "A friend 'elpin' a friend."

"But…" Annie paused.

"But what? 'Spect yer a bit surprised, eh? George Brownrigg's not known for 'is kindness."

"Well, no," Annie said and then added, after consideration, "I don't mean that you're not kind or nothin', just that you're not known for it."

"I am not a kind man. I fear that you are right. But somethin' about you makes me wanna be kind. Or kinder at least." George fiddled with the rim of his hat and stared at the floor. The conversation lulled and then George said, "I really mean it. I don't take to folk easily an' 'eaven knows they don't take to me, but you… well you're different altogether. You lift the darkness that sits within, an' no woman 'as done that for a long time."

"Well that's good then." Annie smiled awkwardly. "And don't be thinkin' that you ain't capable of kindness. I knows it was you what sent Smallcoates." It struck her that, as he stood before her with his hat in his hands, he actually reminded her of a vulnerable little boy and not the brute of a man who had the capacity for extreme violence. Annie had to mentally pinch herself to remember that.

"Forgive me for asking, but is she bad?" said George, looking towards the upstairs room and Bessie.

"The worst. Doctor Smallcoates said that she might die. William Juxon said he's seen the like of this before an' many men perished. We 'ave a long road to travel if she is to recover."

"Smallcoates never did 'ave a good way with words but 'e's a good doctor, and if anyone can save Bessie, it's 'im."

"So it was you what sent 'im. I knew it."

"I may be a bad man in many circles, but I still care about some things. Specially where you an' that little girl is concerned."

"But I don't understand," said Annie. "Why do you care so much when you knows I can't be with you?"

"I got me reasons and that's that."

"Reasons? What reasons? It ain't goin' to 'appen, George. I need that to be plain between us."

Brownrigg stared at her. "You think this is purely carnal?" He shrugged. "Like I said, I got my reasons."

"But…" Annie was cut short.

"Reasons that are best left alone," said George flatly.

"I understand completely if they're private," said Annie. "I wouldn't expect you to trust me. We barely know each other."

"It ain't a matter of trust, girl. It's just personal, that's all."

"I'm a good listener and a very poor gossip. A little understanding can be a good thing, especially where the feared George Brownrigg is concerned."

George didn't respond and just stared at his hat, like it was the most interesting thing in the world. Annie pressed further,

"Do you trust me, George?" she said gently.

George nodded with a sigh, wiped his brow with his trembling hand and said, "I ain't never told anyone this, so what I tell you is between us, and us only. Do you understand?" He glared at her and Annie found herself thinking that this must be what it was like to be on the receiving end of one of his infamous stares. "Promise?" he said.

Annie nodded and George took a deep breath. He went to speak but paused suddenly, eyeing Annie again.

"You can't speak of this to anyone. Not a soul," he repeated. "Not even Mary."

"On the life of my child, I swear it won't pass my lips to another, as long as you wish it," said Annie firmly.

"I can't believe I'm goin' to tell you this," he said. "When I was much younger, maybe twenty years ago, I 'ad a wife and child and they were the most precious things in my life. I was in love, Annie Crowther. Can you believe that?"

"I can," said Annie. "I believe everyone is capable of love. You are no different. Can I ask what became of them?"

"They died." George squeezed his eyes closed and lowered his head as if in prayer. Annie could see that, whatever else was going on in his head, the turmoil of his loss still bore down on him like a lead weight.

She reached out, grabbed his arm and said, "You poor thing. That must 'ave been awful, losing them both."

"It was the worst time in my life. I watched them both die in my arms and there was nothin' I could do." He shuddered, shook his head and looked up at the ceiling. "This world – this life – it is a cruel mistress. It is the cruellest of them all. Have you any notion of helplessness? Of utter uselessness. That's how I felt watching them…" George's words trailed into silence.

"What was it that…?" Annie lacked the conviction to finish her sentence.

"Took 'em?" said George. "Consumption. And do you know what the worst of it is?"

Annie shook her head. "I can't imagine," she said.

"My will to live died with 'em. They may as well 'ave chucked me in the ground too, for I was a changed man after that. I didn't care if I lived or died." Annie could see that he was trembling. "With them in my life, I 'ad 'ope an' purpose, but take all that away – well, somethin' like that changes a man. I buried hope, I buried what was left of my life in that grave with them both," said George sitting at Sam's bench and throwing his hat on the table. Annie sat and waited for him to continue.

"I didn't care anymore... *don't* care anymore," he said. "I looks at the world like it's dead, like I wear a veil of black, an' all the people in it are corpses, empty and rotting." He buried his face in his hands and gripped the sides of his head by the tufts of hair that jutted out, giving them a tug. "Can you imagine that?" he continued. "Seeing the world around you as nothing but bleak?" He slammed his fist on the table, making Annie jump. "I tell you this," he said, "killin' is an act of kindness for a lot of 'em."

"Surely you see some good in this place, or you wouldn't stay 'ere?" said Annie. "The world is not as dark as you would 'ave it, George. You don't see me that way."

"You're different," he said. "You are what keeps me sane. It is you what gives me 'ope. As for the rest..."

"But there 'as to be some 'ope left in you for others?" said Annie.

"Maybe you're right. Maybe I chose to shut the world out. That was until Mary told me about your Bessie, an' that's when I realised that I did care. It hit me like a bucket of cold water to the face, and that's when I knew that I 'ad to do somethin'."

"What were their names?" she asked quietly.

"Rebecca and my little girl was Susan."

"I am so sorry for you," said Annie. "Truly I am. I 'ad no idea."

George shrugged and straightened up, shaking off the cloak of tragedy that had shrouded his muscular frame. He rubbed his face, wiping away the tears and bad thoughts, and it was as if the man before her was undergoing a change of character. As quickly as the wind alters direction, he was back to being the old George. "So, what do we do about your little one?" he said changing the subject.

"Well," said Annie, "the doctor is coming back tomorrow to apply a special balm to her throat and I 'ave some 'oney to soothe her gullet."

"And 'er fever, is it abating?"

Annie shook her head and stared into the distance. "I fear things are as bad as they could be. She is burning up."

"Then we will get Smallcoates to attend to 'er today, and tomorrow and the next if we must. We will do whatever it takes to see that girl right."

"And when she is well?" said Annie tentatively.

"I ain't followin'," said George. "We celebrate and thank the Lord for bestowing such luck upon us."

"The Lord, or you? When Bessie recovers, what then?"

"I still don't follow," said George again.

"What do you want from me? Am I to be indebted to you in – well, *that* way?"

"That way? Oh, I see. *That way.*" George shook his head and smiled. "I am not doin' this to get you in my bed, Annie Crowther. Firstly, I am doin' it for that little girl and for the memory of my daughter. Secondly, I am doin' it to prove to myself that I ain't all bad."

"So there are no conditions?"

"None whatsoever." George held his arms out in a gesture of openness. "Like I said, you make me want to be a nicer person. If there is just the smallest chance that something good exists within me, I want to find it and nurture it."

"I must admit that I ain't never seen this side of you, an' it is a side that fares you well."

George burst into loud fits of laughter. "That's what I loves about you, Annie Crowther… always truthful."

"I always will be too," said Annie.

There was a natural lull in the conversation, as both sat listening to the sounds of the Point drifting into the small house, and the sound of Bessie's heavy breathing in the bed upstairs. Suddenly, George gripped Annie's hand across the table and she could feel the leathery callouses on his fingers. "I can look after you," said Brownrigg staring into her eyes.

"I thought you said that all this 'elp wasn't to try an' get me into your bed."

"Think of it as a business arrangement. I'm 'elpin' out a friend in need. I see the vulnerable in you, in your situation. In return all I ask is that you 'elp out with the business."

"I will never resort to that sort of thing," said Annie.

George threw up his arms and said, "You misunderstand. My depth of feelin' for you would never allow me to suggest such a thing. I meant with takin' supplies to the ships and such. You said that I had a kinder side."

"But…" Her words trailed off.

"Taken you by surprise again, eh? Old George's carin' side?"

"It's nice of you to offer, but…" Her words trailed off again.

"But what?"

"I'm sorry I jumped to conclusions," Annie took a deep breathe. "But like I said yesterday, I'm taken."

"Oh, Annie! Look around you," said George sweeping his arm around the room. "I don't see an 'usband to tend to the girl, or you. I don't see 'im puttin' food on the table or sendin' for the doctor."

"Don't you dare! My 'usband is a good man an' it wasn't 'is fault that he got taken." Annie thumped her fist on the wooden table top and stood suddenly.

"*Is* a good man?" said George. "Are you still clingin' to the 'ope that he will return? 'Ow long as it been now?"

"Too long," said Annie. "But I must believe, for Bessie's sake at least."

"Look, I'm sorry if I spoke outta turn. I always did 'ave an 'abit of speakin' me mind. I didn't mean that 'e wasn't a good man just that 'e ain't around, an' a woman needs a man about the place."

"An' I suppose you're that man, are you?" said Annie.

"I see no other 'ere. What is so bad about me lookin' after you? Maybe one day you could learn to like me, like Sam."

"I didn't *like* Sam, I loved 'im. Unconditional, deep, overwhelmin' love that keeps me starin' out the window at the return of each bloody ship. Keeps me visiting the Camber most nights, come rain or wind.

Keeps me listenin' for the sound of 'is voice or a glimpse of 'im in a crowd at the bar or on the Camber when the boats pull alongside." Annie wrung her hands, and paced the small room. "And every time it turns out to be a false hope and each time I peer upon a boat full of strangers' faces, I resolve that whilst disappointment is still my bedfellow, one day 'e *will* return."

George stood and said, "I'm sorry if I offended you. It wasn't my intention."

"You weren't to know the depth of feelin' that Sam an' me shared," she said.

"Subtlety ain't my strong point. I s'pose it's just my way." He smiled at Annie and said, "I best be getting off." George turned and walked towards the door and, in that moment, she thought that he had shrunk a couple of inches since stepping through her door, and put it down to his hunched shoulders. For such a large man, Annie got the distinct impression that he looked crumpled. She reached out, grabbing his arm, and spun him around.

"Thank you," she said stretching on her tip-toes and planting a delicate kiss on his cheek. She fell back on her heels and said, "I like you this day for what you have done... for what you are doin'."

"*Like*, now that's a start," said George beaming and regaining his lost inches. "What else do you need before I get off?"

Annie said, "The landlord's comin' by later for 'is rent."

"Shylock will know the new arrangement. You don't 'ave to worry about it. I'll speak with 'im shortly, so that you can stay 'ere as long as you need to and not to worry about the rent."

"You won't 'urt the poor man, will you?" she said looking concerned.

"It'll be a business arrangement, is all. Honest."

Annie liked her landlord, Thomas Shylock. This place wasn't a palace but it was dry and Shylock often let her pay the rent late.

George opened the front door, stopped and turned.

"Need anythin' else?" he said.

"Need?" said Annie, "I needs everythin'. Food, wood and beer to name a few."

"Pete Bookbinder will be along later today with supplies." George placed his hat on his head, patting it in place and said, "You concentrate on that girl of yours gettin' better and leave it all to me, got it?"

Annie nodded and watched George Brownrigg trudge across the cobbles and disappear. She shut the door and sat on the bench. Her head was in a whirl. Had that just happened? Had George just showed her kindness? George Brownrigg, the most feared man on the Point, so feared that his reputation extended beyond King James Gate and into Devils Acre. As ridiculous as it was, after all he was just a man, she told herself, she never considered that he had fears and feelings like everyone else.

Bessie called from upstairs. "I heard a man's voice. I thought it was father, returned to us." She sounded distant and weak.

"No, Bessie, it wasn't. Get some rest now." Annie climbed to the top of the ladder and rested on the bed next to her daughter.

"Were you listening? I thought you were asleep," said Annie.

"I was asleep," said Bessie with the faintest hint of life in her sunken grey eyes, "but then I woke to the sound of the voices. That's when I heard you both."

"You forget that man, do you 'ear. 'E's a friend what wants to 'elp an' that's that."

"That man likes you," said Bessie closing her eyes.

"An' I loves you… so be quiet and get to sleep," said Annie kissing her daughter's moist forehead. "Please try an' get better," she said pressing her cheek to Bessie's and rocking her gently. The heat flowed from her daughter into Annie's body but she thought that the temperature had dropped just a fraction. It wasn't anything that she could place exactly, she just instinctively felt the change in heat and knew that her fever might be breaking.

Chapter Six

Mr Brownrigg to the likes of you…

The winter sun started to sink on the horizon as candles burned optimistically in meagre arrow slot windows that dotted the square and Annie was beginning to think that George had broken his promise of help. Then Pete Bookbinder rattled the door. She opened it and let him in. He was carrying a large sack, which he deposited on the table.

"Annie, this is compliments of Mr Brownrigg."

She opened the sack and peeked inside. There was bread, cheese, meat and a jug containing some pottage as well as ale and wood. There was enough food to last her a couple of days.

"Thank George for me," she said. "I am most grateful."

"Mr Brownrigg to the likes of you," said Pete. "Don't be disrespectin' 'im now."

"George to the likes of me, Pete Bookbinder. He told me 'imself that I was to call 'im George."

"Bloody 'ell. What makes you so special?" laughed Pete, placing his cap on his head and looking her up and down. His eyes lingered on her figure and he said, "On second thoughts, need I ask?"

"No you need not ask," said Annie.

That night, Annie ate the best meal that she had in ages. Bessie woke a couple of times and, with each barking cough that rasped forth, Annie raced to her daughter to sooth her throat with more honey. At eight o'clock she bathed her in cold water and tucked her back into bed. When she was sure that Bessie had settled back down, Annie returned to finish her meal. On the table next to her was a small parcel of food that was saved for when Bessie could stomach it and when her throat released its grip on her. As she chewed on a hunk of bread, Annie's thoughts returned to happier days. The ghostly face of Sam smiled at her across the table. Since he'd vanished, his image had blurred in her mind. She struggled to place his features as accurately and feared that, as time moved on, she would forget him completely. The vision before her reached for her hand and she in turn reached out to take his. If only she knew where he was? She knew that the Impress gang had taken him, that much was sure. Men regularly vanished on the Point. Some never came back and some turned up years later, when a frigate or sloop pulled into port. She worried for him, for his mental state. Sam wasn't the warring kind. He was a gentle man, a considerate man and serving in Nelson's navy wasn't something that Annie envisioned for him.

She was so lost in her thoughts that she didn't notice that Bessie had climbed down from her bed and now stood beside her, looking at her with doleful eyes. The little girl slid her hand into her mother's and Annie looked at her daughter. The vision of Sam was gone and all that was there was the drab wall and the face of her sick daughter.

"What are you doin' outta bed?" she said, shaking off her melancholic state.

"I miss father," said Bessie.

"Of course you do, silly." Annie was shocked at just how thin her little girl was. She hid her shock behind a wistful smile, ruffled Bessie's hair and pinched her gently on the chin. "Just as I do," she said. "Now back into bed with you." She stood and shooed the little girl towards the steps

Bessie said, "I want him to come back."

"As do I, girl. As do I." Annie wiped a stray tear from her cheek and looked away for a moment as Bessie climbed the ladder and fell back into the bed. Annie followed her up and pressed her hand to her daughter's forehead.

"Do you feel better?" she said.

Bessie nodded.

"Are you hungry? We have some food."

Bessie shook her head.

"You must eat somethin' soon. Shall I make you some broth?" said Annie.

Bessie shook her head again and laid down on the bed.

"If you need anythin', just call. I'll be downstairs," said Annie blowing her daughter a kiss. She climbed down to the ground floor and sat back at the bench. It didn't take long for her thoughts to stray back to her missing husband and the weeks before he had vanished.

If only he'd joined the Sea Fencibles like I begged, thought Annie. She remembered the conversation as if it were yesterday...

"I don't wanna do it," said Sam puffing on his pipe. "'Sides, there's talk that they 'ave enough volunteers."

"Mary said that Charlie joined and gets a shilling a week. A shilling for one day's work, Sam."

"Boss won't let me off work for one day. I'll gain a shillin' by losin' my situation."

"Charlie told Mary that while you volunteer, Impress can't touch you. Said that 'e's protected under rules."

"I ain't scared of the Press gangs. I'm real careful, see. Always in before they come a sniffin', like a good husband oughta be." Sam smiled at his wife and winked.

Those words now haunted her thoughts like the ghost of a long gone time rattling around a dusty tower. She muttered, "Real careful," and smiled ruefully. "If only that were the case, Sam Crowther," she said to the empty room.

****

The *Squeeze Gut Boys* were assembled in the upstairs room of *The Dolphin* public house waiting for Skinny to speak. He sat in a chair at the front, smoking his pipe and sipping his ale calmly. The murmur of voices suddenly silenced as he stood to address them. Some in the gang were as young as fourteen or fifteen but they were built like men, and they were handy with their fists and could hit as hard as any man. Skinny knew the importance of fresh blood in the ranks. *The Squeeze Gut*

Boys took their name for the slang name of a local alley that was so narrow that you had to *squeeze your gut* to pass.

"This is madness. Brownrigg's a nutter," said Daniel Mercer, one of the newcomers to the gang. "We've been livin' in this area for ages, an' we ain't had no trouble with Brownrigg. Why start now?"

Skinny slammed his tankard of beer on the table and the whole room sat to attention. He glared at the assembled crowd and chewed on the end of his pipe like a snarling dog. Silence descended in the room and only the sound of the regulars downstairs could be heard wafting through the wooden floor.

"Who else thinks that musclin' in on the Point is a bad idea?" said Skinny, pacing like a caged tiger. "Who else thinks that we shouldn't look to 'ave a slice of another man's pie."

Mercer put his hand up and looked around at the other faces in the room. No one looked back at him or followed suit. They were too busy staring at the floor, desperate not to make eye contact with Skinny Jim McDowell. Mercer lowered his arm.

"So, it seems we 'ave a coward in our midst," he said. "Is that what you is? A coward, Daniel Mercer?"

Mercer started to shake and beads of sweat bubbled on his forehead. He'd never dared to speak out before and he knew what happened to those who did. He would have kept quiet as he always did but on this night he'd had conversations with others who shared his views. They'd said that they would speak out as well. Those same men sat with bowed heads and silence as their protector. Regret flashed across his mind like a bolt of lightning. "I ain't a coward, an' you know that, Skinny. I was just sayin' that we're doin' alright as it is and we don't wanna stir no stick in the 'ornet's nest, is all."

"There are over forty one inns and brandy shops on the point. There are drapers, butchers, tailors and brothels. Every ship of the line comes ashore at the Camber. Every known angle is performed nightly to relieve our salty war heroes of their money, every method is employed to sell opium, grog and liquor," Skinny screwed his fist into a tight ball and pushed through the men towards Daniel Mercer. "Every one of 'em sailors has saved up his wages or 'as a share of a war chest and is ready to part with it all too easily." He raised his fist and Mercer steeled himself as he waited for his punishment for speaking out of turn. "An' you wanna pass up this opportunity all because this bastard," he cocked his thumb at Daniel, "don't wanna put 'is stick in the 'ornet's nest?" Skinny crashed his fist into the side of Daniel's face and he toppled off his chair. The men surrounding him scattered and Mercer was alone in a ring of empty chairs with one of the most feared gang leaders standing over him.

"Maybe 'e didn't mean what 'e said," blurted John Knox nervously.

Henry stood beside his brother and nodded. "Maybe it's the drink what's talkin'?"

"Is it the drink?" asked Skinny as he pulled a knife from his pocket.

"Please, Jim, we've known each other a long time. My mum used to take you in and feed you when you was younger. I didn't mean what I said." Daniel held his hands out in front of his face and started to blubber. "I ain't ready to die."

Skinny's hollow façade softened as he smiled and said, "You an' me, we're like brothers. I was just messin' with you, to scare you a bit, see." Skinny offered his hand to the fallen man and he took it. As Skinny hoisted him from the ground, the rest of the room breathed a collective sigh of relief. He pulled Daniel in for a hug and whispered, "You're lucky I don't stick you right now."

"I'm sorry for what I said," replied Mercer. "I'm still your pal, right?"

Skinny Jim paused, pressing his thin lips to Mercer's ear. Eventually he nodded and said, "Yes," and patted the back of Daniel's head.

He pushed Daniel away and he staggered against some empty chairs, knocking them over. He stared at Skinny with wide eyes and wiped his brow as the others started to pick up the toppled chairs. After a few minutes the meeting resumed.

"Now boys," said Skinny, "now that we are agreed, what say we go poke a large stick up Brownrigg's arse and see how that rattles 'im?"

The faces before him nodded, stamping their heavy boots on the wooden floorboards, sending dust and flecks of paint raining down on the drinkers in the bar below. Skinny turned to John and Henry Knox, covered his mouth with his hand and said, "See to it that this is Mercer's last night. I don't care 'ow you does it, just make sure that you gets rid of the body."

"Where shall we take 'im?" said Henry.

"I don't fuckin' know. You can chuck 'im in the brine for all I care. Just see that it's done and no mistakes." Skinny stood and sauntered towards the stairs, disappearing from view. Henry and John made their way towards Daniel Mercer, who was sitting deep in contemplation with his head rested on his hands. He had a far-away look in his eyes and didn't notice the Knox brothers as they drew near.

"Daniel," said Henry, "I'm sorry for what 'appened. Let's get a drink an' forget this night." He held out his hand which Daniel Mercer took and shook.

He stood and said, "Right now I needs a barrel of ale to calm me nerves." Daniel held out his shaking hand to show the brothers. "Do you know I was this close to getting' stuck tonight?"

John Knox said, "Skinny can be a bastard sometimes but sometimes 'e 'as to be. That 'ain't no excuse." Knox threw his arms in the air in resignation and said, "But what the 'ell." He broke into a broad smile and patted Daniel on the shoulder. "C'mon, let's get pissed."

Daniel Mercer left the upstairs room of *The Dolphin* pub flanked by John and Henry Knox. It was the last time he was seen alive.

Chapter Seven

"You are George Brownrigg, are you not, sir?"

Annie poked her head out of the front door and stared in the direction of the Camber. Shouting had diverted her attention from her chores and she was curious to see what was happening. Mary waved to her from across the square and Annie waved back. She strained for a better view but all she could see was a line of oars, standing erect like maypoles, as a small boat glided into the dock. For the first time in years she wasn't gut achingly hungry. Thanks to the kindness of George Brownrigg, she had eaten well and would eat well again today.

In the room upstairs, Bessie slept. Her fever was still present and, although Annie thought she might have perked up after she had said she was feeling better, Bessie still showed only slight signs of improvement. Annie stepped into Bath Square and wrapped her shawl tightly around her shoulders. Mary sauntered over.

"Goin' somewhere?" she said.

Annie nodded. "Just getting' some air. I was distracted by all the shoutin'."

"Looks like someone's in trouble," said Mary.

"Why do you say that?"

"I just been down to the Camber and in that boat is an officer and four lobsters. It must be about that missin' lad."

"What missin' lad?" said Annie.

"Disappeared two nights back. Vanished into thin air outside *The Camber Inn*. I'll wager George and 'is boys are behind this."

"Watch Bessie for me," said Annie. "The doctor is due in a bit. If I'm not back, let 'im in." She rushed away and turned the corner. She had a bad feeling that Mary was right. Without a moment to waste, she trotted towards the Camber at the end of Bath Square and turned by *The Coal Exchange* pub. Tied to the Camber was a Pinnace with four marines and an officer who barked commands at them as they climbed from the launch. They formed two lines on the dock with their flintlock muskets rested against their bright red tunics as the officer straightened his uniform. Number one hundred and two Broad street – George's house – was in front of her.

Annie thought that the marines looked very smart. So did a few of the other women of the Point, who started to wolf whistle and call to them suggestively. Annie drew nearer to the boat and passed the line of Marines, when suddenly a voice called out. "You there," shouted the officer. "Where might I find a man named Brownrigg?"

Annie stopped and faced the officer. She shrugged at him and said nothing.

"Are you mute?" he said. "I asked, where can I find George Brownrigg?"

"I ain't seen 'im," said Annie. "Why you askin'?"

"I seek him to answer questions pertaining to the disappearance and possible murder of one of my Able Seamen. He's known simply as Guppy," said the officer. "Now, I didn't ask whether you had seen him, I asked where he could be found."

"Usually 'e's in the pub at this hour."

The officer said, "But it's barely past first light. Do you people have nothing better to do with your time, other than drinking?"

"Not much else to do in these parts," said Annie. "I'll be sure to tell 'im if I sees 'im."

"Which establishment does he frequent?" said the officer.

"Take your pick," said Annie. "There's over forty."

The officer shook his head and turned to the four marines, barking his orders. They moved forward in a hurried fashion, quick stepping their way down Broad Street with the officer following. When they got to the first pub, *The Union Tavern* on the corner of Broad Street and Bath Square, they entered.

"I must find George," said Annie under her breath, rushing towards George's house and climbing the steps to bang the door. *Murder*, thought Annie, *Mary said he was just missing*. So for all the kindness that he'd shown her and her daughter, George was still the same man. Footsteps echoed in the entrance hall and the door opened.

George stood in his bed clothes munching on a dry biscuit. He smiled and said, "To what do I owe the pleasure, Annie Crowther?"

Annie rolled her eyes at him and said, "T'ain't no pleasure, George. Let me in and be quick about it. There's a party of marines lookin' for you."

George looked startled and ushered her inside. Annie couldn't ever remember seeing George rattled before, so she knew that he was guilty of something to do with that lad's disappearance.

"You're in big trouble," she said, glaring at George as he shut the door. Once in the parlour Annie said, "What's this about a murder?"

"I don't know nothin' 'bout no murder," said George, trying to mask his guilt.

"You're lying," said Annie, carefully reading his expression. "I can tell it is so. When I told you about the marines you looked mighty startled. Tell me the truth, George, or I will go into the street and hail them 'ere in an instant."

"You wouldn't," said George.

"Wouldn't I?" said Annie. "The officer stopped me as I was comin' over. Said somethin' about the murder of a man named Guppy." Annie sat in a vacant chair and George did the same. "I just know you're at the centre of this." She brushed a weary hand across her face.

"Shit!" said George. "Me an' my bloody temper."

"So it's true – you did kill 'im."

"I didn't mean to," said George. "It just got out of 'and. He got a whack for insultin' Mary an' 'e fell to the ground. I didn't know I was gonna kill 'im."

"Just when I thought you had a kinder side, you goes an' does this," said Annie, standing and turning away from George's stare, throwing her arms in the air. She fell silent for a moment to take in the terrible truth. Suddenly, she reeled around, planted both her hands on the table and leaned over him. "What if they take you away? What will 'appen then? 'Ave you given thought to that?" Panic spread across her face instantly as she realised the implications of George's arrest.

"Bessie," she said quietly.

"Eh, what was that?" said George.

"If you gets pinched, what will become of Bessie? She will die without the help of Smallcoates."

"I ain't goin' anywhere. I'm George Brownrigg, remember? King of the Point."

"You're a man, just a thing of skin an' bone, and very little thought," said Annie. "Do you think for one moment that the government, or for that matter the King, cares a jot for your status or reputation?"

"Then my acts of kindness do have a toll to pay. The terms of the arrangement 'ave now changed. You need to 'elp me just as I 'elp you," said George. "You need to say that I was elsewhere at the time of the murder."

"What about William Juxon? Won't 'e tell 'em where you was?"

"Juxon's not the chatty type an' knows the worth of a tight lip."

"I don't believe this is 'appenin' to me," said Annie. "All I wanna do is see my girl right, to see 'er recovered, an' now I'm coverin' up a murder. An' for what? Just so I can keep on your good side, so you keep payin' the doctor's fees."

"This ain't ideal for either of us," smiled George, "but it does serve us both well. I imagine that Bessie is no better? Still in need of medicine?"

Annie nodded. "A little better," she muttered, glaring at him.

"Don't be like that," he said. "It wasn't my intention that we should be shackled in this unfortunate situation."

"No strings, you said. Why is it I feel like I'm bein' controlled like a marionette?"

"You keep to your part of the story an' I promise that I will double my efforts to aid Bessie. You will not miss out, Annie Crowther. Of that I promise."

"Promise? I think I know the value of your promises well and good." She sat back down and crossed her arms. "Let's get our story straight then."

For the next fifteen minutes, George and Annie concocted a version of events that saw him at Annie's house at the time of the murder. He was tending Annie's daughter and there were witnesses who could back up that story. Both knew that Mary would play along, as well as Smallcoates, if he wanted to protect his fee.

"What do we say to explain Guppy's disappearance? It's not like he vanished into thin air," said Annie.

"Don't worry about that," said George. "These men are runnin' away from ships all the time. First sign of land an' they fuck off, never to be seen again."

"But his shipmates will say different."

"Course they will. That's why they're 'is mates. They will invent anythin' to cover up the fact that this Guppy 'as deserted."

"You got every angle covered, 'ain't you?" said Annie.

George winked at her, which infuriated her more.

"This ain't the time to be feelin' so cock sure. Don't you feel anythin' for that lad? You took 'is life, for pity's sake."

George shrugged at her, pausing to consider his response. After a short silence he said, "I ain't makin' excuses, Annie, but I been this way for so long now that it feels normal."

Annie shook her head in disbelief. "I fail to understand why you take such matters so lightly." But then again, she told herself, why should she understand, she wasn't George Brownrigg. Only he knew what went on in that head of his.

"They'll be callin' for me soon," said George. "Best get me finest suit of clothes on. I'll be seein' you, Annie."

"Will you?" said Annie. "When?"

"Later on, when that sailor an' 'is *lobsters* decide to call on you for questions. And when they do, remember that you know nothin' about a murder." George looked at Annie intently and waited for her response.

She nodded at him and turned to leave.

"Annie," called George, "I'll 'ave Pete bring some fresh supplies over. You know, clothes and food and the like, and I'll get Smallcoates to bring some more 'oney too."

Annie paused at the bottom step and nodded without turning around. She waited for the door to shut before she stepped into the cobbled street. The marines were heading towards *The Camber Inn* and she watched as they stooped to enter the low door. The officer took off his hat and stepped over the threshold. Annie ran across Broad Street and turned into Bath Square, heading for home. Mary was out on the front step and looked at Annie as she passed by. She smiled and Annie smiled back.

"We'll meet up later," said Annie as she reached her house.

"What's up?" said Mary. Behind her, Charlie, her husband, stuffed his hands in his pockets. He trudged along Bath Square in the direction of Tower Street and King James Gate, on his way to work in the Dockyard. It was the largest employer in Portsmouth, giving work to almost a thousand men and boys.

Annie said, "You were right about that sailor, Guppy. 'Is shipmates 'ave come lookin' for 'im." She slipped into her house and shut the door.

****

Brownrigg heard the knock at his door. He opened it to see a young lad, sent by William Juxon, the landlord of *The Camber Inn*, to fetch him. "You're wanted, Mr Brownrigg," said the boy, "for questioning by the Master Warrant Officer." Brownrigg smiled at the lad and said, "I'll be there presently." The boy scampered away. George Brownrigg stood in his hallway straightening his collar and making sure that his hat sat up straight on his head. He took a deep breath and stepped into the street. As George trudged across the Camber towards Bath Square, he contemplated the possibility that one day his luck could run out. Ever since the tragedy of his wife and child's death, he had been living dangerously, not caring about the consequences of his actions. Life was about the next ale, the next get rich scheme, the next murder and not giving a damn about any of it. Blank faces watched George as he passed by and he doubted that any of them cared whether he lived or died, and that was fine as far as he was concerned. There was no love lost with most on the Point but there was fear, and George learnt very quickly that fear was almost as persuasive as love. He entered the pub and saw that the officer was seated by the fire supping on a tankard of ale. The officer stood and offered George a seat. George sat and immediately felt the presence of the four Marines close behind him.

The sailor cleared his throat. "You are George Brownrigg, are you not, sir?" said the officer.

Brownrigg nodded and said, "Who wants to know?"

"I am Warrant Officer Chapman of the *HMS Foudroyant*. I have been sent ashore to discover the whereabouts of a seaman named Alfred Fish."

"What's that gotta do with me?" said George gruffly.

"You were seen beating the man outside this very inn. Some of the other crew members had an altercation with locals on the night that Alfred Fish disappeared."

"I ain't never beaten one of His Majesty's loyal sailors. I love the Navy." George smiled at the officer and looked over to Juxon. William knew that it was his cue to serve drinks. "We welcome all 'ere with open arms. Why would we risk damaging the hospitality that we extend so warmly? Men like yours are meat and gravy to a place like this. Maybe – an' this is just a guess – maybe when you find them what beat your men, you'll find out what 'appened to this poor lad."

Juxon placed a full cup in front of Brownrigg and he snatched it up in his huge meaty hands and slurped the ale down in one. He held the cup in the air and wiggled it at William.

"Mr Brownrigg, my men swore that you beat the lad in this very square after an altercation about a woman that he paid for. What do you say to that, sir?"

"I don't know nothin' 'bout no woman. I'm a local businessman of high standin'. I don't consort with the likes of whores." George sat forward and leaned in closer to the officer. "Your men seem to be well acquainted with those types though." He scooped up the refilled cup and sipped his drink, then smirked at the officer.

"I will not have the good name of my ship dragged through the mud. My men are wholesome types."

George snorted. "Wholesome! If they're so saintly, how come you got a missin' man? Seems to me that indiscipline is a problem for you."

"I will not be lectured by the likes of you about discipline and morality," said the officer. He sipped from his drink, wiped his mouth with a crisp white handkerchief and said, "I should like to speak with this woman. Where can she be found?"

"I don't know who you're talkin' about. Like I said, I ain't spoken to anyone of that ilk."

"Mr Brownrigg, who was that woman that you spoke to this morning, on your step?"

"What woman?" George felt a small prickle of heat on the back of his neck. Suddenly, the marines seemed to lean in closer than ever.

"Come now. I saw her from the window of the public house opposite your home. She was taking a great interest in our movements." Chapman placed his hand on his sword and sat back in the chair. "If I was a betting man I would say that she was warning you of our presence." The officer sipped from his cup again and now it was his turn to smirk at George. He placed his cup on the table and stared at George intently. "Think very carefully, Mr Brownrigg before you answer. I have a boat at the Camber and four armed men. If I so wish, that ugly man," and he pointed at William Juxon, "might be that last to see you alive on dry land."

"You wouldn't dare," snarled Brownrigg, slamming his hand down on the table and sitting forward aggressively. The marines stepped in closer to the table and lowered their muskets. George raised his hands and sat back in his chair. "Fair enough. I gets a bit angry sometimes," he said.

"Perhaps it was the same anger that drove you to beat my man to death?"

"Like I said, I ain't guilty. I wasn't even in the pub the night before last."

"Where were you then?" said Officer Chapman.

"At that woman's 'ouse. She 'as a sick child an' I was 'elpin' out."

"The same woman as this morning?"

George nodded. "The very same. She wasn't warning me of your presence, she was begging for my 'elp."

"Such charity," said Chapman. "It warms me to the heart to know that you are such a kind man. Give me her name."

"Her name is Annie Crowther, an' you'll find her in Bath Square."

"What number?"

"Number three."

"Thank you, Mr Brownrigg. That wasn't so difficult now, was it?"

George scowled at Chapman who waved his hands at two of the marines and said, "You two, go and find her. At once, if you please."

Two marines ran from the pub and Chapman said to George, "You may go. I have no further need of you."

****

Annie wiped the crumbs from her small table and dropped them in the hearth. Suddenly, there was a banging at the door, making her jump. She went to the window and peered out. Two marines were at her door and they were armed.

"Annie Crowther, are you in there?" bellowed one.

She opened the door and said, "I am Annie. What can I do for you boys on this fine morning?"

"Your presence is requested by Warrant Officer Chapman. He wishes to ask you some questions."

"Questions? What questions?" spluttered Annie. Across the road, Mary had stepped out of her door. She looked at Annie with a concerned expression.

"I'm not at liberty to say. My orders are to find you and deliver you." The marine took a step nearer to Annie.

"Alright, I'm comin'," she said, slamming her front door. She called across to Mary, "Keep an eye on Bessie for me, will you?"

Mary nodded and waved at her.

Once at the pub, the marines escorted her through the door and Chapman stood, offering Annie a chair.

"Please," he smiled at her. "Please sit."

Annie did as she was told and plonked herself in the chair. Her long dark locks fell about her neck and face and the officer smiled at her.

"My dear, would you care for a drink?"

Annie nodded and Chapman clicked his fingers at Juxon, who rushed over with two fresh beers.

"I suppose you're wondering why I have summoned you this morning?" said Chapman.

"Well, yes," said Annie.

"What is your relationship with Mr Brownrigg? Do you know him *well?*" He emphasised the word 'well' and Annie thought that he was implying that there was something going on between them.

"George is a friend, is all," she said playing with her cup and avoiding eye contact.

"George, eh. How do you know this George?"

"The Point is a small place," she said. "It ain't like the big city, where folk like you comes from. We all know each other's business on the Point."

"Glad to hear it. If that's the case, then you'll know what happened to our missing man."

"Who?" said Annie, playing dumb.

"Alfred Fish, better known as Guppy. He was seen at this establishment last evening but one, and now has vanished."

"I don't see 'ow I can be of assistance. I know nothin' 'bout no missin' sailor."

"Mrs Crowther – Annie – are you a woman of the night, like so many females in this place?"

Annie could feel her bottom lip tremble. She shook her head and said, "No, I ain't, an' I take umbrage with those what insult me in such a manner."

"My dear, are you upset?" There was no hint of concern in the officer's voice. He was mocking her.

"I 'ave a sick child. I was at 'ome tendin' to 'er needs."

"And Mr Brownrigg – George – was he there also?"

Annie nodded. "George 'as a soft spot for my Bessie an' is payin' for a doctor named Smallcoates to attend to 'er."

"This Smallcoates. Where can he be found?" Chapman sipped from his ale.

"Past the gate, in the High Street. Got a small surgery there," said Annie.

"Is there anyone else that can be called upon to substantiate your story?"

Annie nodded and said, "Mary Abbott was there with me an' George."

"Where can she be found?"

"Across the street from my place. I'll fetch 'er for you when I gets back to my daughter."

"Thank you. That would be most helpful," said Chapman. "Tell me, is George Brownrigg a violent man?"

"'E's got a temper, if that's what you mean, but I wouldn't say 'e was a violent man. Got an 'eart of gold that one."

"Such a saintly sort," said Chapman with as much sarcasm as he could muster. "Seems the stories that I had heard about this man are all untrue."

"Stories?" said Annie.

"I was led to understand that this kind hearted, charitable pillar of the community was thick with thieves, smuggling and violence." Chapman leaned forward in his chair, "How can my sources get it so wrong?"

Annie shrugged at him. "I speak as I find," she said. "I don't recognise your description of George at all. Anyway, what's to say that this Guppy didn't run away?"

"Ah, so he ran away?" said Chapman. "Mr Brownrigg said the very same. If I didn't know better, I'd say that you two have rehearsed your stories."

"You do 'ear stories an' the like. All them pressed men getting' a belly full of ale and a head full of freedom. Dry land must be a temptation."

"Alfred Fish was not a Quota man, Miss Crowther. Do you know what that means?"

Annie shook her head.

"It means that he joined the service of his own free will. Why, therefore, would he run away?"

"I don't know. Maybe he got fed up and wanted a new life. Maybe one of your crew did 'im in over a disagreement. Am I free to go now?" Annie stared at the officer and he stared back at her.

"There is something that you're hiding, my girl. You may go, but don't go far. I may need to speak with you again."

Annie stood and downed the rest of her ale. As she turned Chapman asked, "Where can I find Peter Bookbinder?"

The questioning went on for most of the day. Officer Chapman wasn't getting anywhere. As far as the inhabitants of the Point were concerned, Guppy had seized his moment and run for his dear life and the rest of the crew had made up the story about the fight to cover their own tracks and those of the missing sailor. At five thirty, the sound of three bells echoed across the winter sky. *The Foudroyant* was starting the first dog watch. That was Chapman's cue to return to the ship. He left in the Pinnace and slid across the dark waters to the waiting ship. Annie and Mary Abbott stood on the dock side and watched as the boat disappeared from view.

Mary said, "You'd best beware, my girl. If I didn't know better I'd say that officer is spoilin' to arrest someone, an' we ain't 'eard the last of this."

"I know, Mary. I gets the same feelin', but I think I got bigger worries."

Mary looked at her friend and read the expression on her face. "George Brownrigg?"

"You don't know the 'arf of it," said Annie turning and heading for home.

Chapter Eight

"There ain't gonna be trouble is there?"

Skinny spat on the ground, pulled the collar of his coat around his neck and set off towards King James Gate, while the rest of the *Squeeze Gut Boys* hid in the shadow of the square tower. His footsteps echoed on the dank stone as he approached Stanley, the guard at the gate, who stood with his loaded musket, watching the rakish frame of Skinny draw nearer. Stanley raised his weapon and aimed it at the slither of shadow before him.

"Who approaches?" Stanley called into the gloom. "Declare yourself."

"Jim McDowell from Portsea."

"What business do you have at these gates, Jim McDowell from Portsea?"

Skinny was almost at the imposing stone pillars of the barrier and could see that the drawbridge was still down. He sized up Stanley in an instant and decided that he didn't really pose much of a threat, even with a loaded musket. The eyes always gave away fear and he recognised that look in Stanley's.

"I seek entrance to the point," said McDowell.

"What's your business in the Point at this hour?" Stanley trained his musket on the man and took a step towards him.

"Who wants to know?" said Skinny.

"I ask the questions. You won't be crossing through this gate tonight unless you tells me your business."

"I seek someone," said Skinny, eyeing the guard carefully. He was almost as thin as Skinny himself and it looked like his uniform had seen better days. His tunic hung on his reedy shoulders like a child wearing a grown man's clothes. His boots were scuffed and unpolished and he appeared not to have washed or shaved in a week. He was a very sorry looking guardsman.

"Who are you seeking?" said Stanley trying his best to control his shaking hands.

"George Brownrigg, that's who." Skinny pulled a jar of rum from under his coat and took a generous glug. As he wiped his chin, Skinny saw the look of fear in Stanley's eyes melt away to be replaced by a look of want. Stanley licked his lips. "You look thirsty," said Skinny. "Want some?" he shoved the jar at Stanley and gave it a waggle.

"Not while I'm on duty," said the guard, shaking his head but licking his lips again. As Skinny swung the jar from side to side, Stanley's eyes followed its progress like he was tracing a pocket watch swinging in the hands of a hypnotist in a cheap side show. He never let his gaze fall away, not for an instant.

"It's a cold one tonight," said McDowell, shivering and sipping from the receptacle again. "This stuff will keep you warmer than a bed full of whores. Are you sure that I can't tempt you to a drop?"

"I mustn't. I'll get the boot for sure if I'm drunk on duty again."

"Who will tell?" Skinny looked around at the deserted street. "There ain't a soul about and besides, you're among friends 'ere."

"Friends? I don't think we are acquainted."

"Sure we are. You knows my name now, so we must be acquainted," said Skinny.

"I suppose you're right there," said Stanley, eyeing the rum like it was liquid gold. "It is cold tonight," he said, stamping his feet to accentuate exactly how cold it was, "and I do 'ave to stand here for hours." The dark rum sloshed in the jar and the sweet smell of molasses caressed Stanley's nostrils. He looked left, then right, half expecting his commanding officer to be hiding in the tall shadows of the fortifications that surrounded the gates and the guard house. After another quick glance, he lowered his gun and rubbed his chin in contemplation. "You're sure you won't tell?" he said.

"Cross my 'eart and all that. Just 'ave a drop to take away the chill." Skinny held out the vessel and it dangled from his scrawny finger. Stanley looked like a child who had just discovered he'd been locked in a sweet shop. He reached for the rum and gingerly took it from Skinny's finger.

"That's right," said Skinny, "just to take the edge off."

Stanley already had the stopper out of the end of the jar and had tipped a large splash of the alcohol into his mouth. He closed his eyes and waited for the warmth to snake to his gut and Skinny thought for a moment that he reminded him of someone waiting to receive the Almighty in prayer at the altar of a church. His face was tilted to the heavens with a look of pure ecstasy upon it. Stanley opened his eyes and swigged another generous glug.

"That's good stuff," he said with a loud sigh, wiping the dregs that slid down his chin with his fingers, and licking them clean. "Mind if I have another slug?"

"Be my guest," said Skinny. "In fact why don't you keep it? You looks like you could do with it more than me."

"If you're sure?" said Stanley downing a third mouthful of the alcohol. His belly roared hotter than the lame fire that he had lit in the stove in the guard house.

"Here's a thought," said Skinny placing his arm around the guard's shoulders and squeezing him close. "What say you let me an' me mates through an', when we return, we'll bring you some more?" said Skinny.

"More? How much more?" said Stanley.

"As much as you need... but that depends on whether you is opening this gate. Maybe we'll fetch you more than you'll need. Name your price?"

Stanley belched loudly and said, "I'll let you through if you brings me two, and I mean *two*, bottles of brandy. And not the cheap stuff, mind."

Skinny thrust out his hand for Stanley to shake. The guardsman reciprocated. "You have a deal, my friend. Now open this gate."

Stanley slid his key in the lock and turned it. He looked at Skinny with narrowed eyes.

"What time are you planning on coming back through?"

"We'll be back before midnight," said Skinny Jim. "Why?"

"Just so I know when to expect you," said Stanley. "Before twelve it is then." He pushed open the gate and it squealed as it moved. Skinny whistled and the others, who had been waiting in the shadows, ran across the street towards the gate.

Stanley scratched his head. "How many are you taking in?"

"About ten."

"There ain't gonna be no trouble, is there?"

"Trouble?" said Skinny slapping the rum soaked guard on the back and steering him towards the guardhouse. "Don't fret none. We're just gonna 'ave a chat about business is all. Nice an' civilised over a cup or two of ale." As Skinny steered the guard towards the door of the guardhouse, he was frantically ushering the gang through the gate with the hand that he held behind his back. They did as they were told and slid silently through onto the Point. Skinny Jim waited until Stanley had gone inside before joining them and pulling the gate shut.

"That was easier than I thought," he said to the Knox brothers who were standing at the head of the rabble, waiting for further instructions.

The gang made their way up Broad Street. They turned left onto Tower Street and up ahead was Bath Square. The Point teemed with life. Sailors sat in doorways toasting nothing but fresh air, lost comrades and the gods of the seas. Others sang merrily about long lost loves and far-away lands while bare chested women tried to coax them down dirty alley ways. In the middle of the square, a group of raggedy children screamed in delight as they tried to trap a burning rat. It was a popular game to catch a rat, soak it in turpentine and set it alight and, if there was one thing that the Point had in abundance, it was rats. Skinny watched as the rat ran squealing under a stack of crates and the smell of smouldering flesh and wood was hard to ignore. Next to the crates, on a stack of fisherman's nets, a rotund woman rolled around, naked and drunk, howling with laughter at her inability to get to her feet. Beside her, a drunken man tried and failed to stand and put his left shoe on. It didn't matter that he wasn't wearing anything other than his neck scarf and a right shoe, the pair were as brazen as a baby on wash day. Skinny thought that this was the most depraved place he'd ever seen, and he loved it. He squeezed his eyes shut and sniffed in the scent of debauchery and lust, the stench of poverty and greed. At the end of Bath Square was *The Camber Inn*. The lights inside spilled out onto the crowded street.

Skinny turned and faced the rest of his boys, placing a finger to his lips. Henry Knox said, "What do we do now?"

"You and John are gonna go in and see how many there are inside and then draw them out. Keep your ears an' eyes open cos I wanna know which one's Brownrigg."

Henry and John nodded and Skinny patted them both on the back. The rest of the gang watched as John and Henry made their way across the square and entered the inn. The place was packed and the cacophony of bawdy noise spilled out into the Square. Voices echoed off the walls of the pub, making the brothers' ears ring with the din. In the far corner of the room, next to a mean-spirited fire that barely set a glow, a group of seamen sat at a table shouting loudly to each other in a haze of pipe smoke and alcohol fumes. On their knees sat the ugliest whores that the two brothers had seen. Old and grizzled women giggled in the ears of the sailors as they in turn kept them plied with liquor. This scene was repeated at the next table, and the next, and the next. John tugged Henry's arm and pointed to a tall man standing at the bar. He was surrounded by others who appeared to hang on his every word. John pulled his brother closer to the bar to see what was what. Henry stood close by, eagerly listening above the noise for any clues in their conversation.

Then William Juxon sauntered over and said, "What'll it be, lads?"

"Two Ales," Henry replied.

William Juxon filled two tankards, handed them to the brothers, took their money, and went back to his work behind the bar, listening intermittently to the conversation of the group huddled around the man mountain.

A younger man came in and the large man shouted, "Davey, 'ave a drink with us."

Davey shouted back, "Are you payin', Mr Brownrigg?"

George Brownrigg slapped Davey on the back so hard that he knocked Davey off balance and he fell into Henry Knox, splashing ale all over the front of John Knox's coat. Henry slammed down his cup and glared at Davey.

"Look what you've done, you fuckin' plugtail," he shouted. Davey said nothing and just stared back.

"Don't just stand there. Get me another drink, or else," demanded Henry, wiping the liquid from his brother's clothing. "An' get me brother one too."

Brownrigg squeezed himself between Davey and the Knox brothers. Including his Derby hat, he was at least two feet taller than them. He placed a huge hand on Davey's shoulder and glowered at them both. "There a problem 'ere?" he said. Both men knew that they didn't want to get into a fight in the confined quarters of the bar.

"This fool spilled beer down my brother's coat. I wants another," said Henry.

"No one speaks to my mate, Davey Turner that way," said George. "You might wanna think about sayin' sorry, boys."

Henry Knox knew that the odds were stacked heavily against them and decided that this was the time to draw Brownrigg and his boys outside.

"I will do no such thing, you bastard. If you wanna make me, then be my guest," said Henry defiantly.

"Do you know who I am?" said George Brownrigg, removing his hat and tossing it at William Juxon.

Henry looked at John and shrugged. He said, "Should I know you? You ain't the ghost of Horatio Nelson, are you?" John Knox sniggered behind his hand.

"Ever 'eard the name Brownrigg before?" said George.

Both brothers looked at each other and shook their heads. "Can't say that we 'ave," said Henry.

"Well," said George sucking air through his teeth, "what say I acquaint you?"

He raised his club stick in the air, ready to strike the pair. Both men raised their arms over their faces to protect themselves. Suddenly,

Juxon called out from behind the bar and cut through the din. "Not in 'ere," he said. "Please, George, take it outside."

The room fell silent. There was an air of expectation in the crowded room. Drunken men and women were spoiling to watch a good fight at the best of times and it seemed that they were going to get their wish. Racing may be the sport of kings but fighting was the sport of paupers.

One of the women, balancing on a sailor's lap screamed, "Kill 'im, Mr Brownrigg."

John and Henry pushed their way towards the door with Brownrigg and his gang following. They stumbled out into the square and the cold damp air fogged their breaths, dissipating in the darkness. The two brothers removed their coats and threw them on the ground.

"Come on then, Brownrigg. Let's see what you got," said Henry Knox at the top of his voice.

By the time George Brownrigg realised that it was a trap, it was too late. As he stood with his back to the square, facing the brothers towards the Camber, Skinny and the remaining *Squeeze Gut Boys* rushed out of the shadows brandishing their assorted weapons. At the front was their deranged leader with the wildest look in his eyes, and he headed straight for Brownrigg.

"This one's mine," he screamed above the clatter, leaping into the air.

George turned just in time to dodge the swinging arm of McDowell with a gleaming blade in his hand. For a tall man, George was quite nimble and shifted weight from his right foot to his left, leaning back to avoid the blade. As it arched past his face, the blade glinted in the shallow moonlight, taking a nick out of his ear. Skinny was now off balance and had his rib cage exposed to George. He wasted little time in burying his large fist into the skeletal frame of McDowell and Skinny collapsed on the floor in agony, gasping for breath.

The Knox brothers were squaring up to Davey Turner and Pete Bookbinder. Both brothers had their backs pressed together so that they could cover every angle of attack. Henry brandished a hammer and John had a length of heavy chain, given to them by the rest of the gang when they came out of the pub. They lashed out wildly, desperate to keep a distance from their enemies. Davey lunged at them with a length of wood but the brothers were quicker, wrapping the length of chain around the shaft of wood and snatching it from Davey's grip.

"You'll 'ave to do better than that," growled Henry.

Pete grabbed his friend and yanked him out of harm's way in the nick of time. The hammer that Henry brandished whizzed past the young Turner's head, missing by inches.

Brownrigg felt someone jump on his back and wrap a length of chain around his throat. George felt his windpipe snapping shut as the mystery attacker applied the pressure. George shook with all his might but his attacker would not be dislodged. The lack of oxygen made his head swim and he fell to his knees. His attacker still held firm and squeezed even tighter, shouting with delight that Brownrigg was for the taking. This gave Skinny enough time to clamber to his feet and wave the blade in George's face, laughing as he did.

"Know my name?" he said through gritted teeth. "Skinny Jim McDowell is about to finish you."

George knew what was coming and he glared in defiance at the man before him. Skinny Jim stepped in closer and placed his hand on George's shoulder, giving the man clinging to his shoulders the signal to dismount, which he did immediately. Skinny pulled George onto him in his weakened state and plunged his knife into his stomach. Brownrigg went taut as he braced for the impact of the knife and then he slumped forward. Just before George fell face down into the grimy street, McDowell finished the job by smacking him in the face with his wiry fist. Brownrigg fell on his side and groaned at McDowell's feet and Skinny spat on the cobbles and laughed.

"Nice to make your acquaintance, George Brownrigg," he said leaning down and patting the stricken man on the side of the cheek.

The sight of the King of the Point lying on the ground caused the square to fall silent. Bruised men stopped brawling and fixed their stare, first on the injured Brownrigg, and then to the deliriously happy Skinny Jim, who beamed from ear to ear. He stared at the crowd and allowed the adrenalin to rush through him like it was opium. He was elated with his victory and he held out his arms as though preparing to accept his flock like some deity giving a sermon. Then he spoke. "Pointers, listen up. There is a new king now. The old king 'as been deposed. What went before is no more."

"You ain't no king. You're barely a full grown man," shouted a shrill voice from the shadows.

Someone else joined in, "We don't like outsiders. Specially if they's from Devils Acre."

There was now a crowd of almost one hundred people in the square and, save for the ten lads that had crept through the gate, the rest were all 'Pointers'. William Juxon stepped forward and said, "No one comes onto our patch and does this. No one."

"You think I'm not to be taken seriously?" Skinny bent down and ripped the knife from Brownrigg's gut, brandishing it at the crowd. "You see the blood on this blade, and you think I'm not to be feared? Well come on! I'll kill the fuckin' lot of you."

The crowd moved forward and Skinny and the boys edged back. He snarled at Juxon like a feral dog, waving the knife at him. "You'll be first, you ugly cunt."

The Knox brothers swung their weapons at the front row of the horde. "Jim, what do we do?" said Henry. "They won't stop comin'."

Skinny knew their predicament and said, "Keep your 'eads, lads. This lot won't wanna get 'urt like old George there." He slashed at the mob vigorously with the blade. The gang were now on the edge of the Point, cornered on the outer Camber. Skinny looked over his shoulder and glanced down at the cold, murky brine. The crowd pushed forward again.

Someone else shouted out, "Let's get the stink of Portsea out of our nostrils. Kill the bastards."

A huge roar erupted and the crowd broke, chasing the Portsea boys, who started to leap into the dark sea. The Knox brothers followed their friends into the icy waters and started swimming for the Hard. Others followed suit.

Something caught Skinny's attention momentarily among the chaos. He was distracted by an attractive woman, tall and slender with shiny black hair. He watched Annie kneel beside the still body of

Brownrigg and cradle his head to her bosom, and Skinny formulated a plan. Annie glanced in his direction just before he jumped and Skinny winked at her and beamed. Behind him, his gang called for him to jump and jump he would, but in the last dying embers of his criminal coup, with the baying 'Pointers' clawing for his blood, McDowell had a clear and concise thought about the way forward. He smiled inwardly and looked at the crowd that surrounded him. As calmly as a gull drops to the surface of the ocean after flight, Jim McDowell stepped of the dockside and splashed into the sea. As he dropped, a huge cheer erupted from the crowd.

Above the splashing in the darkness of Portsmouth harbour a lone voice wafted back to dry land: "This ain't over. Not by a stretch. We'll be back."

Davey was at George's side the minute that he was sure the attackers had gone. He said to Annie, "Is it bad? Will 'e die?"

She could read the fear in the young man's eyes.

Pete stood over Davy and slapped the back of his head.

"Course 'e ain't gonna die. This is Brownrigg. The toughest man in the world."

George wheezed and groaned as Annie gently tried to turn him onto his back. The wound was visible for all to see. "Sorry," was all Annie could think to say to him. She whispered it in his ear and cradled his head, and briefly his eyes flickered open and a faint smile flirted with his lips.

"I 'ope the blade missed the important bits. 'E's cut bad but I 'ope that's all," said Annie, brushing stray hairs from his forehead. George opened his eyes again and stared up at her with another strained half-smile. Annie couldn't decide if it actually was a smile or if it was the pain that caused him to wince. "Don't speak," she said, wiping dirt from his face.

William Juxon approached and said, "Davey, you take 'is left leg; Pete, you take 'is right. We need to get 'im in 'is bed where he'll be comfortable."

Davey and Pete took up their positions and Juxon said, "Annie, do you know Mudge the tailor?" Mudge had a shop near the entrance to

Tower Alley. She nodded. "Good," said Juxon. "Now go and find 'im, post-haste."

Annie said, "What about Doctor Smallcoates? Wouldn't 'e be better?"

"No time. Stanley at the gate will be sleepin' at this hour and the damn thing'll be locked. Mudge is just up there," said Juxon pointing towards Tower Alley.

Annie nodded and raced in the direction of Mudge's shop.

"You tell 'im that Brownrigg is hurt. Tell him to bring needles and thread," shouted William after the slight shape of Annie melting into the darkness.

"Mudge ain't no doctor," said Pete.

"'Appen not," said Juxon, "but I know for a fact that 'e's 'ad medical training an' 'e's a dab 'and with a needle an' thread. Old George 'ere's gonna need stitchin'."

****

Skinny shivered in his wet clothes as he lay against the damp cobble stones of the Hard. He and the gang were exhausted from their swim to safety and some of the younger boys were a little bit rattled.

"That's that then," said Henry Knox, leaning back on his elbows and taking in huge gulps of air.

"Who says?" said McDowell sullenly.

"You can't be serious. You wanna 'ave another go at it?" said Henry. A few voices echoed his sentiment but quickly fell silent when they realised that their boss was deadly serious.

Skinny climbed to his feet and squeezed water from his coat. He pulled off his right boot and emptied the water from it, repeating the process for the left one. "That Brownrigg has a weakness. He is vulnerable an' we're gonna take advantage of it."

"Weakness? What you talkin' about?" said Henry.

"Yeah, what you talkin' about?" echoed his brother John.

"The dark haired woman," said Skinny.

"What woman?" said Henry.

"That's the difference between you an' me. I keeps my eyes open," said Skinny. "George 'as a woman. We target 'er, and that's how we get 'im to yield to us, boys."

A few heads nodded, while others were preoccupied with wringing out their sodden garments. Skinny Jim continued, "Some among you might see this as bein' a bad night, as we didn't get what we wanted." Skinny looked at the pale faces before him and a few heads nodded. "Well," he continued, "opportunity comes in many shapes, my friends, and our opportunity comes in the shape of a pretty woman."

Chapter Nine

"If Mudge 'adn't patched you up you'd be dead from the bleed."

"Annie, George is awake," called Mary through the open door. Annie sat up in bed and rubbed the remnants of sleep from her eyes.

She called down through a half-yawn, "I'll be there presently." Mary said something inaudible in response and slammed the door shut. Annie watched from her small bedroom as she crossed the square.

Beside Annie, Bessie opened her eyes and stared out from under the blanket. Annie placed a hand on her forehead and gasped.

"The fever," she said excitedly, "it's gone." She leant over and gave Bessie the biggest hug that the little girl had ever had, squeezing her slight frame so hard that the poor thing winced.

"How do you feel?" said Annie.

"I feel better," said Bessie with a smile. In that smile Annie knew that her daughter had returned and was her old self again.

"Hungry?" said Annie and Bessie nodded. That was the best response that she could have wished for. "All you've been livin' on is watered down broth and mashed vegetables," she said. "I'll fix you somethin' to eat, my darlin'," she added as she scrambled from the bed and raced down stairs. In her haste she almost forgot Mary's message about George. She decided that, once she'd fixed breakfast, she would pop over to the house on Broad Street to see him, give him the good news and most importantly of all, thank him. It would be the tonic that he needed, knowing that he had saved Bessie from the grave. Her survival would be his too. This morning, more than any that Annie could remember since Sam's disappearance, she was bursting with so much joy that she was sure she could step off the Camber's edge and walk the waters to Gosport and back without getting wet. Annie looked to the heavens and silently said a prayer of thanks, then set about fixing her daughter some proper food to eat.

****

George rolled in his bed and groaned. He opened his eyes and glanced around the room with a confused look, taking a while to bring his eyes into focus. At first he couldn't work out where the stinging pain was coming from, such was its nauseating intensity. With every intake of breath, he paused and waited for the stabbing finger of pain to hit, and he steeled himself as he exhaled. It was so acute that he'd even felt it in his slumber, but now he was awake the pain had trebled and trebled again. He tried to lean up on his elbows, instantly regretting it, and flopped back to the bed just as the door opened and Annie walked in.

"Be still," said Annie, rushing to his bedside. "You've 'ad a scare."

"Where am I, girl?" said George in confusion.

"You're in your 'ouse. This is your bed, George." Annie placed a gentle hand on his chest and held him firmly, in case he had further designs on trying to sit. She stared at him, lying there half naked, his sheet just covering his waist and below, and her eyes traced the scars and blemishes that were visible on his torso. Large pink welts covered his arms and chest, resembling the marks made by the ropes of a cat of nine tails. George saw her staring and answered her unspoken question.

"The scars are from my younger days. I was caught stealin' when I was ten an' I was sentenced to twenty lashes."

"You poor thing," said Annie.

"Don't think about it much these days," said George. "I think in some ways it toughened me up."

"Do you remember much about last night?" said Annie.

"I remember I was lyin' on the ground with that bastard, Jim McDowell standin' over me. I remember the pain in me gut."

"You've 'ad a lucky escape, George Brownrigg. If Mudge 'adn't patched you up you'd be dead from the bleed."

"Mudge? What was 'e doin' tendin' to me? 'E's a tailor!" Brownrigg looked at Annie and saw that his outburst had startled her. He placed his hand on hers and said, "Sorry, Annie, I didn't mean to shout. Why Mudge and not Smallcoates?"

"Smallcoates is on the other side of the gate. It would 'ave taken too long to get past Stanley, and Juxon was worried that time was against us. He knew that you'd bleed out, so 'e sent me to fetch Mudge instead."

"Stanley, eh?" said George. "I s'pose that Jim an' 'is boys just wandered onto the point unchecked. I'll wager that Stanley played 'is part in this."

"Now you leave that man alone," said Annie. "I won't 'ave any more blood shed, do you 'ear?" She leaned over George and stared at his wound, which was covered with a rag. She lifted the rag and examined the neat line of stitches that crossed his lower stomach. "Looks like Mudge 'as done a good job."

"Then I must thank 'im, soon as I'm back on me feet. An' I must thank you too." George smiled at Annie and squeezed her hand.

"You don't need to thank me. What you done for me this past week 'as been thanks enough. 'Sides, I was just doin' what I was told."

"Even so, you was lookin' out for me," said George with a weak smile. He patted the back of her arm and said, "You are my angel sent to watch over me, an' I am right grateful."

Annie smiled back and then looked away in embarrassment. She wiped her eyes and said, "I didn't take you for a religious man. Found God now, eh?"

"Who needs God when I got you," said George. "It must mean that you like me after all."

Annie stood and snatched her hand away. "George! That is not a question that I should be answering." She stood at the window and stared down into Broad Street at the Camber. Small boats bobbed in the tiny harbour and a group of men shovelled coal into the *Coal Exchange's* cellars. Beyond that, she could just make out the roof top of *The Still Tavern* on the edge of the shore. Blockhouse fort framed the horizon beyond.

"Annie, I didn't mean to embarrass you. I just say it like it is. I make no secret of my likin' for you. I 'ope that this last few days you've seen a different side to me."

"I 'ave that," she said not turning her gaze from the window. "But you're still a murderer. That don't sit comfortably with me."

"That lad was askin' for it. I got a business to protect, or else we'll all be at the mercy of bastards like Skinny Jim McDowell."

"Then maybe we're from different worlds. I will never accept killin' as a means of keepin' shop. It ain't right." Annie turned from the window and looked at George, and for the first time she saw him as vulnerable. He might like the folk on the Point to think that he was invincible but to Annie, George was just a man, flawed, childish and cruel.

She sighed and George said, "After lyin' for me the other day, your world ain't so far away from mine." He paused before continuing, "Maybe we ain't so different after all?"

"I ain't like you in the slightest," snapped Annie. "I got a conscience for starters."

"Look," said George, "I didn't intend to quarrel with you this day. I wanted us to get along."

"Then you must promise me that you will stop the killin'. I can't be friends with someone who does that sort of thing."

"Are we friends then?" said George.

"Stop teasin' me," said Annie. "Will you stop the killin'?"

"Bein' as you asked so nicely, yes, I will stop. But there will still be violence in my line of work. There has to be."

Annie nodded. "I ain't askin' you to stop what you do, just to stop the murderin'. If there 'as to be violence, then so be it. Just don't tell me when it 'appens."

"You 'ave my word, Annie Crowther," said George. "See, I feel kinder already." He broke into a broad grin and the sparkle in his eyes returned.

"I said stop teasin' me," said Annie.

"Tell me, why is it that you are 'ere this mornin' and not with your Bessie. You don't look like you've had a wink of sleep, girl. Are you 'ere outta concern for me, is that it? Or are you worried that if old Brownrigg shuffled of this mortal coil that you'd 'ave no more 'elp and such?"

Annie glared at George. "Such a suggestion indeed. I am ashamed that you think that."

"Annie, I could 'ave died last night. I am a bad man an' I know that. But like I said before, when I'm with you… I can't explain it, but you make me wanna be kinder."

"Kindness is admirable. It's a start, shall we say." Annie pulled her shawl over her shoulders. "I must be off, George. Bessie will be wonderin' where I am."

"'Ow is the child?" said George.

"It is for that reason that I came. She is well again. The fever broke this mornin' an' she's eaten for the first time too."

"I am heartily pleased for you."

"Thank you… and thank you for the 'elp. I am convinced that without you, I would 'ave lost 'er."

"But you didn't, did you?"

Annie shook her head and said, "What a few days. First Bessie, an' now you."

"Never a dull moment, eh?"

"I must be goin'," said Annie pulling open the door. She stopped and looked back at George. "I'm so glad that you are okay," she said. "Gettin' to know you this last week 'as been an eye opener."

"Likewise, Annie, likewise."

"I'll pop in later to see 'ow you are."

"You'll be wantin' more supplies today?" asked George.

Annie nodded. "Don't be thinkin' about that right now. You just worry about getting' better."

She started down the stairs and just before she disappeared out of view, George called, "Annie, wait!" He tried to sit up once more and screwed up his face, groaning in pain. "Annie?" he said again.

She stopped and turned to face him.

"Annie, when you say it's a start, do you mean it's a start for you an' me?"

After the briefest of pauses, she nodded and disappeared down the stairs.

George lay in his bed and stared at his stained ceiling. Sounds wafted in from the street below. He knew that he would need to be up and about today. His status was at stake, especially after last night's attempt to take this place from him, so what better way to show the world that nothing stops George Brownrigg? He needed to let his people know that he was invincible and he needed to be seen and talked about more than ever before.

"Annie said it was a start." He smiled as the words left his lips and fell silent in the morning air. "Annie Brownrigg," he said to himself, "now that 'as a ring to it."

Buoyed by his marginal success with Annie, George decided to attempt standing up. He let his legs fall out of the bed and he gingerly felt for the cold floorboards with his toes. He waited for the pain, which had doubled with the movement of his body, to subside and eased himself to the edge of the bed and stood. George knew that he'd feel unsteady on his feet and he gripped the bedpost to steady himself.

It took over an hour for Brownrigg to get dressed and make his way to the ground floor. He stood in the entrance hall and stared in the mirror. A pale, moistened face stared back, with dark rings circling sunken eyes and lines that had been there the day before, appearing more defined. It seemed to George that he had come closer to death than he or anyone else had bargained for, and the shadow of that close shave still clouded the lines on his face. He straightened up and placed his Derby hat on his head. Whilst dressing, George had taken the time to bind the knife wound with a tight bedsheet, torn into a strip and wound around his midriff. It seemed to be doing the trick, holding the stitches in place, giving George the support that he needed to move about. He grabbed his club-headed stick for support, stepped from the house and stood at the top of the three steps that led from his door to the Square.

"Time to show me face," he whispered and made his way down the steps.

William Juxon was stepping out of Mudge's shop on the corner of Tower Alley, when he saw George walking gingerly along Broad Street in the direction of the gate.

"George!" he called. "Mr Brownrigg, what you doin' up? You'll come to 'arm if you don't rest. Smallcoates is due to attend you this mornin'."

"Ease up, William. I'm fine, see. Never better." Brownrigg smiled at Juxon, straightening his frame to its full height, and passed him by.

"Is 'e in?" he said.

"What, Mudge? That 'e is, Mr Brownrigg."

George tipped his hat at Juxon, opened the door to the tailor's shop and entered. A few minutes later he emerged, with the grateful thanks of Mudge ringing in his ears. Brownrigg knew that the only way to garner loyalty was to be firm but fair. He made sure that Mudge would enjoy a comfortable Christmas. George continued along the street, turning heads as he passed by. Occasionally someone would tip their hat and offer a 'good morning' or remark on his swift recovery. He smiled and tipped his hat back and continued on his way towards the gate. The fortifications and round tower loomed large on his right hand side, with the gate open and seemingly deserted. The drawbridge across the moat was down, so George stepped through the gate and crossed the bridge, approaching the guard house on the right. He banged on the door and waited. When no one came, he banged again. Still there was no answer.

"Stanley?" he called. "You in there?"

Somebody moved inside and then George heard shuffling footsteps. The door opened a little and a scruffy looking man peered through the gap.

"Mr Brownrigg," said Stanley. "To what do I owe the pleasure?"

"Not pleasure, Stanley. More like pain." George leaned on the door and it opened further. Stanley stumbled backwards and Brownrigg entered the guard house. It was a single room with a stove and bunk. The empty jug of rum sat on the table by the bed. George wandered over, picked up the jug and sniffed.

"'Ow's your 'ead this day, Stanley?"

"I'm fine, Mr Brownrigg. Why do you ask?"

George held up the jug and shook it. "Looks like someone had their fill last night. Everyone knows that you likes a drink."

"Not me, sir. Stan wouldn't dare, not on duty."

"This place reeks, Stanley. It reeks of rum an' sweat, an' it reeks of lies and betrayal."

"Betrayal, Mr Brownrigg? I don't understand." Stanley was shaking and he struggled to keep his voice steady.

"Oh, I think you do understand. See, I got this last night," George pulled up his shirt and showed Stanley the wound. The strip of bedsheet was stained red.

"What happened to you?" said Stan.

"McDowell an' 'is boys, Stan. That's what 'appened. He stuck me last night in Bath Square an' left me for dead."

"That's terrible." George could see the guilt in Stanley's shifty expression.

"Now I'm thinkin' to meself, 'ow did a lowlife shit like 'im get onto the Point, specially as the gate was closed and the drawbridge was up?"

Stanley shrugged and looked at the ground, thrusting his hands deep into the pockets of his tatty trousers.

"Again I'm thinkin' that old Stanley will know, as you're the one the keys. So I says to meself, go and see Stanley an' 'e'll clear up the confusion." George stepped closer to the guard and he in turn stepped backwards. He had nowhere to go, the wall stopped his progress. "So 'ere I am."

"Mr Brownrigg, I don't know anything. Honest." said Stanley.

"So you didn't open the gate last night? You didn't see McDowell and 'is boys cross the bridge an' enter the Point?"

Stanley shook his head and stared at Brownrigg with wide eyes. "Wait!" he said. "I knows what 'appened. I was jumped, that's what. Coshed on the 'ead." Stanley rubbed the back of his head to emphasise the point. "That's why I'm groggy this mornin'."

"I can't see no wound. No bump or sore," said George. "I thinks that you're groggy 'cos of the grog. I think you got pissed and that lot just strolled on in."

"Never!" said Stanley. "Not while I wear this uniform. The very thought…"

George pulled out a large blade from inside his coat, and waved it at Stanley menacingly.

"What you gonna do to me?" asked the guard, staring at the blade.

"Well, if you're tellin' the truth, then you ain't got no reason to be scared. But listen good," Brownrigg pushed the blade against Stanley's throat and pressed the tip in so hard that it drew blood. Stanley gulped. "If I finds out that you willingly let them bastards in, I'll come back 'ere an' do to you what McDowell did to me, only this time I'll do it properly."

"Please, Mr Brownrigg, don't hurt me," pleaded Stanley.

George patted Stan's cheek with his large hand and smiled at him. "'Urt you, guardsman? I ain't gonna 'urt you. Not today at least, but you think on 'bout what has passed between us." He took a step away from the guard and slid the blade back inside his coat. Stanley collapsed on the floor in a heap with a wet patch staining his crotch and the smell of urine hanging in the air. George opened the door and stepped into the crisp morning light. As the door shut, he fell against the cold wall clutching his side. He drew three large breaths and stood, looking around to see if anyone had seen his predicament. A small boy sat atop a stack of wooden crates with the mangiest cat George had ever seen perched on his lap. George smiled and made his way down the path, heading for Broad Street.

Brownrigg knew that Stanley had let the boys in the previous night. He was sure of it in fact, but he was in a good mood this morning and so saw no point in ending his life. Besides, Stanley owed him and he would need to return that favour in the coming days. Ordinarily, he would have killed him in a heartbeat, without the slightest hesitation, but something was different inside him, something had softened his stone heart. Annie Crowther was the cause and he knew it. What was it that he had said to her? That he was trying to be kinder, and that was the truth of it. He was being kinder and thanks to Annie, old Stan was still breathing. He marvelled at the way of things. How was it that a woman could have such a powerful effect on things? How was it that his act of kindness was driven by a desire to win this woman's heart? *Stan should thank Annie for his very life*, thought George.

He made his way back through the gate and up Broad Street, taking deep breaths and sniffing in the sea air. The smell was intoxicating. It wasn't pleasant and to the unfamiliar nose it would be regarded as offensive, but it was the Point, it was the smell of the sea and it was George's… all of it. The King of the Point wandered among his people, receiving their congratulations and approval. They told him it was a miracle that he was up and about, and shook his hand.

Mary Abbott was milling around outside *The Union Tavern*, chatting to a group of women by the door. She saw George and stopped speaking in mid-sentence. The other women did the same as Brownrigg approached. He bade them good morning and crossed the square, heading towards *The Camber Inn*.

Chapter Ten

"'Ello little'un. What say you open the door?"

Leaning back onto the rear legs of his spindly chair, Henry Knox rested his head on the wall of *The George Hotel* and puffed out plumes of smoke from his pipe. The place was quiet with just a few locals supping their drinks at the bar and chatting while the landlord kept himself busy. Henry had a far-away look in his eye.

"You still with us, Henry?" Skinny kicked the leg of the chair and it toppled backwards, sending Knox sprawling as the back of his head slid down the wall. The others around the table burst into laughter at this sight, causing the regulars to look up from their drinks at the bar and shake their heads. The landlord wasn't that thrilled that Skinny and his mates had decided to frequent his establishment but they bought drinks and that was all that mattered as far as he was concerned. They had been coming in for the best part of a week and complaints about their behaviour were becoming commonplace.

"What you do that for?" said Henry climbing to his feet and dusting himself down. "You've been in a bad mood this last three days, since you stuck George."

"Woke you up, didn't it?" said Skinny. "Besides, I got to make plans 'aven't I? No one else is goin' to do it. Now take a seat and we'll get down to business."

Knox sat down next to his brother, John, and sipped his drink.

"Now, as you know we stuck that fucker, Brownrigg well and good three nights past but 'e still lives."

"We're not goin' back on the Point, are we? I got beaten bad last time an' don't fancy it again." said James Tuckey, rubbing his bruises gingerly.

"I 'ave somethin' else," said Skinny. "Now I 'ear tell that Brownrigg's sweet on a local girl, goes by the name of Annie Crowther."

"What does that 'ave to do with us?" asked John Knox.

"Lots an' lots. It means that old iron George isn't so invincible. This Crowther woman 'as a daughter, an' that's where I think we should strike next."

"I ain't bein' party to no murder of an innocent girl. That sort of action will find you at the end of a rope, for sure." James Tuckey stood and made to leave.

"Sit down!" shouted McDowell and James did as he was told. The regulars in the *George Hotel* once more looked up from their drinks and stared at the gang.

"No one said anythin' about killin'," said Skinny in a hushed voice, all too aware that the men at the bar could hear them. "I merely propose that the girl disappears for a while. Sorta goes on 'oliday on our side of the gate."

"Kidnap 'er?" said Henry.

"The boy's got brains after all," said Skinny raising his cup in a toast.

"When were you thinkin' of doin' it?" said John.

"Me?" said Skinny. "I'm not doin' it. Henry and James are to carry out the task."

"Why us?" said James. "Why not you?"

"I am known in those parts, am I not? That guardsman Stanley knows me for one thing. I would be struck down not three steps into the Point, you mark my words. This task is more suited to ones less conspicuous, shall we say."

"When do we do it?" asked Henry.

"There is a Frigate pullin' into port tomorrow, *HMS Sirius*. I 'ave it on good authority that this Crowther woman is goin' to be on a launch rowin' out supplies and the like to the ship."

"'Ow do you know?" said Henry.

"Let's just say that I knows, an' leave it at that. I am owed money an' I 'ave called in the debt."

****

"Look lively, girl. The *Sirius* docks later this mornin'." Mary stood in the doorway of Annie's house, blocking the light in the room. Annie and Bessie were sat at the table eating what was left of the previous night's supplies. Mary smiled at the little girl and said, "To see you sat there, as large as life… it's a miracle, an' no mistake."

"I feel much better, thank you," said Bessie through large mouthfuls of bread.

"Brownrigg's as good as 'is word then?" said Mary looking enviously at the food on their plates.

"Better, Mary. 'E can be a real gent when it takes 'is fancy," said Annie. "Why do you need me along for this one?"

"Cos, girl, I need you to carry supplies. Juxon an' Mr George 'ave tasked me with shiftin' as much salt junk an' mutton as possible. Also got some casks of porter."

"Did George ask that I go?"

"That 'e did, sweet."

"I don't know, Mary. Bess is only just recovered an' me leavin' 'er don't seem fair."

"I ain't gonna argue, girl, but don't you think that now Bessie's feelin' better, you should start pullin' your weight in other ways to show your gratitude to George?"

Annie shrugged. "I s'pose you could be right, Mary. I do owe 'im, after all."

"That's the spirit, and Brownrigg will see that you're prepared to do your bit for the business."

"I 'ain't prepared to do anythin', if you knows what I mean," said Annie.

Mary smiled and said, "What do you take me for? I knows that."

"What time do we row out?" said Annie.

"Mid mornin'. I'll come and get you when it's time." Mary waved at Bessie and shut the door.

At around ten-thirty Annie received a knock on her door.

She turned to Bessie and said, "Now you be good an' wait for my return. I won't be long."

"Can't I wave you off?" said Bessie.

"I suppose so," said Annie. "Then it's straight back in the dry for you after. I don't want you catchin' your death again now, do I?"

She opened the door and stepped into the cold day, following her friend to the Camber's edge where a small boat waited. On board, Juxon and one of his lads manned the oars while Davy Turner had control of the rudder. Annie stepped into the boat and settled on a wooden seat next to Mary. Bessie stood on the dock and waved to her mother as the boat pushed off. *HMS Sirius* was anchored between the *Foudroyant* and the *Fortitude*. The little vessel that conveyed them slid effortlessly among the ships in the harbour. It rounded the *Foudroyant* and the calls and whistles of the sailors on board made Annie smile. A boat of women bound for one of the ships of the line after it had been at sea for many months was sure to get the pulses racing. The sailors even had an affectionate name for them, calling them *Solent nymphs.* Since Guppy had disappeared, the Captain of the *Foudroyant*, Edward Kendall, had confined this men to the ship. He was scared that the crew would seize further opportunities to desert and so instructed his officers that if the men couldn't attend the Point, then the Point would have to attend them instead. Mary had been on board the previous night and had made a good sum of money.

The *Sirius* came into view. It was a sleek and handsome ship, unlike the larger first and second rate ships of the line. Frigates were nimble and quick to heel and they had speed and agility.

The launch slowed and pulled alongside the vessel. A rope ladder was lowered and they climbed on board one by one. The supplies were hoisted on hooks attached to long ropes and eased to the decks.

****

Bessie sat at the table in their small home in Bath Square. She was busy dressing her peg dolly in simple rags that her mother had given her. Bess liked to pretend that her doll was a rich lady destined to meet an admiral or sea captain. She called her Grace. As she played, a dark shadow passed by the window but she was too engrossed in her imaginary world of balls, dances and handsome sea captains to notice.

Outside, Henry Knox and James Tuckey listened for sounds behind the door.

"'Ow you wanna play this then?" said Henry to his companion.

"Skinny said to tell 'er we know where 'er father is. Said to bring 'er to *The George Hotel*," said James.

"I s'pose we knock first and see if she comes to the door. Failin' that, we kick the thing down and grab 'er."

"We don't wanna be drawin' too much attention to ourselves though," said Tuckey. Let's just knock first an' see what 'appens." He handed the empty sack cloth that they intended to place over Bessie's head to Henry, and knocked on the door.

Light footsteps approached and the face of the little girl appeared at the window. She looked at them blankly and Henry waved at her and said, "'Ello little'un. What say you open the door?"

Bessie shook her head and carried on staring.

"C'mon' girl, we 'ave treats and sweets," said Henry, giving her his best kindly uncle smile.

James said under his breath, "She 'as the measure of you, my boy. She ain't 'avin none of it." He chuckled and turned to look about the Square. The place was quite deserted. Next door to Mary Abbott's place, an old lady threw scraps to the pigs that lived in the square. She had her back to them and, as far as James Tuckey could tell, she hadn't noticed them. He turned his attention back to the matter in hand.

"Please, I only wants to ask you somethin'. Is yer mother in?" said Henry.

Bessie shook her head.

"It's about your daddy," said James suddenly, shoving Henry out of the way. "Do want to know where he is?"

Bessie expression suddenly changed and a broad grin spread across her dirty little face. She nodded vigorously.

"Then open the door an' find out more, child," said Tuckey.

Bessie's face disappeared from the window and Tuckey winked at Henry.

"Gotta know where the weak spot is," he said.

The door opened and the thin frame of Bessie was all that stood between the men and her tiny house. Both men towered over her as she looked up with excitement in her eyes. James gently eased her into the house and Henry followed, checking left and right down the street to make sure that he wasn't spotted, then closed the door.

"Do you know where my daddy is?" asked Bessie.

"That we do, child. That we do." Henry knelt down to face her and ruffled her hair. "You're a pretty one, eh? Gonna grow up like your mother."

"Can you take me to him?" said Bessie unable to contain her excitement.

"All in good time, child," said James. "Where is your mother?"

"On an errand," said Bess pointing toward the harbour.

"So you's all alone?" said Henry.

Bessie nodded and said, "Tell me where my daddy is."

Henry stood, paused and looked down at her. "Thing is," he said, fishing for the right words, "we don't rightly know ourselves." He could see her expression drop. "No, no, little one – we may not know exactly, but we knows a man that does. We can take you to 'im, if you like?"

"It would be an adventure. Us three goin' on a journey to find your father," said James winking at her.

Bessie nodded and grabbed her shawl. She pulled it on and grabbed Henry Knox by the hand. He squeezed her fingers gently and walked with her to the front door. The sack cloth dangled from his coat pocket. They wouldn't be needing it today. Once in Bath Square, they looked left, then right. To the right of Bessie's house a narrow passage called Rowes Alley ran between the square and Broad Street. The alley joined Broad Street a few doors from the *Fortitude* public house. The two men moved slowly along the alley and, at the end, scanned the street. Broad

Street was teeming with people. Shop keepers chatted with locals as they loaded tables and baskets with their goods, groups of women staggered drunkenly along the cobbles using each other for support. Across the street Henry spotted George Brownrigg, outside his front door, perched on his top step like a king keeping court, chatting to a group of men. Henry pulled his cap down over his face and lifted his collar. James did the same and they ushered little Bessie down the road, keeping her in front so that her frame was blocked from view from behind. To further conceal themselves, the two men stayed close to the shop fronts and pubs that lined the right hand side of the road and soon they were out of sight of George and his men. The gate loomed in front of Henry and James, and mercifully it was un-manned. Stanley was nowhere to be seen as they stepped through, into the old town.

"How far is it?" said Bessie. "I don't like bein' away from my mother."

"Don't fret little 'un, we'll soon 'ave ya back safe and sound," said Henry.

The George Hotel came up on their right and they entered through the large arch that acted as a coach stop for travellers to alight in safety and comfort. They entered the hotel and made their way to a table in the far corner, away from prying eyes.

"What we doin' 'ere?" said Bessie.

"So many bloody questions," muttered James under his breath. He smiled at Bessie and said, "Would you like a drink while were waitin'?"

Bessie shook her head and said, "Waitin' for what?"

"You mean waitin' for who. We are waitin' for the man what knows the whereabouts of your daddy. He'll be here soon," said James Tuckey.

The door opened and a tall man entered followed by another. Henry waved at his brother and beckoned them both over. The tall man removed his stovepipe hat and took a bow in front of the table making Bessie smile.

"Are you the man that we's waitin' for?" she said.

"I am indeed, young lady. An' who might you be?"

"Bessie Crowther," she said.

"Well, Bessie Crowther, my name is Jim an' I'm very pleased to meet you." Skinny offered the girl his hand and she shook it.

"You're funny," she said, giggling.

Skinny pinched her gently on the chin and said, "Let's get you to your father."

Chapter Eleven

What if the moon gets cold?

By the time Annie returned from her trip on board the *Sirius* it was after four o'clock. She waved goodbye to Juxon and the others on the Camber and plodded back to Bath Square with Mary in tow. The sun had now sloped beneath the horizon, melting into the sea, and the point was shrouded in a gun-metal grey dimness. Above Annie, the sky was as clear and brilliant as she could remember, a carpet of stars shimmering like a million tiny flames, except for a thin wisp of cloud that wrapped around the moon like a scarf. Annie had a sudden ridiculous thought and it made her smile. *What if the moon gets cold? Who would begrudge it a winter scarf?*

Mary was watching Annie's face closely and said, "What amuses you, sweet?"

"Oh, nothin', I was just thinkin' to meself," she said, suddenly grabbing Mary's hand and pulling her towards the Square. "I got a large jug of ale in the 'ouse, what say you an' me 'ave a good drink to celebrate Bessie's recovery?"

"Annie Crowther, you speaks the same language as me. I accept your kind invite," said Mary mimicking her best upper class accent.

Both women fell about in fits of laughter. They rounded *The Coal Exchange* pub on the corner of Bath Square and made towards Annie's front door.

"Why is there no candle burnin'?" said Mary pointing towards the darkened window. "Bessie must be sittin' in the dark."

"Bessie, sittin' in the dark?" said Annie. "She's scared of the dark. Has been ever since Sam went away." Annie could feel her stomach start to knot. "This don't feel right."

"Look!" said Mary. "Your front door is open."

Annie bolted for the house and burst through the open door.

"Bessie? You in 'ere?" she called. "My girl, it's me." Silence greeted her. "Bessie?" she called again, poking her head through the upstairs hatch into the bedroom. It was empty and the bed hadn't been slept in. Annie was now very scared. She climbed down the last few rungs of the ladder and stared at Mary.

"She's gone," she said.

"Can't be," said Mary. "She's probably out playin'."

"I knows it, Mary. I can feel it here." Annie jabbed herself in the chest. "My 'eart is tellin' me that somethin's wrong and my little girl is in danger."

"'Ow can you be so sure?"

"I'm 'er bloody mother. I know what she's like, an' she would normally be 'ere. She don't much like bein' out alone."

"What should we do?" asked Mary.

"We need to knock on next door and every other door in this shit hole. That's what we are gonna do."

Annie pushed past her friend, back out into Bath Square and banged on the door to the right of her house. An elderly man answered, holding onto a stick for balance.

"Mr Leggatt, it's Annie from next door."

Solomon Leggatt leaned closer to Annie and stared at her with cloudy eyes.

"What can I do for you, Annie from next door?" he said.

"My Bessie, she's gone. 'Ave you seen anythin' suspicious this day. Anythin' outta the ordinary."

"Girl, this place is full to the brim of suspicious and outta the ordinary. Since when 'ave I had the faculties to spot such goins on." Leggatt pointed to his cataract filled eyes and smiled.

"Never mind," said Annie and knocked on the door next to Mr Leggatt. Mary crossed the square and started doing the same. Nobody had seen anything. Nobody had seen Bessie leave the house and nobody had seen where she went. By the time they'd exhausted the homes in the square it was after five in the evening. The two women sat on a low wall that overlooked the harbour and Annie started to sob. Mary placed her arm around her friend.

"We need to get 'elp," she said. She lifted Annie's chin and stared into her watery eyes.

"What sort of 'elp?" said Annie through rasping sobs.

"We need to see Mr Brownrigg. I bets 'e'll know what to do."

Annie nodded and the two women stood and crossed the square towards Broad Street.

****

Bessie Crowther sobbed in the darkness. The odour of dampness pervaded the gloom. She assumed she was in a small cellar. To her left she could see wooden shelves full of old tools and empty glass bottles of all shapes and sizes. In front of her was the only source of light; a small window, blackened by years of soot and street grime, looking up into the street above affording the dank space a slither of illumination. Bessie assumed that it must be a street that the little window looked onto because she could hear the sound of wheels turning, grinding on thick cobbles and hooves clip clopping along. She wanted to call out but the stained rag that was tied around her mouth prevented her from doing so. It was a dirty rag and Bessie could taste the foul flavours of sweat and salt and it turned her stomach.

She was angry with herself. She was angry that she'd listened to those two kindly men. They knew no more the whereabouts of her father than Bessie did herself, or for that matter, her mother. She allowed her tears to dribble along her pretty cheeks and fall to the dirty ground of the stinking cellar. It stank of urine and worse.

Bessie knew that her mother would be worried and she knew that she would soon start looking for her. That thought alone was enough to bring some solace to her petrified little frame. Footsteps on the wooden boards of the room above her distracted Bessie for a moment and she listened intently trying to hear for clues, for names and places. She heard the voice of one of her kidnappers and then the voice of the one called Jim. They were arguing and shouting and she was sure that she could make out the mention of her name and then she heard Mr Brownrigg's name. Bessie had to get nearer to the floorboards above her to listen to the conversation, so she tried to scan the room but the darkness was too thick for her to see. Her small hands were bound with rope but she was still able to feel in the gloom. Her fingers traced foreign objects like a blind man touching the surface of a face to feel familiarity. Eventually she touched on something wooden. *It's a box*, she thought and dragged it closer, taking great care not to let it scrape along the flagstone floor. She tested its sturdiness with her foot and it held her weight so she stood and pressed her ear closer to the ceiling.

"What makes you think 'e cares about this girl?" said Henry, his voice wafting to Bessie's ear with greater clarity.

"The Crowther woman is 'er mother. He will care. You'll see."

"An' what then? We cannot 'old 'er forever. We'll be found out."

"Henry, you must 'old your nerve. Have faith in Skinny Jim. When Brownrigg comes sniffin', I am gonna stick 'im proper this time. In 'is heart," said Skinny.

"And what of the girl and 'er mother?" said Henry.

"What of 'em? I couldn't care a jot for 'em."

"But they'll tell on us for sure. They'll know we're behind this."

"Then," said Skinny, lowering his voice, "we'll stick 'em too."

Henry Knox crossed the room and his footsteps knocked dust between the gaps of the boards. Bessie breathed in the dust and sneezed loudly. She wobbled on the box, lost her footing and, with an almighty crash, fell into some shelving containing rusty old tools. Above her, the conversation stopped abruptly, as the two men listened to the sounds below them. Bessie screamed and sobbed at the pain. She had twisted her ankle and couldn't stand. "Please find me, please," she said to the darkness that surrounded her, as a heavy footfall echoed on the wooden staircase that led to the cellar.

****

"What do you mean 'gone'?" said Brownrigg, slamming his tankard down on the bar.

"I returned from the boat at about four. Me an' Mary were makin' our way to the 'ouse and that's when we saw that she was gone." Annie wiped her eyes with the heel of her palm and stared at George. He handed her a handkerchief.

"An' yer sure that she ain't out playin' or visitin' on someone?"

"George, I'm certain of it. Bessie is scared of the dark, an' she don't 'ave many friends to speak of. Mary an' me 'ave knocked on every door in the square, an' no one's seen anythin'."

"But who'd wanna take her? You don't 'ave any enemies, do you?" George took back the handkerchief and stuffed it in his pocket.

"None that leaps to mind. Who would do such a thing?" Annie said. Mary threw her arm around her friend's shoulder and gave her a squeeze.

"Mr Brownrigg, sir," she said, "we was 'opin' that you would 'elp find 'er."

"We will find 'er, Mary. I give you my word on that." Brownrigg turned to William Juxon, who had been listening intently to the conversation. "William," he said, "fetch Davy and Pete, an' take these two ladies 'ome." He reached into his pocket and pulled out a shilling. "Take this," he said handing the coin to Mary. "Make sure that you get some food an' drink inside you. It's gonna be a long night."

"Thank you, Mr Brownrigg. I'll stay with the girl 'til first light," said Mary, taking the money. "C'mon, Annie, let's get you 'ome."

The two women followed Juxon out of the door into the December night. As the door swung shut, George suddenly felt helpless. He didn't know what to do or where to start. Annie was having a huge effect on him and on this night he felt it more than ever. At this precise moment he felt love, stronger than before, for her and for her little girl. It was as if someone had taken *his* daughter.

After ten minutes or so, William returned with Davey and Pete.

"Juxon says that the Crowther girl is taken. Is it true?" said Pete.

"Well she's missin', assumed taken, but whichever it is, this is bad business, gents. Very bad indeed," said Brownrigg handing the two men a drink. Both accepted readily and sipped their beer.

"What's to be done?" said Davey, wiping his chin free of dribbles. "Do we know who 'as done this?"

"We don't, Davey me boy, but we's gonna find out," said George with a steely stare.

Juxon nodded and said, "I knows it's rough on the Point, but this…" He fell silent as did the others in the room.

George broke the silence. "We need some 'elp on this. William, I want you an' the boys to ask in the pubs, brandy 'ouses an' grog shops. If there's anywhere where tongues are loose, it is these places."

"I reckon you're right there, George. If ever you wanna know what's goin' on, ask a landlord."

"Good. Make haste, gentlemen. There is no time to waste."

"What will you be doin', George?" said Davey.

"I am goin' to comfort Annie. She needs me more than ever, an' I am gonna see to it that she is cared for. Now get goin'."

The three men shuffled out of the pub and disappeared into the night. George took off his Derby hat and wiped his brow with the handkerchief that Annie had used to dry her tears. He caught her scent on that piece of cloth and held it to his nose, sniffing it in. As far as Annie was concerned, George knew what must be done. The sickness of her daughter and now this had convinced him that she couldn't cope without him. She was vulnerable and he was going to ask her to move in with him, to stay at his place permanently. He placed his hat back on his head, downed the last of his ale and left the pub, heading for Bath Square.

Chapter Twelve

"Is there news already?"

William, Pete and Davey went their separate ways and began the arduous task of scouring the forty-one drinking establishments that filled the point.

Pete went into the *Coal Exchange* to ask if there had been any talk of a kidnapping.

"Little girl you say? I've not heard of such, Pete, but rest assured that I will employ a keen ear and listen out," said the landlord, Robert Brock.

"That would be grand, Robert. Mr Brownrigg 'imself is very angry 'bout this an' wants nothin' more than the safe return of that girl."

Robert nodded and said, "Staying for a quick one?"

"Best not," said Pete as he made his way towards the door. "Got to keep a clear 'ead for the task in 'and."

Pete left the pub and moved along the front of the Point to *The Union Tavern*, on the Broad Street side of the dock. More men moved about in the shadows, recruited to search for the girl. Again, there was no knowledge of the disappearance, or any plot to kidnap the girl.

Juxon had decided to head through the gate and try his luck on the High Street. A hunch told him that this wasn't the work of someone within their midst. He didn't think anyone on the Point would have the guts or the stupidity to try something as bold as this. Stanley, the guardsman was keen to lend a hand in Brownrigg's pursuit of the girl, in a bid to win back favour with the King. He let William Juxon pass without a moment's hesitation.

"You tell Mr Brownrigg that Stanley was only too 'appy to 'elp. You make sure that he knows it?" called the guardsman after William. "And if old Stanley should clap eyes on the mite, he will be sure to deliver her safely."

"Will do," said Juxon heading along the road by the fortification walls, on his way to see an old friend, Valentine Romley. The landlord of *The George Hotel* was well known in the town and had become somewhat famous when the newspapers descended on the area after Admiral Nelson made a visit his hotel for his last meal on English soil. He quickened his pace and rounded the bend at the Square tower, and the smell of animal carcasses suddenly assaulted his nostrils. He was glad that he didn't live down wind of the meat store in the tower and pitied anyone who did. To his left, he passed Grand Parade, which led to the Garrison Church, and on the corner, the impressive building of *Godwin's Bank*. *The George Hotel* was a little way along the High Street on the left hand side.

William stood under the large arch of the hotel and marvelled at its size. To him it seemed fitting that Nelson would come here and feast before setting off to his ship. Juxon had been there that morning, pressed deep into the throng of people, eager to catch a glimpse of England's hero. William recalled vividly the moment that the landlord, Valentine Romley had spotted him in the crowd and beckoned his friend inside. William had found himself in the dining room that morning, staring at the naval hero in the flesh. Oh, how he wished that he had acted on his impulse to shake Nelson's hand. Little did he know that it would be the last time anyone in England would see the great man alive.

Juxon entered and saw Valentine at the bar. Valentine looked up and beckoned him over.

"How are you, Willyboy?" said Romley. He was the only person who called him Willyboy. "You lost or something? We don't see you this side of the gate much these days."

"Old friend," said Juxon, "I come on an urgent errand." Juxon gripped the hand of Valentine and shook it vigorously. "Still tellin' stories of Nelson and the day 'e visited?" he grinned.

"Bloody right. This hotel has been full ever since the great man sat in that chair and ate." Valentine pointed to the far corner of the room at the table and chair that Nelson had sat at. It was now a shrine, denoted by the thin length of rope that sectioned off the sacred furniture from the rest of the room. No-one was allowed to sit there, other than Valentine himself. "What is this errand that brings you to my place?" said Romley. "It is a rare and pleasant treat to see you."

"I come on serious business," said Juxon gravely.

"Spit it out then, man. What could be so grave that you stand before me with that expression?" said Valentine throwing down the cloth that he had been busily wiping the bar with.

"I'm after some information," said Juxon.

"What sort of information?"

"There's been a disappearance on the Point."

"What's so unusual about that," said Valentine. "That's normal for that place, surely?"

"Grown men, sailors, runaways and debtors, yes, but this is a little girl about nine years old with a mop of dark 'air. She vanished this morning and has not been seen since."

"Oh fuck!" said Valentine. "Little girl you say?"

Juxon nodded, leaned over the bar and stared at Valentine closely. "What is it? Do you know somethin'?"

"There was a little girl of that description in here around eleven o'clock. She was with two men and then two others joined them."

"Do you know these men?" said William.

"I should think so, they are notorious in these parts. The tall thin man is known as Jim McDowell. Folks call him 'Skinny'."

William covered his face with his hands and took a long breath. "What about the others?" he said.

"There are two brothers that run with this Jim. They are the Knox brothers, Henry and John. The other lad, I don't know him."

"Where did they go after they left here? Think really hard," said Juxon.

"I don't know," said Valentine, "I didn't see which way they went."

"Do you know where these men can be found?" William was starting to feel very nervous. "This Skinny Jim was the one what stabbed George Brownrigg. If he can do that, then there was no telling what danger she's in."

"Jim sometimes keeps with a woman called Daisy Chapples. She has a place just off Penny Street behind the hotel but a bit further down to the left. She and Jim were in here making merry just the day before."

"Thank you, Valentine. What you 'ave told me this day will hopefully save a young girl's life." William raced for the door and ran all the way back to *The Camber Inn*. He burst through the door and said, "Where's Brownrigg?"

The young boy manning the bar shook his head and said, "Mr Juxon, sir, he left just after you did, sir."

"To Annie's 'ouse?"

The boy nodded.

****

The front door banged and Annie stood to answer it.

"You sit down, sweet. I'll get it," said Mary easing her friend into the chair. "That's why I'm 'ere."

"What if it's Bessie? I must answer it," said Annie trying to stand. Mary shoved her down and went to the door.

The hulking frame of George Brownrigg filled the space where the door had been. He stepped inside and removed his hat.

Annie stood and stared at him with worried eyes.

"Is there news already?" she said.

"News? No, not yet but my boys are out there and they will find 'er."

"It's been hours now and still no word. What if she is lying in a back street with 'er neck snapped? What if she's…?" Annie buried her face in her hands and turned her back on Mary and George. He looked at Mary and ushered her from the room and, as she passed him, George slipped another shilling into her hand for her trouble. Mary paused and stared at him, mouthing the words, 'thank you'. She slipped out of the door in silence and crossed the square to her house. As she reached her front door she turned and glanced back at Annie's un-shuttered window.

"Annie, you must have faith," said George, placing a hand on her shoulder. He spun her round and she looked into his eyes.

"These are not the same eyes that I once looked upon," she said through her tears. "These eyes are softer and kinder. There is human in you, George."

"I am a much changed man," said Brownrigg, cupping Annie's chin in his hand. "I could care for Bessie like she is my own. I am weighted down by the empty space inside me at the thought of her bein' missin' and alone."

"What 'as become of 'er?" said Annie. "Why would anyone wanna take my little girl?" She buried her face into Brownrigg's chest and bawled her eyes out. George held her tightly and smoothed her hair. Her thin frame shook and juddered with every wailing cry and George did his best to soothe her. He felt her pain as if it were his. He wanted to banish that pain and never see its return. Across the street, Mary watched the pair for a moment and then went in and shut the door.

After a while, Annie's sobs started to subside and she fell silent, with her face still buried in his chest. Eventually, she looked up at him and said, "I feel safe in your arms. I feel that no 'arm can come while I am 'ere with you. Do you understand what I am sayin', George?"

He nodded and said, "After I was stabbed, I asked you if there was a future for us. I asked if you liked me?"

Annie nodded. "But what 'as this to do with the safe return of Bessie?"

"Just listen to me, please," said George.

Annie said, "You told me that you wanted to be a kinder man when you was with me and I said that it was a start."

"That's right. Well, I come today to offer you protection. I come to ask if you will live with me at the 'ouse. There's plenty of room and the girl will be given the best of everythin'."

"What will the people say? The Point is awful for gossip."

"I don't care about the people and what they say. I am the Point. What I say goes and if I say you come and live wiv me, then so be it. That is, if you accept of course."

"And you promise that you will get Bessie back. You promise that you will save 'er?"

"As I live and breathe, Annie Crowther, I will do all I can to get 'er back."

"If that is so, then once she is found, we will accept your kind offer and live at your 'ouse," said Annie.

George pulled Annie on to him and embraced her small frame.

"You 'ave made a weathered man feel very fresh, Annie Crowther."

Heavy footsteps approached the house. There was a knock at the door and then another in quick succession. Juxon shouted through the woodwork, "George, are you in there? I have news of the girl."

Brownrigg tore the door open, catching William by surprise.

"What news?" said George pulling him into the room.

"I know who took her and where she might be, George."

"Who told you this information?" said Annie taking a step closer to William, gripping his hand. "Is it a reliable man what tells you this?"

"Yes, Annie. He is one of my oldest friends. He tells it in good faith an' I 'ave no reason to doubt 'im."

"Who took her?" said George, lighting his pipe and blowing smoke in the room. "Who is cold enough, who is evil enough to snatch that little girl?"

"Skinny Jim took her," said William.

Chapter Thirteen

How simple my life would be if he hadn't gone

"That bastard. 'E's gonna get what's comin'," said George, slamming his fist on the wooden table. A half-filled cup of ale wobbled off the top and dropped to the floor.

Annie stooped to pick it up and said, "What will you do?"

"What will I do? Act out revenge is what," said George. "William, get the boys. It's time we paid Skinny Jim a visit."

Juxon nodded. "Give me ten minutes to round them up," he said and turned to leave.

"Wait!" said Annie. "Just wait an' think on it a bit." She gripped George's hand and said, "The last time you met with Skinny, 'e stuck you bad."

"Annie Crowther, your girl is bein' 'eld an' I means to free her, no matter what befalls me." Brownrigg looked deep into her eyes and Annie could see that he meant every word. At that moment, her heart softened towards him a little bit more.

"I'm comin'," she said squeezing his fingers.

"No," said George raising his hands in protest. "You must remain. What good the safe return of Bessie an' the death of her mother?"

"My daughter is in danger, George. You think I could sit an' do nothin'? You know nothin' about bein' a mother."

George gripped Annie by the hands again. "I know it's difficult for you, but you must understand that I may know nothin' of bein' a mother, but you no nothin' of danger. You live in a world of opposites to me. I understand this, cos it's what I do."

"But…"

"No buts," said George. "It means the world to me to see you an' Bessie safe. Everything I 'ave to live for is standin' in front of me." He grinned at Annie and she could see that look in his eyes once more. The look that told her that he wouldn't see any harm come to her.

"George," said William, "what do you wanna do?"

"Get the boys," said Brownrigg, turning to face him, "and tell 'em to meet 'ere and be armed fer a fight."

George turned to Annie as the sound of William's slapping footsteps echoed on the damp cobbles outside, growing ever fainter. "Look, you know I gotta do it. This place needs a strong leader an' they see that in me, Annie. They look to me for protection, specially from the likes of Jim McDowell and his gang. Without it, they'd perish."

"What if I lose her? What if I lose you, like…?" Her words trailed into silence.

"Say 'is name, girl."

"Sam. What if I lose you like I lost Sam?"

"Sam was a good man. He was honest and that's a quality you rarely find."

"He was the best of men," said Annie staring at the ground.

"And me? Where does that leave me?" Even though George knew that he couldn't compete with a memory, a ghost of a man, he still had to hear her say it.

"You an' me – we're at the start of somethin'. I sense the good in you an' that's what I cling to for 'ope."

"Do you see anythin' else in me?" Brownrigg shuffled awkwardly. "Please tell me that there's more to this than 'ope."

"There is, George, but you 'ave to give me time. Truth is, I'm confused and I know I should fear you, but that ain't so. This side that you now choose to share is unfamiliar, you have to see that."

George nodded.

"Look, right now all I can think about is getting my girl back. Succeed, and when you gets back, I will agree to come live with you, if it makes you 'appy," said Annie.

"But does it make you 'appy?" said George.

She nodded and there were tears in her eyes. "Come back safe. Don't make me care for you an' then go an' leave me. I couldn't take it 'appenin' twice."

George gripped her arms and pulled her closer. He slid a lock of her hair from her cheek and tucked it behind her ear. Annie stared up at him and her heart pounded. Was he actually going to kiss her? Was this the moment that she gave in to George Brownrigg, the most feared man in these parts, yet the most kind and considerate man towards her and her daughter? Her head swam with a mixture of fear and excitement. George leaned in closer and she closed her eyes. Their lips touched and it felt like a bolt of lightning surging through her. She could feel him press down on her and she wanted more. She wanted to stay in his embrace for that night and the next but Bessie's face hovered in her thoughts and she pushed him away.

"Not now. Not like this. Bessie needs me, an' that's all I can think about."

"I understand," said Brownrigg.

"George," said Juxon suddenly peering round the open front door, "I 'ave the boys."

Brownrigg didn't turn around but said, "I'll be there shortly. Shut the door and wait outside."

"But you said to meet 'ere?" said William.

"I know what I said. Just do it."

The door clicked shut and George said to Annie, "I got business to attend to." He pressed a key into her hand. "That's the key to my place. You make yourself comfortable till I return with Bessie." He ran a finger down her cheek and smiled at her. "You make me 'appy, girl, like all the 'appiness that I knew before was a pale imitation, a veil of joy that could be blown away on a light breeze. I've never known anythin' like this, certainly not since I lost my..." George shook his head and turned without giving Annie the chance to reply. He stepped through the door and disappeared into the night.

Annie ran to the doorway just in time to see him turn the corner by *The Coal Exchange* pub. Other than the sound of George's faint footsteps and the clanking of the rigging on the ships in the harbour, it was a calm

December night. Annie thought that it was an omen, maybe the calm before the storm. Something in the back of her mind nipped at her conscience like the pecking of a hen in the yard. Could she be the cause of George's death? If he didn't make it back then the Point would lose a leader, a self-styled king and she would be to blame. The people in this god forsaken place may not be the kindest or most deserving, but they needed the protection that a man like George offered. He was right, this place would collapse without his control, especially if Jim McDowell was to muscle in on the Point. She leaned out of the doorway and looked down Bath Square towards the Camber and the sea beyond. A heavy curtain of mist had descended, wiping the star littered sky from view, and it lingered on the water, shrouding the tall ships anchored in the harbour. Faint lights twinkled in that murk and her thoughts drifted from George to Sam. *How simple my life would be if he hadn't gone*, she thought. She straightened up and sniffed back the self-pity, accepting that he had left, and that this was now her life.

A stiffening breeze whistled down the square, almost in answer to her thoughts, banishing the comfort of Sam's memory and catching her breath. She stepped back inside the house and shut the door. *I have to gather mine and Bessie's things*, she thought.

Annie saw the faintest light emanating from the tiny window of Mary's house across the square. She could see her friend staring at her through the grim night. The door opened and the portly shape of Mary Abbott approached and knocked the door.

****

"What's the plan?" asked Davey. He and Pete were now joined by several others in the pub; Old Percy, a half-blind debt collector, Pete's brother, Trent and others that had been rounded up after hearing the news of the kidnapping. Each man came armed with a weapon of sorts. Most had opted for a hammer or the handle of a shovel.

George gripped his trusty club-stick and said, "We knows that she's bein' 'eld in an 'ouse on Penny Street. I suggest that we start there." He gripped the stem of his pipe in his teeth and puffed out smoke.

"What do we do when we find her?" said Pete.

"What do we do? We beat them to death is what we do. I will not have them come an' go as they please on my patch. It's time we taught these fuckers a lesson."

The Camber Inn erupted into a cacophony of noise as the assembled men howled for the blood of their enemies. George led them from the pub and down Broad Street towards the gate. Women and children stared out of the poorly lit windows that lined the street as the gang of men made their way towards the barrier and drawbridge. At the head of the line, George felt like a general marching his men off to war and the watching women who bore witness to their passage reminded him of the wives and lovers who waved their men to their deaths on the battlefield.

Stanley the guardsman saw the shadows approach in the murk and stood to attention.

"No one shall pass this night," he said officiously holding out his hand to halt whoever approached. He puffed out his chest and waited for a response.

"We will pass this night, Stanley or I'll make good my promise," came the booming voice of Brownrigg.

"Mr Brownrigg," stuttered Stanley as he saw the shape of George emerge from the darkness, along with his assembled gang. "Course you shall pass. I didn't know it was you, is all," he said, sliding his key in the lock and turning it.

"Drawbridge?" snapped George at the nervous man and he duly lowered the bridge so that they could cross the moat. Once on the other side Brownrigg said, "None other than us shall pass through this gate tonight." He held up his knife and the shiny blade bounced moonlight into Stanley's face.

Stanley said, "I understand."

The men headed towards the bend at the meat store in the square tower and turned onto the High Street. As they rounded the corner, James Tuckey was leaning against the wall of *The Dolphin Hotel* chatting to a woman. She giggled, placed a hand on his groin and he lent in for a kiss. Something caught his attention out of the corner of his eye, and he stared up the High Street towards the fortifications and the gate. Brownrigg and his boys approached.

"Shit!" said Tuckey bolting as fast as his legs would carry him.

"Get after 'im," shouted George and two of his boys gave chase as Tuckey hurtled along Grand Parade and past the Garrison Church. He made his way onto Penny Street with the sound of Davey Turner and Pete Bookbinder shouting behind him. The shadows of Penny Street with its narrow path and leaning buildings made it easier for James to vanish and, by the time his two pursuers entered the road, he was nowhere to be seen.

"Shit!" said Pete, "Looks like we lost 'im." Behind them, George and the rest of the gang panted to a stop.

"Well?" said George. "What we waitin' for? Get after 'im." He shoved Davey in the back with his club.

"We lost 'im, George," said Davey. "He knows these streets better than us, an' the darkness is 'is friend."

"Ally or not, get down that street an' flush the man out. 'E is all we 'ave to lead us to the girl and if we don't stop 'im, Skinny will be alerted to our presence and move Bessie."

Pete and Davey didn't wait to be told twice and entered Penny Street. George doubled back and went along the High Street in case their target decided to use a back entrance of one of the pubs. He sent the rest of his boys in pairs to comb the surrounding streets.

****

Inside number fifteen Penny Street, Daisy Chapples served her man, Jim McDowell a fresh drink. He barely glanced up as she handed him a full cup, choosing instead to scowl and snatch it from her. When he spilled a little he tutted and licked the residue that coated his fingers. Inside the room were the Knox brothers, both holding out their cups eagerly at the prospect of more alcohol.

"When are you going to move her?" she said with a scowl, cocking her thumb at the cellar door. "She makes me nervous."

"Wipe that sour face away. She will be gone in the next couple of nights, just like I said," said Skinny.

"It's wrong, I tell you. Takin' a little girl from her mother…" Daisy didn't finish her sentence. Skinny stood faster than she could blink and struck her forcefully, sending her and the fresh jug of ale sprawling across the room. She landed against the wall with a thump and her head struck the floor. A small gash appeared on her forehead. The Knox brothers were crestfallen that the ale had spilled and placed their empty cups back on the table.

"Keep yer tongue, woman, before I 'ave a mind to extract it with this knife." Skinny held up his blade. She watched in silence, through matted strands of hair as the light from the candle on the table danced on the shiny surface of the weapon.

"That's it," smiled Jim, "you be good an' silent. Now fetch to *The Dolphin* for some more beer."

"But I'm cut," said Daisy. She touched her fingers to the wound and winced. She showed the blood to Skinny.

"It's a bloody flesh wound. Now get." He snarled and Daisy clambered to her feet and rushed past the emaciated frame of her man, slamming the door behind her.

"Now that she's gone, listen up," said Skinny. "We move her tonight."

"But…" said Henry Knox. He was interrupted by the slapping of shoe leather on stone as James Tuckey skidded to a halt and banged on the door.

John peered out the window and said, "It's James an' 'e looks like 'e's in an 'urry. Shall I let 'im in?" He looked at Skinny and the thin man nodded. John opened the door and Tuckey almost fell into the small room.

"They're 'ere," he said through panting breaths and dripping in sweat.

"Slow down," said Skinny gripping him by the arm. "Who's 'they'?"

Tuckey took three deep lugs of air and said, "Brownrigg and his boys are in the High Street. There's about ten of 'em."

"There's too many, or we'd stay an' fight," said Skinny.

"What next then?" said Henry looking alarmed. John Knox looked no better and fidgeted on the balls of his feet like he was standing on hot coals.

"Get below and fetch her here. Now!"

Henry and John did as they were told and a few minutes later they appeared at the door with Bessie, looking bedraggled and hobbling badly from her fall.

"We're takin' a trip, little 'un. Gonna take you somewhere safe," said Skinny.

Bessie sobbed and shook with fear, staring up at the men with wide eyes. Skinny pulled the rag from her mouth and Bessie said, "I want my mother."

"All in good time. We need to keep you for a while longer," said Skinny. "And then you shall 'ave your mother." He signalled to the two men and John stuffed a rag back in her mouth. Henry slid a sack cloth over her head and Bessie squealed as the world went dark.

"Where we takin' her?" said John.

"Back to the Hard. I knows a man with a hay loft what owes me a favour. We're too close to the Point 'ere." Skinny stood and crossed the room.

"What about Daisy and that jug of ale?" Henry licked his lips at the thought of another drink.

"She cannot know where this girl is. You 'eard 'er. She don't see the worth in such acts. If she knows, she'll tell." Skinny pointed to the door and said, "Now get gone before she comes back."

Bessie was dragged from the room and out into the cold night to be loaded onto the back of a waiting coal cart before it trundled away.

Daisy wandered from *The Dolphin* with a fresh jug of beer and made her way up Penny Street. Her head was hurting and she dabbed away the drying blood with her free hand. Skinny was violent, she knew that, but this… she didn't want to be part of snatching an innocent child. Daisy knew that Skinny was bad but she loved and feared him in equal measure. She supposed that with her influence she could somehow change the man but evidence of that strategy was thin on the ground.

She was sure that he loved her in his own way but sometimes, and tonight was one such time, she doubted that he would ever change. She didn't notice the shape of the tall man approaching as she passed the first row of small houses and the two collided. The jug of ale, not for the first time that night, was spilled from her hand and splashed across the cobbles.

"Mind where you're going," she said.

"I am sorry. I didn't mean to spill your beer," said George. He removed his hat and said. "I was in a bit of an 'urry you see."

"Hurry for what that you're too busy to look where you're goin'?" said Daisy bending to pick up the jug.

"I'm looking for a little girl," said George, "'bout nine or so, with dark hair."

Daisy grabbed the jug from the floor and said, "An' what makes you think I can 'elp you find a girl?"

"No, I don't mean I wants a girl, I'm lookin' for a specific girl what's been taken this night."

"About nine or so?" said Daisy.

"Can you think of any such that matches my description? Or maybe you 'ave 'eard somethin' yourself?" said George.

Daisy could feel her mouth dry and she doubted that the words would come out, so she shrugged and turned to leave but felt a heavy hand grip her arm. George gripped her so hard that she squealed and said, "Let go. You're hurting me."

George whirled her around to face him and stared at her. "You don't answer me," he said. "Am I to take it that your silence masks guilt, or knowledge, or is it that you just don't care?"

"What little girl? I ain't seen no little girl. Let me go."

"There is somethin' there," he said. "Your eyes betray you." George pressed his frame against the woman and said, "I 'ave a good nose, see," and he tapped the end of it, "for sniffin' out lies. If I didn't know better I'd say you was 'idin' somethin'."

"You got it wrong. You're scarin' me is all. I don't know about no girl."

"Where did you get that cut?"

"Fell. Why?"

"An' you live in this street?" said George pointing into the gloom. She nodded.

"You ever 'eard of Jim McDowell?"

Daisy narrowed her eyes and said, "Who ain't?"

"Take me to your 'ouse," said George, shoving her down the street. As they made their way along the path, a drunk man staggered out of the darkness and almost bumped into them.

He belched and said, "My, my, if it ain't sweet Daisy Chapples. 'Ow's Skinny?"

George shoved the man away and said, "So, you know nothing about the girl, eh? Move!" He gave her a rough shove in the back and followed her up Penny Street. Eventually they arrived at number fifteen.

"This is my 'ouse," she said at the top of her voice.

"Why do you shout?" said Brownrigg. "You seek to warn," he said, shoving her away and kicking the door open. It flew off its hinges and he entered the house. On the table were the three tankards. Brownrigg picked one of them up and sniffed. "So you weren't on your own this evenin'? I'd guess that the beer is for Skinny an' 'is lads, which means that the girl must be 'ere abouts." He tore around the small house like a man possessed, upturning chairs and tables and opening doors. Eventually he paused at the door to the cellar and said, "Where does this lead to?"

"To the cellar," said Daisy. George ripped open the door and descended the wooden stairs. At the bottom he scanned the darkened room and something caught his eye, discarded on the floor among the dirt. He bent and picked up the peg doll and wiped dust from its rag dress. He studied it carefully and suddenly rage gripped him. George knew that he was a violent man but this night, this place drove him to want to commit acts so bad that he wanted this lying woman dead. He pounded up the stairs and burst into the room. Daisy stared at him open mouthed. She could see the menace in his expression. She turned to run but George was too quick and he pulled her back. She stumbled backwards, striking her head on the corner of the table and the cups spilled to the floor. George towered over her and gripped her by the hair.

"What's this?" he said showing her the peg doll.

"I didn't want no part of this," said Daisy. "I told 'im that it was wrong, takin' a little girl from 'er mother. I said it was wrong and he gave me this." She pointed to the smeared wound on her head. "He smacked me to the floor because I spoke me mind. Honest!"

"You lie!" screamed George shoving the doll into her face. "Look at it. It belongs to an innocent little girl. She was in your cellar but is now gone. Where is she?"

"She was here," said Daisy. "I went to the pub for some drink and now she's gone. I know not where."

"But she was 'ere." he snarled.

"I'm sorry. I was scared of what might become of me. I fear him as I fear you."

"So you should fear me, for I am no less or more forgiving than Skinny," said George "Well, if 'e 'as our girl, then I see no other end to this. I should kill you and 'ave done with it." George pulled out the blade from his pocket and squeezed the handle tightly in his sweating hand. "It is time to even the score," he said.

Suddenly William Juxon appeared at the doorway.

"Don't do it, George. You can see she is afraid of Skinny. What good is murder?"

George turned around and glared at William.

"She lies," he said. "She knows where the girl is."

"Look at her, for pity's sake. Look at her face, her bruises and cuts," said Juxon. "They are fist sized and I'll wager that the fist what did this belongs to Skinny. This girl is scared of 'im an' that's what drove 'er to lie. Am I right, girl?"

Daisy nodded as tears splashed her cheeks. George stared at Daisy then back to William, taking a moment to ponder. Eventually he released his grip, pushing her away.

"That's it, George, just let her be," said Juxon. "This ain't her fight, nor yours. I know you're upset, but killin' this woman will not find Bessie."

"I'm sorry," he muttered. "I wasn't thinkin' clearly." He held out his hand and she recoiled in fear.

Footsteps clattered down the street in the direction of the house. He heard voices and recognised them as Davey and Pete. Juxon poked his head out of the door and whistled. Davey and Pete approached.

"William? What you doin' in there?" said Davey.

Juxon placed a finger on his lips to silence them both and pointed into the house. Pete peered in and saw Daisy cowering in the corner with George holding the blade.

"Is she 'urt?" he said.

George shook his head. "She's just scared. I threatened to stab 'er if she didn't talk.

"Christ!" said Pete, "What the hell 'ave you done to 'er? She's in a bad way."

"She's Skinny's girl," said George. "It's 'is hand what done this."

"Was Skinny's girl," said Davey. "She ain't gonna be no more. Not after this night."

"Bessie was 'ere and now Skinny has moved her and we're too late." George kicked over a wooden chair and Daisy squeezed her frame further into the sanctity of the shadows.

"No quarrel there, boss. What's Skinny gonna do when he finds out you threatened 'is woman?" said Davey.

"Who cares," said George. "Reckon 'e's had a go at 'er often enough before tonight."

"He'll kill the little-un for sure after this," said Pete.

"He won't," said George. "Bessie is too valuable to be killed. Skinny thinks that while 'e keeps 'er away from 'er mother, there is some kind of 'old over me. 'E thinks that, cos I'm sweet on Annie, I'll do whatever it takes to get the girl back, includin' givin' up my business interests."

"And will you?" said Pete.

"I will do almost anythin' to get that girl back an' see Annie smile again. You knows that, but givin' up my business ain't one of 'em."

Chapter Fourteen

Such harsh words…

"What do you mean she's gone?" Annie balled her fists and glared at George.

"Gone. Not there. Moved," he said staring at her helplessly. "I knows 'ow you must feel," he said softly.

"*Feel!* What do you know about the love between a mother and her child? You poor man, you 'ave no children, you 'ave no one that relies on you for everythin' in their world. My child is out there alone, reachin' for me, an' I ain't there to comfort 'er," Annie jabbed her finger towards the window to emphasise the point. "An' you didn't do what you said."

"Such harsh words," said George. "Did I not open up to you an' tell of my loss? Yet you forget so easily." He paced the room and said "I tried, Annie. Really I did, but they were warned of our arrival."

"This Skinny is far more dangerous than we had given thought to. To outsmart us like that… I fear for her now more than ever."

"I will get 'er back, Annie. It's just that it might take longer than I imagined."

"Longer? Well that's alright then," she said throwing her arms in the air. "Let's all go to the pub an' get drunk while we wait."

"Annie…" said George raising his hand in protest.

"No!" she snapped. "Don't you dare try and make this sound like it'll all be fine. Time is the one thing we don't have, George. Surely you see that?" And then she added, "Or maybe you don't?" Annie could see George start to tremble with anger. "I suppose you wants to strike me now for speakin' to you in such a way?" she said.

"Don't speak like that," he said. "Not such cruel words. This isn't you and I know you don't mean it." She could see his forehead pulse as the rage grew. Annie watched him bite back the anger.

"You don't know how cruel I can be," she said. "You made a promise that you'd get her back. You said that she'd be safe in your care this night and we were to move in here with you." Annie looked at George and he said nothing. "You said that, didn't you?" she continued.

He nodded and looked at the floor.

"Maybe you didn't want to find Bessie at all? Maybe this was your way of getting' me 'ere, into your 'ouse and bed?"

"Such vile words, Annie Crowther," said George balling his fists as tightly as possible. "I will not hear such things."

Annie said, "So, you are outwitted by Skinny Jim and the only thing that you can think of doing is striking me. Is that it?" She thrust her body forward aggressively and continued, "Want to 'it me, eh? Well get it done an' that'll be that. I ain't scared of you no more."

George exploded and smashed his huge fist into the plaster on the wall above Annie's head and dust fell onto her dark locks as she ducked out of the way. She screamed and bolted for the door, ripping it open and rushing down the stairs, heading for the front door.

"Annie, come back. I'm sorry," called George rushing after her, racing down the front steps onto Broad Street… but she was gone.

Annie moved at pace, heading for the gate. The sound of George calling her name echoed from the filthy bricks of the houses and pubs that lined the street. She pushed it to the back of her mind, focusing on her footsteps as they slammed on the wet floor. The sound of her heart beat pulsed in her ears. She didn't know what she was doing or where she was going exactly, but she was intent on being somewhere – anywhere that might place her closer to her little darling. Annie knew that George would follow and try to drag her back.

What does he know of love, of commitment? He's many things, but a parent he is not. Annie knew that only she could feel the despair. Not even Mary could truly understand. She scolded herself again and rued the moment she'd agreed to go on board the *Sirius* and leave her child. No, she told herself, not leave her child, she had abandoned her.

Ahead of her, the gate loomed large. Stanley's silhouette grew more defined as she got closer.

"Who's that?" he called out with a thin voice that matched his stature.

"Annie Crowther," she said flatly. "Let me pass." The guardsman was now within touching distance and Annie doubted that he could stop her passage even if he wanted to.

"The gate is locked, miss." He jangled the keys in the air to underline the fact.

"Unlock it then."

"Can't be done. This gate is to remain locked after seven in accordance with the city rules."

"If you don't let me pass this night, I will see to it that George Brownrigg gets to hear of this and he will exact a vicious punishment."

Stanley blinked and then gulped.

"George Brownrigg you say? What are you to him?"

"Come now, you must 'ave seen me an' George together. I am 'is girl, Annie Crowther, and me an' George are sweet on each other. Now are you lettin' me pass, or not?"

Annie heard George calling her at the top of his voice.

"That's the man 'imself," said Annie trying to hurry Stanley to a decision.

Nervous fingers inserted the key into the lock and turned. He pulled the gate open a crack and, before Stanley had a chance, Annie squeezed through and disappeared towards the square tower and beyond.

She rushed along the High Street, past the tower and along by *The George Hotel*. Annie was sure that, whilst her knowledge of her whereabouts remained a mystery, her maternal bond would lead her to her daughter soon enough. If *he* couldn't find her then she would. Why had she put so much faith in George in the first place? Wasn't *he* just a man after all? Wasn't he weak, selfish, knowing nothing of the bond between a mother and her child. She scolded herself for even thinking that he could keep her safe. Suddenly a terrible thought fell into her head. *What a fool*, she told herself, the dangers that Bessie now faced were revenge for her relationship with George. How could she not have seen it? Before her dalliance with George, her life had been dull and uneventful. Instead of protecting her, her friendship had done the opposite and placed them both directly in harm's way. That's why Skinny had taken her child. If Brownrigg hadn't been in her life, both she and Bessie would be safe and warm in their little house.

Annie passed shops and inns and their inviting lights offered relief to the darkness of the street. Jolly folk sampled the wares inside, with little care for Annie and her troubles. She picked up her speed and crossed the street that led to the Garrison Church and the green. Annie came upon a large group of men at the entrance to *The George Hotel* and decided against entering. They loitered in the doorway, huddled together in quiet conversation. The light above the coach arch illuminated their faces and she thought that she recognised one of the men in the group. She was sure that she'd seen him the night that Skinny and his gang had fought on the Point; the night that George had been stabbed and almost died. That thought, the fleeting moment that passed through her mind suddenly made her realise that George dying had been a real possibility and that, when he'd been stricken in his bed, her thoughts for him were much changed. She'd felt sorrow and sadness at his possible demise, and it was these thoughts that she clung to now. Annie was as confused emotionally as she had ever been. As much as she blamed him for the situation that she and her daughter were in, he was just a man after all and could not be blamed for nature's choice. He didn't know any better and it was a misplaced love that drove his actions. Could she blame him for that? Was it his fault that he was who he was? She had accepted it for the most part, so she, not he, had placed her daughter in danger. She realised in the moment of conflict between the love of her daughter and her fears, that she needed George. *Oh, the irony of it all*, she thought. Without the help of the man at the centre of her turmoil, she might not see her child again. She knew, despite the anger that she still felt, that her feelings still existed for him, now that she'd calmed down a bit. What was she doing here? It was as if she was coming around from a spell. The spell of motherhood that compelled her actions without thought for her own safety. One of the men in the gang looked at her suddenly and her stomach knotted. She did know him and he was a bad man. He said something under his breath and the others in the gang turned to stare. The man she recognised from that violent night on the Point smiled at her and Annie knew that she was in real danger. The group moved along the wall of the arch and drew closer to her.

"ANNIE!" George's voice, laced with thick desperation, chased along the street, skipping from brick to building, to air, amplifying in the winter stillness.

The group of men looked in the direction of the sound and someone said, "Brownrigg."

George approached and saw Annie standing at the entrance to the hotel as still as a statue. She was frozen to the spot, petrified, gripped by fear. George called her name again and this time she looked at him and said, "Run, George!"

The gang pushed past her, knocking her out of the way, and made their way towards George with their weapons drawn. George winked at Annie and pulled out his blade. The group of five men lined up in the street and goaded him with insults. The one that Annie recognised, John Knox, was brandishing a heavy wooden post. Next to him, a knife flashed in the gloom of the night. Annie was sure that George would be murdered this night. She rushed past the line of thugs and drew to a halt in front of him.

"No, George, not here like this," she said desperately. "You'll die." Annie placed her hand on his chest and tried to push him back but he was too strong. He brushed past her without a word, his focus firmly on the ensuing fight.

George squared up to his full height and said, "Let's get this done, boys. Which of you is first?" He tossed his knife from his left hand to his right and back again. John Knox stepped forward and spat on the ground between them.

"I'm gonna enjoy this, Brownrigg." He spat again and circled in front of George, who hunched down and circled in turn matching Knox's movements. Neither took their eyes off each other.

"Stealin' a young-un from the breast of its mother, that's wrong," said George.

Annie called out, "It don't 'ave to be like this. Stop and think about what you do."

Knox snorted in derision, "Shut 'er up for fuck's sake, Brownrigg, or is it that she controls you? I can't think about anythin' else 'sept murderin' you." He jabbed his weapon at George. George smiled back but made no return comment.

"She's bitten you bad, that woman. You suffer with love and that makes you weak, Brownrigg," said Knox, licking his fingers.

"Seems you got me pegged all wrong, don't you?" said Brownrigg with a smile that scared the hell out of the men behind Knox. "Now, is we gonna talk till the lark rises, or is we gonna get down to it and see who's got the courage to see it to the end."

George spotted what he wanted to see in Knox's face. A flash of fear crossed his eyes, fleeting, instantaneous but noticeable all the same. At that moment, he knew that he had the measure of his enemy. He knew that the fight was won.

"You scared?" he said.

Knox shook his head and the same fear crossed his eyes.

George lunged at Knox and he sidestepped swiftly as the blade whizzed past his face. As John straightened up, he brought the wooden post round with all his might and it struck George on the small of his back, making him collapse in a heap on the floor.

Knox skipped from left foot to right and said, "You wanna eat a few less pies. Looks like you're getting' slow in your old age, Brownrigg."

That brought a loud cheer from the others and gave John Knox the encouragement to step in closer to Brownrigg, just as he tried to clamber to his feet. Knox raised the weapon over his head and brought it down at speed. The wood splintered on the cobbles as George rolled out of harm's way and climbed to his feet.

"Who you callin' slow?" said George with a grin.

Once more, John attacked, but this time it was Brownrigg who stepped to the side as the wooden pole shot past him. George's fist landed on the side of Knox's face with a thump and he toppled forward, but not enough to fall. John righted himself and turned to face his enemy. Blood ran from his ear. He spat on the floor again and this time his saliva was stained red. Knox took a step closer to George and lunged again, and Annie screamed out. The wooden post swished through the air, missing Brownrigg by inches as it brushed the side of his face. Knox was off balance and George waited until his enemy was facing the opposite direction, and at that moment he raised the knife and stuck it deep into the side of John Knox. There was a gasp from the other men as they realised what had happened. Knox fell to his knees, clutching his side as his coat stained a deep crimson. He raised his hands in front of his face and saw the blood drip to the floor.

"You've stuck me," he said.

George stepped in closer, shifting his body so that he was directly behind the kneeling man. He gripped Knox by the chin and tilted his head towards the sky.

"Let every man here know that George Brownrigg is comin'. Tell Jim that I'm comin' for 'im." He smiled at them all and they looked back at him in sheer terror. Not one came to the aid of their friend just as George had predicted before the fight. He glared at them and, without looking down, he pushed the stricken man to the hard cobbles. Knox groaned as his face landed on the damp ground and a small track of blood clouded the tiny rivers that collected between each stone.

The other men scattered, running for their dear lives, but Brownrigg was having none of it and chased after them. Annie watched as he caught up with one of the stragglers and pulled him to the ground. George dragged him back down the street kicking and screaming.

"Let me go," screamed Tuckey. "I ain't got no beef with you."

"You are gonna tell me where the little girl is," said George through gritted teeth.

"What little girl?" said Tuckey.

Annie leaned over him and said, "I don't know you and I don't care to, but you know where my scared little girl is and I want you to tell me."

"Tell you? I would rather see my days end than speak against Jim," said Tuckey.

George pulled out his stained knife and showed it to the captured man. "Firstly, I can arrange to make that wish a reality. Secondly, you admit that Jim 'as the child then?"

Tuckey nodded. "She's bein' 'eld in a barn on Devils Acre," spluttered the terrified man.

"Where on Devils Acre?" said George twisting the man's head, applying more pressure.

"I don't know," screamed Tuckey.

"Tell me, or you die," said George.

"It's in Hay Street. Number five."

Brownrigg threw Tuckey to the floor, placed his boot on the side of his face and squashed it into the dirt. George turned to Annie and said, "Go and get Pete and Davey. Fetch Juxon too. This is gonna get sorted tonight. Tell 'em to come armed."

"I will do no such thing. I am not leavin' this place without my Bessie."

"We need 'elp. You an' me ain't strong enough to do this alone," said George.

"What are you gonna do with 'im?" said Annie staring at the dark shape on the ground. "Are you gonna kill 'im?"

"Not yet," said George. "'E's gonna lead us to Bessie. Right now he lives. Now hurry."

Annie smiled at him and dashed back towards the gate.

Chapter Fifteen

She's still alive…

"Where is George?" said Mary.

"With the others, fetchin' Bessie back to me," said Annie. She wrung her hands together and shook with fear.

"And you didn't want to go?" said Mary.

"Didn't want to go? Mary, I would give my life for that girl, but George insisted I stay 'ere."

"Let's both go then," said Mary gripping her friend's hands. "Why listen to that man? 'E ain't Bessie's father, and 'e certainly ain't your husband."

"Do you think we should?" said Annie.

"Think? I *know*, sweet. Get your shawl."

"But George said…"

"Fuck George and fuck what 'e said." Mary pulled Annie towards the door. "You knows your mind and that little girl needs 'er mother."

They stepped out of the door and braced themselves against the chill night. Mary gripped her friend by the shoulders and squeezed as both women exchanged a look of determination and they started on their journey.

****

Hay Street was narrow. So narrow that it was more like a back alley than a street of dwellings that housed many families, crammed in like kindling wood. The houses stretched towards a high wall at the far corner which blocked the road to through traffic. These houses were the poorest excuse for dwellings that the old city knew. So ramshackle and in a poor state of repair were they that George doubted that he would keep the most common of animals in such conditions as these downtrodden people were forced to endure. As Brownrigg and his boys made their way along this darkened corner of Devils Acre, he could feel the knot of tension in his stomach. He gripped James Tuckey by the collar and shoved him along the path. Tuckey scuffed and scraped along the uneven road and muttered insults under his breath. A swift whack across the back of his head soon sorted him out. An old lady peered out the door of a nearby house. She didn't say a word and simply stared. George tipped his hat at her and moved on, hoping that she wasn't some kind of look out.

"Which one?" he whispered into Tuckey's ear. "Just point."

James did as he was told and pointed to the house at the end. It had tiny shuttered windows, and a mean slither of light spilled into the night. Attached to the main building was a two storey barn, a little like a hay loft. There were two large doors that led into the barn and above the doors was another hatch, which George imagined was where hay and goods were lowered onto waiting carts. A rickety washing line crisscrossed the path, hung with threadbare clothes that looked like they were fit for the bin. Tuckey ducked under the lines and George followed suit. Pete Bookbinder, Davey Turner and William Juxon followed from the rear. A cat darted across the road and disappeared under a broken fence, making Juxon jump.

"You looks like you're a bit scared," joked Pete.

"Ain't you then? I'm shittin' meself," said William.

Suddenly George gripped James's collar and pulled him to a stop. They were about ten feet from the house at the end of the row. Brownrigg squeezed past Tuckey and said, "Make a sound – just one – and I'll finish you like your friend." He pressed the tip of the knife against Tuckey's throat and stared at the captured man carefully. When he was satisfied that James was going to comply, he lowered the blade and turned to face the house. Tuckey seized his chance to escape and bolted down the street towards the corner, narrowly avoiding the grasping fingers of Pete and Davey. He moved so quickly that he took the others by surprise and skipped out of their reach, turning the corner and disappearing into the night.

"We don't need 'im anyway," said George to the others.

"What if 'e warns 'em?" said Pete.

"Best we act now before 'e gets that chance," said Brownrigg.

He stood outside the house and listened through the door. He could hear voices, raised and angry. He recognised that one of the voices belonged to Skinny Jim.

"Is it them?" said Pete in George's ear.

He nodded and said, "On the count of three... one, two, three." Brownrigg kicked the door with his heavy boot and wood splinters flew into the gloomy room. Skinny was seated in a wooden chair by a large fire. Beside him sat Henry Knox and an unknown man that George presumed to be the owner of the house. Brownrigg and the others burst in and Skinny stood, along with Knox. The unknown man dashed through an adjoining door that led into the barn. Pete, Brownrigg, Davey and Juxon eyed up their enemies.

"George Brownrigg, I declare," said Skinny with a wry smile playing across his lips. "To what do we owe the pleasure?"

"We've come for the girl," said George.

"The girl?" said Skinny sweeping his arm around the room. "What girl?"

"You wanna play games, do you?" said George. "Funny that... I think your brother wanted to play games with me earlier." He looked at Henry. "That's why I stuck 'im good." George waved the knife at Henry, who took a step towards Brownrigg.

Skinny placed a restraining arm on Henry's chest and said, "He'll rip you apart."

"It ends tonight, Jim," said George. "Give me the girl and I'll let you live."

There was the sound of a struggle in the barn and then he heard a girl scream. *Bessie*, he thought as his heart leapt. *She's still alive.*

Skinny panicked and tipped the table over that stood between him and the intruders, spilling the lit candles onto the floor. One of the candles rolled along the flagstones and came to rest next to a bundle of dirty rags that were piled in a heap in the corner. The candle licked the rags and they burst into flames. Skinny pulled out his knife and lunged at George, but Brownrigg was ready for him. He knocked Skinny aside with ease and sent him flying into the flaming pile in the corner. The flames were now catching the wooden walls of the house, stretching as high as the narrow windows. Acrid smoke billowed up the wall and rolled like a sea of black heat, caressing the length of the ceiling, filling the room with noxious fumes. Jim McDowell clambered to his feet and wiped his stinging eyes with the heel of his palm. He patted out his smouldering coat and glared at George.

"The girl is in the barn if you want 'er," he said. "Take 'er an' fuck off outta 'ere."

"Pete," said George without taking his eyes of Skinny, "go an' fetch the girl." He pointed towards the door that led into the hay loft and barn. Pete dashed into the darkness immediately.

On the other side of the room, Henry Knox was no match for Davey and William Juxon. He was pinned to floor and was soaking up repeated blows from his attackers as they put the boot in. Knox was curled into a tiny ball with his hands over his head for protection. Juxon placed a hand on Davey's arm and said, "If we keep this up, we'll kill the man." He thrust his face close to Davey's and said, "You ain't no killer, and neither am I."

Davey lowered his gaze and stepped away from the squirming body of Knox. Seizing his chance, the stricken man started to crawl towards the front door without so much as a glance back to see if Skinny was all right.

"He's gettin' away," shouted Davey.

"Rats leavin' a sinkin' ship," said William. "Let 'im be; 'e's been beaten enough."

As the door opened and Knox fell out into the street the cold air sucked into the room and the flames leapt taller than ever. The paint on the rough surface of the walls blistered and popped in the heat and the hairs on George's arms started to curl.

Pete emerged with Bessie, who looked weak and shaken, but otherwise unharmed. The sight of her pale face enraged George so much that he lashed out at Skinny and pushed him to the floor. Skinny landed badly, clattering his head against the dirty stone floor. Above him, in the corner, the flames roared with such an intensity that the men in the room struggled to be heard.

Juxon screamed at Brownrigg, "We have to get outta this place."

George beckoned Pete and Davey out of the room and the two, accompanied by Bessie, scampered past the inferno and stepped into the street, gasping for clean air. George said, "And you, William."

"What about you?" William said.

"I'm comin', don't you worry," said George. "Find somethin' to barricade that door." He pointed to the front door and shoved William from the room.

Brownrigg turned towards Skinny who was leaning up on his elbows, still dazed from the fall.

"This is where we part company," said George. "I ain't gonna kill you. Way I see it, you're already dead if you stays 'ere."

George pulled a rag from his pocket and covered his nose and mouth to prevent the ruinous fumes from lining his lungs. He knew that it was time to leave, but before he did, he gave Skinny one last look and said, "If I see you again, I'll kill you." He spat at him and left the room. As the door banged shut, Juxon stepped up and bound the handle with a length of rope that he'd found in the street.

"That'll keep 'im," said William. He looked at George with cinder features and said, "Let's get the little-un back to 'er mother afore this place goes up completely and takes us with it."

Flames licked the air outside the house as the fire searched for the nearest source of oxygen. The barn and hay loft were alight and the smoke that billowed from the inferno rose above the ramshackle street and snaked towards the heavens. A large crowd had gathered in the street, watching with horror on their faces. George pushed through the gathering and led his ash covered rabble down the road, heading back to the point. Suddenly, an explosion from inside the house shot wood and debris into the air and Skinny's screams could be heard over the monstrous growl of the conflagration. George stopped and listened and was sure that he heard his name being called in anger. George turned to watch the menfolk rush to and fro with half-filled buckets of water in a vain attempt to quell the flames and stop the fire spreading to their homes.

"Are you alright?" said George crouching down in front of Bessie. He took her chin and brushed her face gently. She nodded.

"Did they 'urt you, girl?"

She shook her head silently.

George smiled at her and ruffled her hair with his black stained hand. "Let's get you back to your mother."

****

Annie and Mary passed by the gate and the bewildered Guardsman, Stanley. As they disappeared into the darkness, he muttered to himself, "Damn place is goin' bleedin' mad." He scratched his head under his ill-fitting hat and closed the gate.

Chapter Sixteen

Nowhere on God's earth could you see the things that go on in full view on this tiny scrap of land…

The lonely shapes of the two women pressed further into the old city. They made their way up the High Street, past the same inns and shops that Annie had passed by earlier, only this time the lights were extinguished as their occupants slept soundly. In the distance a plume of smoke rose like a dark column, billowing above the city rooftops.

"You should 'ave seen 'im, Mary. He was so mad that I thought 'e would slice the man's throat in the street and let 'im bleed out."

"Well from what you say, it sounds like this man got stuck bad anyway," said Mary looking at her friend. "Why do you care so much? This man that George killed was one of 'em what took Bessie."

"Because I seen that side of 'im that scares the 'ell out of me. Don't you understand? I seen the real Brownrigg and that makes me fear more than the violence of this Jim an' 'is lot. Brownrigg was like a wild animal."

"But you seen the nice too. It was 'im what 'elped Bessie to health again, let's not forget that." Mary halted her friend in the middle of the road and turned to face her. "Never forget what that man 'as done for you. 'E may not be the best of men but 'e is 'ere and that's all that matters."

"You asked why I care so much, now I ask the same of you," said Annie.

"Cos you are the dearest thing to me in this world, you an' Bessie. I wanna see you 'appy an' I think the man you speak of is your best 'ope." She pulled her friend close and hugged her so tightly that Annie groaned. Mary sniffled and tears splashed Annie's shoulder, and she released her grip.

"What is it, Mary?" said Annie. "Why are you so upset?"

"It's all my fault."

"How so?" said Annie. "You didn't take Bessie."

"No, but had I not asked for your 'elp on that day, Bessie might still be 'ere."

"Oh, Mary, don't be thinkin' like that. You couldn't 'ave known what would 'appen."

Her friend wiped her tears and nose with the sleeve of her tattered dress and said, "Because you and that girl are like family. I couldn't stand to see any 'arm befall you."

"Hey, hey," said Annie, "it's goin' to be fine. You'll see."

Mary nodded and stared at the ground.

After a little pause Annie said, "I suppose you are right, you know… about George. Perhaps I can change him for the good. I said to 'im recently that I see a softer side in him that wasn't present before and do you know what he said?"

"No," said Mary, "What did 'e say?"

"'E said that bein' with me made 'im want to be a kinder person."

"Well, there you 'ave it. The man speaks from the 'eart. An' you doubt 'im? If that ain't proof enough that Brownrigg wants to turn a new leaf, I don't know what is," said Mary with a broad grin.

"But what if the tree the leaf is attached to is rotten to the core," said Annie.

Before Mary could answer, distant voices floated towards them. Mary pulled Annie into the shadow of a shop doorway and said, "Listen."

Annie heard the voices and thought for a fleeting moment that she recognised some of them. Shapes appeared in the gloom, faded and insubstantial at first but, as the sound of their voices carried clearer on the winter breeze, so too their shapes took defined form.

"I think that's George," said Annie. "Look, the size of the man is not in question. It must be George."

Annie stepped out from the protective canopy of shadow and called to the approaching group. Mary tugged her back into the doorway.

"What the fuck are you doin'?" she said through gritted teeth.

"I knows it's them," said Annie.

"You'll get us both murdered if you're not careful." Mary jabbed her finger into her friends face and said, "Just wait a bit an' we'll see who we're dealin' with."

The shadows drew nearer and so the names of those present became obvious. After Annie had called to them, William Juxon called back and turned to the large shape and said, "That sounded like Annie."

"I know," came the gruff unmistakeable reply of Brownrigg.

"See?" said Annie to Mary, pulling free of her friend's grip once more.

"George, is that you?" she called into the murk.

"Mother?" called back the sweet voice of her Bessie.

Annie clapped her hands to her mouth and fell to her knees. Tears streamed as she listened to the sound of small feet slapping on the cobbles as Bessie raced towards her and then, the face of her daughter appeared in the night. Annie held open her arms and Bessie leapt at her mother, the two embracing and kissing as though their lives depended on it. Mary stepped from the shadow and placed her calloused hand on the soft dark hair of Bessie, and smiled at them both. Under her breath she whispered, "Well done, George. Well done indeed."

"I always knew I'd find you... that George would find you," said Annie, drawing her face away from her daughter's and cupping her cheeks in her hands. "I never doubted it." She squeezed her child again as hard as she dared and said, "Are you 'urt? Did they do anythin' to you?"

Bessie thought for a moment and then shook her head. George and the others drew to a halt and stood, staring in silence at the moving scene of the mother-daughter reunion. George smiled at her and Annie could see that his face was covered in soot. Suddenly she had a pang of concern for him. What if he was hurt? She let go of Bessie and climbed to her feet, stepping towards him.

"Are you 'urt?" she said gripping his hand.

He shook his head.

"No, Annie Crowther, but the other fella is none too clever."

"You mean Skinny?"

George tapped the side of his nose and said, "Ask no questions." He stared at his blood stained knuckles and blackened clothes, realising that he must have looked a sight and tried to wipe them on his coat. When the blood wouldn't come off, he thrust his hands into his pocket. "Bet I looks a real sight?" he said.

"You do, George, you do at that. Was there a fire or somethin'? What 'appened?"

"There was. It was an accident but it was Skinny what lit the place up."

"Is 'e dead?" said Annie.

George nodded. "I s'pose he is at that." He caught Bessie staring straight at him said, "Not 'ere. Let's get the girl into the warm and get some food down 'er first."

There it is again, that caring side to the man, thought Annie. She was starting to understand that, with George, there were two personalities that vied for space in his head. What did it matter that he was a product of this place, his place, and that he had to be tough to survive? Wasn't it how he treated those close to him, those that he cared about, that stood him apart from the violent man that would rip out the throats of his enemies to protect those same people? Her heart softened a little more towards him. Hadn't he just delivered on his promise and brought Bessie back to her?

Once back at the house on Broad Street, Bessie was washed and readied for bed. She wouldn't sleep on her own, so Annie promised her she could sleep in her bed.

"When will you be up?" said Bessie as she lowered her slight frame into the oversized bed.

"In a bit. Just gotta speak to Mr Brownrigg first," said Annie kissing her hand and planting it on her daughter's forehead.

"Don't be long," said Bessie closing her eyes.

"I won't be," said Annie, placing a lit candle on a small table and turning to leave the room. George stood in the doorway wiping his face and hands with a damp cloth, watching the scene in silence. Bessie opened her eyes and turned to look at him, flashing him a big smile. She lifted her arm out from under the covers and reached for George.

"She wants you to say goodnight," said Annie, welling up.

George stepped into the room and knelt by the bed.

"Goodnight, Bessie," he said softly.

She sat up, threw her arms around his neck and planted a kiss on his cheek. Annie burst into tears and rubbed at her eyes with the heel of her palm. Her Bessie had taken to this man, especially after all he went through to rescue her.

"Thank you," said Bessie in George's ear.

"You're welcome," he said, giving the little girl a gentle squeeze. "Now get some sleep." He let her go and she flopped back on the bed. Once more she was tucked in and Annie and George crept from the room. The candle burned on the table to ward away the demons that came with the darkness.

In the parlour downstairs, George poured a large glass of brandy. He placed it on the table in front of Annie and then poured one for himself. He sat in the chair nearest the un-made fire and sipped the golden liquid, swallowing and letting out a large sigh. He still had dried soot under his fingernails. He stared at the wall and let his thoughts wander.

"Penny for 'em?" said Annie. She sat on the cushioned chair and curled her long legs to her side, gripping the glass of brandy in both hands.

"Penny? You're a bit on the generous side. They 'ain't worth that much," chuckled George.

"What is it that troubles you?" said Annie.

George Brownrigg pursed his lips and thought about what he wanted to say. What he should or could say. After a moment he stared at Annie and said, "Fifteen men."

"What do you mean 'fifteen men'?" said Annie, "I don't understand."

"What do you see before you, Annie?"

"I used to see a man full of hate and violence, but now I see a man that does what 'e can to survive in a dangerous place. I see a man that 'ides 'is true feelings behind a varnish of violence and hate. I see a man that 'as been shaped by circumstance."

"Don't be makin' excuses for me now," said George. "I ain't someone given to passing off my actions as the work of some sorry life what 'aunts me to do these bad things."

"That's not what I meant," said Annie. "We all do bad things when we are cornered or threatened. Survival ain't the same as livin'."

"And you say I 'ides my true feelings? What true feelings?" said George swigging back the last of his glass before standing to pour another. He raised the bottle to offer Annie a top up but she shook her head.

"You're a scary man. You're a killer of men."

"Do I scare you?" said George stopping in mid-pour.

"You did... but not no more. That fear is for others." Annie sat forward in her chair and rested her arms on her knees. "What you do will never sit comfortably with me. But I ain't perfect neither. I didn't treat Bessie right and she caught the fever. I should 'ave been at 'ome lookin' out for her when she got took. These are the things that I 'ave to live with."

"This night, more than any other, I am sick to the centre of my soul with death," said George. "The stench of it stains my nose. I smell it now. Can you?"

Annie shook her head.

"When I should be smellin' sweetness like your scent, all I smell is decay."

"What you tryin' to say?" said Annie, "That you're bad to the marrow? That you ain't for changin'?" She downed the rest of her drink and continued, "Cos what I see is a man what tries to be good, a man what *does* good. That is admirable and somethin' that should be nurtured." Annie smiled at George. "I can be the one to nurture it."

"Or I'll be the one to turn your 'eart black. Maybe you bein' around me ain't the best idea. Maybe I'm the reason why we nearly lost that girl. Do you not see that danger clings to me like the limpets that cling to the hulls of those ships out there in the harbour?"

"That I do. I 'ave thought similar tonight. I blamed you, George, for all of this. But I realised that I couldn't get Bessie back without you. And, once she was back, I knew that you and your world were now our world." She smiled at him. "Don't you see we 'ave little choice. We've been thrown together by fate. My Sam goin' wasn't no one's fault, especially not yours but 'ere we are, so to speak, an' we make the best of it, right?"

"Can you really accept me for what I am?" said George. "Remember what you said about Sam, that he was the best of men. Do you think I could replace 'im an' be an 'usband to you, an' a father to Bessie?"

"After this night, Bessie already thinks that the sun shines outta you. Did you not feel that when she called to you at bedtime?"

George nodded and said, "Why do you make me want to be a better person? What is this magic that you spin on me?"

"You 'ave shown me the kindest side of any man since Sam vanished. Tonight I realised that I've gotta do the best for my girl. As a mother I owe her the best life that there can be."

"But..." George was cut short.

"Let me finish, George," she said firmly. "I am tryin' to tell you that, while there are still doubts and yes, I 'ave fears of what a life with you might bring, I also know that you will treat me proper and Bessie like a daughter. I can't ask for more than that."

Annie stood and crossed the room. She knelt at George's feet and took his bruised hand. She kissed it and caressed it. "I am fallin' for you," she said, holding his palm to her beating chest. "Feel my 'eart. Feel its rhythm. Your touch excites it, makes it beat faster. That is what you do to me."

George leaned forward and kissed her cheek. It was the gentlest of kisses and Annie sighed. He stood and took her hand, leading her from the room. As they climbed the stairs, pausing outside the door to the room where Bessie slept, they both listened to the silence beyond.

Annie peeked inside and saw the face of her daughter sleeping calmly, illuminated by the soft glow of the single candle that burnt on the table.

She smiled and said, "I can't be long. I promised Bessie that I would stay with her tonight."

"Always the doting mother," said George leading her to the room opposite and closing the door. "Are you ready for this?" said George. "I don't wanna force you."

Annie waved away his concern. "I want to," she said, "I needs to feel the warmth of a man tonight."

George watched as Annie allowed her dress to slide from her frame and climbed into his bed. George undressed and followed suit, pulling her onto him, kissing her neck gently and tickling her body with his warm, brandy scented breath.

"You are beautiful," he whispered.

Suddenly, Annie stopped and looked at him closely.

"What troubles you?" said George.

"Fifteen men? You said fifteen men earlier. What did you mean?"

"Not now, Annie. Not as we're about to…" George didn't finish his sentence and looked away.

"What did you mean by fifteen men, George?" said Annie firmly. "If I am to let you take me, you owe me that at least."

"Fifteen men I have killed. That's how many have met their end at my hand."

Chapter Seventeen

"Starboard a little. Steady so."

*The hull of HMS Raisonnable exploded inwards as the cannonball struck, filling
the gun deck with deadly wooden rain. Seasoned, bare chested gunners scrambled for
cover, diving behind whatever they could to hide from the razor sharp splinters that
scattered in all directions. The thirty-two pound cannons shook in their breechings
as the metal rings that fed the hemp ropes that bound them in place, took the strain.
One gun snapped free of its breeching and rolled backwards as the ship tilted. Its bright
red carriage bumped over the bodies of the stricken and rammed into the other side of
the hull. Two tons of weight pounded a hole in the ship and the cannon toppled over
the edge, falling into the sea. As it fell, the rope that held it in position dragged the deck
like a startled snake, snaring a youngster, a twelve year old mid-shipman called Bile,
and he was dragged to his death, toppling into the brine and swirl, sinking without
a trace. Some tried to grab him, as he slid past his shipmates screaming to be saved
but his small fingers gained no purchase. Sam watched in horror, the melee around
him somehow paused, as the boy pleaded for help before sliding over the edge and
plunging to his death. The seabed bound cannon was too great an anchor to fight and
the poor lad sank beneath the waves. Garnet Papkin, gunner's mate, took a slither of
wood full in the face, splitting his skin and bursting an eyeball. He gripped his face
and howled like a wounded dog as blood washed the black soot of the gunpowder from
his bare chest. In the confusion of battle, no one came to his succour and he stumbled
from man to man screaming that he'd been hit. He flopped to the boards, collapsing
in a heap and eventually, the lieutenant and a kindly marine stepped in and pulled
him out of harm's way with the marine given instructions to carry him below deck
to the surgeon. The call came down to 'Stand to your guns' and every able gun captain
stood by their thirty-two pounders. Around them bodies were strewn like drift wood,*

among the debris. Between each cannon, a bucket filled with sand held the 'matches', twisted cotton wicks soaked in lye and smouldering. Boys, some like Bile, as young as twelve, commonly known as Scape Gallowses because many chose a life in the Navy instead of the gallows as punishment for minor crimes, lay dead among the older men.

The ship lurched violently, rolling on the upward wave. The almighty sound of cracking wood, high above the poop deck alerted the men that the mizzenmast had given way under the French fire. The men knew of the French technique of rolling on the upward wave and firing to take out the ships' masts, thus rendering it powerless. It crashed down on top of the officers and men, many diving into the rough seas for safety. Screams echoed on the smoke-filled air as mates and comrades fell or were crushed to death. Through the hatch someone shouted that the enemy ship was in an upward roll and instantly there was a loud whoosh followed by an even larger cracking sound than before. The main top mast teetered above the deck. Someone shouted, "Stand clear." Men scattered as it fell, striking the ship in the centre and spearing through the two gun decks, coming to rest in the orlop deck, or over-lap deck. Once more, the spent bodies of the crew littered the ship. A small barrel of gunpowder rolled towards a fire that raged in the starboard gun ports. Drake, a gunner's mate, leapt towards it, desperate to snatch it back to safety. He knew that it would be fatal if it reached the flames, but he landed inches from it and the barrel came to rest in the blaze, exploding into smithereens. Drake went in several directions, landing among the thirty-two pounders. Sam Crowther saw his leg rip, as a section of the hull struck him, slicing through his limb and landing on the far side of the deck. He keeled over and looked down to see, through blurred, fainting sight, that his leg was hanging at a strange angle, and he knew that it could not be saved. The cheers of the French, their nostrils filled with the burning flesh of the British, was the last thing that Sam could remember before passing out.

Sam awoke in a fierce sweat, to the sound of snoring from the hammock above him. Robert Brock muttered something and slipped back into a deep sleep. The unlit lantern above Sam swayed with the rocking of the ship, creaking a little as it did. He was having the same nightmare that he'd had every night since the battle of Cape Finnistere – the battle that claimed his leg. He lay dripping with fever, his stump wrapped in cloth and a snoring shipmate to keep him from reliving the nightmare. The only thing that Sam could be thankful for was the straw pillow, mattress and the fresh linen that he'd been given to aid his recuperation. His makeshift bed was placed where the mess table would have been on the lower gun deck, between the cannons. The deck was completely dark, save for the thin slivers of moonlight that penetrated the hull and the hawkes-holes, plugged with oakum to stop the sea from finding its way in whilst the ship was moving. Every now and then, Sam could hear the gentle splash of sea water as it always found a gap, no matter how well sealed they were. Down in the lower deck, it smelt of damp. Wet wood, that never saw the warmth of sunlight, soaked up sea water like a sponge and filled the air with its odour. The only other source of light was the *Pursers Glims,* sitting in their tin sconces. Brock rattled out another loud snore and Sam thought for a moment that he would hit him with the makeshift crutch that he had fashioned from a table leg, blown off in the battle. He thought better of it and lay back on his arm, listening to the sounds of footsteps from the deck above. He had time to think, to ponder his situation. He had time to reminisce about all that the Navy had taken from him. Since that damp March night in 1803, he had thought of nothing else other than his Annie and Bessie. The fateful day that he'd refused to listen to his wife was etched on his brain as though the captain himself had ordered him twenty lashes of regret. She had warned him that the press gangs were about, but in his jealous rage, his anger at the unwanted attentions of George Brownrigg, he'd ignored his wife and gone to the pub. *How could I have been so stupid? Annie was loyal to me and wouldn't have entertained a scoundrel like Brownrigg,* he told himself

Sam could hear voices on the main deck and then he heard the master's command to the quartermaster, "Starboard a little. Steady so."

He closed his eyes and Annie's face filled his thoughts as he smiled to himself, imagining his return to Portsmouth. He tried to picture his little girl and how she'd have grown. What a splendid sight she must be. His hand reached to scratch an itch on his sawn limb, before realising that it was a mere phantom. The surgeon had said that this would happen, just before he made Sam swig down a generous glug of rum and bite down on a leather strap. The surgeon soaked his saw in a bucket of warm water and gripped Sam's leg above the knee. A soaking sponge, the same sponge that had cleaned the scars of twenty or so of his shipmates, was dabbed onto the wound. The blood, thinned with the water, stained the sail that he lay upon, used as a makeshift sheet, hastily thrown over the mid-shipmans' chests that were dragged together to make a crude operating table. Sam shuddered as he remembered the surgeon's face, his grim expression and determined eyes. The sweat on his brow was as if he had sawn the mightiest oak in the forest with his bare hands, and yet all his saw knew was the flesh and bone of men. It didn't take long for the thin strip of skin and the last muscles and ligaments to relinquish their hold on what was left of his limb. The surgeon threw the lower half of Sam's leg in the bucket and a small cabin boy scooped it up to throw over the side. Just as the boy was about to leave the room, the surgeon shouted, "Check the wind, boy. Your face will not thank you otherwise."

The surgeon attempted to seal the open arteries with the flame of a candle and Sam could still smell the sickly odour of smouldering flesh, and it turned his stomach. Rum was splashed on the wound to sterilise it and then the surgeon began the crude process of stitching him up. Now he lay in his sick bed and he tried to sit, to see what had become of him. He had little time for tears or sorrow, of lamenting the loss of his limb. He wouldn't get much sympathy here. The king was a cruel paymaster and his shilling was scant reward for a leg no longer attached.

After the battle, Captain Hotham declared that the dead be given over to the sea, as befits a man who plies his trade upon it. The injured were treated as best the surgeon could, and patched up. Those who could fight on, those with minor injuries, such as loss of an eye or fingers and toes were put back to light duties until such time that they would need to be called upon. Those with injuries so great that they were no longer of use to the war effort were sent on the next ship to port and retired with the thanks of the Admiralty. This was how Samuel Crowther found himself on the razee, *HMS Anson*, a forty-four gun frigate bound for Portsmouth harbour for repairs. She had sustained a lot of damage in battle and was in need of urgent attention. *HMS Raisonnable*, flying the flag of Sir Robert Calder's fleet, sailed to Cork after the battle with Admiral Villeneuve's ships and docked. From there, Samuel was transferred for the homeward bound *Anson*.

The journey from Cork was in its second day and Samuel was starting to get used to his amputation. He still suffered the night sweats, but fever on board was rife. Men living cheek to jowl wasn't a healthy place to be when able-bodied, let alone with injury. Sam prayed to the heavens that he would reach dry land alive and that, after all his hardship, he would get to hold Annie once more and to kiss his child. He allowed himself a small smile as he planned their life together. She would be over the moon that he had returned, he was sure of it. Whilst his time away was a black void of silence for her, he knew Annie would understand that he had been taken against his will, coshed over the head and the king's shilling slipped into his pocket. What could he do to remedy the situation? If the Impress gang want you, they will get you. Sam suspected that the landlord of *The Camber Inn* was in on the snatch. He remembered thinking that it was odd that Juxon had disappeared right before he was attacked. Juxon never left his place behind the bar, especially if there were paying customers still. *Come to that*, he thought, *why did he offer me a free drink just as I was about to leave?*

Brock grunted above him and said something about a large breasted woman, then jittered, trying to sit. Samuel watched him from the corner of his eye, the lantern swinging back and forth, squeaking loudly. Hammocks, like chrysalis, hung from the beams above the guns and tables that the men shared at meal times. Robert Brock scratched his chest and yawned, eventually closing his eyes and falling back to sleep.

Suddenly it dawned on Sam that if Juxon was in on the act, aiding the gang, then how did they know he was there? Was it blind luck or had William got word to the gang somehow? Sam remembered the little girl coming in and then leaving with a jar of ale. Had she been the look out, running to alert them that there was an able bodied man waiting to serve Nelson? *Able bodied indeed*, he thought, *what a fucking joke*. There was nothing able bodied about him now.

Another panicked thought rushed through his troubled mind. What if Annie didn't want him? What if she shunned him, or worse still, had found someone else? He had disappeared without a sound, and had offered no word since. He banished those doubts instantly. His and Annie's love was as firm as the rock that their home was built upon. His love wasn't like the sea, shifting and insubstantial. *She'll still be there, don't you worry*, he told himself. Sam yawned and felt drowsiness descend upon him. He didn't have the energy that he once did, not now he was so poorly, but every day he grew a little stronger. He closed his eyes and tried to concentrate on his breathing, doing his best to block out the thunderous rattling of Brock's snoring. They were expected to be in port in a couple of days. Those days he would spend building himself up as much as he could to show his girl that he was the same old Samuel Crowther – minus a limb, but the same nonetheless. He slipped into the calmest sleep that he'd had since the surgery. He dreamed of home, of warm beds and smiles. He dreamed that he and Annie were in each other's arms and that the memory of battle, of death and danger were long since passed; a distant, fleeting moment, a drop in the ocean of their time together. It was comforting to know that tomorrow would be a new world, a new hope, in which he and Annie were going to be stronger than they'd ever been before.

HMS Anson slipped gracefully through the night, cutting the ocean like a hot knife through butter. Above her, the star-filled sky sent millions of lights to aid her way. Like spyholes to heaven, their glow seemed to hint at the irrelevance of man's endeavours. Fixated with dominance of the planet and its resources, man filled his time with accumulation and greed, but this world and the one beyond were never meant to be owned like a trinket, and so it was that man would pass, but the world remained.

Chapter Eighteen

His body told an intriguing story that Annie would one day ask about…

The sound of the Point coming to life echoed in the darkened bedroom. Clattering, chattering and commerce interrupted the silence of the morning. Annie yawned and stretched, waking George. She shivered with the cold, its icy nails scratching her body. He rubbed his tired eyes and looked at her.

"Morning," he said. "Did you sleep well?"

Annie shook her head. "Bessie woke me just past midnight. She was screamin' the place down."

"Again?" said George. "It's been three days since she came 'ome. I thought she was getting' better."

"She is, but she needs time," said Annie. "That first night she was terrified but gradually she is getting' better. She slept on 'er own most of the night. I only attended to 'er when she started screamin'"

"I didn't hear nothin'," said George, sitting up and letting the blanket fall from his chest. Even though George had explained the scars on his torso, Annie noticed other marks that looked suspiciously like lead shot wounds. His body told an intriguing story that Annie would one day ask about. She was sure that each mark, like the lines in a book, would hold some adventure or tale of daring do. "'Ow could you not 'ear. She was bellowin' like the devil came to take her."

"Is she alright now that morning 'as come?" said George, rubbing his finger along Annie's bare shoulder. He lent in and kissed her soft skin.

"George, don't be getting' ideas. There's lots to be done today. The *Anson* is due in port and she will be needin' supplies. Think about the business for a minute, will you?" She shrugged her shoulder away and slipped from the bed, her lithe frame silhouetted in the shafts of half-light that sneaked in through the curtains. George watched her closely as she slipped on her under garments and then her dress.

"My," said George smiling, "such a business brain on you, and a beauty to behold, Annie Crowther. I am the richest man alive."

Annie looked at him and said, "You are the richest man on the Point, that's for sure. I think you're goin' soft on me since we got together. Put *your* business head on and get those supplies sorted. They won't sort themselves."

"I don't want you goin' onto that ship," said George. "You shouldn't be consorting with those men."

"I wouldn't go on that ship if you paid me," she said heading towards the door. "If you remember, it was while I was on the last ship that Bessie got took." She left the room.

George flopped back onto the bed and listened to the sounds of the street below. The pubs would be busy today and for the coming week, what with the *Anson* in port as well as the *Foudroyant*. Ships meant sailors and that meant money. He resolved to pay a visit to the landlords on the Point to collect what was owed to him for his protection and law. Annie and Bessie sat at the kitchen table drinking a cup of milk. Bessie was stuffing her mouth with bread and looked up at George when he came into the room. She smiled and he winked at her.

"Mornin', cheery." he said. "'Ow's you this fine mornin'"

"I'm fine thank you, Mr Brownrigg." she said through mouthfuls of food.

"Good to 'ear it. No more nightmares then?" he said glancing at Annie. She gave him a look that said, *don't rake up last night*, and he frowned.

Bessie shook her head. He could see that she was troubled in her face and he regretted asking her the question. He ruffled her hair. "What say you spend the day with me today? We's goin' to see some men about payments. Wanna come?"

Bessie nodded vigorously and smiled at him.

"That's settled then. Get your coat, it's a cold one today," said George, sensing that he had done the right thing. It felt good knowing that this little girl was happy and content. He wanted to help her settle and he wanted her to love him like he was a father to her.

Bessie scampered from the room and came back with her boots and coat on. "Can we see William today?" she asked. She meant William Juxon, who since she was rescued, had become her favourite person, other than her mother and George.

"Course we can," said George. "Let's go." They left the house and Annie watched them from the doorway as they crossed the street heading towards the *Camber Inn*.

At one o'clock, *HMS Anson* was anchored in the harbour, sandwiched between the *Foudroyant* and the guard ship *HMS Fortitude*. She was a sorry sight, with the mizzenmast split in two and the main mast missing at the top. The rigging was patched up for the journey and the hull bore the scars of war. Her majesty was tarnished somewhat, like a rusted crown on the head of the king. The mighty *Anson* would take months and hundreds of pounds to put right.

Annie watched her friend Mary Abbott waving to the small boat that carried the *Solent nymphs* as it set sail, sitting low in the sea due to the weight of her cargo. She was laden with supplies for the men, and the women were included. She waved at Mary, who waved back. Annie smiled and wrapped her shawl around her shoulders. It was the thirtieth of December and the Point was looking forward to seeing in the New Year with full coffers and lots of satisfied customers. As she watched the boat slink out of sight, Annie suddenly had an odd sensation. She shivered and convinced herself that it was the winter chill. Somehow, she was gripped by the feeling that something was going to happen today. She didn't know what, but she couldn't shake the feeling. To her it was the same feeling that she'd got when she'd seen the front door of her house ajar and swathed in darkness, that day when Bessie had been taken. Her daughter was fine, she was with George, and so it couldn't be that which was bothering her. She mentally shrugged and climbed the steps to the house. She was now engrossed with her chores for the day. She wanted to make sure that the house was clean for when George returned and then she would cook him something nice for dinner.

****

Sam rested awkwardly on his makeshift crutch, wobbling precariously on the top deck of the *Anson*. He stared across the sea to the grand buildings that stood majestically along the shoreline of the dockyard. He scanned along the harbour, past the Hard and Portsea, until his eyes rested on the ramshackle buildings that lined the Point and the Camber. His heart leapt at the thought that he was soon to set foot on soil that he had convinced himself he would never see again. Sam rubbed the top of his shaven head and wondered if he looked smart enough for his grand reunion. He needed a shave, that was for sure, but when Annie had last seen him he'd had a full head of hair. Now he looked like one of those convicts bound for the new world. Sam cursed the captain for ordering that all seamen aboard his ship be shaved to stop lice. Rumours were rife that the men on some of the other ships in the harbour were confined to their vessels but there were no such problems on this ship. Sam was grateful that his navy days were at an end. It seemed the king didn't want cripples in his service.

A small launch drew near and he heard voices. The boat pulled alongside and Sam could see that it was full of supplies and women. Robert Brock sauntered over.

"Looks like the entertainment's arrived," he said, clapping a hand on Sam's shoulder. "You staying to sample the produce?"

"Nah. Got me a meeting with fate."

"Ah, the fabled Annie that I've heard so much about. You'll be lucky if she's still waiting for you."

"Thanks for the encouragement," said Sam. "I'm on the first pinnace. What about you?"

"First one for me too. I'll be in the pub if you fancy drowning your sorrows."

"I'll see you in the pub. I'll also introduce you to my wife if you like?"

Robert chuckled. "I hope you do. I've heard so much about this woman I feel like I practically know her." Brock wandered away to help the crew of the arriving boat, much to the squealing delight of the women on board. Once the boat was unloaded it returned to the Point.

At two o'clock the first pinnace was loaded and slid towards the Point. Spirits on the boat were running high with sea-weary sailors swapping stories of what they were going to get up to now that they were free of the shackles of command. The Point was legendary to the men of His Majesty's Navy. On board were Sam and his friend Robert Brock. The first launch held twenty men as well as four marines and two lieutenants. Sam watched as the Point drew into focus and he could make out the *Coal Exchange* pub next to the *Union Tavern*. He saw Broad Street as it stretched towards the Gate. It was all exactly as he remembered. Excitedly he gripped Robert's arm and said, "My house is just round that bend." Sam pointed towards Bath Square and the row of houses that joined his. His place was just out of view from the direction that the pinnace approached, but Sam could picture it as if he were seeing it with his own eyes. His heart was beating in his chest so hard that he was starting to feel giddy. "I have waited for this moment and many times thought it would not come," he said quietly, as much to himself as to Robert.

"It is a good day and it will get better for you, my friend," said Brock patting Sam's good leg.

"I hope you are right. I hope and pray it is so," said Sam staring into the distance, his mind a whirl of emotions.

"Still," said Brock, "she will be mighty surprised to see you."

"I imagine so."

"The art of surprise might have a wondrous effect on *you-know-what*," said Robert with a wink.

"Is that all you can think about?" said Sam punching his friend on the arm.

"You sound surprised," said Brock, "especially given the time we've been away."

The boat pulled alongside the dock wall of the outer Camber. A rope was thrown up and tied to secure the pinnace. There was a wooden ladder that was fixed to the side of the dock and the passengers of the launch climbed them one by one. Sam was last to exit the boat due to his incapacity. Robert stood at the top of the dock and gripped his friend's hand, hauling him up on his one good leg.

"I should let you go," joked Brock. "It would amuse me to see you swim for shore with one good leg."

"You just keep pulling and I'll forget that you said that. I could still hit you with this crutch." Sam slid his wooden stick over the top of the sea wall and pulled himself onto dry land. Robert lifted his friend and passed him the crutch.

"Now, you go and make another baby with your wife while I drown myself in ale and women," said Robert, sauntering in the direction of *The Star and Garter* pub on Broad Street.

Sam made his way towards Bath Square, teetering on his stick. He hadn't quite mastered the art of walking yet, but he was getting better. He turned by *The Coal Exchange* and stood at the entrance to Bath Square. It was exactly as he remembered it. *The Camber Inn* stood to his right, next to *The Still Tavern*, on the end of the row. On the other side of the square stood his house. His heart leapt at the sight of it, its sorry state, its drooping windows and lop sided door, all exactly as he remembered. It was the same as when he'd left it. Sam noted that the Solent had worn the wooden boarding and rotted the small window frame and door. The paint had all but flaked away and the door was washed pale with sea salt. He made his way towards the house and passed a woman who Sam recognised as being from the square.

"Morning," he said, tipping his hat. She stared at him in silence and passed him by, showing no signs of recognition towards him, which perturbed him somewhat. *Am I that different that my neighbours don't recognise me? What will Annie say when she sees me? Will I have to convince her who I am?* He stood outside the front door of number three and listened for sounds of life. Suddenly he had a very dry mouth and wished that he'd gone with Robert and filled himself up with ale to give him a little false courage. Sam tottered unsteadily as his heart pounded in his chest. He felt the same faintness as he had on the pinnace, pulling into port. He counted to three and rapped on the door. There was no sound from inside so he knocked again. Still no one came to answer the door. *She must not be in,* he thought. It amused him a little to think that he had travelled half-way round the world, fought fierce battles, lost a leg and almost died to reach this moment and curse his damn luck if she wasn't in.

The lady who he had passed before and who'd ignored his greeting now came back into the square with another woman. She looked familiar to Sam although his eyesight wasn't what it used to be. They drew nearer and stopped, and the fatter of the two said, "What's your business knocking on Annie's door?" She was a stout lady with her hair tied in a bun. Up close, he instantly recognised her voice.

"My business?" said Sam. "What business is it of yours, Mary, to enquire so rudely?" he turned and faced them both.

"'Ow do you know my name? I am a great friend of Annie's and I don't want no trouble for 'er. You look mighty suspicious to me."

"Am I that different that you don't see me?" said Sam.

"See you? I see you alright, but you labour under an idea that we knows each other. Have we met before? I live across the square." She pointed to her house, a not dissimilar place with dirty little windows and a tiny front door.

"We 'ave at that. You're Charlie's missus, Mary Abbott," said Sam.

Mary took a step backwards and said, "'Ow do you know me an' my 'usband? What's your name?"

"Look at me," said Sam. "Really look at me, an' you will see who I am. You do know me."

Mary stared at the strange looking man and tried to recall faces locked in her limited mind. "Nothin'," she said. "I declare that I do not know you. Now kindly move along before I call someone to 'elp." Mary planted both hands firmly on her hips, adopting a no-nonsense expression.

"My name is Sam Crowther and my daughter is named Bessie," he said. "I was taken some time past and conscripted to the navy."

Mary leaned in closer to Sam and studied his features carefully. Finally the fledgling signs of recognition entered her eyes and she said, "Oh my fuckin' lord. You're back from the dead."

"From the dead? I was never dead. I was pressed into the navy."

"Figure of speech, sweet," said Mary. "We knew you'd been pressed but we wasn't expectin' you to come back. Annie 'eard nothin' from you, so we thought you was dead."

"Where is Annie? The house is silent."

"She must be out," lied Mary. "Why don't you come over to my place and rest your leg. It looks mighty uncomfortable. I've got a fire lit and, whilst you warms, I'll fetch Annie for you."

"That would be very kind of you," said Sam. "I could do with resting a while."

He followed Mary across the square into her house. The other woman waved goodbye and scurried away to spread the word that Sam was back. The Point was rife with rumour and stories, swapped in pubs and on street corners between gossiping men and women, eager to taste the fortune or misfortune of others; eager to bask in the tainted light of scandal and bad news. It made their pitiful lives somehow more valid and acceptable.

Mary sat Sam down and poured him a cup of ale. Then she left the house swiftly and scurried across the square like a fussing hen, towards Brownrigg's house. Her bulky frame had never known such haste, as her little legs moved nineteen to the dozen. It had started to drizzle and she shivered against the icy blasts of wind that stabbed at her jowly face. For a larger woman she made good speed, dodging among the inebriated and the fornicators. She reached number one hundred and two Broad Street and rapped on the door. From inside, Mary could hear the angelic voice of her friend as she hummed a tune, and approached the door.

The door opened and Annie said, "Mary? What brings you 'ere on such a miserable day?"

Mary stared at Annie and struggled to speak, her mouth flapping like a fish. Her face a picture of surprise and shock.

"What is it?" said Annie, growing concerned. "Is it Bessie?"

Mary shook her head and wiped tears from her eyes.

"Bleedin' 'ell!" said Annie. "Speak woman, or I shall shut this door."

"He's 'ere," blurted Mary.

"Who's 'ere? You make no sense."

"In my 'ouse," said Mary ignoring her friend. "'E's in my 'ouse right now, bold as brass, waitin' for you."

"Who? For gawd's sake, Mary, who's waitin' for me?"

"Your 'usband."

Annie felt her legs buckle at the sound of Mary's words and her head struck the floorboards of with a thump. The last thing that went through her mind before she fainted was an image of her beloved Sam, staring at her and smiling.

Chapter Nineteen

The emaciated man stood…

Crossing that square was the longest journey of Annie's life. Every step felt slow, like she was walking through quicksand. The sound of each footstep was muffled in her swirling mind. It seemed that the quicker she ran, the farther Mary's house got. Familiar faces called out to her as she passed by, but she didn't hear them. Her mind was a muddy mix of confusion and excitement. The thought of seeing her man, of holding him once more, filled her with so much emotion that she was sure she would burst and drop dead at the very sight of him. His face loomed large in her head and suddenly a tiny pinch of anger was added to the mix. What would she say to him and how would he explain the lost time to her? Suddenly she was scared that the frustration of the moment would spill out of her and manifest itself in violence. Would she, could she attack him for what he had put her through? Her heart raced and she swallowed back waves of nausea. Mary followed behind, desperate to keep up. She was taken by surprise at the recovery that Annie had made. After she'd fainted, Mary had sat with her and patted her hand until she came round. Eventually Annie opened her eyes and stared at her friend.

"What 'appened?" she said. It had been clear from her dazed expression that she was struggling to recognise where she was.

"You came over all queer and fell," said Mary.

"Did I dream it?"

"Dream what, sweet?" said Mary.

"That Sam is back?"

"No, Annie, don't you remember? It wasn't a dream. He sits in my 'ouse, large as life."

And so it was that Mary was chasing across Bath Square after her friend as they approached her little house. Annie skidded to a halt and stared at the door like it might scald her if she touched it. She paced backwards and forwards, patting down her hair and straightening her dress.

"How do I look?" said Annie.

"Like a princess. Now what you waitin' for?" said Mary. "Get in there, girl."

"I'm scared, Mary. I'm scared of what he might think of me when 'e finds out about George. I'm scared of 'ow I might be towards 'im. I feel love, but I feel anger too."

Mary hauled her friend away from the door and said,

"Firstly, you say nothin' about Brownrigg." She jabbed her finger in Annie's face, "not just yet anyway. There will come a time but this ain't it. Second, it's understandable that you feel anger. I would too but that will subside quickly and you'll discover that you were meant for each other." Mary gave Annie a shove towards the door. "Now get in there an' get your 'usband back."

Annie turned the handle and pushed open the door. Inside, sat in the chair by the fire, a rakishly thin man with a shaved head and scars on his face stared back at her. *This isn't Sam. This man has lost a leg*, she thought. She turned and looked at Mary in confusion. Mary nodded, pushed Annie into the room and stepped in behind her, slamming the door shut. The glow of the fire made it difficult for her to see him properly and the overcast afternoon wasn't helping to light the room. The emaciated man stood, wobbling a little at first and steadied himself against the chair.

"Annie," he said.

At that moment, hearing his voice, she knew it was Sam. She knew beyond all doubt that her husband had returned. Annie clapped her hands to her mouth and let out a gasp.

"Is it really you?" she said as her eyes filled with tears.

The one-legged man nodded and grinned. "You ain't 'arf a sight for sore eyes, Annie Crowther." He held out his arm and reached for her hand and Annie stepped forward. He pulled her towards him and Annie balled her fists as tight as she could. When she was close enough, she struck Sam in the chest. She hit him again and again, making him wobble precariously and Sam raised his free arm to protect himself from the blows that rained down.

"Annie!" he shouted. "Be calm."

"Be calm?" she spat. "Be calm? You 'ave a nerve, Samuel Crowther. All this time and not a word. Not one note to say you was alright."

"I was at sea. It was war. Surely you can understand that. Besides, you know I can't write."

"My life was turned upside down. And Bessie's. She's been cryin' 'erself to sleep ever since you left. What am I goin' to tell the poor girl?"

"It's been a long time for me too," said Sam. "It was war and it was brutal and the only thing that kept me goin' was the thought that one day I would see your face again." He stretched out his hand towards her and said, "I missed you both so sorely."

"But not a word," said Annie. "I grieved for you like you was dead. Every day I asked myself if you were dead or not. To 'ave to look Bessie in the face and decide to tell 'er that 'er father ain't comin' back. Can you understand that? Do you see?"

"I know and I understand, really I do." Sam dropped his head and stared at the floor. "I ain't 'ere to ask for your forgiveness. I could take a lifetime of punishment if it meant that we were together again." He lifted his face and stared at her. Behind the scars and the shaved head and the lines now etched into his sea-weathered face, Annie could see the same kind eyes of the man she loved more than life itself.

She lifted her fist and thumped him again but this time it hardly had any substance and then the fight drained from her. She dropped her arms by her side and Sam gripped her by the shoulders and looked deep into her eyes.

"You ask what you should tell Bessie? Tell her that her father is returned for good."

She stared at him longingly, the resistance in her eyes melting like frosted grass in the mid-winter sun. Tears flowed and she wiped her cheeks with the sleeve of her dress. "I never thought I'd see this moment. I 'ad you pegged as dead."

"I too doubted that my eyes would ever get to see your beauty again, but 'ere I stand before you, very much alive," said Sam.

"I see your face. I hear your voice… but inside I am still tryin' to convince myself that this is no dream. This is real… I'm awake, ain't I? This is real?"

Sam leaned in closer to his wife and planted a kiss on her lips. "Do you feel that?" he said.

She nodded and ran her finger over the spot on her lips where Sam had kissed her.

He kissed her again and the warmth of his breath tickled her skin.

"You feel the warmth of my breath?" he said.

Annie nodded.

"Then why do you doubt your senses? I am returned and we are to be a family again."

"Do you mean that?" she whispered closing her eyes.

"My Annie, my Annie," said Sam. "You are as beautiful as the day I left." He kissed her lips and cheeks and eyes. Annie clung to him like a shipwrecked sailor clings to driftwood in the ocean. She didn't want to let him go, for fear that she would see him drift away on a tide of agony. Tears of joy streamed down her face and she returned his kisses. Eventually they parted and Annie turned towards her friend, Mary. But she was gone, slipping out of the door unnoticed.

Sam gripped Annie's chin and spun her round to face him.

"I missed you," he said. "There wasn't a day that went by that I didn't think about you."

"I missed you too," she said, sitting down. Sam followed suit and wobbled on his one good leg. He plonked down and Annie could see the pain and frustration on his face. She took his hand and said, "Tell me what 'appened?"

"It was that night in the pub. The night that we argued. Impress got me. Coshed me over the 'ead an' dragged me off to sea."

"It must 'ave been 'orrible for you. Where did they take you?"

"Cork, in Ireland. From there I joined *HMS Raisonnable* and went to do my duty." Sam shuddered at the troubled thoughts that occupied his head. He had seen things that he wouldn't wish for his worst enemy.

"What pains you so?" said Annie, reading the look in his eyes.

"What I saw... the things that I did. They are best kept buried. I feel that if I let them out, they will be the ruin of me." Sam shuddered. "They do not account for the man I am, Annie, nor do they account for the man I will be. I want to leave them at the bottom of the ocean where they belong. The ghosts of the dead will no longer occupy my life now I am returned to you. They are to occupy the other Sam Crowther's head, the man that lies in spirit with his fallen shipmates at the bottom of the sea, and never shall they be a part of my life again."

"You poor man, I cannot imagine what you must 'ave gone through." Annie stood and kissed his forehead and she could feel herself welling up again. She bit back tears. She had to be strong for Sam's sake. He needed her more than ever and she wasn't going to abandon him in his hour of need. Annie sat back down and gripped his hand again.

"A lot 'as 'appened since you went away," she said, staring at Sam's severed leg.

She held her gaze and Sam said, "Does it shock you?"

"Does what shock me?" said Annie doing a poor job of hiding her disturbed expression.

"The leg. You were starin' at it."

"It doesn't bother me, but it will take some gettin' used to, mind. What 'appened?"

"Battle of Cape Finnistere. Got injured so bad that the surgeon chopped it. Would 'ave died otherwise."

"Oh my poor, Sam," she said.

"I 'ave accepted my fate. Some others weren't so lucky."

Had she just heard him correctly? 'Lucky' wasn't a word that she would have used in his situation.

"You think I'm mad for thinkin' I'm lucky? Annie, men better than me got blown to pieces before my eyes. Children, some not much older than Bessie lay dead, crushed, shot or speared by debris." Sam banged his fist on the arm of the chair. "I am bleedin' lucky. I got you and Bessie, and I'm alive. What more do I need?"

"Then we are both blessed," said Annie, "and we are a family again."

"So, I've imparted my news. What of you? You ain't starvin', that's fer sure. What news of your life?"

Suddenly Annie sat bolt upright. In her euphoria at her husband's return, she had forgotten about George Brownrigg. What was she going to do about him? She daren't mention that she was living at his house or that she shared his bed. What would that do to this poor broken man? She had to speak to Mary to make sure that she mentioned nothing.

"Annie, you look like you had a shock or somethin'. What's up?" said Sam, leaning forward in his chair. As he did, he winced and screwed his face in pain.

"I 'ave 'ad a shock. You are returned. Is that not shock enough?"

"I see somethin' else in your eyes. You look troubled."

"Does it 'urt?" said Annie, seizing the opportunity to steer Sam's conversation in a different direction. She resolved that she would have to be straight with George and tell him the truth. He'd always known that Sam was the love of her life and that he would come off second best in her choices, should her husband ever return. Well that moment had arrived and he would have to live with it.

"It does, every now and again. I gets twinges and it runs up me side." Sam sucked in air and tried to slow his breathing. "It'll pass in a bit."

"Sit here and rest. I will ready our 'ouse for your return." Annie stood and crossed the room.

"I can come with you," said Sam trying to stand, the visible pain draining the energy from his battered body. He flopped back down and waved a listless hand at her. "You go. Come an' get me when you're ready." He rested his head on the back of the chair and closed his eyes. Annie watched from the doorway, listening to the sound of his breathing. He didn't sound like a well man to her. His hollow chest rose weakly and his eyes flickered open and shut, almost as if he was about to pass out.

"Sam?" she said and he opened his eyes and lifted his head, looking at her.

It seemed to take the greatest amount of his strength to do it but Sam smiled all the same and said, "I'm fine."

Annie slipped out of the door and shut it quietly. It was drizzling in the square and Mary stood in a doorway across the way puffing on her pipe. When she saw Annie come out alone, she scooted over and said, "Fuck me, girl, watcha gonna do?"

"I can't think straight. Mary, you mustn't say a word to anyone. If Sam finds out, this will finish 'im. That man in there ain't well, an' I fear for 'is 'ealth."

"Annie love, there ain't a thing that 'appens on the Point don't get known about. Brownrigg probably already knows about Sam."

"Please, Mary. I'm askin', just this once to keep it to yourself."

"You 'ave my word, but Sam will find out, not from me mind, but 'e will. And when 'e does, don't say I didn't warn you."

"I need to find George an' Bessie. Can you sit with Sam till I find 'em? I'll send Bessie to yours the moment that I do."

"What are friends for? Course I'll sit with 'im."

Annie gripped her friend by the hands and shook them. "Thank you. Wish me luck, Mary Abbott."

"You don't need luck, sweet. You got your 'usband back."

"You're right," she said. "I do 'ave 'im back."

Annie hugged her friend and then left to go in search of George. It didn't take her long and she found him in Broad Street chatting to Pete Bookbinder. Pete was showing a magic trick to Bessie in which he plucked a penny from behind her ear, making her marvel at how he did it. George saw Annie approach.

"You alright? Looks like you've seen a ghost or somethin'?" said George gripping Bessie's hand.

"I need to talk to you," she said solemnly.

"What about?"

"Not 'ere. Can we go back to yours?"

George nodded and looked at her with growing concern. "What's 'appened, girl? Your face tells of trouble comin' and you've got me worried."

Annie smiled weakly at George and her daughter. It wasn't that convincing and she knew that George wasn't buying it. She could see that he was troubled. She tried to order her jumbled thoughts into some thread of sense. How was she going to do this? She had all but given herself to this man and now she was going to let him down. She hated herself for it, finally realising that her feelings for George had blossomed into something that resembled more than affection. It wasn't the same heart flipping love that she felt for Sam, but Annie knew that had her husband not returned it may have grown into love.

George said goodbye to Pete and trudged back to the house with Bessie in tow. Neither Annie nor George said a word on the short journey back. When they got to the end of Broad Street, by *The Union Tavern*, Annie knelt down and gripped Bessie by the face.

"Bessie?" The little girl nodded at her mother. "I want you to go an' see Mary."

"Why?" said Bessie. "I want to stay with you."

"I've asked Mary to give you a treat. You know that peg dolly that you lost?" Annie hated lying to her daughter. It made her feel cheap and tarnished. Bessie nodded again, her eyes widening, along with the smile that spread across her face. "Mary has a gift for you."

Before Annie could finish another word, the little girl bolted towards Bath Square and disappeared around the corner.

Chapter Twenty

"Sam has returned."

Annie watched as George threw his long coat on the chair in the parlour and stared at the empty wall. There was no window to look through, no view to enchant his eyes and draw him away from the doom that she knew he must be feeling. George made it plain that he knew something was wrong. From his stance, with fallen head and slumped shoulders, it was obvious. Why else would she have sent the girl away? She must have appeared to have had the weight of the world on her shoulders. He placed his hands on his hips and hung his head like a man about to hear his sentence before being led to the gallows. Annie listened to the sound of her heart beating and tried to concentrate on what she was going to say. Her pulse was so strong that she felt giddy, almost as if she were drunk. The sounds of the outside world lifted the silence and drowned the rhythmic thumping in her ears.

"George," she said, "can we sit?"

"You sit, Annie. I feel like standin'," he said without turning around.

"I 'ave some news to impart," said Annie sitting at the table.

"I fear it ain't good news neither. What do you wanna tell me so bad that it can't be said in front of the child?"

"This isn't for her young ears. Besides, she's been through enough just recently."

"You're leavin' me. I can sense it." George finally spun around and stared at Annie with reddening eyes. They had glazed over and threatened tears.

Annie didn't say anything and stared at the same blank wall behind George, looking through him rather than at him. She searched for anything to fix her attention on, so that she didn't have to suffer the sight of his sorrow. There was a stain on the wall, so she fixated on that, trying to fathom how it had got there. She played with the sleeve of her dress, to calm her shaking hands.

"What is it about that wall, eh? Seems that we both 'ave cause to stare at it," said George without a hint of humour in his voice. "What do you 'ave to say to me?"

"You know that I 'ave grown fond of you these past few weeks?" Annie stood and approached Brownrigg.

"What are you sayin'?"

"I once said about us that it was a start. Do you remember?" George nodded. "I said that you were makin' a start at me growing fond of you."

"Annie," said George lifting his face towards the ceiling, biting back more approaching tears, "get to the point. I don't think I can take this, girl."

"Sam has returned."

George staggered backwards as if her words were delivered with the force of a bare knuckle fighter pounding at his chest. A single teardrop ran the length of his unshaven face and dripped on his shirt. Annie stood and approached him but he held out his hands to stop her advance.

"Say somethin'," said Annie.

George turned and faced the wall again and hunched his shoulders. They rose and fell gently. He wiped his eyes with his hand and shook his head.

"Please say somethin'?" pleaded Annie.

"What's there to say?" he said after a long pause. "It seems that I am surplus to needs after all."

"Don't say it like that. You knows that we had somethin'. I didn't plan on Sam comin' back."

"Nor I," said George sarcastically.

"George, you always knew of my unshakeable love for my 'usband. I made no secret of it and I make no secret of it now."

"You gave me 'ope. You gave me a reason to look to the future. For the first time in my life, since the death of my family, I felt that I could 'ave the things that I told myself would never come to a man like me. I lost my wife an' child, an' now I've lost you an' Bessie." George spun round and looked her in the eyes. "Tell me that you could 'ave grown to love me?"

"I could – I was. But Sam is the love of my life and 'e is back, George. Can you not see that I need him in my life?"

"I need you in my life. I need Bessie in my life," said Brownrigg.

"Bessie can still be in your life. I can too. We are friends are we not? We are that at least."

"I don't know if I can settle for second best. I don't know if I can stand the pain of seein' you with another man. Knowin' that you share 'is bed… that ain't somethin' that sits well with me."

"He's my 'usband, an' 'e needs me. You 'ave become the *other* man in this, an' there's nothin' that can be done."

"So that's it? You walk away, back into your old life like I never existed, an' I'm left watchin' you play 'appy families."

"I know this is 'ard, George, really I do, but if you 'ad the tiniest amount of love for me that you profess, you'd understand that I do not ask this lightly… an' believe me when I say that I am truly sorry."

"Does 'e know?" said Brownrigg.

"About us?" said Annie.

George nodded.

"No. I don't want 'im to know. Promise me that you won't speak of this."

"He's gonna find out soon enough. You knows what it's like 'ere. Bleedin' place is alive with rumour. What makes you think you can stop the gossip?"

"*You* can stop the gossip. If you say it, they will obey. Nothin' 'appens in this place without your say-so or knowledge," said Annie.

"Why should I 'elp you? Walk out that door an' you are no longer in my protection." George's voice was cold, steely, determined.

Annie thought she detected a hint of malice in his words. "That sounds like a threat," she said. "I may 'ave to consider movin' away then."

"You only know this place," said George. "Sam only knows this place. Where would you go?"

"Truth is, I 'ave no idea. I know that we can't live 'ere under the shadow of you an' your threats."

"What if Skinny's boys come lookin' for revenge? Does Sam possess the skills to protect you?"

"Is that the only reason that you think I should stay?" said Annie. "Way I see it, Skinny's more likely to come at me while I'm with you. Skinny Jim ain't interested in the likes of me an' Sam."

"Annie, I didn't mean to sound like I was threatenin' you. That's the last thing I wanted. I'm desperate."

"It's the last thing I wanted too but fate is cruel and I must accept what it 'as in stall for me… and so should you," said Annie, turning and heading for the door.

"Wait!" George called after her.

Annie stopped and faced him. "George, this is impossible. I 'ave to accept things whatever your intentions. Love me, 'ate me, ignore me, it's up to you. My priority lies with my 'usband now."

"We cannot part in this way. I really didn't mean to say those words. I'm angry, Annie. Surely you can understand that?"

Annie's face softened and she said, "Anger will not solve this. I need understanding, George. I am willin' to forgive your words, for I am sure they're unfounded, that your threats are empty."

George nodded. "And is there nothin' that I can say to change the course of things? Is there no way you might take some time to consider your decision?" George had the look of a fallen man.

Annie approached and placed a hand on George's face, kissing his bristled chin. "I am resolute. My 'usband is my priority now. There is room in my life for only one man. For the pain, the anger you feel towards me, it is something that I 'ave to accept, as do you, but I am sorry, truly sorry for what I 'ave done to you." She placed his hand on her chest. "See how my heart beats so. It is in sorrow and sadness for you that it pounds. If we are to part, let it not be as enemies. But hear this: I will never give up on Sam, no matter what." Annie stepped out the door and out of George Brownrigg's life.

He screwed his fist into a tight ball as he stared at the empty space where Annie had been. He'd never felt so empty, so crushed. George Brownrigg slammed his fist into the wall and watched as the broken plaster dropped to the floor.

****

Mary saw Bessie running up Bath Square and opened the door to greet her.

"Mary," said the little girl, throwing her arms around her neck, "do you 'ave somethin' for me?"

"For you?" said Mary.

"Mother said that you 'ad a treat for me, an' I was to come 'ere straight away."

"Oh that." Mary did her best to play along. "I do, my girl. Do you wanna see what it is?"

Bessie jumped up and down on the spot excitedly. "Please, can I see it?"

Mary placed a calming hand on the girl's shoulder and said, "What I'm about to show you is very special, but I need to ask you somethin'."

Bessie nodded and said, "What do you ask, Mary?"

"I need to ask that you keep your time at Mr Brownrigg's 'ouse as a secret for now. Can you do that? You know, just our little secret?"

Bessie didn't understand and thought for a moment. "Why?" she eventually said.

"If you can't keep a secret then no treat. I need you to forget that you ever went to live with that man. Forget everythin' about him an' your mother seein' each other. Promise me, Bessie, or no treat?"

Bessie wanted her treat so badly that she nodded and said, "Now can I 'ave my treat?"

Mary stepped aside and said, "Open the door, girl. Your surprise is in that room."

Sam saw the small shape of Bessie silhouetted in the dim light of the open door. He stood and wobbled on his good leg. The door shut and the room was swathed in darkness. Only the fire, crackling in the stove, offered any relief from the gloom. Sam stepped towards the girl and she backed up nearer to the door.

"Who are you? Do *you* 'ave my treat?" said Bessie, slightly alarmed at being shut in a dark room with a strange man.

"Do you not remember me, Bessie?" said Sam.

Bessie paused and thought for a while, then said, "You sound like my father, but you ain't 'im."

"What makes you think that I am not?"

"Cos you don't look like 'im. You've only got one leg."

Sam stepped closer again and his face was partially illuminated in the light of the window. He smiled and something in his eyes spoke to the girl. She smiled back.

"I see my father in your eyes."

"Your father exists in these eyes and in this voice and this body. I have returned, my sweet little girl, an' we are to be a family again."

Bessie's eyes widened and she opened her mouth. His voice was that of her father. His eyes were those of her father. She mouthed words but made no sound.

Sam said, "Bit of a shock, eh? Bet you didn't think you'd see me again?"

Bessie nodded, still unable to add volume to her silent words.

"Cat got your tongue?" said Sam.

Bessie ran at him and threw her arms around his neck, squeezing for all she was worth. She hit him with such a force that Sam fell backwards against the table and toppled onto the floor. As he collapsed, Bessie let out a scream and they both hit the wooden floor with a thump. Mary burst in to find them lying on the floor giggling like drunken fools, at their misfortune. She stopped in the doorway and beamed from ear to ear.

"Look at you two," she said. "You're like a pair of clowns." She held out her hand and hoisted Bessie from the floor and then helped Sam up, gently placing him in his chair and handing him his stick.

"I can hear footsteps," said Mary peering out the small window across the damp square. A thick mist, a permanent fixture of winter on the Point, hung over the rooftops that lined the street. There wasn't much activity out there and Mary easily spotted Annie trotting in their direction. She had her shawl over her head to protect her from the dampness.

"Annie's comin'," said Mary, opening the front door and stepping out. She pulled the door closed and said, "Well?"

"It didn't go well, Mary. He was broken. I told him Sam was my priority and that was that."

"What else did you expect? George has been 'urt and is suffering. That man didn't know what love was until you came along, an' now he knows how cruel love can be. Did you part on good terms?"

"Hard to say," said Annie. "I want to stay friends with 'im but it's up to George how 'e deals with this. I feel bad but I've a chance of 'appiness that I can't walk away from."

"No one's saying that what you do is wrong, but you must understand the pain that George feels."

"I do," said Annie, "more than you'll know." She brushed past her friend and opened the door. Annie stepped inside and shook off the dampness from her shawl. She saw Bessie and Sam holding hands and suddenly she was overwhelmed with emotion. Yesterday her life was very different. There was hope, and the chance of a new start with George. It may not have been the ideal situation, but Annie knew it was the best option. And now her past had returned, and with it, she had a different future to embrace and cling to. Sam brought that; this poor wretched man, bedraggled and emaciated. This poor man with one leg. He wasn't perfect – far from it – and there would be tough times ahead. How were they going to survive without an income? Sam couldn't work, that was certain. She had just walked out on the richest and most influential man on the Point. Her chances of gainful employment were very slim. She could always ask William Juxon to take pity on her and give her a job behind the bar. She stepped into the room and her daughter leapt from her chair and gripped her round the waist with both arms.

"Father has returned," she said excitedly.

"I know, child. Why do you think I sent you 'ere?" Annie lifted Bessie's face towards her and rubbed her nose with her finger. "He is back and we are to be a family again. No more will you cry yourself to sleep. No more fear of the dark, neither."

Bessie nodded. Behind her, Sam stood and hobbled over. He gripped Annie and pulled the two women in his life in for an embrace. They stood in the middle of Mary's room for what seemed like an age and hugged each other. Annie didn't want the moment to end. She was truly happy for the first time in two and a half years. She smiled inwardly and savoured the moment. Never again was her family going to suffer. Bessie would grow up with her father by her side and nothing was going to change that. Annie was going to make sure of it.

Her last thoughts were of George and her request that he keep his word to not mention anything to Sam. Should she rely on him or should she tell Sam herself that she'd shared Brownrigg's bed? She decided that these were issues that could wait. Tomorrow was the start of setting her life straight. Tomorrow was the time for hard conversations. Today was the time for rejoicing and counting their blessings that, unlike hundreds, even thousands of other families suffering because of the violence of war, they were to have a second chance at happiness.

Darkness settled on the Point like a well-worn hat. Night time was the natural order of things. Its security meant that the smugglers could go about their business undetected. Prostitutes could entertain customers in corners and shaded recesses without fear of harassment or embarrassment. Land sharks could fleece the unsuspecting sailors of their hard earned money and disappear into the gloom of an alleyway before the victim could act. The Point had an ally and it was night, in all its gloom and cover. Annie was glad that night was here. She lay in her bed next to her husband for the first time in an age, feeling his head resting on her shoulder. Bessie lay on the other shoulder and slept soundly. Annie looked at them both and felt a sense of relief. She felt complete. She hated to use the comparison, but without Sam, she'd always felt like one of her limbs had been lopped off. Now he was here and he needed her to be strong because of his missing leg. She spied the stars through the un-shuttered window and said a silent 'thank you' to the heavens. To her, the blackness of night was a time for joy and she savoured every moment that she got to spend in that bed, waiting for the new day.

Chapter Twenty-one

George spat on the floor and stuffed his pipe in his mouth…

"I dunno, Annie. George would skin me if he knew I'd given you employment." William Juxon placed the full tankard on the counter and scooped up the coin that sat in a puddle of ale. The man beside Annie picked up the drink and fell into her, almost spilling his beer on her dress.

"Easy, Tom," said Annie, holding him steady. He looked at her with drowsy eyes and sauntered to his table, falling into his seat and spilling more beer in the process.

Annie turned to William and said, "I need the work. You still own this place, dontcha? What right does George 'ave to tell you who you should and shouldn't employ?"

"What right? 'Ave you been livin' in the clouds? He's the king of the fuckin' Point, that's what right 'e 'as. 'Ave you forgotten that, or is true love turning your brains to water?"

"I know and I ain't forgotten but I've seen a softer side to George that you don't see. He'll understand."

"Understandin' – you ain't been around since you an' 'im… well, you know," said Juxon. "This last week 'as been terrible. Understandin'? Now that's a word that doesn't leap to the fore when you mentions Brownrigg's name."

"Please! I'm desperate. Sam is incapable of findin' work an' we needs the money."

William Juxon thought for a moment and scratched his chin.

"It still sits awkwardly with me. What about when 'e comes in 'ere? 'Ow you gonna 'andle that?"

"I will deal with it. Me an' George will deal with it. Please say yes. I got nowhere else to go."

"Alright, stop moanin' on. You can start tonight. And mind," said Juxon, "the first sign that Brownrigg ain't comfortable with the arrangement, you'll be out on your ear."

Annie grabbed William by the arm and pulled him in for a kiss. She said, "You're the best, William Juxon. The sweetest of men."

William blushed and stared away in embarrassment. "I am a fool," he said, "a bloody fool among men."

Back at the house, Sam Crowther was busy trying to set a fire. He eventually got it smouldering and white smoke curled gently up the chimney. He blew on the ball of straw and its core glowed orange as the flames burst into life. Sam reached for the small bits of kindling wood that he'd spent the morning cutting into slithers. He laid them around the flaming centre in a pyramid and they caught too, and heat started to fill the room. Just doing something as simple as lighting the fire made him feel that he had a value and was worthy of his place in the family. Warmth and shelter where the two most basic elements of a husband's responsibilities. The other was food, and Sam was struggling in that department. No one wanted to hire a one legged man. It had been a week since his return and in that time he had never had so many doors slammed in his face. Even people that he considered neighbours and friends were indifferent to his needs. 'What use is a man with a missing limb?' they said. 'Take away a quarter of a man an' 'e ain't a whole person.' Sam reminded each and every one of them how it came to be that he was in this state, how he had fought the French, the Spanish, and served with loyalty and courage. He reminded those good folk that the war was fought at the cost of the little man, the common men and the profit was reaped by the lords and the admirals.

Still the doors slammed.

Sam hated the fact that Annie had resorted to begging for work at Juxon's pub but there was nothing that could be done to ease their situation. The full blown joy of reunion was dampening in the harsh light of another failed day.

Annie burst through the door and stamped her feet. The weather had eased somewhat and the rain was now just a light misty film that penetrated even the thickest of garments.

Sam turned and looked at his wife. "Well?" he said sounding a little more impatient than he had intended. He softened his tone and continued, "'Ow did you fare?"

"'E didn't want to at first. But I can be very persuasive an' 'e relented. I starts tonight after dark."

"I'm so sorry for this. It should be me puttin' food on the table and money in our pockets." Sam screwed up his fist and thumped the table.

Bessie, who had been taking a nap, woke suddenly at the noise and called downstairs, "Father, is that you?"

"Yes, child. Now go back to sleep," snapped Sam.

"Don't be takin' it out on that poor girl. She's been through enough, without you snappin' at 'er."

"I'm sorry," said Sam. "It's just that I feel so 'elpless. Do you know how many people turned their backs on me today? Do you know how many we counted as friends? What use is a cripple, they said?"

"You 'ave to keep a positive bent of mind. Don't let it beat you," said Annie.

"I know," said Sam, "I do try an' think of the good things in my life, but seein' you an' the girl suffer tarnishes what I 'ave. I am startin' to think that I would be better off going back to sea."

"The Navy won't 'ave you. It was them that sent you 'ome, remember? We need the money," said Annie throwing her shawl on the chair near the fire. "I know that don't make it any easier for you to 'ear. Besides, I'd rather 'ave you in whatever state than not 'ave you 'ere at all. Don't ever think that I ain't grateful for you bein' 'ere."

"I know, but if you could just taste the bitterness that I feel at my situation. It stings my tongue and coats my throat. I am a sorry sight, for sure."

"That you are, Sam Crowther," smiled Annie, "but you're *my* sorry sight."

"I don't deserve you," he said.

"Don't place such lofty thoughts of me in your 'ead. There ain't nothin' saintly about me," said Annie.

****

The evening came, ushered in on a stiffening breeze that carried across the harbour and the Point. The streets were packed with sailors braving the freezing temperatures, eager to spend what was left of their wages. The lure of wine and women was too great. Annie said her goodbyes to Sam and Bessie and slipped out of the front door. She crossed the Square and saw *The Camber Inn* in front of her, the sound of bawdy laughter spilling out onto the cobbles. Pete Bookbinder and Davey Turner were huddled by the light outside the entrance to the bar.

Annie approached and said, "Evenin' gents."

Pete looked at her with a sense of pity and disgust. He said nothing, but Davey returned the greeting, much to the consternation of Pete. He thumped his friend on the arm and glared at him, as if to say, 'we don't speak to her anymore'. The pub was packed with drinkers. William smiled at Annie as she entered and he beckoned her over.

"Annie, get yourself ready. It's a busy one for sure."

Annie nodded and removed her shawl. She brushed the dregs of dampness from her long black locks and shouted, "Right boys, who's next?"

A row of arms with tankards attached thrust their empty vessels towards her and she took one and filled it. She was a natural and the customers loved her. The night was going well and the ale flowed. The men seemed to be drinking more than usual and soon it was apparent to William Juxon that Annie was the reason. Each was so keen to see her that they made any excuse to return to the bar, and usually they returned to their seats with a charged tankard and a penny lighter in the purse.

William was glad that he'd listened to Annie and her persuasive talents. He had never known it so busy. All was going well until the one dark cloud that was George Brownrigg blew in on the breeze through the open door, followed by the obedient Pete and Davey. Pete tapped George on the arm and pointed towards Annie and his expression was thunderous. Annie looked over at him and saw that he looked dreadful. His face was a pale crumpled mess and his eyes were framed by dark circles. His clothes hung from him like rags and he looked like he hadn't washed since their split. George approached the bar and threw his hat down on the counter.

William said, "The usual, Mr Brownrigg?"

"What's she doin' 'ere?" He chewed on the words like he was gnawing on a piece of gristle. His eyes never left Annie's face and she did her best to ignore him. She could feel his anger, beaming from those eyes directly at her. Annie hoped that there wouldn't be a scene and resolved that, should it go badly, she would not return to the pub the following night. She owed Juxon that at least, instead of landing him in the bad books of Brownrigg.

"She needed the work, George. What was I to do? Let her an' the girl starve?"

George spat on the floor and stuffed his pipe in his mouth. "Light," he said and William duly obliged, striking a match on the rough counter and touching the flame to the tobacco in the bowl of his pipe. Smoke circled his face, clinging to his hair. He didn't take his eyes off Annie once, not even when William placed a brandy on the bar in front of him. George simply picked it up and downed it in one, slamming the glass back down and demanding another. William pulled the bottle from the shelf and with shaking hands poured a second brandy. He turned to put the bottle back on the shelf when George gripped his arm and said, "Leave it on the bar."

"Yes, Mr Brownrigg," said William.

Brownrigg snatched it up and turned towards the packed room. Annie felt a little relief that he wasn't staring at her anymore. The room fell silent and the gaggle of people parted to let George pass. He made his way to a table by the fire. Tom, who had just downed the last of his ale, squinted through soused eyes at the approaching dark mass. His inebriated state prevented him from focusing properly and he didn't realise that George Brownrigg stood before him. Pete tipped his chair and the old man fell to the floor. The room erupted in loud guffaws as the drunken man crawled towards the bar on his hands and knees. Davey watched him as he passed by and gave his side a shove with his boot and old Tom fell on his back. More laughter filled the room until Annie stepped from behind the bar and stood in the clearing, beside Tom.

"You should be ashamed of yourselves." She glared at Pete and Davey. "Treatin' an old man in such a shameful manner is wicked, an' I thought better of you two."

Pete stared at Annie without saying a word.

"And the rest of you, don't be thinkin' that any of you is any better. Laughin' at Tom while he suffers." She stared at each of the faces in the room. No one made eye contact with her and she stooped to help Tom to his feet.

"There you go, Tom," she whispered, "that's better. Now you come with me an' I'll give you one on the 'ouse."

Tom wobbled to his feet and followed Annie to the bar.

Brownrigg watched Annie and the old man make their way back to the counter in the silenced room. He still ached for her. In that moment he knew that he wouldn't rest until she was back in his arms. The few days since Annie had announced she was leaving him were the worst of his life. He hadn't remembered them, not a single moment. The bottle had seen to that. It numbed and that was good at first, but still her face appeared in his mind, still she spoke to him in his sleep. But at least her voice didn't echo in his head as much when he'd had a skin full. He sat in that big house and stared out the window at the ocean. It rose and fell, shimmering in the winter sun. The sea gave him comfort and mollified his bruised mind.

Brownrigg stood suddenly, catching Pete and Davey off guard. He straightened his coat and hitched his belt. Davey and Pete stood beside him, waiting to see where he was going. George strode across the room towards Annie and Tom. He kicked chairs out of his way and again, people scattered out of his path.

Annie was handing Tom a fresh drink when the shadows in the room grew darker behind her.

"What can I get you, Mr Brownrigg?" said Annie without turning. She knew it was him.

"I wants to buy old Tom a drink an' apologise for these two." He cocked his thumb at Pete and Davey who stared back at him with looks of incredulity.

Annie turned and said, "Old Tom would like a brandy, an' I would like one too." She stared at George without a hint of fear in her pretty eyes and waited for him to speak.

"William," he called, "a brandy for the old man and one for Mrs Crowther."

"So I'm Mrs Crowther now, am I?"

"It wouldn't do to address a married woman in the wrong fashion," said George.

Annie took the glass of brandy from Juxon and downed her drink in one, wiping her chin with her arm. George didn't take his eyes from her face. Annie could see that his were ragged, blood shot and grey.

"You look like you could do with some sleep," she said.

Suddenly Brownrigg was angry, flaring his nostrils and grinding his blackened teeth. "Sleep?" he said, bending so close to her that she could smell the foulness on his breath. "An' just how do you think I'm sleepin' these days?"

Her heart was pounding and she wondered if George meant her harm. He could do it. She had seen it happen to others. Not just men but women too. This man before her displayed none of the attributes that she had previously found attractive. It seemed to her that he was making up for the kinder moments of their previous lives by doubling his cruelty and nastiness. He was the George that she'd known before he had softened her heart. She stared at him as he swayed before her, in the grip of intoxication, and she wondered whether she would ever know him like she did before. She had done this to him. Her and her alone. It struck her that the power of the man was fickle and easily broken, that it was the power of love, above all else that had done this to him.

"Spare me your pity, Annie Crowther," he snarled. "You are the one what's done this. You 'ave filled my 'ead with notions that are not to be, an' now you pity me."

"It was not my intention. I 'oped that you'd understand," said Annie.

"The only thing I understand is that, not content with ruining me, you seek to work in the very place that I come to drink away the memory of you." George spat on the floor and turned to William Juxon. "Juxon? A word if you please?"

Juxon followed Brownrigg into a room at the back of the bar. It was usually used for card games and storing stolen booty. Brownrigg liked the landlords that he extorted money from to play their part in his criminal family and, in return, he would let them off a week's protection money. The door was slightly ajar and Annie could see through the small gap that they were deep in conversation. Brownrigg was thrusting his arms around and gesticulating at Juxon. She leaned in and tried to listen to their conversation. She could just make out snippets, the odd word. She tried to block out the raucous laughter in the bar and focus on the men in the room, but she was interrupted by a drinker at the bar slurring for a refill. She duly obliged and quickly returned to her spot by the door.

"What's the 'arm, Mr Brownrigg? She's good with the customers," she heard William say.

"'Ave you forgotten?" said George. "Well? It's too dangerous 'avin' 'er about the place."

"She won't find out," said Juxon. "I'll make sure she don't. Trust me, Mr Brownrigg."

"I trust no-one these days. Specially not the likes of 'er. What if she finds out?"

"She won't. She ain't gonna find out. The only ones what know is you an' me, an' we ain't tellin'."

Annie listened at the door with a growing sense of unease. What were they talking about that she mustn't know? Annie felt a heavy sense of dread settling in her stomach. It sat there like a serpent, curled in her gut, waiting to poison her with its malice and ill feeling. She strained even harder to catch the rest of the conversation.

"On your head be it then," said George. "I 'ave little patience left in the matter. It's irrelevant now that she an' I are no longer together. She asks that I keep her dalliance in me bed a secret, an' so I shall, but should she know what we done, well that would be the end for 'er, an' that cripple of an' 'usband."

"Surely not. You wouldn't do such a thing," said Juxon in horror.

"Afore I was bewitched by 'er beauty I wouldn't 'ave thought twice about it. It's time old George got back to business and stopped fretting over lost love." Annie watched as George lit his pipe and straightened his coat. He prodded William Juxon in the chest and said, "You make sure that for 'er sake she remains ignorant of the facts. 'Er life depends on you keepin' our secret." He turned and paced towards the door. Annie jumped and ran back towards the bar and started filling empty tankards. Old Tom was asleep, his head resting on the ale-soaked counter. He dribbled and blew bubbles every time he breathed out. The door opened and George stepped back into the bar. He placed his hat on his head and turned towards Annie.

"You keep your distance from me. Understand?" He accentuated his words by jabbing the sodden end of his clay pipe at her to underline the point.

Annie nodded and said nothing.

"Pete, get Tom 'ome and meet me at the 'ouse."

"You don't touch 'im," snapped Annie stepping towards Tom and squaring up to Brownrigg.

"Fuck me. 'E ain't gonna 'urt 'im, just take 'im 'ome is all."

"You promise?" said Annie.

"My word is my word. I realise that keepin' your word don't mean shit to the likes of you, but me, I don't go back on what I say." George glared at Annie for a moment, then left the pub with Davey in tow. Pete let Tom rest on his shoulder as he slowly walked the drunken man home.

Annie was determined to get to the bottom of what George had meant by 'secrets'. She finished her shift in near silence and, by the end of the night, William asked her if she was okay.

"You seem a little quiet, girl," he said.

"Just tired is all," said Annie, trying not to make eye contact. Her curiosity was threatening to overwhelm her tongue and she knew that, if William pressed her on her mood, she would crack and ask him outright what they had been talking about. She turned and wiped down the bar with a beer-soaked cloth.

"Maybe you should get yourself on home. Sam will be pleased to have you returned safe and sound."

"Maybe I will, if you don't mind?" said Annie, throwing the cloth on the counter and making for the door. The last words that she heard before the door closed were William calling goodnight to her. She didn't call back.

Chapter Twenty-two

It was cool and wet and it soothed his aching head…

"Calm down, Annie," said Sam. "You've been in a right state ever since you got back from the pub."

Annie sat in the chair wringing her hands, unable to sit still. Sam placed his hands on hers and said, "What bothers you so?"

"I 'ave some news. Somethin' that I learned tonight at work."

"What is it? Tell me. You've been sat in that chair chewin' on your thoughts like they was a hearty meal. It's not like you, girl."

"They 'ave a secret but I don't know what."

"Who 'as a secret?"

"Brownrigg and Juxon. I overheard them speakin' in the back room of the pub. George said that I couldn't know their secret, that it was dangerous 'avin' me workin' there."

"Secret? What did they mean?" said Sam sitting forward in his chair. He winced at the pain in his leg but did his best to not let it show to his wife.

"That's just it," said Annie throwing her arms in the air, "I don't know. It's somethin' bad, I can feel it in my gut."

"Brownrigg 'as lots of secrets. Men like 'im always do," said Sam reaching for his wife's hand again. She stood and snatched her hand away. "What is it? What did I say?" said Sam looking at his wife closely. She did her best to remain composed but she knew what secrets Brownrigg had and hearing her husband say it only made her feel worse.

"You've not said anythin' wrong. I am worried that they mentioned me, like I was part of this deceit. Me! What 'ave I ever done to be dragged into such schemes?"

"I'm tellin' you, men like Brownrigg 'ave more to 'ide than most. It's probably just that 'e don't want you snooping while you are there."

"No, this is different. They 'ave done somethin' bad an' they don't want me to find out."

Sam sat bolt upright and opened his mouth to say something.

"You alright?" said Annie.

"It can't be..." he said then shook his head. It seemed that adding volume to his thoughts made them feel more ridiculous than if he'd kept them buried.

"What is it?" said Annie.

"That night I was taken," he said through dry lips, "Juxon had a strange look in his eyes. Sorta furtive and sneaky. I remarked on it at the time and he said that it was because business was bad, cos of the impress gangs."

"Go on."

"Well, 'e offered me a free drink, on the 'ouse, and Juxon's never offered anythin' free before. The man's as tight as a drum."

"An' you took this free drink?" said Annie.

"Course I did. It was free. It's just the timin' that sits at odds with me. I was about to leave when he offered it to me an' then, just after that, the Impress came in and I got took." Sam paused, then said, "If I didn't know better I'd say that he almost wanted me to stay, for whatever reason."

He looked at his wife who said, "You think 'e wanted to keep you there so the Impress could get you?"

"If I'd refused that drink, I would've been tucked up at 'ome, safe an' warm."

"If you'd not been such a fool and stormed out on me that night, you'd 'ave been tucked up warm in your bed too."

"I think I've paid the price for that act many times over," said Sam.

Letting the comment pass, Annie said, "So you're sayin' that Juxon 'ad somethin' to do with it?"

"It's a possibility, don't you think?" said Sam. Annie thought for a moment and then clicked her fingers.

"It couldn't be so. 'Ow did Juxon know you was comin' in that night in the first place?" said Annie. "If 'e planned for you to be snatched, 'e would 'ave known you was comin'. An' let's face it, you didn't go out after dark at the best of times."

Sam rested back in the chair and pondered what she had said, eventually conceding that she must be right.

"I think you was just unlucky… or careless," said Annie. "Take your pick which one."

"Okay, so he couldn't 'ave known I was there, but that look…" Sam's words trailed into silence and he stared straight ahead, deep in thought.

"William Juxon 'as the strangest look of anyone on the Point. If that's the only evidence that we 'ave to find 'im guilty then there would be a line of people waitin' to convict 'im on the basis of a strange look."

Sam sat bolt upright again and blurted out, "The girl!"

"What girl?" said Annie.

"A little girl, Hawkchurch's girl, entered the pub. She came in to get some ale for her father," said Samuel.

"And?"

"What if she warned the Impress gang? What if she was a lookout? No one would suspect a little girl."

"So you think that Juxon, or the Impress employed the services of Kitty Hawkchurch to spy on you,?" said Annie placing her hands on her hips.

"It's possible. Why else was Juxon so keen to keep me there?" said Sam. "That little girl could 'ave warned them I was there."

"And George Brownrigg?" said Annie

"What of 'im?"

"I said that Brownrigg told William that *I* – that's me, Sam – couldn't find out their secret. *Their* secret!"

"I don't see 'ow George could 'ave anythin' to do with it. I didn't see 'im that night," said Sam trying to search his memories.

"Just cos you didn't see 'im, don't mean that 'e couldn't 'ave been involved."

"That's stretching the thread a little thin in this theory, don't you think?" said Sam with a wry smile. "I admire your imagination."

"Don't make fun of me, Samuel Crowther. I knows Brownrigg better than most. 'E is capable of anythin', mark my words."

"Okay. Let's say 'e was behind it. What possible reason could 'e 'ave for getting' me pressed into service?"

"What reason would Juxon 'ave, come to that?" said Annie.

"Money. Juxon is as tight as they come. But Brownrigg…'e ain't short of brass."

"I can think of one reason," said Annie feeling sick to the core. If this line of questions followed their natural course, she would have to admit to Sam about her affair and her and Bessie moving in with Brownrigg. Maybe she had no choice and it was time he knew the truth. After all, as Mary had said, he was going to find out sooner rather than later. What if Sam was right and Juxon was behind it all it? She knew that it wasn't a massive leap to link William Juxon with George Brownrigg. It was starting to make sense and unbeknown to Sam, Annie knew that George had a very good reason for removing her husband from the scene. She took a deep breath and contemplated her next words like they were the sad ending to a love note, the sort that gets left on a table for the spurned lover to find, signifying the end of the relationship.

"What reason?" said Sam.

"Me."

"You?" he said, staring at his wife. "You?"

"Yes," snapped Annie. "Me, me, me."

"I don't understand and I'm not sure that I wanna understand. Why would George 'ave me taken because of you?"

"That night, when you stormed out, can you remember what it was about? Can you recall what it was that made you so angry?"

Sam nodded. "Remember? I'd never forget something like that. George Brownrigg," he said quietly.

Bessie stirred in the room above, calling out in her sleep. Annie rose, thankful that there was a pause in the conversation, taking the time to gather her thoughts. She climbed the ladder and peeked through the hatch at her daughter. Bessie was mumbling in her sleep and tossing. Annie pulled the covers over her child and kissed her own fingers, placing them on Bessie's face. She climbed back down the ladder and saw that Sam was standing, leaning on his chair.

"What are you doin'?" said Annie. "You'll fall. Where's your stick?"

"I wanna hear what you gotta say while I'm standin'. You ain't tellin' me somethin' an' I gets the feelin' that what you ain't tellin' is the key to everythin'"

"Sam, please, keep your voice down," said Annie. "Bessie gets precious little sleep as it is, an' I don't wanna wake her."

Sam plonked back in the chair in resignation. He had the most doleful eyes and the saddest expression that Annie wanted to scoop him into her arms and cuddle him until he begged to be released. She sat back down and said, "If I tells you, do you promise me that you won't do anythin' stupid?"

"I don't know what you're about to tell me. 'Ow can I make such a promise? Just tell me what this 'as to do with that bastard, Brownrigg?"

Annie took a deep gulp and ordered her mind. She knew what she wanted to say but not how she should say it. Her main concern was trying to explain it in a way that didn't make it look like she didn't love Sam, and that she hadn't ever given up on the prospect of him returning. "We was poor, once you'd been taken," said Annie, "You gotta understand that. Bessie an' me were starvin'"

"What's that gotta do with that man?" said Sam, ignoring the suffering of his wife.

"I'm getting' to that," she said, lowering her voice.

"Get there a bit quicker then."

"Right! We was poor, an' I 'ad no prospect of employment. It was a case of find work or go to the poor 'ouse." Annie bit back tears as she spoke and wiped her nose on the back of her sleeve. "The poor 'ouse is a shockin' place. A place of disease an' death. A place of deceitful people makin' profit from babies. I couldn't... I wouldn't take our daughter to a place like that."

"So what did you do instead?" said Sam.

"I went to Brownrigg."

"Now we get to the truth." said Sam. "What did you *do* for George?"

"I did what any woman in my position would do, I fell on 'is mercy," said Annie. "I knew 'e wanted me, but I didn't 'ave a choice." Annie wiped her eyes with her hand and sniffed. "The final straw was when Bessie got sick. I couldn't afford the doctor but Brownrigg could, an' without 'im Bessie would 'ave died. I'm sure of it."

Sam stood suddenly and toppled to the floor, landing on his bad leg and gave out a loud whine. Annie remained seated and looked the other way ignoring his plight.

"Don't you 'elp me no more?" said Sam holding out his hand for assistance.

Annie relented and stood, pulling him up. "I see the look of disgust on your face, Samuel Crowther," said Annie.

He sat back down in his chair and said, "What look would you 'ave me adopt? I 'ave just discovered that my wife shared another man while I was away." He glared at the floor.

"That's right, *while you were away!*" Annie struggled to contain her wrath. "You should know that your wife, whilst her 'usband was away, was – is – a mother first. A mother's job is to protect her child. You weren't here to aid me, so what was I to do? Let our child starve? Let her waste away while the fever squeezed the life from 'er?" It was Annie's turn to raise her voice and she banged her hand on the table. "Look me in the eye," she said. "What would you have done in my position?"

Sam shrugged and said nothing.

"Thought as much," she sneered. "I am not proud of it, but I am also not sorry. I didn't know where you were, or if you would come back at all. I couldn't sit and wait for your triumphant return. Life was goin' on, an' it was in danger of killin' me an' that little girl up there." Annie stabbed her finger towards the ladder.

"An' that's where Brownrigg comes in?" said Sam sullenly.

"It was protection, it was stability but most of all, it was about savin' our daughter."

"So you save our daughter at the risk of killin' our marriage?" Sam shuddered as he spoke, just as if the words made him physically sick.

"Killin' our marriage? The fuckin' Navy did a good job of that." Annie held her hand up. "Look at this," she said, "what do you see on that finger?" Her wedding ring glinted in the light of the fire. "That's right," said Annie. "Still there, ain't it? This ring never left my finger in all the time you were away. I needed money, food, warmth but the most precious thing I own stayed right here with me."

"But Brownrigg?" said Sam. "Of all the men."

"Oh, so another man would 'ave been fine, eh? What difference does it make which man it was? I 'ad to save our daughter an' 'e had the means."

Sam glared at his wife and she could see he was shaking with anger. The veins in his forehead pulsed and his eyes had the look of madness in them. "You filthy little whore," he spat. "You let that man 'ave is way with you, an' you only think to tell me now."

"I tell you now not outta choice. If I 'ad my way you'd still be in the dark about the whole thing."

"So you would keep up this falseness, this deceit?"

She nodded. "Tellin' you what I 'ave, I don't expect you to understand. I don't expect that for one moment there is any part of you that can find it within to look at me as a strugglin' mother an' wife, before you see me as a whore."

"What 'appened to my sweet girl? My sweet innocent girl?"

"She died on the wall of the Camber, crying her eyes out for the return of her 'usband. You think that I would 'ave chosen any of this?" A stray tear fell onto Annie's cheek. "What 'appened to my carin' 'usband? Where did 'e go?"

"I didn't ask to be taken from you," said Sam quietly.

"Neither did I," said Annie. "But you were. So fate 'as dealt us both a cruel blow, but what would you 'ave done in my position?"

Sam slumped in his chair, stared at her and shook his head. "I need time, Annie. Time to chew on this an' come to terms with it in my own way. You can understand that, can't you?"

"I just want us to be a family like we was before all this. I don't blame you for anythin', an' I hope that you feel the same. But the truth is that we were both copin' in our own way with the circumstances."

"Please fetch my stick," said her husband.

"Where are you goin'?" Annie rose and scooped up his crutch from its place by the fire side. She handed it to him and Sam snatched it from her hand.

"Where are you going?" said Annie again.

"I need some air. I need to be away from you at this moment." He stood and sucked through his teeth.

"Sam," pleaded Annie, "please sit. That leg still 'urts."

"There ain't no fuckin' leg, see?" said Sam, pointing at the place where the lower half of his limb used to be. "It ain't there. So no, my leg don't 'urt." He hobbled towards the door and opened it. The damp air rushed in and Annie shivered. The flames in the hearth, albeit dying away, suddenly sprang back into life. Sam paused before stepping through the door.

"Did Brownrigg ever say 'e loved you?"

"Never," said Annie.

"Did you ever say you loved 'im?"

"Never," she said again.

Sam Crowther stepped outside and shut the door on his wife's tears. The Point was deserted. Not even the sailors who usually staggered about the place were foolhardy enough to brave the chill that this cold night brought with such a vengeance.

Annie had no idea where he was going or what he would do. All she knew was that he had taken the news badly and she feared for his safety. She would give him some time to clear his head and then she was sure that he would return to her bosom, full of understanding and regret. That was her Sam and she knew him well enough. She settled in her chair and rested her chin in her hands. Upstairs Bessie snored in deep sleep. At least she hadn't been awake to witness the argument, thought Annie and for that she was thankful. The fire crackled and spat as the last embers of wood glowed dark and red, sending playful flames dancing along their smouldering forms.

****

Sam was hurting like he'd never hurt before. The pain in his heart was threefold the pain that he'd felt when he lost his leg. To him, the last two years had been a holiday compared with how he felt right now. He lent against the wall of the house and placed his forehead on the weathered boarding that covered the brickwork. It was cool and wet and it soothed his aching head. Tears flowed in steady gulping streams. He loved her, that much he knew, but this... this? It was Juxon who'd had him taken and it would be Juxon who would confess to Sam in person. Sam was not going to let him get away with it.

He pushed himself off the wall and made his way slowly up Bath Square towards the outer Camber. Even as he turned by *The Coal Exchange* and eventually reached the more exposed part of the Point, he walked with a purpose that had all but deserted him since his injury. On this exposed point the wind whipped in from the sea enthusiastically, carrying the drizzle that stung his face. He stared up at one hundred and two Broad Street as it perched on the very edge of the island like a diseased tooth in the blackened mouth of this whore of a place. It was a massive Georgian pile, the last house in Portsmouth, as it overlooked the Camber swathed in darkness. Sam imagined Brownrigg snoring in his bed, oblivious to the heartache that his actions had caused. Men like him didn't see the world as normal men did. To Brownrigg the world was a tree full of ripe apples and every last one was his to be plucked, regardless of the consequences. Sam imagined standing over him in the shadows and, in his imaginings, Sam still had two good legs. He could see Brownrigg's face and smell the stench of brandy as he snored like there was a thunder storm in the room. Sam knew that nothing was going to wake this man. He knew that by the time he sliced George's throat, it would be too late for Brownrigg. He might open his eyes and get a good look at his killer. Sam hoped that he would, so that he knew that revenge was sweet. In his head, he mouthed the words, 'that's for Annie, you bastard'. The sound of the wind whistling through the rigging of the ships anchored in the harbour drew him back from his murderous thoughts and he smiled. The war had changed him and he felt that change within.

"For now, I see Juxon," he whispered to himself and pressed on towards *The Camber Inn*.

Chapter Twenty-three

"You want me that bad, then fuckin' do it."

William Juxon woke with a start at the banging on the door of the pub.

"Who the 'ell is knockin' at this hour?" he grumbled as he climbed from his bed and peered into the Square. *The Camber Inn* was situated on the very edge of the Bath Square, opposite *The Coal Exchange* and next to *The Still Tavern*. A shadow moved in the street below. Juxon couldn't make out who it was, so he crept out of his bedroom and descended the stairs to the bar below. He didn't move as easily as he used to and his bones took longer to cope with the demands of his sudden leaping from the bed. He grabbed a thick club that he kept behind the counter in case of emergencies. The last time he'd felt the need to employ its use was when the *Squeeze Gut Boys* came onto the Point to cause merry hell. The banging came again, followed by the shouts of a solitary man.

"Juxon, I knows yer in there. Open this door an' face me like a man."

William recognised the voice as Sam Crowther's. *What could he want at this hour?* he thought. Juxon gripped the wooden club and reached for the top and bottom bolts. He slid them across and pulled open the door.

****

George Brownrigg stood at the window of his bed chambers and stared at the one legged shadow weaving in the road across the square. In the distance, beyond *The Still Tavern*, out into the harbour, the *Foudroyant* and *HMS Anson* dominated the seascape, framed beautifully by the winter moon. George could see that the figure below was Sam Crowther, and he listened as Sam screamed at the empty night, commanding that Juxon open up.

"That boy is going to get 'imself killed if 'e don't watch out," said George to the empty room of long shadows. He tutted and yawned. *It must be nearly one in the morning. What the hell is Crowther doing at this hour?* George knew that Sam must suspect something and, if that were true, then he feared the worst for the Crowther family, especially Annie. He was banking on her not finding out their secret, but it seemed that it was a foregone conclusion. Somehow, that one-legged fool must have worked it out. *Why don't he let sleepin' dogs lie?* he thought to himself. George saw the pub doors open and the flickering light of a single candle lit the entrance. Brownrigg could just make out the shape of William Juxon as he ushered Crowther into the pub. The door shut and all was silent.

****

"Bloody wake the 'ounds of 'ell with all that 'ollerin," snapped William as he shut the door and stared at Sam. "What is it that you need that can't wait till first light?"

Sam was incandescent with fury. He could barely contain his temper. He slammed his fist down on a nearby table and said, "It was you."

"It was me? What are you talkin' about?"

"Don't pretend you're all innocent. You knows full well to what I refer," snarled Sam.

"I don't know to what you refer, an' I say this, Samuel Crowther, you'd best be makin' yourself clear or I'll throw you out." Juxon moved towards the bar and stepped behind the counter for protection. He didn't fear the man before him. Sam was not a man of violence, and with only one leg, he wasn't much of a threat. What William didn't like was the mad eyes that stared out of Sam's skull. He hadn't seen eyes as mad as that, not in all his years working in one of the meanest, most dangerous places in the country. They had a look that said *kill*. Maybe the years of war had changed him and he wasn't the same man that had left this place all those years ago. Juxon placed the lit candle on the counter and stared at Sam.

"What 'as become of you? You are a cripple an' you bear the scars of war. Some I see an' some are not visible to the naked eye."

"I bear the scars of a war that had no right takin' me. I shouldn't have gone," said Sam, "but then you'd know all about that, wouldn't you?" He jabbed his finger at Willam and stumbled.

"Sit down before you fall down," said Juxon.

Sam shook his head and said, "I want to stand an' face you, man to man." He shifted his weight and almost fell. The only thing that stopped him was his crutch, which he managed to wedge into the floorboards, taking his weight.

"Face me? You can barely stand. Now sit down before I push you over," said Juxon. Sam fell into the nearest chair and sucked air through his gritted teeth. "Now, what is all this about? Why seek me out for special blame?"

"That night, here in the pub-you knew they were comin' for me."

"How the 'ell could I have known?" said William throwing his arms into the air. "You were 'ere with me the whole time. 'Sides, I didn't know you was gonna walk into my place that night."

"I don't know how, but I am convinced that you knew."

"You ain't talkin' nor thinkin' straight. Talk like that's gonna get your poor wife the sack."

"You doin' that to please Brownrigg? I knows that you're 'idin' somethin'. I knows that you two are tryin' to conceal a secret. An' I know it involves Annie."

"There ain't no secret." William pulled two cups from under the bar and walked to the large barrel on the shelf. He turned the stopper and dark ale flowed into both cups.

"'Ere," said Juxon, "take this and get it down your neck." He walked round the counter and slid the tankard along the table next to Sam and the liquid slopped over the side and spilled. William sat at a nearby table.

"What's this?" said Sam. "Another free drink? I remember the last free drink that you gave me. If I'd refused that drink I would 'ave been safe in me bed when the Impress came."

"So that's what you pin your argument on, is it? One free bloody drink."

"You never gave anythin' for free. Why that night?" said Sam. Juxon shifted awkwardly and Sam added, "I seen that look in your eyes before."

"What look?"

"Shifty, uncomfortable," said Sam. "Same as the look in your eyes on the night I was taken."

"So, a free drink an' a fuckin' look is what you bring forth as evidence?"

"Tell me I'm wrong," said Sam.

"Nobody other than you can be blamed for what 'appened. You alone must carry that burden." William stared at Sam and thought that he had aged beyond his years. Gone was the fresh-faced man who many women on the Point would have prized as a partner. Here before Juxon was an emaciated wretch of a man, filled with as many bad memories as he had physical scars.

"I trusted you," said Sam. "I thought you were my friend."

"I was – I am still. We needn't quarrel about what you suspect but cannot prove. I give you my word that I 'ad nothin' to do with you getting pressed into service. It was just bad luck."

"I don't believe you. I 'ad to see your face to know the truth, an' now I do, I want revenge."

"Revenge? For what? You must stop this, Sam."

"Why did you an' Brownrigg say that Annie couldn't find out your secret? What secret do you 'ide? Is Brownrigg involved?"

Juxon wagged his finger at Sam and said, "You are steppin' on dangerous territory there. Hush your mouth and look elsewhere for your retribution."

"You're scared of 'im, aren't you?" Sam smiled at William but it wasn't a joyous smile.

"Shit scared. An' so should you be. That man would kill you for lookin' at 'im the wrong way."

"I'm already dead. Look at me. I am a ghost, a spectre of a man. I ain't scared of dyin'."

"You gotta remember what you got, not what you lost. You got a wife an' child. If that ain't worth livin' for, then I don't know that you deserve either," said William.

Ignoring him completely, Sam said, "Perhaps I should go an' see Brownrigg. Get a good look at 'is face an' learn the truth. Shall I say that you sent me and that you sang like a caged canary, tellin' me everythin' that I needed to know?"

"If you do, you'll get us both killed. Think about your wife an' child. What you do is dangerous and foolhardy." William Juxon leaned forward on his elbows and said, "Annie 'as already lost you once, don't make the mistake of it bein' a second time. You won't come back to 'er if you do what you say."

"If you tell me what I want to know, I won't say another word about it." Sam placed his empty cup on the table and slid it towards the publican.

Juxon stood and yawned. He snatched the tankard up and said, "It's late." William went back behind the bar and refilled the cup, then turned to Sam and said, "This is the last one of the night. I cannot tell you what you want to 'ear."

"If you can't, then you give me no choice." Sam stood and grabbed his stick.

"Where you goin'?" said William, the panic in his voice evident to Sam's ear.

"I will wake Brownrigg an' see what he 'as to say on the matter." Sam hobbled towards the door.

Just as he placed his fingers on the handle Juxon said, "Wait!"

Sam turned and faced him. "What is it, William Juxon? Tell me, why should I wait?"

"Sit down, an' if you promise not to do anythin', I'll tell you the truth."

Sam made his way towards the chair that he'd just vacated and once more rested his bones. He hadn't quite mastered the art of sitting yet and, as he lowered himself, he fell into the chair. "The truth, mind," said Sam, narrowing his eyes at Juxon. Juxon nodded in silence and waited until Crowther was settled.

"What I say to you cannot be repeated. I cannot risk my business or my life."

"I give you my word," said Sam.

"It was me what got you snatched that night." Juxon took a huge gulp and waited for the information to sink in. He knew that if he took the blame, he stood a chance of coming out of this alive. He daren't let Sam know the whole truth, that Brownrigg had Sam removed because he had desires towards Annie. Sam would get himself killed and that wouldn't be what he or Annie wanted. He had only one option and that was to say that he was entirely to blame.

"You did this alone? Then why was Brownrigg askin' for this to be kept from Annie?"

"Brownrigg was profitin' from the Impress. Like everythin' else that 'appens 'ere, Brownrigg was gettin' 'is cut."

"Cut? How did 'e profit?" Sam could feel the veins in his temples start to pulse.

"Each pressed man had businesses or belongins and George sold 'em on for profit."

"An' what of my belongins?" said Sam. "My Annie and Bessie…. were they treated as goods, fit for sale?"

"I never intended for Annie to get 'urt," said Juxon.

"My wife fell into *his* arms, my daughter nearly starved to death and then got the fever. My family was torn apart."

"I'm sorry," nodded William Juxon.

"So what she tells me is the truth. I had hoped that this was some fabrication, a cruel joke. I see now that it was not."

William looked at the ground.

"An' she was s'posed to conjure food for the table outta thin air, was she?" continued Sam. "What did you think was gonna 'appen when you 'ad me taken?"

"I didn't think too much about it. I was told that the Impress demanded a body for their quota. George promised them a man and it was my job to deliver." William rubbed his ashen face and yawned. "I didn't know that it was gonna be you."

"So it wasn't planned? It was all left to chance?"

"When you walked in that night I 'ad all but given up on success. Rumours of the Impress 'ad cleared the streets. None other than drunkards or those what were too old braved the pubs and brandy shops. Then you walked in…" William let his words trail off and the room fell silent.

"And that's when you ruined my life," said Crowther. His words sounded hollow. "If I wasn't a cripple, so help me, I'd run you through."

"I feel so bad for what I did that I would let you too." William stood and leant across the bar, fishing for something. The glint of the blade reflected in the flame of the single candle that burned. William approached Sam and handed him the knife. "Here," he said, "now you 'ave your chance. Get the revenge that you desperately seek."

Sam reached out with a shaking hand and took the dagger. He stared at the blade, mesmerised by it, the silver surface showing him his own reflection. "You don't mean it," he said.

Juxon tore open his night gown, revealing his hairy chest. He stood before the seated Crowther and gripped Sam's arm, pushing the tip of the knife against his own chest and said, "You want me that bad, then fuckin' do it."

Sam couldn't take his eyes off the knife. He watched as it pressed against Juxon's flabby chest. All he had to do was push. One simple act and it would all be over. William Juxon would get his punishment and Sam would get his retribution. If that were so, then why did it all feel so wrong? Sam didn't want to be like this. He wasn't a killer of men; never was and never would be. The knife remained poised, indenting the skin.

"What are you waitin' for? I give you my permission to do it," said William.

Sam released his grip and the blade clattered to the floor. He drew back his hand slowly and said, "I cannot. I am no murderer."

Picking up the knife, Juxon said, "Brownrigg is a murderer, an' if you confront him he will stick you for sure. You are a good man, Sam Crowther an' I am sorry for what I did to you, but Brownrigg was not directly involved. Do you understand?"

Sam nodded in silence.

"Now it's time you left. Get on 'ome an' never speak of this again."

Crowther stood and made his way unsteadily towards the door. He was a shell of a man. Broken in so many ways and now unable to exact the revenge that had eaten him up inside. All the visions from earlier, the murderous thoughts that bobbed like a ship on an ocean of bitterness, they were no more. The ship had sunk and with it the hope of a man unable to find work, unable to avenge the wrongs that had been brought on his family in the name of profit. He opened the door without looking back, stepped into the night, and allowed the door to slam shut.

Chapter Twenty-four

Man could not fight God...

The rain fell in waves, plummeting towards the earth, driven on a determined wind. Each droplet of water exploded with such a force that, to the naked eye, they looked like thousands of tiny explosions. The wooden tiles of the ramshackle roofs that lined the Point echoed with the ringing of the raindrops and the streets were soon awash with torrents of water, rushing along inlets and gullies, finding the easiest course to the harbour and out to sea. No stars dared brave this torrent; those gentle lights that hinted at heaven's beauty were gone, hidden by the dark mass that were the storm clouds. Even the moon, usually so resplendent in all its majestic glow was dwarfed by a black carpet of cloud that settled over the Point.

Annie was starting to grow anxious at the late return of Sam. So convinced was she that he would come back once the cold air had quelled his hot temper that she waited a full thirty minutes before deciding that she should venture out. She was soaked in the deluge, but rain drenched nights were nothing new for a woman who had spent many dark hours on the harbour's edge, hoping and praying. She passed the buildings at the end of the square and rounded the corner. Up ahead she saw the faintest light in the upstairs window of George's house. Dare she go there? Dare she fall on his mercy once more? Should she try and warn him that Sam intended to act out revenge for his suspected ill doing or would that make matters worse? What if her Sam had already taken matters into his own hands and acted on his fury at Brownrigg. That thought alone was enough to send her racing towards George's front door. She banged the heavy knocker and waited.

****

Sam Crowther wandered aimlessly, away from *The Camber Inn*, heading in the direction of the gate. Confusion swam in his already swirling mind. What he had learned this evening would change his perception of the place he called home, of the people he called friends and the time stolen from his family. He balled his fists and stopped to listen to the rain drumming on his head. Ahead of him, the dark mass of the gate awaited, but where would he go? When would he stop running from the truth that he was a failed man, a cripple in a world of sneering indifference? And his wife, the one person who he should have felt for was as bad as the rest. He lifted his face to the skies and let the globules splash over his skin. It reminded him of a storm that he had witnessed whilst out at sea. He'd been on board the *HMS Raisonnable* as she approached the blockade of Brest. It was a night, much like this, only in the middle of the ocean the waves rocked and tossed the giant hull of the sixty-four gun, Ardent class ship like it was a cork in a bucket. The ship had listed dangerously as the order was given to lower the sails. Men clung to whatever they could to stay safe and alive. Animals in the hold, deep in the belly of the ship, squealed and whined in pain as they were buffered from side to side. The two ton cannons, fixed into position by their breechings, had groaned under the strain of the onslaught of the sea, battering the wooden hull. The hawse-holes, plugged with oakum, sprang leaks and sprayed salt water over the men who cowered from the fury of Mother Nature. It had been an angry cyclone, the sort that seamen feared over almost all other things. Battle and its many dangers were one thing. Man could fight man and stand a good chance of winning. The odds were at least reasonable. Man could not fight God. The wind could not be stopped with a cannonball or a musket. And many a sailor ended their days sinking to the bottom of the murky brine on a night such as this.

Sam turned away from the gate and hunched his shoulders against the wind. He headed back towards the Camber and the sea, so he failed to see the shape of his wife entering the door of his rival in love, George Brownrigg. He stood at the edge of the dock and stared into the dark swirling mass of the sea. Waves crashed against the wall and sprayed over the edge of the harbour, wetting him further. Its power mesmerised him. Sam was transfixed by its yawning depths... its blackness. Suddenly, soft words, splitting the commotion, echoed gently in his ears and Sam knew who it was that spoke. It was the voice of Bile the mid-shipman who had sunk to his death in the heat of battle. Sam listened intently as the voice grew louder...

"Just one small step, Sam. That's all it would take. One small step and then nothing. Annie would be free to live her life unburdened by a cripple and Bessie would be able to remember you as the able bodied man you once were and not the pathetic creature standing here."

"Is that you, Bile?" Sam's words carried on the wind. "Is that you come to take me?"

"You are done with life," said the spectral voice, *"life is done with you. Would you not be better letting her go back to him and his money?"*

"How can you know such things? Do you see me now as I stand here?"

"I see you always. I hear your thoughts and feel your pain. Step off, Sam and join me down here."

"Did it 'urt when you died, Bile? Will it be the same for me?"

"It was as easy as falling asleep. I'm here to make things better for you. Step off, step off and allow the waters to claim you to their bosom."

How hard can it be? thought Sam. Many men lost their lives at sea. He shuddered at the memory of Bile, so fresh and vivid in his mind and of the time he saw Royston Graystones, a cabin boy no older than twelve, sink beneath the wash, claimed by Poseidon's mighty claw as it rose and curled itself around his slight frame. At first, Sam could only see fear etched on the poor lad's face and then, just as he was claimed, his face was serene and calm, almost as if he was willing to accept his fate. Sam knew that by the time Royston sank he was unconscious and probably never knew what was happening. He knew that it couldn't be that difficult to do. Just a small step over the edge and the dark swirling mass below him would do the rest. All he had to do was close his eyes and wait for the bright light that welcomed him into the arms of his maker.

Slats of driftwood crashed against the Camber walls and foam lifted on the increasing winds and drifted like snow over Sam's face. He shuffled towards the harbour's edge, balancing on his stick and peering down. Bile's voice urged him on.

"*We are here, waiting for you,*" said Bile. "*Step off.*"

****

Inside George's house, Annie waited for him to speak. His initial greeting had been cold and disdainful. He barely summoned the will to look her in the eye. She listened to the storm slamming into the Point and thought about her poor man, out in the wet and cold, laying in some gutter, possibly in a pool of his own blood. She knew what Brownrigg was capable of and loyalty was no guarantee of safety where he was concerned. Annie knew that she'd killed her chances of ever remaining friends with George. She'd hurt him more than any other had before and he was now her enemy. But fear compelled her to see him this night. She needed to know that he hadn't done anything to Sam. Annie took a deep breath and waited for the silence to be broken.

"What do you want?" he said flatly.

"George, I need your 'elp. You ain't seen my Sam tonight, 'ave you?"

"Mr Brownrigg to the likes of you," he said, ignoring her question.

"Please. I need to find 'im," said Annie, throwing herself on his mercy, if there were any for him to give.

George said, "Why should I 'elp you?"

"'Ave you 'urt 'im?" said Annie

"Sam? Why would I 'ave done 'im 'arm? I ain't seen 'im tonight."

"You promise? Sam suspects that you 'ad somethin' to do with 'is kidnap. Said that he was gonna come and set the record straight an' get the truth."

"Like I said, I ain't 'ad cause to speak to your man."

"I need to find 'im," said Annie plonking in a chair and allowing tears to stream down her face. "I'm worried, George. 'E wasn't in the

220

best frame of mind when 'e left. I think 'e's bent on destruction an' 'e don't care."

The sight of Annie bawling her eyes out softened Brownrigg's heart a little and he placed a calming hand on her shoulder.

"I seen 'im not half hour ago, bangin' on Juxon's door an' shouting 'is mouth off."

"I saw the light in the window at the pub. Do you think that they're still there?"

George walked along the hallway and opened the front door as rain splattered his face. "Light's off in the pub. 'E must have gone."

Suddenly he called to Annie.

She raced along the hallway, squeezed past him and stepped into the street.

"Look!" called George. "I see a figure." He pointed towards the Camber and Annie followed the line of his arm. There on the edge of the harbour, the slight frame of Sam could just be made out in the squally rain and wind.

****

Sam shifted his weight onto his good leg, tossed the stick into the water and watched it sink at first then re-emerge on the violent waves that bounced and danced. It disappeared again, stolen by the surf, but Sam didn't care. He had no need for it anymore, not where he was going. He would soon be reunited with his missing limb. Sam closed his eyes and allowed himself to topple forward. He fell headfirst into the breakers and vanished under the water. The icy temperature caught his breath, gripping his chest like a tourniquet, and he found it hard to breathe. Annie's face popped into his head and instantly he regretted his decision. What was he thinking, trying to put his beautiful wife through hell again, and for what? His cowardice to deal with the troubles of life? Something struck the back of his head, slamming into him with such force that it dazed him. He could feel the back of his head stinging and knew that he was bleeding. It was a large hunk of wood, scooped from the bottom of the deep and spat out by the cruel ocean.

Sam screamed for help and tried to cling to the wooden ladder that was attached to the side of the Camber. He reached, as the swell thrust him with force into the stone blockwork and his numb fingers brushed the wooden slats. The sea dragged him back out as the waves undulated violently. He could see the wall growing farther away, as he struggled to keep his head above water.

"Annie! Please, someone, help!"

His voice was weak and barely registered above the roar of the wind and the pelting drops of rain. He called again, this time more weakly as his strength waned in the relentless grip of the freezing sea. The swell smashed him into the sea wall again, cracking his skull and knocking him unconscious. He lay face down, as inanimate as the debris that tossed and bobbed on the surface.

****

"Oh my god!" gasped Annie. "It's Sam! 'E's fallen in the water."

George pushed past her and sprinted towards the Camber. Annie followed, screaming out for her husband. As she approached the spot, she saw the still shape floating face down, tossed on the waves like the driftwood that massed in the mouth of the Camber. George Brownrigg jumped off the wall without a moment's hesitation and landed with a huge splash. Annie searched the dock for something to help George fish out her husband. She saw a pair of oars leaning against the wall of a ramshackle shed. She grabbed one and stretched it over the side, into the sea. George had managed to grab hold of Sam and had turned him on his back with his face above the surface. His pale skin seemed to glow in the darkness and she thought he was dead. Even with his immense strength, George struggled to keep his grasp on Sam from slipping and splashed like a drowning man. He disappeared below the surface and Annie thought that she might lose them both. Seeing George risk his life for a man that he must hate showed her that he was good deep down.

"Grab the oar," she yelled above the din. She lifted the oar again and splashed it into the sea beside Brownrigg's head, narrowly missing him.

He reached out and gripped the smooth wooden shaft just as he was about to disappear under the brine again.

"Pull!" he shouted through mouthfuls of salt water. "Pull, damn you!"

Annie used her last reserves of power and started to draw the oar towards dry land. Brownrigg still had hold of Sam and he still had hold of the oar. He was close enough to grip the wooden ladder that was attached to the stone blockwork on the side of the Camber wall. He let go of the oar suddenly and, as the swell thrust him towards the sea wall, he managed to get enough purchase on the ladder and there he stayed, clinging for dear life. The limp body of Sam was a dead weight in his arms and, try as he might, George couldn't get up the ladder.

"Get Juxon," he gasped in sheer exhaustion. "Be quick! I cannot hold him for long." Annie raced towards *The Camber Inn* and bashed on the door. She glanced back at the water and saw George's head just above the line of the dock. She banged again and paced the step. Suddenly a window opened above and William Juxon peered out.

"For fuck's sake, Sam, will you just go 'ome," he shouted into the darkness.

"It's Annie," she called up. "Come quick. It's George. 'E needs yer 'elp."

"What's up?"

"Come quick, George is in the water."

"In the water? What for?"

"Trying to save my Sam."

The window slammed and Annie waited for Juxon to emerge through the pub door. It flew open and he raced into the street in his bare feet.

"Where is 'e?" he said staring left and right. Annie pointed towards the spot where the ladder jutted above the sea wall and William raced over.

"George, give me your 'and," he said, reaching down and grabbing at Brownrigg's sodden night shirt.

George opened his listless eyes and stared up at William. The faintest smile traced his blue lips.

"Annie, help me get him up," called Juxon, pulling with all his might. Annie reached down and tugged with him.

"George, listen to me, I need you to climb the ladder. We can't lift you on our own," called William.

George nodded and moved his legs. His foot gained purchase on the lower rung of the ladder and, with the help of Annie and Juxon, he slowly hoisted himself and Sam up. Eventually, Brownrigg was level with the dockside and he was able to crawl onto the hard ground, dragging Sam with him. Both men rolled onto their backs. Sam's eyes were closed and there was no sign of movement, but George lay there looking up at the driving rain. He coughed up water and tried to sit but Juxon pushed him back down.

"Stay there, George. You need to get the water outta yer lungs," said William, laying him on his side. "Annie, lay Sam on his side."

"'E's not moving," she stammered. "'E's not moving. 'E's dead."

"Annie! Do as I say. Now!"

Annie turned Sam onto his side and started to copy what William was doing with George. She massaged her husband's back, pushing like she was kneading the weekly laundry in a bowl of soap and water. Sam coughed and water splashed out of his mouth. He coughed again and more sea water flowed from his lungs.

"You're alive!" yelled Annie in relief. She kissed Sam's wet lips and swept muck and seaweed from his face. He opened his eyes and stared around in confusion. He tried to speak but his throat was red raw.

"Shh," said Annie, "stay silent. Let's get you into the warm."

"George is alright," said Juxon as he sat Brownrigg up and let him wipe the dribble from his chin. Brownrigg stared at Annie and Sam, and said nothing, but the look of relief on his face that Sam was alive said it all. He smiled weakly at Annie and tried to stand, but only succeeded in toppling into William, who tried to steady him.

"Let's get them back to George's 'ouse," said Juxon to Annie, placing Brownrigg's arm across his shoulder, gently steering him in the direction of number one hundred and two. Annie managed to get Sam to his feet and followed William. Sam hobbled weakly and progress was

very slow, but eventually they reached the door of George's house and
went inside.

Chapter Twenty-five

The light was waning…

The soothing light of the dawn spilled through the dirty windows of the bed chamber. Shadows vanished as the warming yellow glow reached into every corner of the Point, banishing the memory of the night storm that had ravaged, clawed and pounded the harbour. The waves were so large that the Point was waking to a scene of water-filled streets that stretched all the way to King James Gate and the moat. Water, three feet deep, lapped at the doorways and walls of the rows of town houses that lined either side of Broad Street and Bath Square.

From his bed, Sam sat and rubbed his throat. He coughed and Annie stirred in the chair beside the bed. Slowly she opened her eyes and took a moment to familiarise herself with her surroundings. Her husband's face came into focus and she sat bolt upright.

"Where am I?" said Sam, swallowing hard and gripping the base of his throat.

"George's 'ouse on Broad Street," said Annie with a stifled yawn. She rubbed her eyes with the heel of her palm and waited for the remnants of sleep to disappear. She knew that she must have looked a sight for sore eyes as she had barely slept. Her vigil by the bed had kept her awake until almost four as she watched over her man.

"What 'appened?" said Sam

"What 'appened?" said Annie. "You ask what 'appened? You tried to drown yourself last night is what 'appened."

"I remember the voice calling to me and then I fell into the water." Sam shivered and closed his eyes briefly. "I don't remember much after that. That water was so cold that I thought my 'eart was gonna stop with the shock."

"What voice?" said Annie.

"It was Bile, returned from the deep to claim me."

"Who's Bile?"

"Young lad who died on my last ship. Fell into the sea and drowned."

"An' you 'eard 'im? It isn't possible," said Annie sitting forward in her chair. She was more worried for Sam now that he said he had heard voices.

"It don't make much sense but I swear it was 'im. Kept on tellin' me to step off an' join 'im."

"I don't understand. This ain't like you at all. Why would you want to kill yourself?"

"I thought that you an' Bessie would be better off without me. I was 'urt by what you said, by what you were forced to do in my absence." Sam avoided making eye contact with his wife. He half smiled and, in a bid to lighten the mood said, "Looks like a nice day."

Annie stood and snorted.

"A nice day that you wouldn't have seen if it weren't for the bravery and quick actions of Brownrigg and Juxon."

She saw Sam flinch at the sound of Juxon's name. "Don't speak that name to me," he growled.

"Juxon saved your life. I think you should be thankin' 'im," said Annie, staring out of the window into the street below. The Camber was a wreck, with debris floating in the still waters that remained after the sea had withdrawn at the end of the storm. Broken windows were being boarded up at *The Coal Exchange* pub and *The Union Tavern*. In the harbour, the sloop of war, *HMS Pickle*, returned with speed from the battle of Trafalgar to report on the death of Nelson, lay on her side with her main mast snapped half way along its length. Barrels and other items from inside the hull of the topsail schooner floated in the water. Further out in the bay, a captain's gig lay upside down, its dark blue livery visible above the water line. The crew of the *Fortitude* were busy rowing around the harbour scooping up the debris and supplies that had fallen into the glass-like calm sea.

"William Juxon may 'ave saved my life," said Sam, "but it was 'im what had me taken."

"You don't make any sense. What do you mean?" said Annie facing her husband and sitting back in the chair.

"It was 'im what 'ad me taken all those years ago. So you see why I'm not joyous at the sound of 'is name."

"Did he admit it then?" said Annie

"Last night in his pub. I wasn't leavin' till I 'ad answers. He said that he 'ad me snatched and that George wasn't involved." Sam threw back the sheet and tried to stand, but wobbled precariously on his good leg and flopped back onto the bed.

"You must rest. You ain't strong enough to be outta bed," said Annie

"I need to be up. Fetch my stick," he snapped.

"You threw it away last night. It is in the sea somewhere," said Annie. "What else did Juxon say?"

"'E said that George was profitin' from the Impress but 'e didn't 'ave anythin' to do with my disappearance."

"Do you believe 'im?"

"I s'pose so. Got no proof that he was behind it, 'ave I?"

"You need to thank George for savin' you last night. What 'e did was brave. The man almost drowned 'imself in the attempt to save you."

"Where is 'e now?" said Sam.

"Downstairs in 'is chambers."

"And Juxon?"

"Back at 'is place I s'pose," said Annie. She stood and dragged the sheet over her husband's chest. "Get some sleep. You need to save your energy today." She bent and kissed him on the head.

Sam gripped her by the arm and said, "I'm sorry, Annie. I wasn't thinkin' straight is all. I shouldn't 'ave done what I did."

"I ain't gonna pretend that I've forgiven you, but that's a conversation for another day," said Annie.

"It was the voice. It held me like I was in the grip of a stronger power, compellin' me to do it, tellin' me that it would all be fine if I did. I believed it, thinkin' you'd be better off without me." Sam kissed her hand and said, "I am sorry."

"I know that, but you put me through 'ell yesterday an' I never wanna go through that again. Do you understand?"

Sam nodded and let his grip loosen on her arm. She made to leave the room and just before the door shut behind her she turned and stared at her husband. As he lay there, Annie thought about their daughter and what she'd nearly lost. She saw the pained expression on Sam's face just before she left the room. What was he thinking? He must know that he was lucky to be alive and he owed his life to George? As soon as he was strong enough, she would make him make peace with Brownrigg. They were never going to be friends, but at least they could be civil to each other, especially as they shared a common bond together. That had to count for something after all?

****

The light was waning. Faces grew distant and blurred. Something was dragging him down, deeper and deeper until the sun's rays that danced on the surface of the water above felt like they were miles away. Sam wanted to swim to the surface, to kick as hard as his good leg would allow. He knew that the air in his lungs would empty soon and the cold salt water would fill his chest. Why was he sinking so far? It didn't make sense to him. Speckles of golden light danced above him and he could see the underside of the boats that criss-crossed the harbour, carrying troops, sailors, supplies and goods. *I don't want to die*, he told himself. Hadn't he promised never to try and kill himself again? Annie made him promise.

Suddenly something grabbed his leg and yanked him downwards. He stared down at the pasty face of Bile as he gripped Sam's leg. Sam kicked out with his other leg without thinking and then remembered that it shouldn't have been there, but it was. Bile's voice echoed in his head. *It's alright down here. You get used to it*. He was bloated and his skin hung to his bones like ribbons. His eye sockets, now empty, eaten by the fish, stared up at Sam, reminding him of the ghoulish masks worn by the children of Cork during snap-apple night, their version of all hallows eve. Bile smiled at him and, as he opened his mouth, a large eel slid out of the dark orifice. Sam was now face to face with the shell of Bile, the cadaver that gripped him just a human wreck of his former being, no different to the hundreds of hulls that lay in the silt and mud at the bottom of the murky brine.

"Leave me be," screamed Sam. "I want to live."

The words acted like a battering ram to the ghost of the deep. Bile's grip loosened and Sam felt himself rise slightly. He kicked again, and looking down, he noticed that his leg was no longer there.

"Let me live," he said again. "Let me live."

Further he rose, towards the warming light that grew brighter, nearer. Sam reached out and stretched every last sinew, muscle and bone towards the glow. It was changing before his eyes, morphing from dapples of radiance to firm lines. Lines that formed a face, the face of the woman that he loved. Suddenly he broke the surface of the water and warmth flooded his chilled body. He opened his eyes, took a huge gulp of air and stared wildly around him. Annie stared back, soothing his cheek with the back of her hand.

"There, there, my sweet. You were 'avin a bad dream." She smiled and her eyes twinkled with love for him.

"Oh, Annie, it was terrible," said Sam, now bathed in sweat. "I was at the bottom of the sea and couldn't get back to the top. I was being dragged down by this-this..." His words trailed off and he fell back into silence.

"It was just a dream," said Annie. "I got back 'ere an hour ago and you was fast asleep so I sat and waited. You're safe in bed."

Sam's chest rose and fell and he could feel the colour returning to his face. "I thought I was goin' to lose you," he said. "But this time I didn't see 'ow I was goin' to make it back."

"I'm right 'ere. No one is losin' anyone, not today, tomorrow nor any day," said Annie, smoothing Sam's damp hair. "I'll fetch you some water an' food," she said, standing and walking towards the door.

"You will come back?" said Sam in a state of fright. Annie nodded. "Be quick then," said Sam flopping back on the bed.

******

Three days had passed since Sam had attempted to give himself to the sea. His strength was returning and he told Annie that he was itching to get home. At first she had made sure that he was confined to bed for the most part whilst at Broad Street and now, with the help of a replacement crutch, he was exercising every day. He was capable of walking around the bed several times and spoke confidently about tackling the stairs. Annie did her best to quell his enthusiasm until she was absolutely sure that he wouldn't come to harm in his attempts to recuperate. Sam told Annie over and over that he was desperate to thank George for his kindness and bravery, and that he thought it a snub on his host's hospitality that he'd been in the house for three days and was yet to see his saviour.

******

The day was bright and sunny and it felt like the perfect time to venture to the floor below and seek out Brownrigg. Annie had said that she had some errands to run and wouldn't be there that morning. Sam was starting to get the feeling that she didn't want the two men to meet. Not just yet anyway. Sam recalled the conversation yesterday when he'd asked if she was hiding something...

"You seem awful determined to keep us apart," Sam had said balancing on his new stick. He moved slowly towards the window and faced her. The light that streamed in created a halo effect around his head and shoulders.

"I ain't tryin' to keep you apart. If you remember, it was only three days ago that you was shouting your mouth off about Brownrigg and Juxon an' I was the one what said you 'ad to thank 'im."

"But that was before I changed my opinion of the man," said Sam. "Now I owe 'im me life, girl. A thank you is the least I can do."

"An' you will, all in good time. Just not now. George is busy at the moment, what with the storm, an' keepin' business up." Annie had walked towards Sam and put her hand on his shoulder. She stared deeply into his eyes. "The Point was battered the ova night an' Brownrigg needs them pubs to stay open so that 'e can keep the customers 'appy."

"Well if not now, when? I been cooped up 'ere like I was locked in the bleedin' tower or somethin'. I yearn to see the outside world once more."

"Bloody 'ell. Two nights past you was preparin' to see your last night on this earth an' now you yearn for the outside." Annie let go of Sam and started to smooth the sheets of his bed. As she bent, Sam saw the curve of her backside and he felt something stirring down below.

"Are we alone in the 'ouse?" he'd said, moving closer to her. He rested his hand on the small of her back.

"Apart from the mice an' spiders, yes we are," said Annie without looking up.

Sam slid his fingers down her legs and between her thighs. She clamped them shut and said, "Don't be thinkin' that we're getting' up to anythin', Samuel Crowther. You ain't got the strength, an' I ain't got the time." She stood and straightened her dress, placing a small peck on the disappointed face of her husband. "Maybe later," she said with a smile...

Sam smiled, rueing that missed opportunity. He would have to pick his moments more carefully next time. He opened the door that led to the stairs and the house below. His bedroom was on the top floor and there were two further flights of stairs to negotiate before he reached the ground floor. He stretched for the hand rail and used its reassuring sturdiness to balance himself at the top of the staircase. He counted to three and started his slow descent. It was easier than he thought and soon he was on the middle floor. There was a long corridor that ran along and, after a few steps up, turned left and stretched towards the back of the house. The walls were flaking and plaster had turned to dust, leaving small piles of dirty white powder on the painted floorboards that stretched the length of the landing. An elegant spindled staircase with Georgian turned oak handrail descended to the floor below. Sam stood at the top step and listened as the house settled. Above the sound of floorboards settling and the noise of the street outside, Sam could hear voices and they sounded like they were coming from the end of the landing, up a set of small steps that led to the left. Sam made his way along and climbed the steps. The voices were getting louder. It sounded like Brownrigg was talking to a woman. The closer Sam got, the more he recognised the woman's voice as his wife's. *What was she doing here?* he asked himself. *I thought she had errands to run.* The voices were coming from behind a faded and cracked grey door at the farthest end of the corridor. He moved as quietly as he could, pressed his ear to the wooden panel and listened.

"I release you, Annie Crowther," said Brownrigg. "You are a free woman."

"What you did the other night was beyond brave. You saved the love of my life, an' I will always be in your debt," said Annie.

"The debt is settled." George moved across the room and from behind the door Sam could hear the boards squeaking under foot. "You gave me more 'appiness than you will know those few moments when we were a proper family."

"You showed kindness to me that I did not deserve, George. Takin' me an' Bess in like we was your own. That was the sweetest thing that anyone could 'ave done."

Sam caught his breath and his heart started to pound. Were his ears deceiving him, or had he just heard his wife say that she had moved in with *this* man while he was away at war? He pressed his ear to the door again.

"It was what many would 'ave done. I always loved you, you know that, don't you?"

"I didn't at first but I came to realise it. Do you remember when I said that it was a start?"

George laughed haughtily. "I do, girl. I do. An' do you remember when I said that I 'oped that you grew to love me too?"

"I was getting' there, George. I was very fond of you."

Sam's mind swirled with confusion. He stepped away from the door and turned, almost falling in the process. Slowly he made his way along the landing. *Did she just say that she was falling in love with this man? But she'd said... she'd said that she never loved him and that it was all for convenience.*

Back in the room the conversation continued...

"But Sam was always the one, wasn't 'e? Even when 'e wasn't 'ere, it was as if 'e still was." George coughed and cleared his throat. "I cannot pretend that I am 'appy with 'im bein' back. But back 'e is an' I ain't never seen you 'appier."

"Sam is the love of my life, George. You will always be in my 'eart. But Sam, he means everythin to me."

"I'm glad that he lives this day, but I make no secret of my disappointment that you are lost to me."

"Thank you for not tellin' 'im about movin' in with you."

"I did as you asked. The less Sam knows, the better."

On the landing, Sam made it to the stairs that led to his chambers. In his haste and shock he slipped on the bottom step and his stick clattered on the wooden boards. Suddenly the voices stopped. Sam picked up the pace a little and made his way to the top floor bedroom. He was half-way up when he heard footsteps thundering along the corridor. He heard George say, "There was definitely someone there. I 'eard their footsteps."

Annie's voice followed. "Maybe the 'ouse was settlin'. Maybe it was the sound of Sam upstairs movin' about."

"No, girl. This was not the ghosts of the 'ouse, nor was it Sam. There was someone outside on this landin'."

George's footsteps echoed as they descended the stairs to the ground floor. Sam made it to the top of the flight and pushed open the door to his chamber. He hobbled towards the bed and climbed on top. Annie's footsteps rattled on the stairs outside the door and then she stood in the doorway. Sam did his very best to remain calm and not show the shock or disappointment on his face.

"Was that you movin' about downstairs?" said Annie.

Sam shook his head. "I ain't brave enough to take on stairs just yet," he said.

"George thought 'e 'eard someone in the 'ouse."

"This old place creaks and groans worse than your mother's bones," laughed Sam. "Best blame the 'ouse for the noise rather than some mystery intruder. There's more to this of brick an' plaster than there is skin an' bone."

"You are right, I'm sure. But George is a nervy sort an' 'e won't be told. Get some rest, Sam. Tomorrow we go 'ome." She blew him a kiss and Sam smiled at her. As she shut the door, he was already formulating all the things he was going to do to get his revenge on Brownrigg. As far as Sam was concerned, Brownrigg had only saved his life so that he might take his in revenge. He was determined that he would see George dead before the night was over.

Chapter Twenty-six

She blew him a kiss and disappeared from view...

Annie left the house just after seven. She said that Bessie needed her tea and that Mary Abbott couldn't sit with her tonight as she was needed by Brownrigg to service the sailors that were expected on the Point. It was perfect timing and Sam found himself waving his wife away with a great big grin. Once she was gone, nothing would stray him from completing his task. He waited for the door to slam and he watched from his chamber window as Annie crossed the Camber and turned on the corner of Bath Square by the *Coal Exchange* pub. Just as she turned the corner, Annie looked back at the house and Sam waved to her from the window. She blew him a kiss and disappeared from view. Sam's heart started to thump and his mouth went dry. He didn't have a plan of how he was going to do it, but he just knew that he would. He crossed the room and fished in the pocket of his coat. Inside was the folding gully knife that he'd carried every day whilst at sea. He felt its weight in the palm of his hand and smiled. It was a trusty tool for the common sailor and it was used for everything from eating his food at night to cutting fouled rigging. Sam pulled the blade from its wooden housing and ran his finger along it. *As sharp as the day I bought her,* he thought, folding the knife away and slipping it back in his pocket.

Sam decided that the best way of tackling a man like Brownrigg was to wait until he was asleep. He couldn't take him on in a man-to-man fight. George was massive and so much stronger than Sam that he decided that he would sneak into his bedroom once the big man had slipped into a deep sleep and then he would slice him from ear to ear.

He pictured the moment in his head, the moment that the blade slid along Brownrigg's neck in a clean straight line. Sam could visualise George's eyes snapping open and his mouth flapping as he gasped for air.

Wait. That was all he had to do. Sit and bide his time and then, at the hour of his choosing, he would end the life of the man who had saved his.

The point was teeming with life. Sailors fell in and out of pubs, some with a woman on their arm, some with two. The waters of the storms had receded and there was hardly any sign of the damage from the other night. Laughter in the street caught Sam's attention and he crossed the darkened room and stared out of the window. In the doorway of the *Union Tavern*, directly opposite the house, Mary Abbott was whispering something into the ear of a grizzled old sailor. The sailor laughed and Mary slapped his arm playfully. Sam thought of Annie doing the same with George Brownrigg and it turned his stomach. He balled his fists and thought about all that had happened since he'd been gone

"Gone?" he said to the shadowed room. "I didn't leave, I was taken." The sound of his voice focused his mind. Once he'd sliced George, Juxon would be next. It was because of Juxon's action that his beautiful Annie, his innocent wife, had to resort to climbing into Brownrigg's bed. If Sam had still been around then none of this would have happened. Maybe it was William Juxon who deserved to be killed first? Maybe Sam was focusing on the wrong man? A voice in his head corrected him. She'd slept with George and that was that. There was no way that it could be said that would sweeten the sour taste it left. Of all the men it had to be him. Sam could still picture George's smug face as he sauntered past him that fateful day all those years ago.

Sam nodded in agreement with his inner voice. He knew that George deserved it. More so than the landlord of *The Camber Inn*. A heavy thud drew him away from his thoughts and he realised that it must have been the front door slamming again. He hadn't seen Annie return and hoped that she was still at their house with their daughter. He didn't want her to see what he was going to do. Sam listened for the sound of voices but the house was silent. *It must have been George then.* The thick shape of Brownrigg trudged across the square, passing Mary as she was in a deep embrace with the sailor. Sam watched as George passed the point on the Camber where Sam had tried to kill himself and Brownrigg stopped, peering over the side at the charcoal sea. He thrust his hands into his pockets and spat over the side, then turned in the direction of *The Camber Inn.*

It served Sam well if Brownrigg came home the worse for wear. If he was drunk then there would be a better chance of him succeeding in his task. Sam made his way to the bed and sat, trying to avoid toppling onto his back. He stared at the space where his leg had been and added another mental gripe to the list that was growing. Not only did Juxon have him taken, it was the battle that had claimed part of him forever. Again, that was another score that needed settling when he was ready to mete out Juxon's punishment. Sam laid back and watched the stars through the un-shuttered window. Unlike the night of the storm, Heaven's jewels were polished and on full display. The sky was alight with millions of glimmering diamonds that reminded Sam of a celestial crown. How could such beauty and wonder sit above such shit and squalor? *Such filth and ugliness in the world and yet within sight is the majesty of God and Heaven.* He pondered that through as the shadows danced on the flaked ceiling of his bedroom. Sam could feel his eyes drooping, becoming heavier. The shadows were replaced by the insides of his eyelids and he lost the fight to stay awake. The noise of the Point drifted in and out of earshot as he sank into a deep sleep.

The thud of the front door slamming snapped Sam from his slumber. He sat up a little too fast and felt the tingling sensation of giddiness. He waited for the speckles in his eyes to clear, all the while listening for sounds in the bowels of the house. He heard footsteps, not heavy enough to be George's and then the sound of small feet climbing the stairs. Sam climbed from the bed and, as quietly as he could, he made his way to the door, opening it just enough to hear more clearly. It was definitely the sound of a woman's footsteps, of that he was sure. Then he heard the sound of humming and the woman's voice was instantly recognisable as Annie's. Sam called out.

"Annie, is that you?"

"Yes. I came back for my shawl. I left it 'ere earlier."

"Is George with you?" called Sam, making his way down the stairs to the second floor to see his wife.

"No. I thought 'e was with you. 'As 'e gone out then?" said Annie staring at her husband in the dimly lit corridor.

"I saw 'im cross the square not long after you left. Went to the *Camber* for a drink."

"I would sit with you, for company like, but Bess needs me at 'ome." Annie half smiled at Sam and squeezed past him. "You gonna be alright 'ere on yer own?"

He nodded.

"I got an idea," said Annie suddenly, her eyes lighting up, "why don't I fetch the girl 'ere?"

Sam shook his head. The last thing he needed was his family in this house, this night.

"Let the poor thing rest. Fetchin' 'er at this hour will do nothing but interrupt her sleep."

"She's awake and askin' for you," said Annie.

"Tell 'er I am well and will return tomorrow," said Sam.

Annie pondered what he said for a moment and then said, "Still, George will be back soon an' maybe then you can 'ave some company."

"You've changed your tune. What happened to ''e's a busy man, Sam'?"

"My tune 'asn't changed. It's your imagination is all."

"Well, I'm lookin' forward to chattin' to George. 'E must 'ave so many stories to tell."

There was an edge to Sam's voice that rattled Annie somewhat and she said, "Is everythin' okay. You seem a bit agitated?"

"What 'ave I got to be agitated about, girl? Unless you can think of somethin'?" He stared at her and the corridor fell into silence.

"Best be getting' on," said Annie, breaking that silence, "Bessie will be wonderin' where I've got to." She kissed him on the cheek and noticed that he seemed a little wooden, somehow aloof towards her. She shook off her concerns and descended the stairs. Sam watched as she disappeared into the gloom of the stairwell and then vanished altogether. The front door slammed again and she was gone.

Sam was convinced that it would be the last time that he would see her. Once George was disposed of, he would be wanted, by both the authorities and the criminal friends of Brownrigg. So what that George was able to have his way with another man's wife? That was fine to the highest in the criminal pecking order that laid claim to running the Point, but if that husband should seek revenge, to exact punishment as befits the crime committed against him, then no, that wasn't the done thing and the criminals would surely close ranks. Sam was ready for it all. The dregs of hope that he thought would be rekindled by love were now as damp as the waters that filled the harbour.

Love! Love was just a word, given by common language. The language of man... and love could be taken away, snatched at the slightest moment, never to find its way back into your heart. And who was it that took that love? The same as gives it... man.

Sam clenched his free fist as tightly as he could. The veins in his head pulsed with anger. He didn't want to lose this wrath; it was good. It was fuel for the task ahead. He remembered when on board ship, as a fresh-faced sailor, one of the older men taking him aside and giving him guidance.

"Anger will keep you on your toes. Let it run through your veins as the blood does now. In battle, anger will be your ally. But never let it spill into rage. They are two completely different things." Then Sam had nodded at the old sailor. "Good. Now listen, Sam," he'd continued. "Rage clouds your judgement, it leads you into situations that are dangerous. You must understand that if anger gets loose and remains unchecked then it turns to rage. That's when you die."

Sam never forgot those words and, as he stood on the dark landing in George's house, he allowed the anger to run through his veins like blood. He climbed the stairs, closed the door to his bedroom and took vigil by the window, waiting for George to return.

George eventually sauntered unsteadily out of the pub and the chimes of the clock on the mantel told Sam that it was quarter to midnight. He stretched and followed Brownrigg's steps as he made his way along the Camber. A dark shape left the pub and called to George. It was Pete Bookbinder. The two men chatted for a moment then Bookbinder set off in the direction of the gate at the end of Broad Street. Sam's heart was racing. This was it. The moment that he'd been waiting for. All he had to do was bide his time. Doubts suddenly shot through his head. What if he had misheard them? What if he'd got the wrong idea? After all, Annie and Brownrigg were having the conversation long before he listened in from the other side of the door. He was about to end a man's life, and not just any man. Brownrigg was the man who'd saved his life. Was that the way you thanked someone who'd saved your life?

Sam held his balled fists to his temples and started to moan. He couldn't stop now. Not ever. He banged his clenched knuckles on his temples and tried to block out the doubts. In the street below, Brownrigg had stopped once more to have a piss. He wobbled left then right as he tried to not splash his shoes with urine. He failed and, when he was done, he wiped his boots on the backs of his trousers and shrugged. Sam's intended victim was now on the steps of his house. The front door slammed and Brownrigg was back.

Chapter Twenty-seven

A smile danced on his lips as he stared at the knife…

Heavy boots echoed on the bare boards of the hallway. Sam crept as best he could and opened the bedroom door, listening for the sounds of his intended victim's return. George stumbled up the stairs, muttering incoherently to himself about someone owing him money. Sam heard his feet thud on the landing as he made his way to his chambers. The door slammed, bouncing noise around the house and he knew that he wouldn't have to wait that long. He crept downstairs, his wooden crutch scraping on the stairs. Half-way down, he stopped and listened. George's room was silent of movement. He continued until he was outside the bedroom door, pressing his ear to the wooden panel and heard George's laboured breathing. He seemed to be asleep already. Sam's heart was now so far in his mouth that he was sure that he could reach in and touch it. He suddenly went very cold and felt like he was going to faint, so he bent double and scooped air into his lungs, closing his eyes, waiting for the dizziness to pass.

George was now snoring loudly in his room. *The time is now*, Sam told himself, *not a moment to waste*. He turned the handle and the door opened with a faint squeak, making him stop and listen. To Sam's relief, George hadn't roused from his alcohol infused slumber and snored as loudly as ever. The knife, gripped in his hand, gave him the confidence to enter the bedroom and creep towards his intended victim. George slept on his back with his head facing away from the door. He was still fully clothed and the stench of booze and sweat hung in the air, permeating from his pores. He had one boot on and the other lay on the floor where it fell. George's trousers were open, presumably from a drunken attempt to undress before he'd passed out. Sam crept in, making sure that his stick didn't make too much noise, and stood over the bed. He unfolded the blade of the gully knife and waved it over the shape before him.

"This is for my wife, the woman that you tried to steal," whispered Sam.

George stopped snoring and muttered something in his sleep, again incoherent. He suddenly threw his arm over his face and turned slightly making it difficult for Sam to get at his neck.

"Damn it," said Sam. He leaned over as far as he could on his good leg to see if there was any of Brownrigg's neck on show under his arm, but there wasn't. He would have to move it, there was nothing for it. Sam tugged on George's shirt sleeve as gently as he dare and dragged the arm back over his face. Movement in George's eyes stopped Sam in his tracks and he froze, breathing carefully through his mouth. The flickering eyelids were still and George resumed his heavy breathing once more. Sam let out a small groan and started pulling the sleeve again, dragging the arm further across George's face. The arm suddenly flopped over the edge of the bed and Brownrigg's knuckles rapped the bedroom floor. Sam held his breath as his intended victim opened his eyes and looked around.

"What's goin' on?" he said, rousing from his groggy slumber. His heavy eyes fixed on Sam's startled face and he said, "What you doin' 'ere?"

Crowther was now in a state of panic. He held the knife behind his back, keeping his composure, and said, "'Eard you come in and wanted to 'ave a word with you. But you was asleep."

George looked first at Sam's hidden arm, then at his face and said, "What you 'idin' behind your back?"

Sam shrugged and said, "Nothin'."

"Show me."

Sam held out the knife and George's eyes widened as the glint of silver danced in his expression. "And that? What's that for?" He now sounded very sober. His now alert eyes darted from Sam's face to his hand. The game was up. Sam knew it was now or never.

"I know," said Sam

George sat up, now fully awake, the misted look vanished from his face. "Know what?" he said.

"Don't try and come it with me, Brownrigg. You an' Annie is what."

"There ain't nothin' goin' on. You've got the wrong end of the stick."

"I 'eard it from your own lips. You said it in this very 'ouse."

"So there was someone there outside the door. You!"

Sam nodded. "Me. An' now, after all this time, I'm goin' to get my revenge." He waved the knife in George's face and Brownrigg moved as far away up the bed as he could.

"Listen, Sam. I didn't mean anythin' by it. She needed 'elp. You was gone an' she 'ad no one to turn to."

"What an angel you are," said Sam with a mock sincerity. He wobbled on his leg but steadied himself quickly. "The great George Brownrigg, friend to the people, helper to the husbandless."

"She needed me. Her and Bessie. They were goin' to starve. It's not like you think."

"I bet you couldn't wait for me to not be around. I seen the way that you looks at Annie. I seen the way you leer at 'er." Sam could feel the anger coursing through him and he remembered the advice he'd been given about not letting it turn to rage. He was struggling and was in danger of losing his grip on sanity.

"You went," said George. "You went, and what was the poor girl to do? Wait for her 'usband to return, or get on with 'er life?"

"Me goin' must've been so convenient for you, what with your likin' for Annie," said Sam. Suddenly a definite thought landed in his head. This was all too convenient for Brownrigg. What better way to get at the husband's wife than removing the husband.

"It was you," he said, glaring at George. "You 'ad me snatched. I don't know 'ow, but I knows it all the same."

"Don't be stupid," said George. "'Ow would I do that? You were warned by Annie that the Impress were on the prowl, an' you – that's *you*, Sam – didn't listen."

"You wanted my wife from the moment that you laid eyes on 'er. I bet you only saved me from drowning so that you would look good in 'er eyes."

"That's not true. Is this 'ow you repay me for riskin' me life? Some thank you."

"You slept with my wife. You played happy families while I was at war. What the fuck do you want me to say?" Sam suddenly swiped the knife through the air wildly at George and missed, spinning on his leg. The stick gave way, slipping on the wooden floor and Sam fell backwards. George spotted his opportunity and leapt from the bed before Sam could right himself properly. The larger man slammed into the cripple and both crashed to the ground. In the confusion, the blade sliced into George's arm and blood started to flow in thick crimson streams. Ignoring the pain, George clambered on top of Sam Crowther, pinning him to the floor under his considerable weight. Sam gasped for air and stared wildly at his captor. The knife, with its blood-stained blade, lay next to George's leg. Brownrigg reached down, picked it up and said, "Looks like you fucked up this time." A smile danced on his lips as he stared at the knife, then at Sam. "I gotta get some of me own revenge." He wiped the stained blade on the back of his sleeve and continued, "What a pity. I thought that you an' me was goin' to be friends."

"We were never friends and we never will be," spat Sam.

"Oh well, I suppose the truth will never out. It will be our little secret an' you will take it to your grave." George pointed the tip of the blade at Sam.

"So it's true. You did 'ave me taken away. It was you."

Brownrigg nodded and laughed. "Samuel Crowther, the honest man with a beautiful wife. She's far too good for the likes of you. I don't know what she sees in you anyhow."

"She sees the honour and integrity. She sees the good in me. That's what Annie does, George, she sees the good in people."

"She called it a start, did your Annie," sneered George. "She said that I 'ad softened 'er a little towards me. I am sure that if you'd not shown up, she would be Mrs Brownrigg and that pretty little girl of yours would see me as 'er father."

Sam tried to buck under the weight but George wasn't going anywhere.

"Easy now," said George. "we wouldn't want you getting' away. You might tell Annie."

"Are you goin' to kill me?"

"Yes. That much is inevitable. I'm goin' to kill you an' bury your pathetic body on Rat Island. Then I'm goin' to make it look like you done yourself in. Annie will think that her dear 'usband, 'er dear but sick in the 'ead 'usband has finally gone and topped 'imself."

The dawning realisation that Brownrigg might actually follow through with this started to seep into Sam's mind. He imagined them, George and Annie, with Bessie gripping his shovel sized hands, standing by his gravestone, dressed in their mourning finery. He pictured the little girl placing a small posy on the fresh grave and wiping away tears. He could hear George's voice telling Bessie to hush and that once they went home everything would be okay. *Forget this man*, said George. *He is no longer a part of your world.*

"She'll know," spat Sam, as his eyes bulged with rage. Pure unadulterated rage that had long since quashed anger. If Sam was going to die it wouldn't be meekly.

George laughed and shifted his weight. "How will she know? You ain't goin' to tell 'er."

"She'll work you out, an' when she does, you'll 'ave nothin'."

"I'll still 'ave life. That's more than you," said George. "I'm willin' to take that risk. Right now, your little wife thinks I'm the best damn thing on the Point... after you that is. But still, you won't be around for much longer an' then I *will* be the best thing on the Point."

Sam tried to hit George in his wounded arm but the villain was too quick, catching his flailing arm before Sam made contact. He trapped it under the weight of his meaty leg and pressed down on it with all his might. George pressed the blade of the knife against Sam's chest and said, "Stop fightin' me. It's gonna 'appen an' nothin' can be done about it."

Sam knew that the final moment was upon him. It was the end. He closed his eyes, determined that his last view on earth would not be that of George Brownrigg. Annie's face smiled back at him. How he wished he could hold her again, just one last time, and kiss his daughter.

"I love you, Annie Crowther," he whispered.

George pushed on the knife and Sam could feel the cold steel slide into his skin. He gasped at the pain, gritting his teeth so as not to give his killer the satisfaction of seeing him suffer. The blade slid easily under Brownrigg's weight and Sam tried with all his might to press his chest to the floor, away from the blade, but it did little to help. He started to feel drowsy and could feel his chest cavity fill with blood. A massive shooting pain shot through his torso as the knife reached its target and Sam arched his back, opening his mouth and letting out a gasp of air. Fibrillation-spasms started across his heart and the blood flow ceased to his other vital organs. Sam Crowther rolled his eyes in their sockets and felt the world fade, like a person vanishing in the distance. Annie's face, so fixed in his mind, was growing fainter. He tried to cling to her image mentally, but the blurring of his brain made it impossible. Sounds were muffled, like he had a pillow over his face. He struggled to breathe and the blood that had filled his chest cavity started to spill out of the wound and dribble onto the floor. Sam's last image was his Annie, walking away from him, hand in hand with his darling girl, Bessie. The sky around them was dimming, like the flame of a waning candle. There were sparkles of light filling that sky, stars that exploded with dazzling brilliance, silhouetting his fading family. Sam heard a voice, not an earthly voice, filling every inch of his head. It was Bile and he welcomed Sam as warmth flooded his being. Annie and Bessie were gone, the sky was black and then there was nothing.

****

Annie sat by the light of the fire. She couldn't sleep. Something tugged at her thoughts like an insistent child at a toy shop window. *Wake up* said a voice. *Wake up.* She sat in Sam's favourite chair with her legs drawn against her chest so that she could try and hug some warmth into her bones. The street outside was quiet. Most of the seamen had either gone back across the harbour to their ships or had bedded down in the many guest houses or inns that littered the Point.

Annie was alone in the house, save for Bessie, who slept soundly. She slept well these days, ever since Sam had come back. It was the trigger that she needed. Her faint breaths travelled down the ladder to the room below and Annie smiled. Tomorrow was the day that she was most looking forward to. She was bringing Sam back to his own home. She would care for her husband until he was back to full health. And then they would live their lives in happiness until they both grew old. Old and content.

She jumped at a knocking on the door. Mary's face appeared at the small window and waved. Annie beckoned her in and the door opened.

"Up late, sweet?" whispered Mary, stepping inside and shivering.

"Couldn't sleep."

"Me neither. Charlie's a bugger in bed. All elbows an' knees. Specially with a drink inside 'im."

"I think I can't sleep cos I got used to 'avin Sam in the bed. It's not bein' jabbed with 'is elbows that's keepin' me awake." Annie laughed and uncurled her legs from the chair.

Mary sat in the chair opposite and held her hands out towards the meagre flames of the fire. She smiled at Annie wistfully.

"What?" said Annie.

"Just lookin' at my beautiful friend," said Mary. "Who'd a thought that we'd be sittin' 'ere talkin' about Sam again, waitin' on his return in the mornin'? You are a lucky girl, Annie Crowther. Many in your position won't see the return of their men at all. Many won't even find out what 'appened to 'em."

"I know," said Annie, "I am blessed. Sam is back an' that's the best that I could 'ave wished for."

"'Ow is 'e? You know... since the other night?" said Mary, preferring to not give voice to the suicide attempt for fear of upset.

"Better, I think," said Annie with a weak smile. "'E's got demons, Mary. Some of the things that happened to 'im this last couple of years, and the war... it changes them, you know." Annie stared at the flames as they danced in the hearth.

"I can only imagine the 'orror of war. Losin' a leg as well. These things scar minds. Not like body scars that can be wrapped and treated," said Mary.

"Why would 'e want to take 'is life? Are me an' Bessie not enough? Isn't that what he wanted all those years at sea, to come 'ome to his wife and child? "

"Course it is, sweet, but you gotta draw the poison out of 'im. Whatever's in that brain of 'is – an' let's face it, it ain't a big brain, c'os men don't 'ave 'em – you need to talk to 'im an' understand the pain."

"I tried. I thought we were getting' somewhere, but yesterday he seemed more distant than ever. Like we were talkin' but there was a solid wall of brick between us. Do you know what I mean?"

"Sort of," said Mary.

"You know when you talks to Charlie an' you tells me it goes in one ear an' out the other, like there's nothin' in his 'ead."

Mary laughed loudly. "There ain't nothin' in 'is 'ead, sweet."

"I'm bein' serious. When I talked to Sam, it was as though he was miles away, in some far off land. I coulda stripped naked an' 'e wouldn't 'ave noticed."

"What time's 'e comin' 'ome?" said Mary.

"First thing, thank God."

"Don't you get nervous that 'e's up at Brownrigg's place? What with you not wantin' Sam to know an all."

"Sam knows."

"What? How does 'e know?" said Mary.

"Told 'im meself. It just happened that way. We was chattin' bout 'im disappearing and next thing I was tellin' about George. I figured that he'd find out sooner or later. At least me tellin' 'im means that it's the truth and not some exaggerated tall tale."

"What did Sam do? What did 'e say?"

"That was the night that he tried to drown 'imself."

"Shit," said Mary. "Does Sam know that you moved in with the big fella?"

"No. I couldn't bring myself to tell 'im that part. Knowin' that George an' me played man an' wife would tip 'im over the edge. I couldn't do it."

"What a fuckin' mess," said Mary.

"So you see why I think he's perfectly safe at George's? George promised me that our secret would remain so, an' I believe 'im."

"S'pose George ain't gonna save Sam an' then ruin your life. Don't see the point," said Mary. She patted Annie on the knee and stood, stretching. Her bones cracked and she winced.

"Ooh," said Annie, "you'd best be gettin' those ancient bones to bed."

"Cheeky bitch," winked Mary. "I'll pop you some grub in in the mornin'." Mary opened the front door and stared at her friend. "It'll be fine, you just wait an' see."

"I know," said Annie. "I know," she said again a little less certain, as if trying to convince herself. Mary blew her a kiss and closed the door. Annie stood and watched her through the window as she slipped into her house across Bath Square. *What a truly wonderful friend Mary is*, thought Annie. She yawned, feeling the onset of drowsiness flood her body. Trudging wearily across the bare floor, she started up the ladder to bed. Tomorrow was the start of her new life. She would nurse her husband and make him of sound mind. Annie smiled as she crawled under the blanket and cuddled into her daughter.

Tomorrow is a new day.

Chapter Twenty-eight

Even the weather couldn't dampen her disposition…

"Why's it always us?" Davey Turner dipped his oar into the silky black water and pulled the boat silently towards land. Next to him, Pete Bookbinder did the same.

"It's what we do," said Pete. "Now stop moaning, or do you wanna tell Brownrigg that you've 'ad enough?"

Davey shook his head and stared at his friend. "It's that place," he said, pointing towards their destination, Rat Island, in the near distance. "You know it scares me."

Behind the island sat Priddy's Hard, the main site for naval stores and armaments. Burrow Island, as it was officially known, was nearer to the shoreline of Gosport than it was to Portsmouth. The island was accessible at low tide via a natural banked path that led directly to it. Many prisoners of war ended their days on the island, suffering disease and injury too severe to be treated. Pete could see two bright red tunics, like lit match heads in the darkness, as a couple of Marines paced the banks of Royal Clarence Yard to the left of the island. He tapped Davey on the shoulder and pointed. Davey nodded and sank deeper into the boat. Luckily for both, the moon was cloaked in a thick layer of cloud, or they would have been lit up like a beacon. The boat glided to a halt as the bottom scraped the shingle beach that surrounded the island in the shallow waters. Both men leapt silently from the vessel and dragged it up the bank. Under a large sack cloth was the body of Sam Crowther.

"I can't believe that George killed Sam. Annie will be beside 'erself," said Davey.

"When we're done, we're to drop 'is coat and stick in the 'arbour to make it look like the man done killed 'imself proper this time."

"Why not just dump 'is body in the sea?" said Davey.

"Because," said Pete rolling his eyes, "Sam has a big gash in 'is chest that tells more of a murder than suicide. The coat will do the trick. Folks will thing the poor man 'as sunk to the bottom of the water."

"An' you don't feel bad about this?" said Davey.

"Course I do," said Pete. "I feels as bad about this as you do. Sam was a good man an' I got a soft spot for Annie and the girl, but this is what George does and business is business. Brownrigg is a man who gets what 'e wants, so shut up an' do yer job."

"Even so," said Davey, "this is all wrong. Sometimes you gotta speak out."

"I'll be sure to alert George's ear to your protest. Be sure to speak clearly now," said Pete, bending and grabbing Sam's good leg. Davey took his arms and both men hoisted him over the side of the launch.

"Light as a feather, this one," said Davey.

"Good! My back's killin' me," said Pete.

"Do you think that someday you'll be cartin' me to my grave if George takes a dislike to me an' kills me?"

"Someday? 'Ow about this day, if you don't shut the fuck up?"

"I'm bein' serious. Sooner or later someone upsets George and that's when this place takes you."

"Maybe," shrugged Pete. "Anyhow, don't be so morbid."

"Will you dig me a good grave, for old time's sake?"

"Grab the shovels," said Bookbinder, ignoring his younger friend.

Both men dragged the body off into the thick woods. They were searching for the site where they had buried Guppy. They knew that the ground would be soft there. Something moved in the undergrowth and Davey froze.

"Keep movin'," said Pete. "It's just the wildlife."

"I don't know. The stories are true about this place. Strange lights are seen at night," said Davey.

"Probably another couple of bastards like us, buryin' another body." Pete chuckled and threw down the shovel. "This'll do. I think this is where we buried Guppy."

"Looks familiar," said Davey, throwing his shovel down and lowering Sam's arms. He shook his head and said, "I still can't believe that 'e did it."

Pete pointed at Sam's lifeless form and said, "What more proof do you need? You'd do well to remember just what could 'appen if you let your tongue wag like the tail of a playful puppy. I'd advise you to consider that."

"I know," said Davey. "I don't get like this usually." He shrugged and said, "It's just that we knew this man an' we gotta look Annie in the eye an' pretend like nothin's changed."

"That's exactly what we gotta do," said Pete kicking the soil with the toe of his boot, checking for a soft patch. "You pretend like your life depends on it, Davey my boy."

Both men started to dig until there was a hole big enough to take the body. When the job was done and the hole filled, Davey sighed. "Sam was a good man. Shame really."

"Good men die just like bad ones. Sam was mixed up an' never should 'ave tried to kill George."

"Do you think 'e feels anythin' at all for the deaths?" Davey wiped his muddy hands on the back of the coat that they had taken from Sam just before they put him in the hole.

"Hard to say. If 'e don't feel anythin', then I suppose 'e's not human. Can't kill someone without there bein' some weight that sits in here." Pete pointed to his heart and prodded.

"I'm glad I'm not George. I wanted to be just like 'im once, but not no more."

"Davey," said Pete, "no one *wants* to be like George. What 'e is ain't through choice. A man like 'im 'as a black 'eart, made of cold stone."

"S'pose," said Davey. "Come on, let's get outta here. Like I said, it gives me the willies."

****

Annie banged on George's door and waited. She was in such a good mood this morning that she felt like she glowed brighter than the sun.

Even the weather couldn't dampen her disposition. Her Sam was coming home for good and that was enough to put a smile on the saddest of souls. The door opened and Brownrigg filled the space in front of her.

"Annie," he said, moving aside.

"George," beamed Annie stepping into the house and squeezing past him. She made her way to the kitchen at the back of the house and George followed.

"Is Sam up?"

"Dunno. Just woke up meself." He yawned and scratched his bristled chin.

"'Ave a skinful last night, did ya?" said Annie with a wry smile.

"'Ow do you know?"

"Cos I can smell the stale beer on your breath and you looks like shit."

"That'll be the truth of it, girl. That Juxon knows the worth of a full cup."

"That's why 'e runs the *Camber* an' not you," said Annie, heading for the door to the hallway and the stairs. As she passed George she gave him a smile. "If you ran the place the barrels would be as empty as the profits."

George nodded and said, "What's that smile for?"

"You know. Savin' my Sam was a brave thing an' today 'e comes 'ome. We are to be a family again, thanks to you." She reached out and grabbed his hand, giving it a squeeze.

"You think too much of me, girl. I ain't nothin' special."

"You mightn't think it, but to me, you'll always be the saviour that was there for my Bessie and my Sam." Annie released George's hand and left the room. Her footsteps echoed on the bare steps that led to the top floor chamber, the room where her husband was sure to be waiting. She had to pinch herself that this day had come. Three days ago her world seemed very different, but today, nothing was going to spoil her mood. Even the clouds looked like they would melt away and allow sunshine through.

Annie reached the landing and the door to Sam's room. She knocked and waited. There were no sounds that followed the knock. No movement on the bed, no sound of his stick tapping on the floorboards. She knocked again.

"Sam, it's Annie, come to take you 'ome."

There was no reply, so Annie turned the handle and stepped into the room, expecting her beloved to be in a deep sleep. The bed was unoccupied and the sheets were too smooth to have been slept in.

"Sam, are you in 'ere?" She rushed to the other side of the bed, fearful that he'd somehow fallen in the middle of the night and was unable to get up. The floor was empty. It really didn't look like the bed had been slept in at all. A winding knot of fear settled in the pit of her stomach. She didn't want to think the worst, but after the other night…

"George, come quickly!" she shouted down the stairs.

George thundered up the stairs two at a time. His footsteps were so loud he made the whole house shake.

"What is it, girl?" he said as he entered the room looking short of breath.

"Sam's not 'ere," said Annie staring at Brownrigg, wide eyed. She had the look of a woman on the brink of a breakdown. "I don't think 'e's even slept in the bed."

"Nonsense," said George placing the palm of his hand under the blanket to feel if the sheet was warm. "Maybe 'e went for an early walk?"

"With one bloody leg?" said Annie. "Something's wrong, I tell you. When did you last see 'im? "

"Same as you, just before you left last night. I went to the pub, an' the next thing I know, you're knockin' on my door." George scratched his chin and looked at Annie with a puzzled expression.

"Sam couldn't have disappeared. Not in a silent house in the middle of the night." Annie started to pace the room wringing her hands. "You must have 'eard somethin'?"

"Calm down," said George. "I was pissed when I got 'ome last night. Passed out in my clothes an' didn't wake up till early hours to take a piss. That's when I got undressed an' went back to sleep."

"I need to find 'im. I gotta bad feelin' bout this," said Annie, pushing past Brownrigg and flying down the stairs. George followed, trying to keep up. Annie rushed out of the front door, closely followed be George. She ran towards the *Union Tavern* and burst through the door. At the bar was a collection of sailors and whores, getting the hair of the dog. The landlord looked up from his seat behind the bar and smiled at Annie.

"You seen Sam?" she said. "'As anyone seen 'im?"

The landlord shook his head and took a deep draw on his pipe. "Been quiet this morning, Annie. If he comes in, I'll tell him you're looking for him."

Annie left the pub and scanned the Camber. It was quiet on the Point. Nothing unusual about that. The Point was a night time place and, as such, the day didn't really get going until after mid-day. The masts of the assembled boats just of the shoreline bobbed in the water. Next to the spot where Sam had tried to kill himself was a pile of fisherman's nets. A thought dropped into her head. It was one that she didn't want any part of and she did her best to push it away. But this thought was too strong. *What if he's killed himself?* She raced towards the water's edge and peered over the side.

George caught up with her, panting and doubling over to catch his breath. He said, "What? You think that 'e's gone an' done it?"

"I don't know what to think," said Annie, "but anythin's a possibility."

The green mass of water that stroked the sides of the Camber undulated gently as the flotsam and jetsam of harbour junk sat on the surface. Annie peered into the dark mass, trying to see anything that resembled a body. She caught a glimpse of something fair, something that looked like blonde hair and she clasped her hand to her mouth.

"I see 'im... there, under the water." She pointed and George followed her arm.

He lent as far over as he dare without falling in and said, "That's frayed rope, girl. Don't think it's Sam."

"What's that?" she squealed.

"Where?" said George scanning the depths.

"By that boat. It looks like a coat." Annie clamped her hands to her mouth once more and gasped. "Tell me it isn't."

George grabbed a long pole that lay next to the pile of nets. He reached down and tried to hook the end of the coat but failed.

"Try again!" snapped Annie.

"I'm doin' me best," said George, splashing the end of the pole back into the water and poking it under the fabric of the sodden coat. He lifted the pole and the coat was raised from the brine. George flopped it onto the dockside and Annie was onto it in a flash. She knelt down, turning it over in her hands and pressing the waterlogged cloth onto the side of her face. George knelt beside her.

"It's 'is. I know it." She looked at George and her lips started to tremble.

George placed a hand on her arm and said, "Check the pockets."

Annie fished inside the pocket that was nearest to her while George did the other one. He paused as his hand closed around a small item.

"What 'ave you found?" Annie was barely able to contain her anguish now. Large drops of water teetered on the rims of her eyes, before sliding along her long lashes and dropping onto the back of her hand.

"It's a knife," said George pulling it free from the pocket. He stared at it in the morning haze and turned it over in his hands.

"Give it to me," said Annie, holding out her hand. She opened and closed her fingers impatiently. "Please," she added.

George plonked the small wooden handled knife into her hand and sat back on his heels. He knew what the object was. He knew it well. It was the same knife that Sam had attacked him with the previous night and it was the same knife that George had plunged into Sam's heart, ending his life. He looked away, too ashamed to see the face of the woman he loved in so much pain. He stared at the rays of the morning sun dancing like sea fairies on the murky brine. They twinkled and bounced like fireflies and for a moment, George was distracted. He waited while Annie opened the knife from its wooden handle and read the initials scratched into the blade.

S.C.

Annie threw the knife on the floor as if it had scalded her hand, staring at it with wild eyes and scuttled away from it. Eventually she stopped and drew her knees up under her chin and started to moan.

"Annie?" said George, dragging himself towards her. "What is it?"

She pointed with a shaking hand at the knife. Her groans were getting louder and it sounded like she was finding her voice, in the same way that an opera singer might start low and then build, until there was a crescendo.

George picked up the blade, knowing full well whose knife it was. He didn't need to read the initials inscribed on the blade, but he did all the same, keeping up the pretence.

"Annie, this is Sam's knife and that is Sam's coat. I think – an' I don't wanna be the one to say it out loud – but Sam must 'ave drowned."

At that moment, Annie let out a curdling scream that took flight on the morning air. It echoed over the small peninsula, drawing the attention of those who had ventured out at such an early hour. *The Coal Exchange* pub emptied of its regulars, as did the drinkers in *The Union Tavern*, all came to see what the fuss was about. George grabbed Annie and squeezed her tight as her small frame shook with the uncontrollable grief.

"Shhh," whispered George in her ear. "I'm so sorry."

"He's gone!" wailed Annie. "My Sam 'as killed 'imself when 'e promised not to."

"Don't do this now. Let's get indoors."

Suddenly Annie stopped sobbing and her grief turned to anger. She bashed George with a clenched fist and pushed him away, climbing to her feet, swaying with rage.

"Bastard!" she screamed. "Bastard, bastard, bastard!" Annie clenched her fists and marched up and down the quay side. "How could 'e? After all 'e said. After all we went through. This is 'ow we get treated?" Annie spat on the ground and wiped the long dribble of saliva on her sleeve. "I 'ope you rot in 'ell, Samuel Crowther for what you've done."

"Annie, *please*. Not 'ere. It ain't the time, nor the place," said George peering around at the bemused faces of the onlookers. He rounded on them and snarled, "What? Your lives not interestin' enough that you gotta be standin' 'ere, starin' at this poor woman in her moment of grief?" He moved towards them as they scattered back into the pubs and houses. "That's it," he spat. "Get on outta it, you bunch of fuckin' leeches." George shook his fist and turned towards Annie but she was gone and the coat was gone too.

"Annie?" he said. "Annie!" This time it was his turn to scream. He rushed to the edge of the Camber and peered down, half expecting to see Annie's thick mop of dark hair floating below the surface of the water. His heart leapt when the harbour was empty. George decided to count to ten, just in case his beloved was at the bottom of the sea and might rise to the surface. He counted and still she didn't appear. He knew that she had not drowned herself and so turned towards the point, staring down Broad Street and Bath Square, both of which were fairly deserted and showed no signs of Annie Crowther.

Chapter Twenty-nine

Churning emotions like they were butter…

Annie wandered in a daze. The world around her was as flimsy as the fabric of her tattered dress. People, some she knew, passed by mouthing words to her, smiling and waving, but Annie's world was silent. She didn't know where she was going and didn't care. All she could think about was her dear dead husband. Her mind was a tumbling mess, churning emotions like they were butter. Had she missed something? Was there a sign that Sam was still intent on taking his own life? Was she such a failure as a wife that he was so desperate to be rid of this world… of her? She would never know now but it didn't stop her trying to unpick the logic of the situation all the same. Blame had to be apportioned and Annie knew that she would bear that burden fully. She could have stopped him, she could have been there, with a kind word and a shoulder to rest on. It was the least that she could have done, especially as Sam had suffered demons that she hadn't given sufficient credence to. Annie ran through the last conversations that she'd had with Sam, straining her memory for clues to his intentions, but there was nothing. He had promised her that it wouldn't happen again, that he was stupid for even trying in the first place. And yet, here she was, wandering along Broad Street, approaching King James Gate, with the world staring back at her as if through muslin cloth. Onward she pushed, intent on being as far from the harbour's edge, as far from his death place as possible.

Stanley tipped his hat towards Annie as she crossed over the small bridge that accessed the High Street and beyond. Annie muttered something barely audible to Stanley and carried on her way. She passed the square tower and turned onto the main part of the High Street. She passed Godwins Bank on the corner of Grand Parade and stumbled past a group of men who wolf whistled at her and jeered. She was oblivious to everything around her. It was as if she were frozen in grief, that time had no bearing on her situation. She felt as though the clocks had stopped ticking and she was trapped in this suspended wasteland, both physically and mentally.

****

The man watched from across the road, as Annie staggered down the High Street. He didn't want to be seen, not yet anyway, so he kept to the shadows and doorways that lined the thoroughfare. He was a reedy, wreck of a man, with scars on his face, one that ran the length of his cheek. His complexion was blackened by fire and layers of charred skin peeled from his forehead and chin. His left eye was all but closed, puffy and reddened, and he limped badly. His clothes hung from his wiry frame and there was an odour about him that was less than pleasant. As he moved along the street, passers-by gave him a wide berth, muttering behind concealing hands.

Annie was on the other side of the road, a little way up in front. The man followed, gripping the small stem of his pipe through bent and blackened teeth. Plumes of sweet smoke followed him as he made his way from window to door, sliding along the walls of the shops and pubs.

Annie looks like she's in trouble, he thought, spitting brown saliva onto the ground. He wiped his chin with his raggedy sleeve and popped his pipe back into his mouth.

Poor Annie. Poor, poor Annie.

The last time he'd seen her she'd been in fine fettle. A better specimen of womanly beauty you would scarcely find. The Annie that he watched now with all the care of a cat stalking a pigeon, was bedraggled and lost. He could see from the way she tripped along the road, staring vacantly at the world around her, that she was in the grip of some kind of madness. He pulled the collar of his tattered coat around his throat, hiding the nasty burns. He was lucky to be alive and he knew it too. If it hadn't been for the old woman and her daughter pulling him from the burning house, he would have perished. That woman nursed him to health, until he was well enough to escape his sick bed in a brief moment of isolation and venture back into the streets that he used to own. He knew these streets and the people like the back of his hand. There wasn't a pub, ale house or grog shop that he hadn't frequented, hadn't threatened or extorted money from. But now things were different for him. He was anonymous, as invisible as the air that filled his burned but grateful lungs. His face, so disfigured from the flames, was unrecognisable to those who passed him by. To them, he was a vagrant, a waif, a stray, less worthy than the scrawny cats that fed from the scraps tossed into the street. He was someone to scorn and stare down their noses at. Once, he'd been a king, like George Brownrigg on the Point. Once, the mere mention of his name had struck fear into the men and women of old Portsmouth. He had killed for money, and he had killed for the hell of it. He didn't feel anything for those who died at his hands, because that was part of living for him. He delighted in his notoriety and revelled in the fear that came at the mere mention of his name. At least he used to. Delight was no more. Fear was a thing consigned to yesterday's memory.

He moved gingerly along the path, past *The George Hotel* and peered in. He licked his lips and thought of nothing else but a cup of ale. He saw the landlord behind the bar and thought that he might venture in. The landlord knew him, the old, powerful him. Perhaps he would be recognised once more? Perhaps he had stooped so low that he might throw himself on the landlord's mercy? The reflection that stared back at him in the window made his mind up and he discarded that idea, turning instead to watch Annie's progress along the High Street.

Annie lay on the ground in a heap. Her limp body looked like a pile of rags that might be swept up and discarded. No one came to her aid, choosing instead to step over her or make a beeline around her. She was still, and he feared that she might be dead. He approached and with a great deal of pain, bent to move the dark locks of hair that covered her pretty face. He tapped her on the cheek and Annie's eyes fluttered open briefly.

She wasn't dead, just fainted.

"Annie?" said the man. "Can you 'ear me?"

Annie groaned and said something incoherent. The man thought he heard her mention a man called Sam.

"We need to get you inside. My place is round the corner." The man patted Annie's cheek again and this time she opened her eyes, staring listlessly up at him. Her face was bruised from the fall and she was cut just above her right eye.

"Can you stand up?" said the man.

Annie nodded and sat. Her face had a ghostly pallor and it took a while for her to gather herself sufficiently before attempting to stand. The man offered his long twig-like hand. His three surviving fingernails were charred black from the fire. Annie took his hand and he hoisted her to her feet. She wobbled and almost went over again, but the stranger stopped her from falling.

"Take it easy," said the man. "You've 'ad a nasty fall."

"Who...?" said Annie in confusion.

"Am I?" finished the man. "You know me. My name is not a pleasant one, I fear."

Annie shook her head and life danced back into her eyes. She snatched her hand away and took a step backwards.

"Who are you?" she said again. "You are a stranger to me."

The man removed his cap and gave a small bow. His head was half bald, his hair had been burned clean off his scalp on one side, and on the other, greasy matted locks lay against the enflamed skin like wet leaves plastered to a window pane.

"I'm Jim... Jim McDowell," said the man. "Folks round 'ere used to know me as Skinny Jim."

Chapter Thirty

"I know things, girl. Lots of interestin' things."

Annie sat in the small room fiddling with loose threads on her dress. She was starting to regret her decision to come here at all. If she hadn't been so lacking in her faculties, she would have run a mile from this man. Opposite, Skinny Jim McDowell sat staring at her in quiet contemplation, with his scrawny fingers pressed together below his chin. Even though he was a shadow of his former self, a grotesque caricature of the man he'd once been, she still feared him. The shell that carried the thoughts and deeds of the man may have been tarnished and damaged, but inside, deep within him, the heart of a cold-blooded monster still beat. She knew that he was capable of almost anything and that set her nerves on edge. His good eye, so piercing, still shone brightly with coldness, telling Annie that, inside, Jim was the same, and Annie wanted nothing more than the chance to rip out the heart of this man for what he had done to her precious Bessie. She stared back at him with steely determination, pondering her reasons for allowing him to escort her to this hovel that he called home.

"You'd like to see me dead," said Skinny, finally breaking the silence.

Annie said nothing and continued to stare at him.

"I 'ave no doubt that if I gave you the chance, you'd do me in yourself." A thin smile stretched across his lips and to Annie it looked like a grimace. "Shall I lend you my dagger? Shall I open my shirt and allow you to run me through?"

"Don't ever give me that chance, for it will be a pleasure beyond my wildest dreams to see you dead."

"Ah, behind that pretty exterior there beats the 'eart of a bitter woman," said Skinny.

"Bitter? Have you no compassion? What you did to my family, to my daughter… I could never forgive you." She narrowed her eyes and glared at the skeletal figure opposite her. "What part of you is human? I see nothing that betrays such. Are you so damaged that there is no remorse or feeling?"

"What I did was business. Nothing more, nothing less." Jim swept his arm before him theatrically to make the point. "I was never gonna see the girl 'urt. I am a bad man, but I am not without sensibilities."

"I see you have profited well from your business," said Annie staring around the spartan room.

"Alas, yes, I have fallen somewhat from my former status, I'll grant you that," said Skinny. "But things will not always be as they are."

"You took my daughter. She was terrified that she was goin' to die. She didn't sleep for a week after." Annie knew this wasn't true but didn't care. She wanted this man to know the pain he'd caused

"I did it to get back at Brownrigg. He was the target. Always was."

"So you thought upsettin' the well bein' of an innocent girl, a girl already distraught at the loss of her father, was justification for what you did?" Annie stood and made for the door. Skinny grabbed her arm as she passed and she recoiled at his touch, ripping her arm from his grip. "Keep your filthy 'ands off me," she snarled. Her eyes danced with rage.

Jim sighed and lowered his head and, for the first time, his mask of false bravado slipped. "Annie, I realise that I am abhorrent to you. It seems these days I am to so many people. But I can 'elp you."

"Help? What could you possibly do to 'elp me?"

"I know things, girl. Lots of interestin' things."

****

George Brownrigg gulped down his gin, gripping the glass tightly. It was his fourth of the morning and William Juxon was worried. He hadn't seen Brownrigg this bad. It was barely lunchtime and George was already well oiled. He lent on the bar counter and said, "What's got your thirst?"

George downed the last of the drink and slammed the glass onto the bar. He slid it towards Juxon and stared at him in silence. George's eyes were dead, devoid of expression, of feeling. William refilled his tumbler and placed it down in front of Brownrigg.

"It's fine if you don't wanna talk. I got enough gin to float a second rate ship of the line." Juxon poured himself one. "Got enough gin to drown a man, and all 'is sorrows. Judgin' by the way that you're gettin' through the stuff, I'd say that you got some pretty big sorrows to drown."

Suddenly George chuckled and said, "Drown... now there would be a thing."

"I know it's none of my business, but what's 'appened to put you in this mood?" said Juxon.

"She's gone," said George flatly. His voice was quiet and distant, like he knew what he said was the truth but he didn't believe it. He wiped his face with a listless hand and rubbed at his eyes. If William didn't know better, he'd swear that Brownrigg had been crying.

"Who's gone? You mean Annie?" said William.

George nodded.

"Mr Brownrigg... George, that's not news. She went the day that Sam came back."

"No. She's really gone. Disappeared this mornin'." George swallowed the fresh drink in one and slammed down the glass again. Juxon filled it while shaking his head in disapproval.

"Does Sam know?"

"Sam? I doubt that very much. 'E's dead." Brownrigg glared at the publican.

"Since when? What 'appened?" Juxon nearly dropped the bottle of gin.

George grabbed William's sleeve and pulled him closer. He lowered his voice and Juxon got a full blast of alcohol fumes. Brownrigg stared around the pub, and once satisfied that he wouldn't be heard, he said, "That crippled little fucker tried to run me through with a knife."

"Surely not! Not Sam. He wasn't a violent man. He was the calmest, most composed of men. Murder's not something that springs to mind where Sam's concerned."

"As I stand 'ere now, that bastard was ready to see me dead. He waited for me to fall asleep." George shook his fist.

"I ain't never seen you like this before, George. Not this bad. Somethin' more 'as 'appened to set you off like this," said Juxon. George stared at him, saying nothing. "What 'ave you done, George?"

"I 'ad no choice. I stuck 'im with it. Through the heart, and 'e's dead."

"Jesus, George! Is there no one that you won't kill to get your fuckin' way?" William pulled away from his grip and stared at him in disgust.

"I 'ad no choice. It was me or 'im, an let's face it, it was never gonna be me."

"So Annie's run away c'os you killed her 'usband? I knew that you was capable of almost anythin', but this? Killing the husband of the woman that you love... this is bad, even for you."

"She thinks 'e drowned. I 'ad the boys bury 'im on Burrow Island last night and first thing this mornin' they dropped 'is coat in the water to make it look like 'e did 'imself in."

"That poor girl," said William. "'Ain't she been through enough? First you 'ad Sam snatched away just so you could get your way with Annie and, when 'e comes back, you kills 'im."

"Like I said," George raised his voice a notch, "it wasn't planned or nothin'. It was self-defence. That man came at me with a knife. What was I supposed to do?"

"You could 'ave overpowered Sam. A one-legged man is no match for you, an' you knows it." Juxon could feel the heat of anger flush his cheeks. "I don't normally speak out of turn, but this really is the worst thing you could 'ave done.".

"I tried," said George. "But there was no reasoning with the man. He wanted me dead."

"'E 'ad one fuckin' leg. Couldn't you 'ave just pushed 'im over?"

George shrugged and emptied his glass, sliding it towards Juxon. Juxon shook his head and slid the empty vessel back.

"No more today, Mr Brownrigg. I think you've 'ad enough."

****

"What do you know?" Annie waited for Skinny to speak. The very sight of him repulsed her, so she opted to stare at the wall beyond him.

"Can you not bring yourself to look at me? Are my scars that repugnant?"

"It 'ain't the scars that repulse me. It ain't even you. It's what's inside the man that disgusts me."

Jim laughed and to Annie it seemed inappropriate. This situation didn't seem even slightly amusing to her and it made her feel even more awkward.

"What's so funny?" she said with her hands on her hips.

Skinny waved away her question and said, "Don't mind my sick humour."

"What do you know?" said Annie repeating the question. "I'm not 'ere for the company, so start talkin'."

"I know who's your friend an' who ain't."

"What do you mean by that?" Annie crossed her arms.

"There are people who ain't what they seem, is all."

"Riddles and tricks! You don't have anythin' do you, Jim?"

Annie went to leave but just as she opened the door Skinny said, "I know who's betrayed you, Annie Crowther."

Annie stopped in her tracks and turned slowly. She saw his smug face and all she could think of was hurting him. She did her best to bury the urge to scratch his eyes out and said, "Speak!" Annie took two steps back into the room. "Come on… speak and prove that you're not just a murderer, kidnapper and thief. Prove to me that you're a liar too."

"The day your daughter was taken, who was it made you leave her that day? Who insisted that you row out to the boat?"

"George Brownrigg needed the 'elp. It was my way of repayin' 'im."

"Ah, the loyal woman, ever the pet of George to the last." Skinny laughed heartily and suddenly Annie felt really uncomfortable in his presence. What was she thinking? Why had she allowed herself to be lured in by this gutless wretch?

"Don't laugh at me. You are a sorry sight, Jim. Your reign of terror is at an end and that is worth laughin' about."

"But don't you see?" Skinny clasped his long fingers together. "You need what I know. You're going to thank me when this is done."

"Never!"

"Then walk out the door. Never look back and do not enquire of me again." Jim crossed his arms and leaned back into his chair. "But be warned, you have been betrayed once and you will be again. I only 'ope that no one gets truly 'urt next time."

Annie paused and Skinny leapt on her indecision. "Accept that what I 'ave is of no use to you… or you could sit and 'ear what I 'ave to say."

She sat down on a bench near the door and said, "Tell me what you know."

"Glad that sense has prevailed. Now… where to start?" said Skinny drumming his fingers on his cracked lips.

"You said that I'd been betrayed, that someone made sure I was on that boat the day that Bessie was taken."

"So I did. Well, let's cast our minds back, shall we? Can you remember who it was that was so insistent that you board the *Sirius* that day?"

Annie thought hard, trying to recall conversations from what seemed like an age ago. She knew that George needed help with taking the supplies and goods to the ship. "I owed him for his kindness," she said. "Mary told me that. She said we needed to repay George by helping out where we could and that I should come with her to the *Sirius* and that she wouldn't take no for an answer." Annie's eyes widened at the dawning realisation. "Mary Abbott?" she said looking at Skinny and hoping her words would be greeted by a shake of the head.

His eyes lit up and she knew. "Mary Abbott," he said.

"But Mary is my friend. She 'elped me out. Got me out of a sticky patch."

"Seems that Mary 'elps quite a few people," said Skinny. "Let me tell you about your friend, your dear, sweet friend, shall I? She was in debt to me. Well, her 'usband Charlie was, to be exact."

"Mary owed you money?"

"Charlie did, an' couldn't pay. I decided, rather than cuttin' Charlie, Mary's closeness to you would be more useful. An' that's when I came up with the idea that she get you outta the way."

Annie shook her head in disbelief. "But, she was my…" Her words trailed off and she fell silent as her hand started to shake so badly that she held it still with the other.

Jim stood and crossed the small room. He placed a charred hand on her shoulder.

"So you see, Annie of the Point, we are gonna 'elp each other." Annie stared up at him and tears splashed her cheeks. "Don't go getting' yourself all upset now. This is a good day. You found out the truth about your friend and I've made a new acquaintance." Jim smiled at her and his twisted black teeth poked out.

"What do you want with me?" said Annie.

"Well, there will come a time when I shall want much with you. But for now, I want you to go back to your old life an' act like nothin 'as changed."

"Everythin's changed!" Annie stood. "This mornin' I discover that my 'usband, the man I thought loved me, 'as gone an' killed himself."

"I'm sorry to 'ear that," said Skinny looking genuinely contrite for the first time since she had met him.

"There is a human side to you," she said.

Jim chuckled. "For now my glory days are absent," he said. "I have learnt the value in bein' 'umble. But the good times will return, of that have no doubt."

"And you want me to return to normality, but for me nothin' is normal anymore. My 'usband comes back from the war an' decides to kill 'imself."

"A war that he 'ad no business bein' involved with," said Skinny.

"What do you mean?" said Annie. "Sam was impressed into service. It wasn't a choice that 'e go."

"Such a brutal thing, the Impress, and fate can be such a cruel maiden. Who knows the loaded hand that she deals. I bet Brownrigg does."

"Loaded? Do you know sumfin? Cos the way you're talkin' it seems you do. What's George gotta do with this?"

"Name me somethin' that George Brownrigg isn't involved in?"

"This wasn't George. I said didn't I, that it was the Impress? Sam was stupid, drinkin' later than normal. That's when they got 'im."

Skinny sat back down and crossed his long legs. Annie stared at his face and noticed that he really was in a bad way. He had no eyebrows and the burn marks had charred him in shades of brown and pink.

"I ain't too pretty, eh?" he said.

"You never were," retorted Annie. Little snipes gave her satisfaction, especially as she saw the smallest amount of hurt in his expression.

"I'm lucky to be alive. If it weren't for a kindly lady and 'er family, I'd be dead, burned to a cinder. George's 'andy work again."

"George saved Bessie. You took 'er, an' 'e saved my little girl from your clutches. Don't expect me to feel any sorrow for you."

"George didn't save Sam though, did 'e?"

"Why do you think Brownrigg was behind Sam's impress? What do you know?"

"Mary Abbott again, I'm afraid. She knows Juxon, an' she knows what 'appened. The night your man went to sea was the doin' of Brownrigg. Not directly, mind, but it was 'im what tipped off the Impress an' told them where Sam was." Skinny sat forward and said, "You alright, girl?"

Annie could feel her stomach start to heave. She was struggling to maintain her composure and the room started to spin. She felt her eyelids close and she struggled to open them. Annie started to rock backwards and forwards as nausea rose and fell in waves. Eventually, she slipped from the bench and landed heavily on the floor. Her last thoughts were of Mary and George and their betrayal. Was this true? Did they know more than they were telling?

When Annie came round, she was laid out on a narrow bed, with a scratchy straw filled mattress and pillow. She sat up and looked around frantically. Darkness had descended on the world and the room she found herself in was swathed in shadow. A dark shape in the chair in the corner stirred and Annie heard Jim McDowell's voice in the blackness.

"You fainted," he said. "One moment I was tellin' you about Mary an' George, an' the next you was on the floor, out cold." Jim leaned forward and the moonlight from the single window draped his emaciated face, picking out the scars and faults in a cruel way. The pale light made Skinny look like he'd been dug up from his grave and re-animated.

"Where am I?" said Annie vacantly, waiting for her eyes to adjust to the dimness.

"Still at my place. I put you in my bed... but I left your clothes on." The way Skinny said that last part of the sentence hinted to Annie of someone who had fought with their conscience about removing her clothes. She wrapped her arms around her torso and thanked her lucky stars that Skinny had decided not to take advantage of her.

"Thank you... I think," she said.

"I told you that you'd thank me when we were done. I didn't expect it this early."

"Are we done then? Is that what you wanted to tell me, that the one person I trust above all others is a cheat an' a liar, an' the man that I shared a bed with is the reason that my 'usband disappeared all that time?"

Skinny nodded and slipped his pipe into his mouth. "Just think it's right that people like us stick together. I told you I knew some interstin' stuff." He struck a match and hovered the flame over the bowl of his pipe. The tobacco crackled and glowed with plumes of sweet smoke encircling his head and filling the room. He shook out the match, plunging the space back into complete darkness, save for the glow of the burning tobacco and the moonlight through the window.

"Like us? We ain't alike, Jim McDowell. I am nothin' like you."

"Maybe you're not," said Jim with smoke billowing from his nostrils, "but now that your eyes 'ave been opened, I bet we're more alike than you think."

Annie stood and said, "It's late, an' Bessie will be wonderin' after me."

"I will be in touch," said Skinny. "You be safe, Annie of the Point, and trust no one."

"No one? Includin' you?"

"I'm the only one that you can trust. Seems odd don't it, that we two would 'ave somethin' in common? That you want to see them bastards pay for what they done to you."

"I will be speakin' with them both, you mark my words. I'm gonna see their faces an' then I'll know what you tell me is the truth. Only then will I trust you, Jim McDowell. Only then."

"You'll see that it's true, of that I 'ave no quarrel. Just be careful."

"I will. It'll take more than George Brownrigg and Mary Abbott to stop me." Annie left the room and made her way downstairs without looking back. She heard a door shut and assumed that he had gone back inside. Quickly she moved, in haste at finding out the truth and desperate to escape the same air that Skinny occupied.

Inside his room, Skinny felt a twinge of admiration for Annie. She could certainly look after herself and was a survivor. He wondered what would happen in the cold light of day, when Annie confronted the two conspirators in her life. He wished he could be there to finally see George's crushed expression. To see the man who had nearly ended his life finally having fate's hand dealt to him, and there being nothing he could do.

"You reap what you sow, George Brownrigg. What you sow…" said Jim to the empty space. He lay on the bed and sniffed the blanket that still held the scent of Annie, taking long breaths. Skinny pondered the amusing possibility that Annie would be the weapon that he used to get at George after all. Maybe there could be a future for them both? The minute that the thought entered his head, Skinny pushed it away. "Don't be a fool, man. No one will want you. You are a freak, an abomination, an' that's the price you pay for breath in your lungs."

He closed his eyes and listened to the sounds that seeped in from outside. His breathing grew laboured and slow as he slipped into a deeper sleep. Suddenly, flames licked at his eyeballs, burning the hair in his nostrils and stripping his eyebrows. He screamed and tried to sit, but the pain in his chest, from the smoke inhalation sent a bolt through his skeletal frame, knocking him back down. The stench of cooking flesh was so overpowering that it made him sick and he started to gag. His legs were on fire, and he could feel his toenails burning white hot and dropping off his toes one by one.

"Please, help me!" he screamed. As he opened his mouth, burning smoke flooded his lungs and singed his insides. He gripped his neck and gasped, sucking more smoke deep into his chest. Above his head, he could see more flames, orange and white, licking their way across the ceiling, consuming the wood as it burned. Thousands of combustions danced like a moving, living sea, rolling in on a tide of inferno. It was strangely dazzling and McDowell lay there, mesmerised.

Skinny sat bolt upright and clawed the sleep from his head. He thrashed the blanket from his battered body and stared around the room wildly. He was back in his lodgings, soaked to the core in sweat. The flames were gone and so was the smoke. His lungs didn't burn anymore and his toes weren't melting before his eyes. He gulped and held out his hand. It shook like a drunkard's hand before the first drink of the day. This was to be his curse now. Bad dreams, vivid and terrifying, forcing him to re-live that night inside the burning house, every time he closed his eyes. Jim had to suffer the bonfires of his subconscious mind, the flames of his memory, and the scorn of those who were unfortunate enough to lay eyes on him.

He couldn't have sunk any lower. At that moment he was less a man than he'd ever been.

"But tomorrow... that is a new day," he whispered to the shadows. "Tomorrow is a new day."

Chapter Thirty-one

Annie always knew what Brownrigg was capable of...

The Point was packed as Annie made her way through the gate, marching past Stanley, ignoring his cheery greeting and crossing the drawbridge over the moat. Stanley muttered something under his breath, locked the gate behind her and watched her slim frame disappear into the distance. He made a mental note to tell Mr Brownrigg in the morning that he'd seen her and that she didn't seem herself. In fact, he thought that she was positively troubled. There was something detached and aloof about her and it whet Stanley's quizzical appetite. Mr Brownrigg would hear about it for certain and that would keep him in his good books, and if there was anyone that you needed to stay on the good side of, then George Brownrigg was he.

Annie passed familiar faces as she made her way along Broad Street. She turned into Tower Alley and turned again, entering Tower Street. She passed the tiny *Black Horse Tavern*, almost barging into a swaying sailor as he fell out of the front door.

"Pardon me," he said drunkenly, watching Annie disappear down the street. "Come back, sweetheart. I got something for you." He gripped his groin and thrust at her suggestively.

Annie barely heard a word. She was wrapped up in her thoughts. What was she to do? She did think that, for the time being, she would pretend that she knew nothing. She didn't want to give her enemies the advantage of knowing what she knew. That would be her weakness and could be fatal. Why let them have the element of surprise over her and remove her advantage? It seemed strange to refer to Mary as her enemy, but she was angrier that she'd been betrayed by the woman that she thought was her friend. That's what pricked her antipathy the most, more so than George's betrayal. In her heart Annie had always known what Brownrigg was capable of. She'd seen his cruelty with her own eyes, so why should she be shocked to learn that the bastard had her husband snatched for his own gain. What stuck in her throat was the fact that she'd allowed that man inside her; that she'd been taken in by his kindness and benevolence. Was it just out of guilt that he'd done those nice things for her, or was it all part of his master plan to win her heart? She had given him what he craved and all the time he must have been laughing at her. There was a part of her that wanted to grab Sam's knife and kill them both. Just stab them in cold blood and that would be that. Annie knew that it was a bad idea the moment it entered her head. She could take the consequences of her actions. She was a grown woman, but Bessie couldn't. She needed her mother by her side, not hanging from a rope like the criminals and deserters that the authorities hanged from the round tower as a warning to those who followed similar paths.

Up ahead, Annie saw Mary, leaning against the doorframe of her small house. She clenched a pipe in her teeth and sucked smoke into her lungs. Beside her, Bessie played with a small piglet as it rolled and grunted in her lap. The scene should have lifted Annie's heart, but it did the opposite, leaving her cold and bereft of love for the woman she used to call her friend. Just the sight of her made Annie feel revulsion and rage. It took every last shred of self-control for Annie to wrench her hatred just before it boiled to the surface. She stopped and checked her reflection in a window, practising her composed expression. She had to present the old Annie to Mary or she would suspect something. She had to greet her with the warmth of the naïve, gullible Annie; the Annie who Mary thought could be used as a bargaining tool to release her own husband from his debts.

Bessie looked up and saw Annie staring down the street, motionless. She raised her arm and waved, shooing the piglet from her lap and raced towards her with her arms wide open. Her face lit up with a beaming smile. Mary looked after the running girl and saw Annie. She waved her arm in the air and Annie found herself waving back without giving it any thought. Suddenly, Bessie was upon her, launching herself at Annie with such gusto that it knocked her backwards. She gripped her daughter and hugged her close, taking in the scent of her hair. It was a familiar, reassuring smell and Annie drank it in, wrapping both arms around her for support. Eventually, Bessie let go and Annie eased her to the ground.

"Is it true, about father?" said the little girl, staring at her mother's tear stained face carefully.

It dawned on her that she'd been selfish for running away and not being there to see her daughter's reaction when she was told the terrible truth. She added it to the growing list of failures that she kept stored in her heavy heart. Annie nodded.

"Yes, child. It is." She bit back more tears and wiped her face with the heel of her palm. "He drowned himself."

Bessie blinked away her own tears. It seemed to Annie, that her daughter was trying to be brave, to be grown up so that she didn't upset her mother. Eventually, she looked up at her mother.

"Didn't he like us anymore?"

Behind her, Mary was moving towards them and Annie held out her hand and waved her away. The grief of her daughter was enough to deal with let alone the anger felt towards a former friend. Mary nodded and retraced her steps towards the house, closing her front door behind her.

Annie stared down at her daughter and shook her head. "Daddy was sick, that's all. He wasn't able to cope with the bad things that lived in here." She pointed to her head.

"What bad things?" said Bessie, sniffing.

"Let's go into the 'ouse and I can tell you all you wanna know there." Annie held out her hand and her daughter took it, giving it a gentle squeeze. Both made their way to number three Bath Square and shut the door.

****

"Annie's back!" said Mary Abbott, tapping George Brownrigg's shoulder.

George turned slowly and stared at Mary with listless, drunken eyes.

"'Ow long's 'e been like this?" said Mary to William Juxon, taking a step backwards.

"Since this mornin'. Annie disappearin' drove 'im mad. Been at it since about ten o'clock, an' 'asn't stopped." Juxon threw his hands in the air in exasperation. "Tried to stop 'im drinkin', but what George wants, George gets."

"That's right," said Brownrigg spinning round to face the barman, turning so quickly that it took a little while for his focus to catch up and he toppled sideways. Mary reached out and steadied him, to avoid him crashing into a table nearby. "What George wants, he fuckin' gets."

George composed himself, straightening his coat, slicked down his messy hair and slammed his hand on the bar. Everyone in the place jumped out of their skins. This made George laugh loudly and he did the same again, thumping the beer soaked wooden counter.

"Mr Brownrigg, Annie is back," repeated Mary in slow deliberate words. "Came back this night and sits at 'er 'ouse."

"I need to see 'er," said George, grabbing his hat from the bar, trying to place it on his head and missing. It fell to the floor. Mary and William watched as the giant of a man bent, with one arm still gripping the wooden counter. His right leg stuck out behind him as his left arm swung like the pendulum on a grandfather clock trying, but failing, to snatch up the hat. In the end Mary bent and picked it up, and handed it to him. He took it placed it on his head and straightened up.

"Time to see Annie," he said.

"I think you should see 'er in the mornin' Mr Brownrigg. You looks tired."

At the mere mention of being tired, George gave out an almighty yawn, as if on cue.

"See," said Juxon, backing Mary, "you looks like you could do with a good night's sleep. Best see 'er in the mornin', when you 'ave a clearer 'ead."

"I wanna see 'er now. I needs to explain," George stumbled backwards and barged a man at the bar, spilling his drink. George didn't even notice and the man said nothing, and moved down the bar, wiping the dregs of his drink from his sleeve.

"You look worse for wear. This ain't no way to be visitin' a lady." Mary took Brownrigg's arm and led him towards the doorway. Behind her, William Juxon held George upright, squeezing him out of the door. The wind whipped about their faces and served to sober Brownrigg up a little. Mary and William made across the square, past the Camber and up the steps of number one hundred and two. George fumbled for his keys, dropping them on the ground and muttering. Juxon searched the floor in the dark, eventually seeing a dull glint of metal in the dimness of the moon's glow and scooped them up. He slid the key in the lock and turned, pushing the door open.

Eventually, both William and Mary made it to the first floor and George's bed chamber. After a struggle, pulling off the man's boots, finally they were able to throw a blanket over him and tip toe from the room serenaded by the sound of his rattling snores. When the door was shut, Juxon said, "You did well there, Mary my girl."

"I didn't think it was the best thing if George visited Annie in 'is state, especially knowin' what Annie's been through today. If I'd known 'e was that pissed, I would've kept me mouth shut."

"You don't know the arf of it," said Juxon, turning and descending the stairs to the ground floor.

"Wait up," called Mary. "What d'ya mean, 'the arf of it'?"

"Ignore my loose tongue. I shouldn't 'ave said anythin'." William opened the front door and went to squeeze through, but Mary grabbed his sleeve.

"Are you sayin' there's more to this than meets the eye? Is that it? Is that what you're sayin'?"

"You can't know. It could get you killed," said William.

"What I already know about this fuckin' shit 'ole could get me killed, an' I can only be killed once." Mary snorted. "Another secret to add to my collection ain't gonna give me sleepless nights now, is it?"

"Not like this. This is bad, like the worst thing you ever 'eard." Juxon stared at Mary and studied her features. He looked deep into her eyes and saw that she was determined to hear what he had to say.

"Worse than some of the things I've done? I don't think so, William." Mary stared right back at the publican. "If goin' to 'ell is s'posed to scare me, I got a first class ticket and a place reserved at the head of the table next to old Lucifer 'imself."

"S'pose we all done bad, seen and 'eard bad things," said William with a shrug. He beckoned for Mary to step out of the house and pulled the door closed behind her. "Not in there," he said. He took her by the arm and led her across the Camber to the spot where Sam was supposed to have drowned.

"Where you takin' me?" she said.

"Shut up, will you? You said you wanted to know, well I gotta show you somethin' first."

The pair drew to a stop next to the large pile of fishermen's nets and Juxon pointed to the sea. "That's where 'e drowned. Found 'is coat this mornin'."

"I can't imagine what must have been goin' through 'is mind. To actually do it…" Mary shivered and stared at the dark waters. She wrapped her arms round her torso and shook her head.

"That's just it," said Juxon, "it weren't 'im what done it."

"What do you mean? Who else was it then?"

"Brownrigg." William Juxon clenched his fists and spat on the ground. He waited for Mary to gather her thoughts. Suddenly, she stared at him open mouthed.

"Brownrigg drowned Sam?" she said.

"Shh! Keep your voice down," said Juxon, staring behind him at the stragglers who swayed along the street, making their way back to lodgings after a night's drinking. "You start sayin' this shit out loud an' that'll be the end of you… an' me, no doubt."

"Sorry," whispered Mary.

"Sam didn't drown," said Juxon, leaning closer to Mary.

"But I don't understand," said Mary. "Everyone's sayin' that Sam drowned in the wash."

"That's cos George staged it that way. In 'is drunkenness I got the full confession. Told me that Sam was stabbed last night in 'is bed chamber." Juxon pointed to George's house. He let his stare linger a little longer than he intended. Mary pulled him back from his thoughts.

"Stabbed? Why did Brownrigg kill Sam?"

"Cos," William lent in closer still and their foreheads nearly touched. He lowered his voice. "an' I 'ave no way of tellin' if George is speakin' the truth, but 'e said that Sam was goin' to kill 'im first."

"Sam wouldn't kill. That man isn't…" Mary corrected herself, "*wasn't* capable of murder."

"George is adamant that it was self-defence. Davey and Pete buried the body on Burrow Island next that fella named Guppy that they was lookin' for. Sam's coat was thrown into the brine to make it look like a drownin'."

"'Ave you spoken to Davey and Pete about it yet?"

William nodded and said, "Both came in the pub earlier. I pulled them away from George an' asked them direct."

"What did they say?" said Mary.

"At first they denied it. But I knew. I could tell from the shifty way they looked at me that they was lyin'." William wiped his face with his hand and stared out towards the dark mound that was Burrow Island. "Breaks my 'eart to think that Sam's lyin' in the ground out there, all alone." Mary could see that Juxon had tears in his eyes.

"What will you do now?" she said.

"I don't know. All I know is that this fuckin' business is eatin' me up." William stabbed a finger towards the Brownrigg house. "An' 'e sleeps like a baby without a care in the world."

"Don't do anythin' stupid now," said Mary taking William by the arm and leading him away from the edge of the dock.

"I been doin' stupid things all me life," said William, "usually at the command of that man. I'm tired of all this wickedness and figure maybe this is my chance to actually do somethin' good."

"What you got in mind?"

"I should tell Annie what I know," said William, turning and making his way towards Bath Square.

"Is that a good idea?" Mary pulled Juxon to a halt and turned to face him. "Annie thinks that Sam drowned. You know that ain't the case, but – an' 'ere's where it counts – the man is still dead. Tellin 'er won't bring Sam back."

"No, but it will lighten the load on my conscience. I don't think I can keep this one quiet."

"If you tell Annie, George will kill you. You know it, an' so do I."

"Then so be it," said Juxon. "He can't kill all of us." His words were flat and Mary noted there was an air of finality in them. An air that there were to be no second chances and no more lies. Juxon strode towards the square and paused outside his pub. Mary followed closely behind.

"You seem resolute in your path, William. I ain't never seen you so."

"A sweet girl is deprived of her love, an' for what? So a bully, a murderer and cheat can 'ave his way with 'er. She shouldn't suffer this." Juxon kicked out at the side of the pub. He fell forward and rested both his hands on the weathered boarding that lined the exterior of the *Camber Inn*. Staring at the floor he said, "This is all such a mess. The whole thing." He turned towards Mary. "You are in this up to your neck as well."

"Me?"

"Yes, you. Don't be thinkin' that you're innocent. You knew that George 'ad Sam snatched."

Mary bit her lip and stared at him with wide eyes.

"I see you behind those eyes," said William, "I see the real Mary. You are no friend to that girl. If you were, you'd 'ave told 'er the truth by now."

"I can't tell the truth." Mary paced the damp cobbles. "You may be right. I may not be what I seem, but I do care for 'er."

"Horse-shit! If you did, you'd come clean."

"Okay, so maybe I need to confess. And then what? That poor girl gets even more to deal with. And that really 'elps, don't it?"

"I didn't mean to snap," said William. "It ain't you that I'm angry at." Again, he stared across the Camber at George Brownrigg's silent and dark house. "It's 'im that we should be shoutin' at. We need to do somethin' about this."

"You wanna take on Brownrigg?" said Mary. "I know you said you were tired but I didn't think you meant tired of livin'."

"This ain't a joke, woman," said Juxon with a steely expression. "That man needs to be brought down a peg. Today it's Sam that we mourn, but tomorrow it could be someone else. What if it was Charlie that was lyin' under dirt on that rat infested island?"

Mary shuddered and said, "It don't bear thinkin' about. But you can't fight 'im. Not alone."

"I was hoping that I could count on your moral support. Then I gotta work on Pete and Davey."

"That'll be a challenge," said Mary. "Both are loyal to the man. Look, let's talk about this in the mornin'. I'll drop in on Annie an' see how she is, then we can decide what to do from there."

"I will avenge Sam's death," said William. "If only to get back at Brownrigg." He turned towards the door of the pub and Mary pushed him inside.

Chapter Thirty-two

His head pounded louder than a cannon at the battle of Trafalgar ...

Annie heard footsteps approach her door, followed by a soft rapping.

"You up, sweet?" called Mary.

Annie rolled her eyes. Mary was the last person that Annie wanted to speak to. She contemplated blowing out the candle but that would be too obvious. Annie knew that if she stood face-to-face with Mary she would not hold back.

Mary called again and Annie stood, slowly making her way to the door. She clenched and un-clenched her fists to control her anger, but the sight of Mary's face through the small window by the door did little to quell her temperament. She pulled open the door and stood there staring at Mary in silence.

"Evening, sweet. Got room for another?"

"Not tonight, Mary," said Annie folding her arms. "I just wanna be on me own tonight." She went to close the door and Mary stuck her booted foot in the way.

"Ease up, girl. It's me, your old friend Mary." She beamed at Annie again. "What's 'appened is bad for us all. It fair shocked me too. I think you'd benefit from a friendly ear."

"If it's all the same to you, I'd rather not talk tonight." Annie gave Mary a weak smile and tried her best to hide the strain. Even in the obscurity of the room she knew that Mary wouldn't be fooled. Her eyes were stinging red surrounded by dark outer rings. Mary held out her hand and grabbed Annie's arm. She recoiled, snatching it back instantly, as though Mary's touch was somehow going to burn her. Annie ran her fingers over the spot where Mary had touched her.

"Is there anythin' else that troubles you?" said Mary. "You're actin' like we are strangers."

"I discovered that my 'usband would rather be dead than be with me." Annie was building her anger into a wave of fury that, once released, would be difficult to quell. "So," she said, squeezing out of the door, pushing Mary away and pulling it closed behind her so that she didn't wake her daughter, "you tell me 'ow I should be actin'?"

"I didn't mean it like that," said Mary.

"Then what did you mean? Cos I'm listenin'."

"Well... I meant... that's to say..." Mary let her words trail off.

"Thought as much," said Annie. Her fury was now uncontained and in a sick sort of way, she was enjoying this confrontation. It was very satisfying indeed. "Why don't you fuck off back to your living, breathing drunk of a man an' leave me be."

"But I wanna 'elp. You're my friend," said Mary reaching out again.

"Friend? That's rich comin' from you." There it was. Annie had said too much and now was in danger of revealing what she knew. All logic had deserted her. "And since when did you ever 'elp me?"

"I am your friend. I loves you like a sister." Mary's face bore looks of consternation and hurt, in equal measure.

"An' Bessie? You love 'er like a daughter, I s'pose?"

"You know I do," said Mary. "Why are you sayin' this to me?"

"Cos I know," said Annie glaring at her former friend.

"Know what?"

"About you an' Skinny. About Charlie's debts."

Mary gulped and the colour drained from her face. Her eyes looked panicked and Annie could read every thought in her head like they were printed on one of those public notices that were pasted to the pub walls. Mary's mouth opened and closed but no sound came out.

"What's the matter? Someone snatched your voice away?" said Annie

Eventually Mary managed to muster some sounds. "Who told you this? Was it George?"

"Did George know about it?" said Annie stepping towards Mary aggressively.

"No, but it's the sorta thing he'd tell you to break us up. It's all lies."

"Really? None of it's true then? Charlie didn't owe money to Skinny Jim?"

"Well – yes, 'e did. But that 'ad nothin' to do with Bessie bein' taken. The very thought that I was involved is madness." Mary clasped her hands together and pleaded with Annie.

"Do you still owe that money to Skinny?"

"I promise on my life that I 'ad nothin' to do with it."

"Are you free of debt now?" snapped Annie, prodding her finger at Mary. "Tell me the truth, or I will know." She stared at Mary, long and hard.

Mary nodded and her bottom lip started to tremble.

"Say it, you bitch," said Annie. "I wanna 'ear it from your lyin' filthy mouth."

"I am free of Skinny's debt," said Mary.

"Thought as much. An' why would that be, I wonder?"

Mary's shoulders slumped and the fight drained from her. "Skinny cleared 'em. Said that, because we'd done as 'e asked, we were free of his debt."

"So it's true then. The one woman that I thought I could rely on turns out to be my enemy."

Mary staggered backwards gripping her chest as if in the throes of a heart stroke. The very word seemed to drive home the situation to her. "Enemy?" she spluttered. "Enemy? Surely you don't mean that. Not after all we've been through."

"Been through?" said Annie. "After all we've been through. What exactly 'ave *you* been through, Mary? My man got snatched at the behest of Brownrigg and my daughter got snatched at the behest of my friend." Annie pushed Mary in the chest and she fell backwards, slipping on the damp cobble stones.

"It weren't like that, honest," said Mary

"What did you lose? Tell me?"

"I lost my friend," mumbled Mary with tears streaming down her face.

Annie shoved her again and this time Mary fell to the floor, hitting herself hard on the wet stones. Annie laughed hollowly and said, "You didn't lose a friend. You sold me to Skinny for silver. Friends don't do that, so don't fret about it, Mary Abbott. Tomorrow the sun will rise an' another friend will come along. After all, we seem to be two a penny to you."

"Annie, please listen to me. You have to believe me."

"I wouldn't believe another word that fell from your lips." Annie turned and pushed her front door open. Before shutting the door, she glared at Mary, who was still sat on the damp ground staring back at her with red eyes.

"I never want to see you again. And if you breathe a word of this to Bessie I will kill you." Annie slammed the door and blotted out not just the light from the small house that had spilled into the street, but the light and hope that Mary once had in her heart.

Annie pressed her back hard against the door and waited for her heart to slow its drumming beat. She bit on her lip and listened to the sounds of Mary wailing outside. Annie peeked out of the window and saw that Mary was still sitting on the floor where she'd fallen. Her face was buried in her arms and she rocked backwards and forwards with each piercing shriek. She sat there for what seemed like an age but no one came to her. The candle in the room was extinguished and Annie left Mary in darkness.

Bessie called down, "Is everythin' alright, mother?" She saw her daughter's face stare down the hatch and then she descended to the ground floor. "I 'eard a noise. Sounded like Mary," she said.

"It was Mary, my sweet. She won't be visitin' for a while," said Annie.

"Is it somethin' that I've done?"

Annie scooped up her daughter and squeezed her tightly. "Whatever gives you that impression?"

"I 'eard you shoutin', an' I 'eard my name."

Annie planted the biggest kiss on her daughter's cheek and said, "Mary is a stupid woman what did somethin' very bad. Somethin' that can't be forgiven." She placed Bessie on the ground and said, "You needn't know what, but trust me when I say, it is bad enough that she'll not be my friend anymore."

Bessie started to cry. "I love Mary," she said. "She's kind to me."

"An' I thought the same until recently. Mary 'as done bad to you an' me, so from now on, it's just us two against the world. Can you promise me that you will obey my wishes an' not speak to 'er?"

Bessie thought for a moment, looking into her mother's eyes. Eventually she nodded. "Good girl," said Annie. "Now let's get you back to sleep or else it'll be mornin'."

****

Mary waited for William Juxon to answer the door. She hadn't slept the previous night. Not after she had lost her dearest friend. But she was determined to make amends and she needed William Juxon's help. The last time they had spoken was when they had stood at the spot where Sam had supposedly drowned. Juxon was resolute in his disgust and anger for what George Brownrigg had done. She knew that he was the cause of all that was wrong with the Point and their lives. Mary was under no illusions that she had done really bad things to Annie but she wanted to prove that she could do good things for a change. Her plan was simple; find Juxon and then the two of them would search for the obvious source of Annie's information: Skinny Jim. She shivered at the prospect of meeting such a slimy, snake of a man, but needs must.

"What?" said William blinking away the brilliance of the winter sun as it hung low in the cloudless sky. The Point was enjoying an unusually crisp morning.

"I'm in," said Mary.

"In with what?"

"Gettin' back at George. I'm with you."

"Mary, I know I said I need your moral support last night, and I was angry. But I mean to bear this myself." Juxon grabbed Mary by the arm and dragged her into the bar and bolted the door. "I was resolute, and remain so, but you... you could get 'urt."

"Don't care. I am a shitty person an' I gotta do this to put things right with Annie."

Juxon grabbed Mary again and said, "Annie? What does she know?"

"She knows I was behind Bessie getting' snatched. She knows that Charlie owed money to Skinny and that 'e called in a favour."

"You 'ad the girl snatched?" William rubbed the back of his neck and stared at Mary in confusion. "But she was your best friend."

"I know. Skinny was threatenin' to run Charlie through with a knife. I 'ad no choice."

"Even so... Bessie! She's a child, Mary. You treated 'er like your own."

"I ain't proud of what I did." Mary couldn't bring herself to look at William Juxon's face and stared at the ground.

"Alright," he said. "I s'pose we all done bad things. I am no better, knowin' what I do. What did you have in mind?"

"We find Skinny Jim."

"Find Skinny?" said Juxon. "Are you mad? 'E's dead already. Saw 'im burned in a fire."

"Skinny's alive. Annie as good as told me so," said Mary. "Way I see it, Skinny is the only man that 'as the wherewithal to take on Brownrigg."

"Did she say 'e was alive?"

"Not exactly, but the things she knew were known to one man only. It has to be Skinny."

Juxon turned and raced up the stairs without warning.

"Where you goin'?" called Mary.

"Getting' dressed. We need to get lookin' and not waste another moment," yelled Juxon from his bed chamber.

He returned moments later and Mary said, "Where do we find 'im then?"

"I last time I saw 'im was at the 'ouse of a woman, on Penny Street, number fifteen I think. Chapples was 'er name. We'll start there."

****

George Brownrigg sat unsteadily on the edge of his bed. He hadn't felt this bad before, not even when he was young and carefree. He rubbed his tired, stinging eyes and pondered how he'd got back to his bed last night. The last that he could remember was someone tugging his arm and someone shoving him from behind. He supposed that Juxon had a hand in it and resolved to go and thank him later. For now, he had other matters to deal with. He needed to see Annie and salvage what was left of their relationship. He knew that he was smitten with the girl because the fact he drank enough gin to float the galleons that floated like corks on the horizon off Spithead told him so.

George stood and wobbled, throwing his arms out to his side to steady himself. When he was satisfied that he was going to remain standing, he mustered the courage to take a step forward. His head pounded louder than a cannon at the battle of Trafalgar and his mouth was so dry he was sure that he could drink the entire contents of the harbour and still have need of more. George was going to clean himself up and then go to see Annie. He stood at the window and saw that it was a clear bright morning. The sun's haze reflected on the water like it was on fire as the millions of golden flames danced on the swell. George looked out over the bay, shielding his eyes from the glare and counted the ships that lay at anchor. *One, two, three...* and then he stopped counting. There must have been twenty or thirty vessels of various sizes filling the waters that stretched from Spithead round to Priddy's Hard. As he followed the lines of ships his gaze passed Burrow Island and he stopped. George gulped and rubbed his bristled chin with a shaking hand. Sam was at the front of his mind, his stained face, white and ghostly. The more that George squeezed his eyes shut, trying to push the image away, the stronger it became. Sam stared at him with dark eyes, eyes that were lifeless. Dirt clung to Sam's face, clogging his nostrils and ears. Mud was entwined in his hair and it hung lank and heavy on his head.

"Leave me alone!" shouted George thrusting thick balled fists into his eye sockets and rubbing. "You are dead," he said.

The face melted away and Brownrigg took a long breath, letting his body relax. He opened his eyes and looked down into Broad Street and saw William Juxon and Mary Abbott rushing towards the gate.

Where are those two goin'? he thought, watching their hasty progress. He watched them as they approached the gate but that was as far as his eyesight would allow him to see and their forms melted in the distance.

George yawned and stretched. Today was a good day for new beginnings and he was confident that Annie would come back to him by the end of it.

****

"I ain't 'is keeper," said Daisy Chapples leaning on her door frame wearing next to nothing. She was a gaunt woman with dark hair that hadn't been washed in months, maybe years, and her features were thin and unfriendly. Juxon surmised that she was a woman well versed in the art of a pursed lip.

"Do you know 'is whereabouts?" said Mary.

"Last I 'eard 'e was lodgin' somewhere at the end of the street." Daisy leaned out of the door and cocked her thumb towards the end of Penny Street, leading towards the back of *The George Hotel*. It ran parallel with the High Street. "Don't expect 'im to be in a good way."

"I learned of his survival from the fire just recently," said Mary with a meagre smile.

"When you see 'im, you tell 'im that Daisy Chapples wants nothin' to do with 'im. Tell 'im that he is dead to me."

"We will pass on your message," said Juxon with a small bow. "Come, Mary, we 'ave what we want." He led Mary Abbott gently away from the house and the pair made their way towards the back of *The George Hotel*. The hotel had a gate that led into a small courtyard. This was the same route that Lord Nelson had used to slip away before embarking the *Victory* to sail to Trafalgar. To the left of the gate was a brick building that had narrow windows and a door. To the left of the door was a set of steps that climbed to the right and away from the hotel.

They led to the top of the neighbouring building and looked as shabby as anything that the pair had seen.

Juxon nodded towards them and started up the steps with Mary in tow. There was a small landing where the stairs turned right again and rose further. Here, in the corner was an old man, snoring noisily, hugging a half-empty bottle of some strong liquor. The stench of urine permeated the enclosed space and offended Mary's nostrils.

"This place is awful," said Mary holding her nose. "I ain't no queen and I'm used to smell and squalor, but this is awful."

Juxon nodded and carried on up the steps. On the top floor, there was a small window that threw welcome light into the dingy landing. At the end was a door that was ajar. The painted surface was a faded grey and the paint had peeled so much that in some parts the bare wood was visible. The bottom of the door had rotted away. Juxon pushed it and it gave out a loud squeak.

"Who is it?" said a familiar voice. "You enter at your own risk."

"Is that Skinny Jim?" said Mary, straining in the shadows of the room to see the shape that belonged to the voice. She saw something move in the corner.

"Who wants to know?" came the reply.

"William Juxon and Mary Abbott," said William.

The shape laughed, then burst into fits of coughing. "Brownrigg's people. Did 'e send you?"

"Please, is that you, Skinny?" said Mary pushing further into the room.

"Far enough," said the voice. "Now, did George send you?" he said again.

"No. We come to seek your assistance," said Juxon. He held out his hands with his palms open to show that he was unarmed. "We have no grudge with you."

"So you seek 'elp when once you would 'ave seen me burn, landlord."

"That was before I learned what I know now. I seek your 'elp, if indeed you still 'ave the stomach for it."

Once more the voice rasped a laugh and coughed. "The stomach for it, you say? Let me show you somethin' and you'd best hope *you* have the stomach for it." The shape moved into the light of the room and speckles of dust floated in the illuminated air like thousands of thunder flies. Skinny's face appeared first and Mary held her hands to her mouth and gasped. Juxon swallowed back his own cry of disgust and stared at the ghost of a human before him.

"So, you seek Jim, and behold," Skinny did his best effort of a bow, "you have found 'im."

"Indeed we 'ave," said Juxon, pulling out a chair for Mary to sit. He followed suit and the pair watched Skinny move a little closer.

"Not a pretty sight, I'll be bound," said Skinny with a humourless smile. "So, you seek my assistance?"

Mary nodded. "Brownrigg needs to go. Annie is distraught at the death of 'er 'usband."

"Such sweet friends," said Skinny. "I never knew that you cared so much for this poor creature?"

"Just because we done bad things to that girl don't mean that we can't make amends," said Mary. "Includin' you, Jim McDowell."

"Redemption… what a thing of beauty. Forgiveness too."

"Don't mock us," said Juxon. "We come to you in good faith. We ain't the only ones lookin' for a path to follow. I suppose you've considered the impact on the area if Brownrigg goes?"

"The thought has kindled ambitions, shall we say. I need to recuperate fully first."

"We can 'elp. Why not lend us your support and in return, we'll support you," said Mary.

Skinny nodded and looked out of the window. The sun's rays, although weak with the winter, still burned at his flesh through the small panes of glass.

"What's Brownrigg done that I don't know about?"

"He killed Annie's 'usband. Stabbed 'im and buried 'im on Burrow Island."

"Well," said Skinny rubbing his hands together in joy, "I knew the man had a nasty nature, but killin' a man to 'ave 'is wife, now that is delightfully cruel."

"So you see why Brownrigg has to go. It could be one of us next time," said Juxon.

"I will be in contact," said Skinny Jim, standing suddenly and gesturing William and Mary towards the door. "I'm tired and need some sleep."

"Will we 'ear from you?" said Juxon as he was ushered into the hallway at the top of the stairs.

"When the time comes I shall seek you out. Now that is my last word on the matter." Skinny slammed the rotten door and a large piece of wood snapped off the bottom and fell to the floor.

"Well," said Mary, "I suppose we do as he says."

Chapter Thirty-three

There was a slight air of relish in his voice…

"Where in the name of God is she?" muttered George as he waited for the door to number three Bath Square to open. He rapped again, this time more aggressively. Inside, Annie cowered in the upstairs room with Bessie squeezed tightly to her side. She held her finger to her lips to show Bessie that she had to be a good girl and remain silent.

"Annie Crowther?" called George in the street. "I know you're in there." He banged again, making the cowering pair jump. Tears welled up in her daughter's eyes and Annie could see the fear held in them. It hadn't been easy for the little girl. To lose her father twice was tragic and Annie marvelled at how she coped. In some strange way, the tragedy of the last couple of years had pushed them closer together.

"Annie, please," called Brownrigg. "I don't know why you're avoiding me. I only wanna help."

Annie leaned as near to the window as she dared and peered down into the street. There was a crowd gathering as the noise of George shouting attracted unwanted attention. Suddenly he looked up at the window and Annie snatched her face away hoping that he hadn't seen her. She held her breath and squeezed her eyes shut.

"I ain't gonna be made a fool of," shouted Brownrigg at the top of his voice. "I am the king of this place, an' I will not be ignored." He kicked the front door and the whole house shook but the door remained resolute in its task of blocking his access to the house. He booted it again but still it didn't budge. Annie heard voices and realised that Pete Bookbinder had arrived to try and soothe the temper of Brownrigg. She peeked out of the window once more and saw George gesticulating violently, jabbing his finger into Pete's chest. Pete simply took the abuse, knowing that he couldn't cross George, or he would meet a grisly end. After a little while, Pete led Brownrigg away, but not before George threw one last glance back at the house. Once more, Annie ducked down and hoped that he hadn't seen her. Both of them sat there, gripping each other tightly until night fall. Annie wished that she could wind back the clock, to happier times. How she ached to hold her man again and tell him that she loved him. How she ached for his scent, for his warmth.

When she was sure that it was safe Annie stood and descended the ladder to the ground floor. She opened the front door just a crack and stared out into Bath Square. The Point was quiet and few people milled about. Annie needed to get out, just for a moment, to clear her head and order her thoughts. She knew that George would come back tomorrow and if she didn't see him then, he would break the door down and drag her kicking and screaming into the street.

She slid along the line of ramshackle dwellings that ran along Bath Square leading to Tower Street and then Tower Alley. Two sailors whistled at her as she passed, one of them shouting out, "Come 'ere, darlin'. I ain't never seen such beauty in such an ugly place."

His companion said, "Is you an angel fallen from the sky an' lost?" He thumped his pal on the arm and grabbed his crotch. "This needs an' 'ome as much as you, sweet angel."

Annie ignored them and carried on down Tower Alley, which linked Broad Street and Bath Square. The passage was so narrow that it was barely wide enough for an average sized person to fit down. A shadowy figure approached Annie as she squeezed along Bathing Lane. There was something familiar about this person's shape. How they walked slowly and deliberately, hunched over and looking like they were in pain. The figure was wrapped in a dark blanket, covering its head and torso, but even so, Annie could make out the basic shape and knew that this person was emaciated, almost gaunt. There was only one person that fitted that description.

"Is that you, Skinny?" she called out quietly.

The figure stopped and raised its head. Slowly, the covering that masked its features slid away and Annie could see the scarred face of Skinny Jim. He held a finger to his lips and moved slowly towards her.

"You mustn't alert anyone to my presence," he said, staring at her with his one good eye. "I am dead in the eyes of my enemies and I would like it to remain that way for the time being."

"But George will soon know that you are alive. Specially when you kills 'im," said Annie.

"Not *I*," said Jim, "but more like *you*."

"Me?" said Annie, "I haven't the stomach for such violence."

"Oh you will when you learn what I have this day."

"What is it that you know?" said Annie.

"Sam didn't drown. He was killed," said Skinny. There was a slight air of relish in his voice, as if imparting this information not only struck a blow for Brownrigg but also for Annie.

Annie felt her knees buckle and she reached out to steady herself against the wall of the house that lined the narrow stretch of road.

"Killed? I don't understand." Her head swam with images of Sam and she felt sick. Her stomach rose and fell like a wild sea and she doubled over, gagging as its contents splashed on the cobbles next to her feet. *Killed? How could this be... and who could have done such a thing?* One man's name popped into her head and instantly she knew who was capable of such an act. It was obvious to her now. The man who had gone to such lengths to have Sam removed from the Point had now resorted to the ultimate act to have her Sam silenced forever. Well, he wouldn't be silenced and Annie would have her revenge. She could feel anger coursing through her like she had swallowed red hot coals and they were snaking their way to the pit of her stomach. She clenched her fists and straightened up to face Skinny.

"Brownrigg did it, didn't he?" she said.

"He did," said Skinny Jim.

"How did Sam die?"

"Mary Abbott and William Juxon tells me that he was stabbed and buried on Burrow Island. He lays there now, food for the worms and such like."

"Mary and William came to see you? Why?"

"They seem to 'ave designs on doin' Brownrigg in themselves. Seems that he ain't too careful about who 'e pisses off."

"So they knew all along that Sam wasn't drowned?" Annie could feel the anger in her stomach turn up a notch and she started to shake. *How dare they not tell me? And to think that I once counted them both as friends.* Once she had dealt with George, she vowed to turn her attention towards them. They would not get away with it.

"I don't often speak up for others but them two came to see me out of guilt. If there's one thing I knows about, it's guilt. I think they were tryin' to make amends."

"It's too late for that," spat Annie.

"Careful now," said Skinny. "A word of advice; Juxon is a connected man and would be a good ally in this place. Mary ain't worth shit, but Juxon… that's another thing all together. And remember, he did come to see me to solicit my 'elp."

"I would see them both dead," said Annie. "I would see them buried on that God forsaken island."

Skinny nodded and said, "You say that you have not the stomach for violence? How about now?"

"I would gladly stab Brownrigg while he slept. I would rip out his eyes and cut out his tongue. I would cut off his cock and feed it to the chickens in the yard."

"So, Annie of the Point, you have the stomach for death, but the method you choose is vulgar and dangerous."

"How else would I kill 'im?"

"Poison is so much crueller. And men like Brownrigg deserve to be poisoned."

"Where would I get such a thing? Unlike you, I am not steeped in a world where death and violence are commonplace," said Annie.

"Open your 'and," said Skinny.

She did as she was told and a small folded paper envelope landed in her palm. She examined it closely and said, "What's this?"

"Be very careful, Annie. That is white Arsenic. Sprinkle the powder into 'is ale and 'e will know its effects."

"Won't 'e suspect somethin's wrong?"

Skinny shook his head. "That's the beauty of the stuff. It's tasteless, odourless and colourless. 'E won't know a thing about it until it's too late."

"When shall I do it?" said Annie, sliding the package between her breasts, concealing it in her dress. Skinny's good eye lit up as he watched her.

"You must do it tonight," he said. "Juxon and Abbott are expecting to hear from me very soon and I wouldn't want you to miss out on your chance of revenge."

Annie shuddered at the thought of speaking to George again. She didn't want to be anywhere near him and she was sure that her hatred of him would rise to the surface and reveal itself.

"You don't look too pleased at the prospect of seein' George then?"

"I don't wanna do it. Can't I just set fire to 'is 'ouse or somethin'? I liked the idea of stabbing 'im."

"You would still 'ave to get close enough and that would require some pretence. I see nothin' different with my suggestion, other than the fact that I guarantee 'is death. You'll probably miss with a knife an' end up getting' yerself killed." Skinny chuckled.

"Okay. I'll meet up with him tonight an' give 'im the poison."

"Good girl," said Skinny. "An' don't forget that once it is done, you owe me."

"I know that. What do you want?"

"Brownrigg 'as a fine operation on the Point. I should like to have a slice of that pie. But first I must return to full health."

"And in the meantime who runs the business?" said Annie.

"Well now," mused Jim, "I see no reason why you couldn't do it."

"Me? I am no criminal. I wouldn't have the first idea about what to do."

"You may just surprise yourself, Annie of the Point." Skinny bowed, pulled the blanket over his head and started to make his way back down the alley. Annie didn't go after him or continue their conversation. Her head swam with the events of the night and what was still to come. How she had misjudged Mary. She didn't know when it was that she had become such a bad judge of character. Was she really as gullible as she felt or was it just that she trusted people too easily? She followed Skinny's slow progress along Bathing Lane before entering Broad Street. Skinny shuffled in the direction of King James Gate, back to his lodgings. If someone had told her that she would be thick with Skinny Jim McDowell and acting against George Brownrigg just a couple of days ago, she would have laughed in their face and told them that they were set for a spell in the mad house. But here she was, and there was Skinny, disappearing into the night.

Annie turned and faced the other end of Broad Street and started towards George's house. She could see flickering lights in the unshuttered windows and she knew she would find him at home. As she drew closer, Annie went through her preparations, setting her mind to the task of hiding what she knew; of suppressing her deep desire to scratch George's eyes out and do him harm. One hundred and two Broad Street was now only two doors away. She stopped and composed herself, taking deep breaths. A group of men stumbled out of *The Star and Garter Hotel* very much worse for the wear. They giggled and pointed at her but Annie ignored them. She was in her own little world, concentrating on the events to come. Firstly, she would smile sweetly and apologise for disappearing, reiterating her staunch trust of George. She would then thank him, and complement him on the way he had helped her over the years. Finally, they would celebrate with a cup of ale, to toast their new future together.

Annie didn't know how she got there, those last few steps up to his door a blur of fragmented sights and sounds, but at his door she was, and she slipped into character. Goodbye angry, bitter Annie. Hello gullible, easily tricked Annie. She rapped on the door and swallowed hard.

The sound of footsteps echoed on the bare boards of the hallway as Brownrigg came to the door. He yanked it open and said, "Annie!"

"Hello, George. I have returned to you."

Chapter Thirty-four

The man doesn't even know the meaning of contrition…

"Come in, girl, come in. Don't stand there in the street," said George, stepping aside.

She squeezed by him, catching the faintest whiff of beer on his breath as she passed him. *That's good*, she told herself, *he's already half-cut."*

George followed her down the narrow corridor that led to the parlour and kitchen at the back of the house. He offered her a seat and George sat himself. On the table was a half-full cup of ale. She eyed it nervously and glanced back at George.

"Came by your place yesterday an' if I didn't know better, I'd say you was ignorin' me," he said.

"I know, but I couldn't face seein' you. With the loss you 'ave suffered, you of all people must understand my grief. I 'ave just lost my 'usband for the second time," said Annie. "So yes, I 'eard you knockin', but then again, I think the whole street 'eard you."

"I was worried about you. When you ran off without a word… anythin' could 'ave 'appened."

"There's a small part of me that wishes somethin' did 'appen," said Annie.

George smiled at her and said, "Still, you are 'ere now and that's all that matters."

"You're right," she said trying to avoid eye contact. "I am returned and that is all that matters," she said flatly and shifted nervously, staring at the floor.

"Are you quite yourself?" said George. "Only you seem sorta jumpy, like."

Annie looked straight at George, bit back her unease and smiled. "I was nervous about seein' you. I didn't know what you would say, or do. I spent my time cryin' for what I lost and not thinkin' what I got already."

"Are you that wary of me? Am I that scary that I put the fear of God in you?"

"You were angry yesterday, when you came to my 'ouse."

"I'm overjoyed that you're 'ere, girl. When you disappeared, I thought that I'd lost you." George stood and kissed her on the head. She went stiff at his touch and she was sure that he had noticed. Annie tried with all her will to relax and not snatch her head away. She closed her eyes, feeling numb as his lips pressed gently to her forehead. Brownrigg failed to notice and he went to sit down. "So," he said, "where did you go when you ran off?"

"I went for a walk. I 'ad to clear my 'ead. Truth is, I still don't understand what 'appened and why 'e did it."

"That, I'm afraid," said George, "is the puzzle of an unhinged mind. Sam wasn't well an' we all knew that. But to try an' make sense of a man suffering illness of the brain is impossible."

Annie gritted her teeth and managed her best excuse of a smile. *How dare this man, this murderer, describe my beautiful Sam as suffering brain illness.* She nodded and said, "It was that very fact that returned me to you. I realised that I had somethin' worth fightin' for. Sam was my 'usband but 'e chose death over life with me an' Bessie. For that I shall always resent 'im."

"You mustn't blame 'im, Annie," said George kindly. "If he'd been of sound mind, none of this would 'ave 'appened, an' we wouldn't be here today in this room. In a strange way, I should be thankin' your dear departed 'usband."

Annie gulped back her anger. *Thanking him? What brazen words this murdering bastard speaks. There isn't a hint of guilt on his face. Not a drop of remorse in those cold eyes. The man doesn't even know the meaning of contrition.* "Then a drink, perhaps... to celebrate," said Annie.

"Why not. I'll fetch some ale from the kitchen. I've just had a fresh barrel delivered." George stood and crossed the parlour, heading for the entrance to the kitchen. As he passed Annie, he stopped and stared at her. "You 'ave made a lonely man very 'appy."

Annie bit back the truth, smiled sweetly and said, "And you, sir 'ave made me very 'appy too."

The minute that George left the room, Annie seized her chance and fished the small packet of white Arsenic out of her dress. She ripped the corner from the tiny envelope and dropped it into George's cup, picked it up and gave it a swirl until the powder dissolved without a trace. She sat back down with her heart racing, listening as George rummaged in the kitchen and then to the sound of his footsteps as he returned. He carried a small wooden barrel with a tap hammered in the end. He had a fresh cup for Annie which he placed on the table next to his own half-filled one. Brownrigg held the barrel over both vessels and turned the tap, filling them both to the brim. Annie made a mental note of which cup was hers. She watched carefully as George picked them both up and handed one to her. Thankfully, it was the right one and she accepted with a small nod of her head.

"To us," she said.

"To beginnin's," said George winking and raising his drink to his lips. Before he took a sip, there was a bang on the front door. Annie almost let out a shriek.

"I said you was jumpy tonight," said George, placing the drink on the table. "Who the 'ell could that be this time of night?" He made his way down the narrow corridor and approached the front door.

"Who's there?" he called out.

"Officer Chapman," came the reply. "Kindly open the door."

George turned to glance behind him at Annie who now stood in the doorway of the parlour in silence.

"What the fuck can 'e want?" he said.

"Dunno," shrugged Annie. "Are you goin' to let 'im in?"

George shook his head and turned back to the slab of wood that stood between him and the Royal Navy. "What do you want?" he called.

"Mr Brownrigg," said Chapman, "I assume that you have no desire to converse your business so the entire place can hear?"

George said nothing.

"I will give you a moment to decide if you are going to open the door of your own free will or if you want me to employ brute strength."

"What should I do?" said George, who for one of the rarest moments, looked like he was genuinely scared.

"S'pose you'd best let 'em in," said Annie.

Chapman thumped the door again impatiently. "I will give you to the count of three, Mr Brownrigg but be aware that I have six marines with loaded muskets and I will not be denied entry."

George reached for the door and pulled it open. There stood Warrant Officer Chapman on the top step, flanked by three marines on either side of him. Beyond the uniformed men, a small crowd had gathered to see what was going on.

"So glad that common sense has prevailed," said the naval man without the slightest hint of humour or good will. "Now, kindly step aside."

George did as he was told, as Chapman and the small group entered. They made their way to the parlour and, upon seeing Annie, Chapman removed his hat, gave a small bow and said, "So we meet again."

"So we do," said Annie. Wasting no time she said, "Am I to be kept here, or can I leave?"

"You may leave, Mrs Crowther, unless you had some involvement with the death of Able Seaman Guppy?"

"None whatsoever," said Annie grabbing her shawl. As she passed the marines, she glanced at George and said, "I must be off."

He grabbed her arm and said, "Stay." She nodded and went to sit back down.

"How touching," said Chapman. "This woman will not ease the truth that you are a murderer."

"I ain't no murderer," snarled George, pressing his considerable frame towards the diminutive figure of Chapman. Immediately, the marines pressed closer to their officer and blocked his path.

"Now, now," said Chapman, "I was hoping we could do this the quiet way."

"Do what the quiet way?" said George.

"Come now, Mr Brownrigg, surely you cannot keep up this pretence forever? You and I both know that you killed Guppy and had him buried on that patch of soil you affectionately term 'Rat Island'."

"I ain't guilty and there's nothin' you can do to prove otherwise," said George.

"Interesting," said Chapman rubbing his gloved hand on his smooth chin. "So at what point do you think I need proof?"

"To make the charge stick you is gonna need evidence," said George, looking puzzled.

"Oh, I see." Chapman started to pace the room. "So the King's Navy will bend to your will now? The King's Navy is to operate on your terms, is it?" Chapman gave a small laugh and turned to face Brownrigg. "I know you killed him. Everyone in this rat infested place you call home knows that you did it. Even this woman," and he pointed at Annie, "knows you are guilty, so what evidence do you suppose it is that I need?"

"You cannot take me to trial without proof," said George.

"Trial? I need no trial, Mr Brownrigg. I am the Navy, *we* are the Navy. If we want you then we will have you, do you understand? But, as you say, evidence would be most helpful to the situation. Let it be said that the Navy is honourable in all its dealings."

George Brownrigg started to tremble. Annie could see him boiling with rage and pressed herself deeper into the chair. She knew this would not be a quiet affair as Chapman had hoped.

The naval officer took two steps towards his captive and said, "You *are* under arrest, Mr Brownrigg, for the murder of Able Seaman Alfred Fish. His body was discovered on Burrow Island earlier today after we received some information from a local of his resting place."

"Lies!" screamed George, clenching his massive fists. "I told you I 'ad nothin' to do with that lad's disappearance."

"And I am calling you a liar, sir." Chapman placed his hat back on his head and this was the cue for the marines to surround George with their muskets ready.

"Look," said George trying to soothe the situation, "what say you an' me 'ave a seat an' discuss this like gentlemen?" He offered the sailor a chair which was ignored.

"I would like nothing more than to discuss the situation with you, Mr Brownrigg but any further discussions will be had on the *Foudroyant*. Place him in irons." George exploded and grabbed one of the marines, hurling him towards the furthest wall in the room. As he flew through the air, he knocked the table over containing the drinks. The marine hit the wall with a thud and slid to the floor in a heap. George bolted for the door, shoving the others out of the way. Chapman screamed, "Get after him." Annie watched the front door burst its hinges as the massive frame of George leapt at it and fell into the cold night outside. The marines were close behind with muskets raised. Chapman screamed "Fire at his legs!" and the acrid smell of spent gunpowder filled the air.

George stumbled, holding the back of his leg and then fell into a heap on the stony ground, writhing in pain. The marines caught up with their target and started pommelling him with the butts of their muskets. Annie could hear George scream for them to stop but it didn't matter to her. She knew that he was getting the same dose of violence that all of his victims had met at his hand. She was now as close to George as she dare get. Chapman approached and stood before George, leering down at him with a smile on his face. He said, "You and I are going to become well acquainted over the coming years, Mr Brownrigg. It is going to be a long time before you clap eyes on this place again." He nodded his head and George was hauled to his feet and dragged towards the waiting boat. As he was pulled past Annie, George looked at her with pleading eyes. He said, "Wait! At least let me say goodbye."

Chapman raised his hand and the marines stopped, leaving George facing her. "I suppose this is goodbye then," he said reaching his manacled hands for hers.

She snapped her hand away, took a deep breath and said, "I hope they leave you to rot in 'ell."

Brownrigg looked stung by her words and said, "Wait. What do you mean? I thought we were…" His words trailed away.

Annie leaned closer and said, "You thought we were what? Did you think we were goin' to start a fresh? Is that it, a fresh start, like nothing' ever 'appened?"

"But... well, yes," said George. "I don't understand. You came back to me. You said you 'ad returned."

"An' 'ere I stand, don't I?" said Annie. "I came back to do one final thing and that was to finish you, George Brownrigg. I came back cos I knows what you are and what you done to my Sam."

"Sam drowned. You saw that with your own eyes," said George.

"I saw 'is coat, but I saw no body. You murdered 'im and dumped 'im on that island with the others... with that poor boy, Guppy."

"No," said George. "Don't do this to me. I cannot go away without the thought that you would wait for me. That would be like a waking death."

"Then so be it," said Annie. "For no one in this God forsaken place would give a fuck about you when you are gone." She turned her back on George and said, "Take him away. I 'ave nothin' further I wish to say to him."

A firm hand shoved George in the back as they dragged him through the assembled crowd, towards the edge of the Camber and the waiting pinnace. Chapman paused as he passed Annie. "Madam," he said, "I am heartily sorry for your loss. I will see that Brownrigg pays for his crimes, of that you have my word."

She turned and said, "Thank you. I just want to be with my daughter now and to bury my 'usband properly."

"I will have some of my men search the island for his body and, if indeed he is responsible for a second death, he will pay for that also." Chapman gave Annie a small bow and climbed down the steps that led to the launch. With a shove away, the boat slid through the water towards the *Foudroyant* with George screaming Annie's name as it went. She turned, pushed through the throng and walked back to the house on Broad Street, climbing the steps. The door was hanging off its hinges and she resolved to get it mended in the morning. Once she was back in the parlour, she sat and contemplated what had just happened. Suddenly, she let out an almighty wail and the emotion of the last few weeks flooded from her in waves greater than the breakers out in the harbour. All she could do was picture the mud stained face of her man, pale as the moon and colder than the December sea, lying there among the weeds and worms on that scrap of land. He was all alone in the world and that saddened her more than anything. She would need to give him a proper burial once they had found his body. On the floor in front of her the wet stained boards were starting to dry near the spilt drink. A small powder stain was forming on the surface. She stood, rubbed her eyes dry and picked up the cups, placing them both on the table. She surveyed the dark room. George wouldn't be needing this place for a while and besides, he did say that she and her daughter could move in, and that gave her rights. A small smile cracked onto Annie's lips. For the first time, something good had happened to them. Both she and her daughter would now be comfortable living in the grand surroundings of number one hundred and two Broad Street. Annie brushed her hand over a shelf as she left the room and resolved that in the morning she would start by giving the whole place a thorough clean and then Bessie could choose which room she wanted as hers. Annie did her best to close the front door, even making sure that the lock turned and she slid the key into her corset, climbing down the steps. The crowd watched in silence as she stood on the steps of the house.

"No one is to enter this 'ouse. It is mine now," she said. Still the crowd were silent. Annie nodded and said, "Good. From this moment George is no more. I am the new boss of this place and I will be fair, I will be firm, but the killin' will stop." She stepped into the assembled crowd and some patted her on the shoulder or back, others tried to reach out to her just to touch the woman who finished off the mighty George Brownrigg. She passed through without a word and headed for her daughter. Before turning onto Bath Square she looked out into the harbour and the dark shadow that was the pinnace holding Brownrigg slid towards the mighty *Foudroyant*. Annie wondered how long he would be away for and if he would ever return. She decided that now wasn't the time for worrying about the future, it was the time for fresh starts and hers was well deserved. She made her way to her old house, eager to tell Bessie the news.

Tomorrow would be hers and she would be known as Annie of the Point.

Epilogue

Mary glanced behind her at the sea of faces…

Pete Bookbinder walked in silence. He didn't like what he was doing one little bit. Up ahead was his companion Davey Turner and in between them, Mary Abbott and her husband Charlie dragged their few possessions in a small wooden cart. Stanley stood with his back to the approaching party as a sign of disrespect. King James Gate would be open to the Abbotts for the last time. Next to Stanley stood Annie Crowther, the new Queen of the Point, as she watched her former friend approach with an expression of stony resolution.

Mary glanced behind her at the collection of faces that stared at them down the street. It seemed that the whole of the Point had turned out to witness the humiliating last walk of the Abbott family. Some spat on the ground as Mary passed by. These were the same neighbours, friends and confidants that Mary had once counted as close. She didn't want to look at them anymore than they wanted to smile at her or wave or forgive. Forgiveness was in short supply on the Point. It always had been an unforgiving place. Doors slammed in protest as the forlorn party approached the gate.

"S'pose this is it then?" said Mary to Pete Bookbinder.

He nodded. "You look after yourself, Mary." He gave her a hug and turned to Charlie, extending his hand. Charlie shook it. "An' you look after her," he said to Charlie.

"Does it 'ave to end like this?" said Mary. "I said I was sorry. It was me what tipped off the Officer on the *Foudroyant*. Don't that count for much?"

Davey shrugged his shoulders and looked at Pete. "'Fraid not," he said. "Annie's word is final. She's the boss round 'ere now."

"Well maybe one day I can return to my 'ome?" Mary said more in hope than expectation. She knew that her bridges were well and truly burned where Annie was concerned. She had seen a change in Annie since Brownrigg was taken. Now there was a void on the Point and at first, with William Juxon's help, she eventually convinced Pete and Davey that she was the one to fill it. She was the law, she was the money maker and she was in control.

Mary drew to a stop by the gate and stared at Annie.

"Is this it then? You really are banishin' us," said Mary.

"Open the gate, Stanley," said Annie, standing aside. "This woman wants to pass through." She didn't take her eyes from Mary's face, watching her former friend closely.

"But I said I was sorry," Mary pleaded with Annie. "Why forgive Juxon and not me?"

"Juxon is of use to me. You are not," spat Annie.

Mary gave a wry smile and nodded. "I understand," she said. "I understand."

Both Mary and Charlie stepped through the gate and watched as Stanley slammed it shut and turned the key. Ahead of them was the old part of the City. Behind them was what was left of their old life. Now all they had were memories and an ever dimming image of a place that in time would dull to nothing more than a mist of the mind, faded beyond all recognition, no matter how hard Mary or Charlie might try and remember.

Mary looked at Pete through the metal bars of the gate, as he turned to walk back towards the Point. Davey did the same. Neither looked back.

And that was that. Mary Abbott was on the wrong side of King James Gate and the place she had called home had turned its back on her for good.

The only person who watched as the pair shrank into the distance was Annie.

Eventually she turned and strode towards the Camber.

Printed in Great Britain
by Amazon